ALSO BY FRANK DELANEY

FICTION

Venetia Kelly's Traveling Show
Shannon
Tipperary
Ireland

NONFICTION

Simple Courage

THE MATCHMAKER OF KENMARE

The Matchmaker of Kenmare

A Novel of Ireland

FRANK DELANEY

RANDOM HOUSE
NEW YORK

Copyright © 2011 by Frank Delaney, L.L.C.

Published in the United States by Random House, an imprint of The Random House Publishing Group, a division of Random House, Inc., New York.

RANDOM HOUSE and colophon are registered trademarks of Random House, Inc.

LIBRARY OF CONGRESS CATALOGING-IN-PUBLICATION DATA
Delaney, Frank
The matchmaker of Kenmare: a novel of Ireland / Frank Delaney.
p. cm.
ISBN 978-1-4000-6784-8
eBook ISBN 978-0-679-60433-4
1. Irish Folklore Commission—Fiction. 2. Missing persons—Ireland—Fiction. 3. Man-woman relationships—Ireland—Fiction. 4. Self-realization—Fiction. 5. Ireland—History—20th century—Fiction. I. Title.
PR6054.E396M38 2011 823'.914—dc22 2010035301

Printed in the United States of America on acid-free paper

www.atrandom.com

2 4 6 8 9 7 5 3 1

FIRST EDITION

Book design by Dana Leigh Blanchette

To the Goodwin brothers,
David and Ben

Author's Note

The word *neutral,* from *neuter,* originally meant "neither masculine nor feminine." Time and its upheavals created a new and political meaning: *neutral* meant staying out of a war.

In 1939, Ireland, a small island with a diminutive military capacity, declared itself neutral between Britain and Germany. The Irish felt in danger from both sides—with good reason. Winston Churchill wanted to shelter his warships in Irish ports (some feared he would do so by force), thereby inviting German bombing; Adolf Hitler was known to view Ireland as a possible base from which to attack England.

The arguments raged inside and outside the country and continued for many years after the war ended. How could a defenseless island make a difference one way or another in such a huge military theater and thus invite ruin? The opposing point of view insisted that there can be no such thing in life as a neutral position; faced with uncalled-for aggression, everyone must take sides.

This debate echoes a smaller, more intimate, and much older conundrum, closer to the origin of the word: Can a man and a woman ever be "neutral" toward each other? Can they achieve a deep friendship that remains platonic, or will one or the other want to move it along to a livelier or more committed state?

Naturally, these issues have never been resolved, globally or personally. Nor are they likely to—which is to the benefit of drama and story-telling, because the word *neutrality* has many shades. For example, official papers, released long after 1945, show that Ireland did, in fact, exploit the war politically and contributed many actions to the Allied cause. As to affairs of the heart, who would ever dare to define where friendship should end and passion begin?

PART ONE

The Strange Potency
of Cheap Music

1

The Matchmaker of Kenmare taught me much of what I know.

"If a giraffe isn't weaned right," she said once, "you'll have to provide twenty gallons of fresh milk for it every day."

Another morning she told me, "If you're going out in the rain, always butter your boots. It makes them waterproof."

She knew a terrific card trick, but she refused to teach it to me. "Big hands are for power," she said, "not trickery."

At our very first meeting she asked, "How can you tell whether an egg is fresh?"

If it doesn't bounce when you drop it? In those days, I had a sardonic inner voice, my only defense mechanism.

She said, "Put it in a pan of cold water with salt, and if the egg rises to the surface it's bad."

You must have seen a lot of bad eggs, said my secret voice. I think I was afraid of her then.

She went on, "If you're hard-boiling an egg, a pinch of salt in the water will stop it cracking."

A pinch of salt, indeed.

"If you ever want to catch a bird," she said, "just sprinkle salt on its tail."

How useful. You just have to get close enough.

"Not too much salt," she added.

Does it depend on the size of the bird?

Could she hear what I was thinking? "But don't do it," she said, "with an ostrich. Ostriches hate salt."

Hoping to sound tactful, I asked, "Are there ostriches here in Kerry?"

"Ah, use your imagination," she said. "They're around here all right. But you have to know where to look for them."

I nodded, in confusion more than agreement.

"Do you have a strong imagination, Ben?"

"I do," I said, "but I'm not sure that I trust it."

"There are only two words," she said, "in which I put my trust. Magic and Faith."

Some of her grip on me came from the conflict of opposites. Whereas I had always leaned toward the scholarly, she belonged to the demotic. For every line of Horace and Virgil that I savored, she had a snatch of cant, and from the moment we met I began to note many of her sayings and old saws. They still addle my brain; this morning, as I sat down to work, I remembered a fragment from a spelling game that she'd learned as a child: "Mrs. D. Mrs. I. Mrs. F-F-I. Mrs. C. Mrs. U. Mrs. L-T-Y."

"Patience," she murmured another day, "is the Mother of Science."

I would swear that she often spoke in uppercase letters.

Since she rarely left her stony Atlantic headland, her knowledge of the world must have come from some popular encyclopedia of arcane and unconnected facts. Giraffes, ostriches, and eggs—they formed no more than an introduction. She knew about the lives of ants; how to gut a fish using a sharp stick and your thumb; training a cat to play dead; the healing properties of sour milk; the fact that honey is the only food that never goes off; where to find a stone that retains heat for twelve hours; how cloves grow; the number of bones in an eagle's wing; why a cow has four stomachs; how long to boil the tar for caulking the hull of a boat. She was a walking, talking library of vernacular knowledge.

She loved music, but she couldn't carry a tune in a bucket. Her eye had the familiar speed of a child raised in the countryside—she could identify a bird thousands of yards away. She had a sense of color so strong that she could tell one shade of black from another. Her capacity to quote from Shakespeare suggested wide reading of him—even if some pages seemed to have been missing from her edition of the *Collected Works.*

Moreover, she had one specific gift that I still can't fathom. It has never ceased to puzzle me; she used it a number of times in my company, always with astonishing results, and if it can't be called "magic," well, nothing can: She could find people by looking at a map. And we shall come to those moments when I saw her pull this stunt, trick, sleight of mind, or whatever it should be called.

Although she spoke three and a half languages, she had never been abroad. And however delightful in its innocence, the part of her that remained in her own homestead also made me wince, with its homespun charm, its greeting-card sentiment.

"Ben, do you know what the difference is between Friendship and Love? Friendship is the photograph, Love is the oil painting." And she uttered it in the declarative way she had of saying things that made me hesitate to contradict her.

Her words often sounded so shallow that I dismissed them, and later found to my displeasure that her mushy sentiments had lingered and were staggering around in my mind like a drunk at a wedding. In that sense, she possessed in trumps the strange potency of cheap music, and I know that I caught some of it from her.

However, from inside all that phrase-and-fable stuff, she served up a philosophy that had an alluring power. For example, she brought into my life a belief in something that she called "Referred Passion"; I even lived by it for a time.

"Do you know what I mean by 'Referred Passion'?" she said one day about a year into our relationship. And, as usual, not waiting for my hopeless stab at a reply, she went on. "Do you know what a referred pain is?"

Is it when I feel so stupid that I could kick myself?

"I'll explain it," she said. "Your shoulder is injured, but you feel it in your chest. Or you've hurt your spine, but your hip is carrying the ache. That's referred pain. Well, Referred Passion is when you're in love with one person, but you fiercely embrace another. That's us," she said. "That's me and you. Friendship is a choice," she said. "Love isn't."

What else can I tell you about her? She had a phenomenal passion for handkerchiefs. She kept her hair tucked behind an ear like Rita Hayworth. She taught me the words of bawdy old country rhymes, most of them too salty to repeat here. Also, she had the most peculiar recipes for things.

"If you have the hiccups," she told me one day, "bend down, put your hands on the floor, and look back between your legs at the sun."

My inner voice said, *Is that all you'll be able to see?*—but I asked her, "And what if it's the middle of the night?"

She said, "Then you're in worse trouble."

And I was—but I never picked up the warnings.

As I sat down to write this memoir, I had an opening paragraph in mind; here it is:

> *I wish I could tell you about the greatest friendship of my life; I wish I could tell you how it developed beyond friendship into something for which I have no definition, no terminology. But the moment I begin to tell it (and I must: I'm mortally committed to telling this tale before I die), I know that I'll enter what I call the "Regret Cycle," and the "What If Cycle," and the "If Only Cycle," and I'll end up nowhere again.*

As you can see, I abandoned those opening sentences, and the direction they proposed—yet I'm nevertheless going to write it all down for you. I'm old enough now to deal with the regrets, the what-ifs, and if-onlys, and whatever the subjective faults you may find in this remembrance, at least I can describe how I, who knew little about anything beyond my own narrow concerns, learned to become a true and deep friend to someone. It may prove important to you one day. To the both of you.

She, of course, was the one who taught me this magnificent skill—as she taught me something else extraordinary, the greatest single lesson of my life: She taught me what blind faith looks like. And blind faith is why I'm writing this account of her life, and how it affected me.

Kate Begley was her name, and she was known as the Matchmaker of Kenmare long before I met her. She and her grandmother shared the title, and Kate was as pretty as a pinup. I was twenty-nine, she was twenty-five when I met her, and she had a grin like a boy's.

See? See what's happening to me? *Pretty as a pinup;* and *a grin like a boy's*—the moment I begin to describe her, all these decades later, I become sentimental about her, and I fall into language that I would never use in my ordinary life.

I who for years wrote uncluttered and austere reports of ancient countryside traditions, I who studied with joy the most powerful scholars of old Europe, I who pride myself on my unadorned simplicity of purpose—here I am, forced back into her way of thinking. And I squirm, because at·these moments her greeting-card remarks will flood through me again like a maudlin old song. I've just heard one of those corny echoes: "You have to believe me, Ben," she said. "Love is not a decision. But Friendship is."

Why am I telling you all this? You'll see why. You'll see how she affected my life, and you'll grasp the implications of that effect upon all of us whom this memoir concerns. You'll see how she was the one who made the determinations; where we would go, no matter how dangerous; what we might attempt, no matter how bizarre; and yes, she decided too the balance of love and friendship between us.

I followed, and she led me into trouble so deep that my own father wouldn't have found me. Older than she in years but younger by centuries, I'd never intended to be so commanded, but some people snag you on their spikes, and you hang there, flapping helplessly, and—I admit it—fascinated.

When I met Kate Begley, the Second World War had been under way for four years. In Ireland, we called it by a wonderful, ameliorating euphemism—"The Emergency." We were one of the very few countries in Europe immune from the conflict, because we had taken up a position of neutrality. Controversial among our geographical neighbors, and sometimes even among ourselves, I agreed with it. Its moral simplicity suited what I like in life.

I also liked its military practicality; who were we, on our tiny island, to fight among such vast regiments? We hadn't even replenished our slaughtered breadwinners from the previous war, in which we'd lost tens of thousands of men. Thus, we had learned to stay out of such things, or so I believed.

And yet, because I took Kate Begley at her word, because I surrendered myself to her philosophy of friendship, that is to say, Referred Pas-

sion, the war sucked me in. When it swept her from that brilliant Atlantic headland where she lived, and from her generally innocent life, it
took me with her.

2

July 1943 ·

Here is my note of our first meeting:

*She always serves tea to her callers—to break the ice and soften the
difficult opening questions: "Did you ever court a girl?" And, "What
kind of girl would you like?"*

*The men usually answer no to the first question, and to the second
they might say, "Well, a girl who likes a laugh," or "A sturdy girl, she
won't object to hard work," or "A girl steady in herself"; or, if they were
fishermen, "A girl who knows the sea, can work the nets." Miss Begley
remarked, "At this point I might say that I know just the person." And
she added, "Whether I do or not."*

*The cottage hovers in a pocket above the ocean; there are no other
houses on Lamb's Head. From the red door you can see for miles across
open water. Stone grows everywhere—all around, up the hill, down to
the water, where rocks litter the foreshore, their white patches like
medals in the sun.*

*By land she can hear people coming up the battered lane. If they ar-
rive by sea she can look down on their heads as they moor at the little
jetty. Miss Begley says that since she was a very young child she has
watched for the boats, and to this day she runs back to the house to tell
her grandmother how many men have made the journey. They commonly arrive on a Sunday, she says, striding up from the sea through
the high, scrabby grass, quiet men, she says, "shy and big-boned."*

*One of the first things they see is a photograph on the mantelpiece,
of a little girl with a ribbon in her hair and a middle-aged woman
dressed in black. Dated 1923, it was posed some twenty years ago in a*

studio in Kenmare, the nearest town. Both are looking at the camera; the grandmother, Mrs. Holst, a widow, purses her severe lips; the girl is a little overfed and has a cautious smile; a potted palm sits on a column in the vague "Egyptian" background. There's no doubt that it's grandmother and granddaughter; she says that visitors comment upon the resemblance.

For as long as Miss Begley can remember, the grandmother, before she undertakes to make any introductions, delivers a lecture—which Miss Begley has adopted: "Marriage is very important. Marrying a girl is the most important thing a man can do. Never mind business or politics or sport or any of that, there's nothing so vital to the world as a man marrying a woman. That's where we get our children from, that's how the human race goes forward. And if it's too late for children, there's the companionship of a safe and trusted person."

Miss Begley says that she has listened to those fireside words of her grandmother all her life, a speech that ends on a declaration: "Marriage is the gold standard of all relationships. It's the currency by which everything else is valued."

I asked, What do the visiting men think of all this? She told me, "Very often the father speaks for the son, who is usually asked to leave for a little while, and he'll wander out of the cottage and look at the sea." Then the father describes the son's work as, say, a fisherman on the Atlantic—the small boats, the freezing winds, the catch that might drag you overboard; and the absences lasting all night and perhaps several days if they were following herring shoals, or a field of cod far out. "A woman," he'll announce, "would have to put up with that. And the living is hard, no doubt there. When the ice gets onto your hands, it doubles the size of your knuckles."

Next come some more questions: Is there any insanity in your family? Would your wife say that you yourself were a generous man or a mean-spirited man? Is your son a decent man? Can he be depended upon not to strike a woman? That's a very cowardly thing to do, to strike a woman, who hasn't the same strength as a man.

If the father looks uncomfortable she'll ask him, "Did you ever strike a woman yourself? Did you ever hit your wife?" If he says, however sheepish and apologetic, that yes, he did, the grandmother—or Miss Begley—will rise and say, "Well, sir, I'm afraid—'like father like

son'. That's what we believe in this house. And we can't do business
with you. What I mean is—we won't do business with you. So go on
your way."

Their visitors showed up, Miss Begley said, "throughout the whole
year, except in the time of the gales, March or September, or the worst of
the cold rain in January and February." Sometimes, as many as four and
five seekers of marriage came to that house on a Sunday, in boats tied up
below the headland, or by road in hackney cars from Kenmare.

"And by the time they left," she said, "we had shaped the rest of their
lives."

3

On that first visit, I had taken care to introduce myself, lest they mistake
me for a suitor.

"God save all here. My name is Ben MacCarthy, and I work for the
Folklore Commission. May I come in and speak with you for a while?"

Miss Begley was on her knees in her doorway. Without looking up,
she continued to draw a fat line of white chalk around the doormat.

"This is to keep out the ants," she said. "Ants hate chalk. It makes
them vomit."

The grandmother rose from a chair at the table, came rustling in long
black skirts to the door, peered at me, and seemed disappointed.

I tried again. "My job is to gather traditions that have lasted. And I'm
particularly interested in matchmaking."

Miss Begley, on her knees, replied, "Good."

I looked down at her. She finished framing the doormat with her
chalk line and raised her head. Hands on hips, she looked up at me, her
eyes searching every inch of my face.

"Here," she said, and held up a chalky hand for me to raise her to her
feet. "Did you bring this glorious weather with you?"

Within sight of the ocean, we sat on a bench outside. I prepared my pen and record book, and she adjusted the pace of her words to my note-taking. That's when I took down the note you've just read—about questioning men who sought wives. Later, I made an unofficial entry in my private journal:

> *She has unblinking eye contact. When she's asking a question, one eye-brow rises at an angle like a shrewd lawyer's. She seems to have as much energy as the wind. I wish I'd taken a photograph of her. She also has the gift of affection: From time to time, she reached out and touched me on the forearm, as though to draw me closer to her. I find it very moving—Venetia used to do it.*

Miss Begley grew up speaking the Irish language; it was the family and neighborhood tongue. The local school in Caherdaniel educated her to the age of eleven and balanced her Gaelic speaking with an excellent schooling in English. From there she boarded with the nuns in Killarney until the age of eighteen. With a better-than-good basic education—excellent French, a strong modicum of German, comprehensive Latin—she came home and stayed home. Her grandmother began to fail a little in health for a time, and Miss Begley took over their world.

They lived—and lived well—on the grandmother's three incomes. Childless, now long widowed, formerly a nurse in Chicago, Mrs. Holst had a social welfare pension from the United States. On top of that, small investments and a pension from the long-dead Mr. Holst, a bank employee, had delivered beyond expectations. And she also made money from arranging marriages—to which skill she had apprenticed her granddaughter.

I asked, "Is it an art, a craft, a profession?"

"It's a life," said Miss Begley.

"It's a business," said the grandmother.

A serious business too: In a time of difficult economics, marriage often laid down the path to survival. Ireland, a nation barely twenty years old in the 1940s, had little social help to offer any of its people. Poverty was the national quicksand; widespread and easy to step on, it sucked people down rapidly. But a practical woman could help a man to build up a farm or a business. She could cook and bake, make clothes for the family, plant a kitchen garden, tend animals and account books, help with harvests—many a husband boasted that his wife equaled two men.

"There's another thing," said Miss Begley. "A single girl with a job but who still lives at home has no money for herself."

"Doesn't she work for a wage?" I asked.

"Yes. But she has to throw it into the family pot. They keep nothing for themselves. Very bad for their morale."

They found their clients by different routes. While Mrs. Holst stayed at home and waited for clients to come to her by word of mouth, Miss Begley went out and searched for anybody who wanted a spouse.

She said, "I have an easier task with the girls because most Irishwomen want a man of their own. They want children. And it isn't just for practical reasons, it's romantic too. Most of the men, on the other hand—they don't really know they want a wife. Until we tell them."

4

An expanded version of those first notes from Lamb's Head can be found in my report, *Matchmaking in Rural Ireland 1949*, complete with social information. I didn't use the Ediphone; I wish I had, because we'd now have a record of Miss Begley's voice, but I was clumsy with the device— I broke too many of the cylinders or jammed the machine. So I noted down such interviews in my own kind of shorthand and at night wrote them out in full. Where possible I read my notes back to the interviewee and rarely found inaccuracies; on that count I praise myself.

For the report, I interviewed more than twenty matchmakers all over the country, and one in London, an upper-class woman named Claudia— of whom more later. A man in County Mayo, a portly fellow named Stephen O'Leary, called himself a "marriage broker." One lady in the midlands near Roscommon parlayed her experience into a newspaper advice column for the lovelorn and called herself "Sue the Soother."

All of them, no matter how they did it, aimed at the same goal—to

bring together a pair of strangers who might make a successful life part-
nership, discover deep affections, and breed many children.

They saw no irony in viewing themselves as, in the words of one, "As-
sistants to Destiny." Mr. O'Leary said to me, "We erase loneliness."

None had the life force of Kate Begley. Of them all, she alone understood that matchmakers come from the foundations of the universe. She
believed that the talent for arranging marriages has no boundaries and,
as she said, "Unto those who hold that gift it gives extra power, if they
but knew how to find it in themselves."

From her I learned some of the traditions: that matchmaking was a
priestly duty in more than one faith.

"A Catholic priest or a Jewish rabbi—they're all at it one way and another. There's matchmaking in all societies," she said, "rich or poor." The
rich, she claimed, often pursued it most ardently of all, in order to protect their estates.

In some countries, she told me, those seeking to marry would make
offerings to a matchmaking god, and that same god was often the Man
in the Moon. Or the reflection of the moon in the river or a lake or the
sea. Or a fixed star in the south of the sky.

Magic, she claimed, also plays a large part.

"Well, it must be magic!" she said to me with that indignant shake of
the head. "If two complete strangers have trusted the power of a stranger
to bring them together—what else is that but magic?"

To reinforce the point, she told me that she also doubled as a fortune-
teller.

"It's a very useful thing to be able to see into the future of the people
you're introducing to each other. I read a palm once of a girl from
County Limerick, and I saw in her hand, clear as day, the face of a fellow
from down the road here, in Templenoe. They have eight children now."

The more I pressed her, the more I learned about her view of her
power and its place in the world.

"There's a tribe in Africa," she said, "and they have a matchmaking
feast every seven years. They call on the matchmaking gods to find husbands for the seven most marriageable young ladies at that feast. And lo
and behold! At noon next day without fail, from all points of the compass, seven tall, handsome young warriors stroll into that village."

"How do you know this?" I asked.

"Nana told me. Every matchmaker worth their salt knows that story."

All that first afternoon, I sat and listened to her. Matchmaking, to her, was part of the machinery that drives the universe, and she captured my heart with one detail.

"There's a legend," she said, "and I'm one of the very few who know it—that says all couples who are meant to marry are connected by an invisible silver cord. The matchmaking gods tie that cord around their ankles at birth, and in time the gods pull those cords tighter and tighter. Slowly, slowly, over the next twenty or thirty or forty years, they draw the couple toward each other until they meet."

5

Now let me tell you how I found Miss Begley—and let me tell you too that the man who first told me of her existence, a decent fellow, was the same man who would one day wreck my life.

Our nation has a gift for the bizarre, and I'd gone to see a gentleman in Limerick who advertised dentures for hire. I wanted to collect stories of the occasions—weddings, funerals, and so on—for which people hired false teeth. A potential customer crashed into me as we both tried to step through a narrow doorway. As I write this now, I can see that Miss Begley would call it Fate. With the uppercase *F*.

His name was Neddy; he had a deep, thick accent and empty gums; we stepped together inside the dark, wooden rooms of MR. MACMANUS—OCCASION MERCHANT, as the sign on the wall said. When his bell jangled, the said merchant walked from the rooms at the rear of the premises.

Neddy—full name, Edward Joseph Hannitty—pointed to his mouth, and Mr. MacManus beamed.

"Oh, I've plenty of teeth. I could play a tune for you."

Which was Mr. MacManus's joke; he ran his finger across his own top row alternating black and white, and they did indeed look like piano keys.

"But you want a few teeth for yourself?"

"I do, sir." Neddy nodded.

I can tell you that he didn't look like somebody who would one day change three lives profoundly and forever.

"Is it for a wedding? We do a lot of weddings. I'd a man in here last month," said Mr. MacManus. "He was looking for a parrot to take to a wedding, the bird had learned to say 'Shut up, you hoor,' and he thought it'd be a great joke to bring it to the wedding, and I never got the bird back, the bride's father killed it, so they didn't get the joke I suppose."

Neddy said, "There's a woman, down in Kenmare, like. She's a matchmaker, and she told me if I had any teeth she'd get me my choice of select ladies."

Now began a search of the premises, and to my delight Mr. MacManus invited me to help him. Behind the storefront stretched long, slender rooms with narrow bays containing myriad articles. I read the broad, coiling handwritten legends on the boxes. "Secondhand Ladies' Corsets," said one box. At the edge of another shelf sat "Implements for Removing Thorns from Flesh (Human)" while next to it sat a bigger box of "Implements for Removing Thorns from Flesh (Animal)."

He had thousands of crutches, including a tiny pair.

"For a child?" I asked, charmed in this cave of treasures, and he said, "No, actually. For a midget. I had a little customer who lost a leg in the last war."

"They had dwarves in the war?"

"Running messages in the trenches. They were below the parapets, the snipers couldn't get them."

The next exploration brought us to a room of stuffed creatures.

"I bet the teeth are in here," he said, and as I was about to ask, this heavy-breathing man with the pleasant and willing air explained his method of filing his inventory.

"Now, you're saying to yourself, 'What in the name of God is he doing keeping false teeth with stuffed animals?' and 'tis a valid question enough. Well, some of the teeth have to have repairs, like, and I don't ever get any tooth on its own, so there's times when I take a tooth, like, from a stuffed animal and glue it to a denture plate and it works fine. There's a man here in the city and he has five teeth from a young wolf in his mouth. He's so thrilled with 'em he gave himself his own nickname—'Wolf' O'Brien."

Among stuffed foxes, badgers, ferrets, and a squirrel, Mr. MacManus climbed on a ladder and began to take out a large drawer from a high cabinet. I feared that the weight might topple him, but he cheered with success.

"I have 'em," he said, "the buggers," and he came back down the ladder holding a cardboard shoe box. "And there's teeth in here should be the right age for him."

At Mr. MacManus's directive, Neddy sat in a chair and leaned back. Both sizes, the too-large and the too-small, had their problems. For the large, Neddy's helpfulness led him to make wide, face-threatening contortions; the smaller sets ran the danger of being swallowed whole or in part.

Lanky as a goose, shy as an owl, embarrassed to be alive—those were the terms I was enlisting for my notebook to describe Neddy Hannitty with his mouth open in hope.

"Don't we all have to help a man who's looking to get married?" said Mr. MacManus as he sifted the pink devices. "Ah, God is good!" he then exclaimed. "I knew it'd be this pair."

He wiped a set of tombstone dentures on his sleeve and began to fit them to the willing drover. After some jiggling and juggling, and a gentle amount of drool from Neddy, a triumphant Mr. MacManus held up a mirror.

"You're fixed," he said. "Smile."

Neddy smiled—but, force of habit, smiled with his hand almost covering his mouth.

"I'll hire them out to you for six months," said Mr. MacManus.

Then he stood at his door and waved us off, proud as a parent.

On the street I asked Neddy, "How did you fall into the hands of a matchmaker?"

"I'm forty-five," he said, "I'm a cattle drover to every farmer in the south of Ireland, and there isn't a hill I haven't climbed over, and I never thought of marrying, but I noticed that if I saw a good pair of legs I always felt the day was improving."

Enter Miss Begley. One wet morning, Neddy had been driving cattle from the village of Sneem to the town of Kenmare. I'm familiar with that Atlantic rain; it seeps into every pore, drenches every follicle, drips cold down your neck. When the rain got so heavy that he'd had to take shelter, a woman got off her bicycle, ran through the puddles to the same tree, and complained about the weather.

From a capacious bag she pulled a flask of tea and shared it with Neddy the Drover while the cattle grazed the margins of the road. She began to chat to him—where he came from, where he was going, asked him his destination, where he called home, his age, and so forth. Within minutes she had him talking about himself as never before.

"And you've no wife," she said.

Neddy harruped a little cough, to overcome his embarrassment.

"And then she says to me, 'D'you know what, Neddy? You're a damn nice fella as it is, but if you had a few teeth, sure you'd dazzle us all.' "

I'd been heading southwest anyway, and two days later, I paid my first visit to Lamb's Head. Now, as I sit here, looking back, I have the thought: *What unfriendly god, what cosmic system, sent this man into my life, this simple cattle drover who's as honest as a horse, this dear fellow with his rented teeth?*

6

At that time, July 1943, I viewed myself as a man alone and grieving, with those night soldiers, doubt and fear, hammering always at my door. I believed that my constant pain didn't show in my face, yet when I'd finished my note-taking and was making ready to leave, Miss Begley said, "Tell me about yourself. You look a bit lonely. Might you be looking for somebody yourself?"

I nodded, mute as a leaf. My internal gentleman, for once, said nothing. She pressed, an eyebrow raised like a semaphore.

"There's something wrong, isn't there?" and she put her hand on my arm and said, "Tell me about it. How can I help you? You're a fine-looking man. Nobody has to live a lonesome life."

I nodded again.

After looking at the distant sea for a moment she put on her professional mode. "Here's a question for you," she said. "Would you marry a girl with, say, only one leg?"

"I'm already married," I said.

She barked. "I don't do that kind of thing, and you should be ashamed of yourself." And she turned away, sniffing like an aunt.

"No, no," I said. "That's wrong, that's not right. I *was* married. It's just that I don't know if I still am."

I told her the story as briefly as I could, and I explained that every day I asked everybody I met if they'd ever seen "this beautiful woman, the actress, Venetia Kelly. She was—is—my wife."

As Miss Begley peered at the fraying photograph that I took from my pocket, I could see that she understood. In fact, she summarized my pain—to have had it all and lost it.

"Oh, you poor man." She took my hand. "Here," she said. "Come on in. I'll make a fresh pot of tea and we'll talk like old friends."

As the afternoon went on, I relaxed and opened out my life story a little more. Time and again, she said, "Oh! Oh, that's too bad. Too bad altogether. It's a wonder you can stand upright with that weight of grief. Oh, poor you."

Although the police had insisted that I set down a record of all the events surrounding the disappearance of my wife, and although on many a morning, noon, and night, I'd shouted my grief from the hilltops, I had never until that moment told any human person how I felt. On that entire subject I had uttered scarcely a word—never dared to, because I didn't think that anyone would understand, and I didn't want to weep in front of strangers. Now this girl, a few years younger than I, took my hand and held it and warmed it in hers.

Kate Begley then told me of her own loss. When she was four years old, her parents "failed to come home from the sea." As they returned from a wedding in Waterville, a squall raced up along Ballinskelligs Bay. The spars from their ransacked boat washed up at Sheehan's Point a few days later.

"I even remember the dress my mother wore to the wedding. Soft and gray. Had a small, round collar made of lace that she crocheted herself."

Sitting in the sunlight, with the same deadly sea beating down there, racing like a herd of dragons along the rocky shores and snarling up at us as though we might be their next meal, we leaned on our chairs toward each other and exchanged views of eternal seeking.

I told her of my long search: "Every village is a cave, every town a forest."

She told me of her own eternal quest, prowling the headlands of the ocean, the beaches, still looking: "And, Ben, I say to myself, 'Haste the day when they'll walk up the cliff here and stand in the doorway, cheerful as mice.' "

She squeezed my hand and said, "You know—people with loss are meant to meet. So that they can help each other."

At last I had found somebody who would understand my whimpering anguish. Or so I felt. For a decade and more, I had been immersed in a daily search for a dearly beloved person who might be dead—but equally might be alive. In any given phase of my travels, I might be passing through the town, village, or parish where Venetia lived. No wonder I had known days when, out of sheer pain, my toes felt the curve of the earth.

Yet, I have to be careful in this memoir; I must retain a balance. Much though I took comfort from Miss Begley's soothing empathy, had that conversation not happened, what else might have not?

Many things. I doubt that I'd ever have run from a bursting shell in a French village. Or stumbled through that dreadful snow in Belgium. Nor would I ever have stood among the fearful, tearful wives standing aghast on the docksides of New York. Or killed a man. Or groomed a giraffe. Or sat wide-eyed in that dank room in Dachau, listening to the frightful court proceedings dominated by the word *danke*—as though saying, "For such atrocities I thank you," and my heart simmering with rage on behalf of my two dear friends.

In time, when her own loss made Miss Begley into a searcher too (the world is more full of them than you know), she and I met many people who understood. We met them in army camps, on mountainsides, in village cafés, on battlefields, on boats, on trains. We who search are identified by our quietude—and, I believe, our dignity, because while helping one another, we also try to keep our yearning to ourselves.

Nevertheless, we are perceived as clearly by our anxiety as though a black cross has been daubed on our foreheads.

7

My record of Kate Begley is comprehensive and it's augmented by her own journal, to which she gave me uncensored access. I'm its custodian, and for some time now, while I've been pulling this story together, that diary—a large red ledger—has been as big as an animal on my desk. From her entry for that August day, here's her account of meeting me:

A lovely young man collecting folklore for the government came to see myself and Nana today. Luckily, I was wearing my gray dress and my fuchsia scarf, and the bracelet I borrowed from Mama's top drawer. He is tall, he has hair the color of a brick, and he has suffered a big loss; he keeps plucking at his clothes. Yet when he sits down to talk and listen, there's something calm in him, like the Sea of Tranquillity that I've heard about on the moon.

He has such a sad face. His dear wife was kidnapped from him over ten years ago, and may have been murdered in an act of revenge. Or she may still be alive and is being kept somewhere so that he'll never again find her. She was expecting their first baby.

I'm going to include him in my prayers tonight. But he's in poor condition. I wanted to tell him to shape up, to stop pitying himself. He's very handsome and I'll help him get new clothes. I've told him that he's to shave every day, and he's to cut down his drinking. Nana says he may be dangerous, she thinks he has a fierceness. But I think there might be gold in him too. I'll have to repair him.

He had a hole in the upper of his shoe, and I could see that one foot had no sock on it. But no matter what his sadness may have done to his behavior and general appearance, he knows about a good, clean life, because his official journal looked as black and pure as a prayer book, and his pen was perfect.

8

I stayed the night in the long little house at Lamb's Head. Next morning, I asked if I might sit in one day on a matchmaking session.

"If I say yes, will it bring you back here soon?" she asked.

And I replied, "I'll come back anyway."

"I have to be in Killarney Saturday week," she said. "If you're there, we might go and buy you some clothes."

Down beside the winding Lamb's Head road, I retrieved my tools. When approaching a dwelling, I always hid them, to avoid being asked, "Why do you carry a shovel and a garden fork on your bicycle?" I didn't care to tell people that, as I went from place to place, I also dug in every wood I found.

At that time, the notion seemed to contain a wild logic. Venetia and I had first embraced beneath trees. Leaning against the cool cylinders of their trunks, we'd first kissed under the velvet shelter of their branches.

Then one afternoon, during the blackest of those far-off days after the Disappearance, I met a traveler on the road who told me that he believed she'd been buried beneath a tree. He was a one-legged man, cruel-faced, with a slash of a mouth. At the time I put his meanness down to how much he must have suffered in the loss of that leg. He cackled at me like a wizard as he looked at her photograph. "A tall, blondy one, wasn't she? Venetia Kelly. I went to her show once. And the dummy she had, Blarney, he was a scream altogether." He cupped his filthy hands to his chest. "And she had big diddies on her."

When it occurred to him that I might slug him for the disrespect, he smiled, as one-sided as a shark, affected a sad air, and through his thin lips told me what he thought he knew.

"Well, what it was is this. I was coming through Dromcollogher one day about not long ago, and I was taking a shortcut off the road near Broken Bridge heading for Kilmeedy, and I was up in a wood, up the side of a hill, and there was people there, and they was burying something, I thought it might be a dead calf or something, it was that big, I can tell you the place."

When he lifted his eyebrow, that side of his face went up with it.

"I waited," he said, "hiding myself, and when they were gone, I went over and looked, and they'd covered the ground with old sticks and stuff, rotten leaves and that, but when I poked around, 'twas clear, like, there was a burial, now why would you need to cover the tracks of a burial if 'twas only a calf? I never told anyone, not a soul, until yourself now this minute, a gentleman like you, you'd know what to do."

Kilmeedy. Dromcollogher. Broken Bridge. Not more than a few miles from Charleville, the town from which they took her at midnight. I purchased a gardener's trowel that day, a shovel, and a fork, and strapped them to the bar of my bicycle; and I went and lived in that wood for weeks until I had dug it up.

Soft, pliable earth beneath me, and intense fungi that looked like magic or gangrene or both; cold cushions of moss; ancient roots; the long disused sett of a badger; a soft hollow with some traces of red fur where a family of foxes had played and rested—I found many things: an old pot, part of a wheel, the broken-off tine of a fork, green bottles caked with dirt. But I never found a burial. Perhaps I had dug in the wrong forest.

Often thereafter, in part to get away from the question "Have you seen this woman?" I would ask in jovial conversation, "If you were burying a body, where would you do it?"

Many people answered, "Oh, inside a wood," and I would hear this desperate thought tolling like a leper's bell: *How many forests must I excavate?*

As I rode the narrow winding road back to Kenmare, my mind raced so fast that I scarcely looked at the open sea on my right hand. I'd not spent time alone with any young woman since Venetia's death. Now the force of Kate Begley's impression upon me challenged my memories of Venetia and brought back images.

I'd first seen her on the stage of a dank old hall in Cashel, a few miles from home. She played Portia in an excerpt from *The Merchant of Venice* and the audience fell into a hush when she sauntered on. In a long, black velveteen gown, her silver blond hair falling to her neck, she looked to her right, then her left, and in three or four paces reached center stage. Like truly great performers she had all the time in the world and from the moment she delivered her first lines she owned us.

When I next saw her, she wore a towel around her head and a mask of white cream on her face, as she prepared for bed in the opulent house where she lived with her mother. Two meetings after that, she was standing with me in our woods at Goldenfields, under trees that I loved. I touched her satin hair and she kissed me.

But these are memories, and they don't convey Venetia, they don't tell you the power of her calm, the consistency of her warm nature, the stability given to her by her talent. To sit with her was to be rendered serene; to wake alongside her was to know that a lovely world awaited. If I have to give you one image of your mother as she was when she and I first married, it will be the moment she stepped back onto the quayside in Galway. The law allowed a ship's captain to marry us offshore, and I will ever remember Venetia in a dress of pearl silk, a flower behind one ear, and her hand taking mine as she put her head on my shoulder. She was almost as tall as me, and the western light made her shine like a diamond.

9

August 1943

To this day, the streets of Killarney feel like a minefield under me. I've always been troubled there, and I used to avoid the town if I could. The remarkable beauty of the surrounding countryside made me ill, because I associated the place with flickering images of old silent films, their curly words flustering the screen. Venetia had been a child actress with one of the companies that made miles of film in and around Killarney in the 1910s.

At that time I hadn't yet seen the film *The Courage of Esmerelda,* all seven minutes of it, but I knew about it, she had told me. And now I had to brave again the town where its young star, my passionate love, had lived between the ages of ten and fourteen. No wonder the appointment to buy clothes went so wrong.

Miss Begley had suggested meeting at four o'clock in the afternoon, and we would go shopping. I came in from the village of Rathmore, a strenuous push up through the purple mountains, and then the dizzy reward of a freewheeling, reckless swooping down through lands of gorse and heather, past dark pools of silent water. She'd be punctual, I felt, and she was to stay in the town that night. The Farmers' Dance, an annual early harvest affair, was a big date in her calendar.

"A fertile ground," she called it, "for Seekers of Love and Romance." It didn't begin until ten o'clock, and she said, "I want a leisurely meal before meeting new clients."

Too leisurely—that's how a bad evening began. I got to the Great Southern Hotel at about noon and fell into conversation in the bar with people who had already been drinking. Lively company makes me drink quickly, never a good thing. When Miss Begley arrived four hours later, she showed displeasure, excessive in my view. Taking me away from the bar by the arm, she walked me out into the hotel gardens and insisted that I pace. Up and down, up and down; every time I laughed she cut into the chortle; every time I sat on the ground she made me stand and pace again. Naturally, she lectured me.

"I've seen too many men who drink too much."

Inside I said, *Some days, there's no such thing as too much.*

"Drink too what?" And as the words left my mouth I began to sing: "How can you buy. All the stars in the sky."

She said, "God almighty, a child or a dog knows when it's had too much of anything."

I followed through with, "How can you buy Killaaaaaarney."

She stamped her foot. That stopped me a little.

"How old are you?" she demanded.

Older than the hills and twice as bleak. But to her I said, "Twenty-nine. And lookin' good." Another song welled up inside me. "When Oirish eyes are smilin'."

"Stop this!" She stood back, looking shocked. "Twenty-nine? You look forty. And if you go on like this when you're forty, you'll look sixty."

I am sixty. And I'm eighty. And a hundred. And you, little-Miss-Rita-Hayworth-look-alike, you are a child.

I stumbled a little, recovered, and decided to sit on the ground. At least now I couldn't fall. She stood in front of me, wagged a finger, and began to lecture me. I tuned in and out and in again, but my head was wavy and my eyes were tired. She didn't care. This haranguing from her lasted an hour and included a walk to the cathedral and back again. I refused to go in, and soon she came out saying, "I lit a candle for you. Not that it will do much good unless you try to help yourself."

Any moment now she'll say, "Send forth a candle into a naughty world." And I'll say, "Stick a lighted candle up your backside to give yourself that inner glow."

My guards were indeed on duty that day. And I had stopped singing.

We went to eat. "There's no point in going to buy clothes with you sweating and shaking and stinking like this," she said.

Horses sweat, and men perspire, but ladies merely glow. And sweating and shaking and stinking—can we have less of the alliteration, please, Miss B.?

She asked the restaurant for a pot of very strong tea, and she watched over me as I drank one, two, three, four cups of tea so strong a mouse could trot on it. Then she ordered my food—stew with a double helping of mashed potatoes. She sought, she said, "to soak up the poison" in my stomach. Next she made me drink pint after pint of water: "Wash everything out."

Ah, yes, Miss Begley-of-the-bouncy-bosom, but have you ever washed your face in the morning dew? I have, and it's one of the world's healing miracles.

We ate a long, slow meal, and by then I had recovered most of my faculties, with no lingering symptom worse than a strong headache.

She asked me as dinner ended, "Do you think you'll ever get over your loss?" And when I shook my head, she said, "But isn't it better to be cheerful?"

I said, "Either my wife is dead or my wife is alive. And which is worse? If I knew she was dead, I could mourn her. If I knew that she was alive, and living somewhere, and not coming to find me, that would hurt. But it wouldn't hurt as much as not knowing what to believe."

"Just like me with my father and mother," she said. "We all need bodies. You can't mourn nothing."

I wanted to change the subject. "How many marriages have you made?"

"There's one couple that has stopped speaking to me."

"Why haven't you yourself married?"

She said, "A surgeon doesn't operate on himself."

"Are you saying you'll never marry?"

Miss Begley put down her knife and fork and gave me her full attention.

"I meet all these men, and you'll see some of them tonight at the dance. But I haven't met one that would be right for me."

"How do you know?"

"My grandmother is keeping an eye out for me. But the male customers—they're usually older. And they've usually lost the marriage race. We get the washed-up ones, both sides."

"But you're sure they want to marry?" I said.

"I have questions that I ask. To gauge how desperate they are."

"You asked me if I'd marry a girl with one leg."

"That's my grandmother's first question to a man. And if you'd been looking to become a client she'd have asked you four more questions."

"To measure desperation?"

"Loneliness. That's what cripples people."

I remarked, "As if I didn't know."

Miss Begley said, "Stop turning everything toward yourself."

"What are the other questions?"

She counted them on her fingers. "If I told you there was a little insanity in the family, would you still want her? How do you feel about a woman who never stops talking? Supposing 'tis a girl with a blemish, say a port-wine birthmark on her face, but a very nice nature? And the final question is: Will you settle for someone as flat as a boy or do you want a woman with a bosom?"

"And if a man answers 'Fine' to all five questions?"

She said, "Well, he's a desperate man."

I looked at her with an amazement that I later reflected in my notebook.

Their (extraordinarily basic) matchmaking questions for men are: One leg; flat-chested; facial disfigurement; madness somewhere in her blood; a chatterbox.

"Do you have questions that you ask your female clients?"

Miss Begley laughed. "Oh, God, yes."

"Are they very different?"

"They also establish levels of need." She counted them on her fingers. "A drinker or a sober man?" And of course she looked at me with a wicked eye. "Quiet or bad-tempered? Teeth or none? Though I try to fix that if I can. Fit or lame? Illiterate or not?"

Now I used my fingers to make a list: "So, if a woman will settle for a bad-tempered, toothless, lame heavy drinker who can't read or write . . ."

Miss Begley cut in. "—That's a lonely woman. Or a very hurt one. Or one who's desperate to change her circumstances. Or all three."

"What about hair? Baldness?"

"A detail," she said. "Like teeth."

"What will you accept? For yourself?"

"We're not talking about me," she said.

And I said, "But you're afraid of the question?"

She took her time, then gave an answer that, I guessed, had been worked out a long time earlier.

"It'll be immediate," she said. "I'll know the minute I see him."

"And what if he's a rogue? Or not available?"

She looked at me as though I had hawked and spat.

"Ben, don't ever trample on people's dreams."

When we stood up, she waited for me to move the table out of her way. I followed her out of the restaurant and fell in step beside her.

She said, curt as a teacher, "You're walking on the wrong side. Walk outside me please."

And I did—and for many years.

10

We had time and plenty of it to get to the Farmers' Dance. As we walked, she kept looking at me out of the corner of her eye, assessing me, sizing me up.

"Look how easily we fit together," she said. "We could easily marry each other."

This jarred me. I first knew that Venetia and I suited each other because of how we'd walked side by side. For the next few minutes Miss Begley and I walked in silence.

"Look, Ben," she next said. "Change the way you go about your life. Go on searching by all means, but try to do less moping. It puts people off. Put some chop into things, some energy. And I'll never stop telling you to slow down on the drink."

Uneasy, my head hurting, I began to feel criticized, and though not enough to protest it, I yet saw a surly mood coming toward me like an angry dog. My inner guards had gone to sleep—exhausted, I supposed.

"What's going to happen here?" I asked as we drew near the dance hall.

"A lot of chat," and she laughed. "Shyness in this place is always translated into jokes. You'll not see my business being transacted, because I have to make sure that the women I approach don't get jeered at by the men. Or worse, by the other girls."

Here are some observations of that night, notes that I couldn't have made without sharp attention—so I can't have been too much the worse for drink.

She talks a great deal, even more than my father does. Has a habit of pursing her mouth when listening, and moving her lips in time to the other person's words. Has another habit of "dramatizing" an account, meaning, if she's reporting dialogue, she "plays" it. She's very effective and authoritative. Slightly hooked nose—it quivers when she gives an order. Which is often. Beautiful, pointed shape to her bosom. She gives me the kindest smiles, even if she's irked. If she wants something to work, no effort is too much. She controls her feelings, and won't permit black moods. Eats huge amounts of food. When she laughs, everyone else laughs too.

11

How did a man so naturally ascetic, so given to reason and intellect, so comfortable with the austere and rigorous—how did such a man learn to drink so much? My long answer adds up to a complex of reasons: grief, occupational hazard, fear of self, fear of feelings. A shorter answer is: I fooled myself that I liked it.

I tried to idealize it, give it some style, pretend that I was a seasoned man of the world. *Whiskey is my tipple,* I'd say, all merry and lordly; *Irish whiskey,* I'd emphasize. Were it Scotch I'd have the spelling different—*whisky.* To compound the rakish image, I drank chasers, that is to say, when I drank a pint of stout, I made sure that I always had my little tumbler of golden liquid standing by the big, black glass like Mercury sits near the moon.

But whiskey drops a sourness on me—and not solely on the palate. And I took that sourness onto the dance floor in Killarney, among the men full of drink who eyed the women full of hope.

My head had cleared enough to study this social curio, this corner of existence. Judging from their hands and faces, most of the men worked the land. They wore boots mainly, and oiled hair—*brilliantine,* I believe it was, or *Macassar,* a sticky, honey-type hair oil that in warm rooms runs down collars and the sides of faces, leaving golden trails.

The women had made more of an effort. Hair stiff with fixtures, skirts that would swirl if danced fast, dresses as pretty as their world had for sale—in their lines, six girls deep, dwelt the night's color. But I also saw, like glassy currents on the surface of the sea, their drifts of inferiority, embarrassment, shyness, as though they believed that they could never be attractive.

I had some inside knowledge of how women should rustle up confidence. My mother-in-law, Sarah Kelly, spoke of herself as a great beauty. She had taken Broadway, Hollywood, and the Abbey Theatre in Dublin "without firing a shot," as she put it. Her daughter, the love of my life, had then excelled the mother—because Venetia had higher intelligence and purer, finer purpose than Sarah.

Those Killarney women—they could have done with Venetia's guidance, her poise, her sense of her own good looks. She'd never have stood mute, waiting for some boy to slouch across the floor and stammer his invitation to waltz.

How did folks ever get to know one another at these events? How did they overcome that ingrained diffidence that soused both sides? Yet Miss Begley told me that more than half of the marriages in the hinterland had come of people meeting one another at this annual thrash. She herself had made some successful "connections," and she'd been there only three times.

Among my impressions of the night, here's a note I made on the music:

Every year they choose the same band—an upright piano; a set of drums and cymbals; one clarinet, one trumpet, one trombone, one man on a bass fiddle, and a huge accordion played by a woman big as a church, who smiles like an optimist and keeps time with her foot. The singer is "John the Vocalist," taller than a tent pole, face white as powder, hair black as tar.

They gave the dancers little time between numbers—"Hurrying along the romance," as John the Vocalist put it, and the musicians surged behind him.

Somebody grabbed my arm from behind—Miss Begley was squeezing her way through her potential customers, the raw men of all ages who stood eight deep along the wall.

"Come on, show them," she insisted.

"But I can't dance."

She said, "You will by the time I've trained you."

Why she chose the difficult quickstep rather than the relatively easier waltz puzzled me, and she answered, "Start with the difficult and when it gets easy, everything else is easier."

I soon understood that she was, in effect, saying to the men, *Look— if this dirty big fellow can do it and he's half drunk, so can you. Give it a try like he's doing.*

We wheeled and spun. Sometimes we were awkward. Once or twice we danced lovely steps. The fellows with the hair oil looked on and whistled. Wild and salty, they catcalled, "Cycle into her!" Good-natured, they shouted, "How's she cuttin'?"

And then the trouble began.

I knew these men. They lived in the houses that I visited. Their grandparents sang me the country's songs and told me its lore at their firesides. Night after night, I wrote down the story of their ancient soul.

None lived in wealthy circumstances. A "strong" farmer supported the family entirely from his land. In a poor fisher cottage, a sack on a clothesline divided the entire dwelling. A few had held on to some form of farm wealth down centuries of oppression. Others, primitive and withdrawn, echoed Europe's Stone Age.

So I was completely on their side at that dance. I felt for them, identified with them. Traveling the country brought me closer to them. I saw them as warriors. Of impoverished agriculture, of poor land. Generally unmalicious. Shy and contained men who would do any kind deed for a neighbor or a stranger. But not for a government official. Or a policeman.

In their houses I drank tea. I drank whiskey. I talked with their parents. And with their siblings—who included the girls on the other side of the ballroom.

Yet I lost my control among them, these men whom I loved. Because some fool skated across the floor and wrenched Miss Begley away. He was bigger than I. His friends shouted him on. He grabbed her too tight. He held her too close. He all but trampled on her feet.

I stood there as she wriggled. Then I stalked them across the dance floor. I watched as she tried to push him back. He grinned and ignored her.

"Go back a bit," she said to him.

He grabbed tighter.

Another oaf joined in. From the edge of the deep throng he threw an empty bottle. Intended for me, it hit Miss Begley on the shoulder. Not, thank God, on the head. In fact it did no damage—except to my temper.

She knew too late what I would do. She could see me around the shoulder of her new dance partner. She made the big fellow halt. But she couldn't stop me.

The men parted like a little Red Sea. I ran at the grinning idiot who'd launched the bottle. He held out his hands and smirked. And I hit him; I hit him hard.

Do you know what it feels like to land a punch? Hard bone or soft squelch—it might be addictive. I knew it well. There had been incidents, I don't deny it. A kick here. An argument there. I have red hair, I flare. I'd never, though, taken on a man among his friends. Big mistake. As I hit him again, in the face this time, they landed on me. Including the big dancer.

You don't feel their punches. Not until later. In the first brawl of my life, a stand-up fistfight with my father, I took some heavy blows. I didn't know their true force until that night. And some of that was emotional pain anyway. These fellows, though, hauled and kicked and hammered. Boots stomped on me. Fists pounded on my head. A hand tried for my throat.

Then the scream rang out. And everything stopped. Miss Begley was standing some feet away, could see only my legs, and guessed that these men wouldn't be able to cope with a woman screaming. Her shriek pierced even the music, which ground to a sluggish halt, and when some women from across the floor began screaming too, the banshees took over the world.

The men stopped their kicking and punching and stepped away from me. Now a new standoff developed. Somebody hauled me upright by my hair. He bent me back like a bow. The bottle thrower stepped in front of me. He landed a punch deep to the stomach, but the force of my recoil dislodged the grip on my hair.

The fellow had no experience. He could have sent me into kingdom come. He could have knocked me out with an uppercut, chopped me on the throat—he could have killed me. So I took control.

You can do anything to a man once you've got him by the hair. If he has a lot of hair, you hold tight and twist. The pain is savage. So I grabbed his head and twisted like a lunatic. I ran this fellow out onto the dance floor. I turned him around and around, hauling on his hair. I dared any of his friends to come after me: "Come on! Watch him lose an eye! Or an ear!" I confess that I've cleaned up what I yelled.

Nobody expected what happened next. What happened next was Miss Begley. She strode forward and she slapped my face. Very hard.

Twice. *Slap-slap.* And then twice more. She pulled my hand from the bottle thrower's hair. She shoved him away, then turned him around. She took his fist and mine and made us shake hands.

"Pair of schoolboys," she said. "Ridiculous."

But we squared off again. I threw the first—and vicious—punch. Right into his stomach below the sternum. Would have killed an older man.

That was the moment at which two strangers walked into the dance hall—and that was the beginning of so many things, and the continuation of so many things, and the end of so many things.

12

If I'd seen as many films by then as I have since, I'd have laughed out loud—because they arrived like the cavalry. Except that they were infantry. Their names, not that it matters, were John and Hugh; one tall, one short. Clean as whistles, funny, relaxed, and curious, they wore the uniforms of American soldiers and said to us, "C'mon, guys. Cut it out."

Typically in an Irish brawl, the antagonists will forget their differences, turn on the outsiders who try to stop the fight, and derive their enjoyment from kicking them. We didn't. Perhaps it was the uniform; perhaps it was the American accent, reminding us of all those emigrant dollars that had kept our country alive for decades now; perhaps it was the clean authority that the two soldiers offered. Whatever the reason, my opponent and I looked at each other foolishly and shook hands.

Miss Begley said, "Go outside and cool down. Talk to each other," and to me she hissed, "Don't interfere with my work."

One night, more than a year later, when she was in low straits, I reminded her of "the night of the fight in Killarney" and it made her laugh, but she didn't find it amusing at the time.

Outside, my enemy told me his name—Sean Durkan, a young sheep farmer, and he'd had too much to drink, and I said, "I was drinking all day," to which he said, "Where would we be without it?"

Loiter is a good word to describe how we stood. Dancers would keep arriving until long after midnight, as the dance didn't end until four o'clock in the morning. We greeted people whom we knew or thought we knew, and then Sean Durkan threw up for a while, and then we loitered some more, smoking cigarettes, and making useless but pleasant conversation, mostly about farming, fiddle music, and drink.

The fight, though, must have stirred something in me, because after a lull, during which Sean Durkan had been chatting with some of his newly arrived friends, I heard myself say to this youth, "Did you ever meet a fellow by the name of Cody?"

I had never mentioned his name to anybody—except the police.

"Cody?"

"Raymond Cody. Ray Cody."

He dragged on his cigarette. "What's he like?"

"Did you ever see a water rat?"

Sean Durkan laughed. "There's a lot of them around. It'll be hard to spot him."

But he'd picked up something in my voice, he'd detected a cold shift, because he recoiled a little and added, "Jesus boy, I don't want to be there when you meet him."

That was all. He knew nothing about Raymond Cody, he knew nothing about me, yet he felt the menace.

In time, the two American soldiers came out from the dance to see us and smoke a cigarette. They told us that they were stationed "in Londonderry," which they described as "more than a hundred miles due north" from where we stood in the dark of the night, cigarettes glowing, distant music floating its way to us.

Their uniforms attracted passersby, curious and friendly. Every household in the country had relatives in the United States, and therefore people couldn't have felt warmer. And those open-faced, calm young men made it easy for everyone, chatting, offering cigarettes, looking for beer, asking about the girls—the things soldiers do all over the world. As an encounter it seemed normal, pleasantly interesting, fine.

During this, and all through my alfresco conversation with Sean Durkan the sheep farmer, Miss Begley had been emerging now and then from the dance, and always with a lady in tow. That was more or less what I had expected to see. She kept these women out of earshot, but I could see from the heads bent toward each other, and the intense body attitudes, that she was conducting intimate and powerful conversations with them. At the end of each talk, she took from her small white clutch purse a notebook, and in it she wrote things, then handed the women pieces of paper—her name and address.

My professional interest kicked in. Who were these women and girls? I knew who they were—the future wives and mothers of the southwest. Kate Begley was, among other things, the broker of the next generation.

13

As a consequence of my fight, she told me, Miss Begley changed her plans; she decided not to stay Saturday night in Killarney. With no more than a quick introduction to the two young Americans, she arranged for a hackney driver to take her back home. She insisted that I go with her. En route she sat as far away as she could from me in the back of the car and spoke not at all. I, dabbing my split lip, feeling the sore bumps on my head, speculated that she might have been disgusted.

Dawn had almost broken on the coast. As the hackney clattered and rattled away back down the lane, Miss Begley halted at the door and didn't lift the latch. She laid a hand on my arm and a finger to her lips. And then I heard what she was hearing: the ocean.

We stood there for long minutes, amid the beating and shushing noises, with now and then a seabird's call. When she stepped forward on the little plateau outside the house, I followed. A low sea-mist had draped the coast in a long gray stole. Above its shoulders, offshore and inshore, I could see the hundreds of scattered rocky outposts, fragments of the ancient mainland.

Maybe it's the pure vision of hindsight, but I swear the ocean at that moment represented something. My personal history had left me charged up by words such as *destiny* and *fate* and I began to feel as

though I were standing on the edge of something else enormous, something that would prove as far beyond my control as the white breakers
below.

Kate Begley felt it too. I know it, I saw it. She covered her face with
her hands as if she'd had a sudden surge of emotion. I eased forward for
a better view of her, and for the first time I saw her vulnerability. I saw
the child who had lost her parents and who had countered that loss using
such tools of life as she could muster—courage, skill with people, any
small power she could get her hands on. Most of all she relied upon a
blind faith that her lost parents would return to her one day.

Standing there with her, in the gray, tremendous silence, remains one
of my most powerful images of our relationship—which, in all its myriad forms, began in earnest that dawn.

14

I slept so deeply that she had to shake me at noon. My head and stomach hurt.

"Every pain is a lesson, don't you know that?" But she giggled as she
said it. (By the way, it seems that she destroyed her notes regarding the
brawl at the Farmers' Dance; there's evidence of pages ripped from her
journal around that date.)

The house, when I reached the kitchen, had the same air of blue cool-
ness looking out on brilliant sun that you'll also find in deep France or
the American Midwest. August on the southwest coast of Ireland offers
two seasons at the same time—deep summer and rising fall; that morning, they had merged again. I lurched straight for the open door, across
to the mouth of the steep little pathway, paused, and sucked in ozone to
clear my head.

Miss Begley followed, sidestepping spiky yellow gorse. On the fast
slope, I feared losing my footing but I didn't want to stop. Yesterday's
drinking and last night's fight had now begun to stab me; remorse is a
knife that twists when it's in you. As the familiar abuse ramped up inside

my head, I walked harder—but I began to slip on the steep grass. The waves lashed up, too close for comfort, their menace a cold cobalt on that heavenly, serene day.

"Where d'you think you're going?" she called down.

Outwardly, I didn't answer. Inwardly: *To perdition,* muttered my mind. *To the green, cold safety of the seabed. To oblivion—again.*

"If you fall," she shouted, "you'll slide down onto those rocks and into the sea. I won't be able to help you."

I halted and turned back.

"What are you doing?" She had her hands on her hips. "Are you trying to run away from me?"

I said, "I'm sorry."

True emotional pain is internal. We keep it to ourselves. *Sorry. Yes, sorry, I'm sorry. Sorry am I that my spirit has died. Sorry's the name of the horse I ride.*

"Ben MacCarthy, what's up with you?"

I repeated, "I'm sorry. I want to apologize. The fighting and that."

"Did you think I was going to scold you?"

"But I was badly behaved—"

She wouldn't let me protest. "Come on, Ben." She held out both hands, like a forgiving mother to a small child. "Come on. You've had enough trouble."

I said, "But I didn't behave well."

She said, "You got me home safely, didn't you?"

I began to climb back up the pathway, saying good-bye to some vague notion of shriving myself in the chilling sea. She took my hands.

"You'll be all right. We'll get you there."

Light on her feet as a pony, Miss Begley turned and went ahead of me.

Back inside the house, Mrs. Holst sat at the fireplace. She said nothing, didn't even glance at me.

Hey, Mrs. Holst. It's me, Ben. Come on, you old bitch, look at me. Tell me why you don't like me. If I told you that I'll one day likely inherit four hundred acres of prime Tipperary land—you'd look at me then, wouldn't you?

I hadn't seen her on my pained way through, and I apologized.

"My head isn't very clear this morning, I'm afraid, but that lovely day out there—it'll clear soon."

Well, we don't have to speak to each other, you disapproving old sow.

———

No electricity in that house, and no running water; they cooked on the fire, which even now in the late summer smoldered with peat, not too hot, and aromatic—most comforting.

At lunch, I ate little and remained as silent as good manners permitted. The women chatted to each other, principally about the dance. Miss Begley's smiles for her grandmother, her touches—a hand on the shoulder, a fetching of food, an adjusting of her shawl—warmed, I felt, not just that kitchen, but the entire coastline back as far as Dingle.

I had notes to write and returned to the room in which I'd slept. Through my open door I could hear Miss Begley tell Mrs. Holst about the girls she had interviewed. She made her grandmother laugh out loud many times—and she never mentioned my regrettable antics.

A couple of hours later, when the afternoon had grown quieter, the rest of our lives began. We all heard the engine, we all listened from our respective chairs, and I swear to this day that I knew who had arrived— the two young American soldiers from last night. A third man rode with them, and he was the world changer.

15

For the moment, I'll stick to the simple facts of what I saw in him that day. I saw a serious, considered fellow a few years older than I and some inches bigger. His name, he told me, with a handshake of oak, was Charles Miller. He had a grave, open face and large eyes.

By now, since so much is over and done with, I can say what the grandmother, Mrs. Holst, told me years later: "From the moment Miller walked through that door," she said, "I sensed the power and felt the fear."

She was like that, Mrs. Holst; I tend to scoff at all claims of hindsight. In that case, however, I'm inclined to give the old woman the benefit of the doubt.

Some years later when we were discussing it, Miss Begley said that she too had been anticipating "something." Maybe she was, but there's no trace of premonition in her diaries, whereas from the moment I met Charles Miller, I made notes about him in my personal journal.

In my preparations for writing this account for you, I've looked back at those entries and I find that they're characterized ambivalently—by admiration and unease, by love and fright. I like to think now that I got him right, though, because here's one sentence from a remark that I wrote about him some months later: *Have I heard too many legends about heroes, and the uncaring gods whom they serve?*

And they did look like heroes, those three young soldiers—they gleamed in the cottage kitchen, as strange and marvelous as from a shiny planet. The fuss of welcome, the apologies for arriving unannounced, the reminiscence of the previous night, the introductions—our warm hub-bub died down and we settled into the visit.

That's when, with a shock, I observed something new—Miss Begley had begun to blush, and she frisked like a dog. In my brief acquaintance with her thus far, she'd planned every move she made, got everything under her control, and the more I knew her, the more I confirmed that. That afternoon, though, spontaneity took her over as though glamour had asked her to dance. She began to flutter here and there like a warm breeze; she talked fast and high, she laughed with delight, she teased.

"Oh, but you should see the ocean when the gales come in. The spray drenches the house, doesn't it, Nana?" And "It's considered a great feat to row across the bay—I bet none of you fellows could do it." And, "I don't suppose you'll leave us that old crock of a car you're driving—sure it doesn't even have a roof."

A coquette of the kitchen, she commanded her own stage—positioning the cups and saucers on the table; offering richness in a blue pitcher of white milk; slicing a voluptuous pie; prancing across the stone-flagged floor—while eliciting all kinds of information without seeming to pry, as when she asked, "Now, do you know anybody from Kansas?"

The young officer, Charles Miller, eyeing Miss Begley like a woman eyes a sable coat, said, "That's the very center of the United States."

"My grandmother's late husband was from Kansas, wasn't he, Nana?" And turning to Miller again, she said, "I hope some of you are farmers, because we have farmers all 'round us here. Of course the farms are very small—" and immediately the young officer told us that his father owned five thousand acres, but the Great Depression had hit the farmers hard.

She elicited details of their posting—a U.S. military camp in the far north, near the Donegal border.

"We all believe the Yanks will come into the war, don't we, Nana?"

John, one of the two younger soldiers, said, "Well, ma'am, that's what we've been told to expect." At which the others shot him "shut up" glances, thereby confirming what I thought—they were in Europe under marching orders.

Throughout this hospitality, I also observed Miss Begley's exchanges with her grandmother—eyebrow lifts, subtle nods, tiny hand gestures, and I wondered if I were seeing an operation in progress; were the Matchmakers of Kenmare sizing up?

They were. Easy to tell from their attitudes—and, next, their questions.

"Is it hard being away from your loved ones?" asked Miss Begley, but the soldiers gave no hint of wives or sweethearts.

"Of course it is," encouraged the grandmother. "And fine young men like you always have girls waiting for them."

"You didn't dance away with any of the girls last night," said Miss Begley.

"I'd say they're still in that dance hall waiting for you all to come back," said the grandmother.

Other than pretty blushes, mumbles, and shrugs, the two women got nothing out of the three men.

That night, I wrote my observations of Lieutenant Miller:

He might indeed be a farm boy, but not the kind I know. College-educated? Maybe. Hasn't been on a farm in a while—look at those hands, big as shovels, bigger even than mine, but perfect, level fingernails. Sharp fellow; thinks before he speaks, that little pause before he answers a question. Does he laugh much? His face is too smooth to tell. Does he perhaps have something of the winter in him, a certain bleakness?

He's perfectly turned out. Uniform spotless; pant creases like blades, even after traveling down from the north. Height? Six feet five inches is my guess. He's smart enough, I can see that; he glances around him,

he takes in everything. How does he look at Miss B.? With definite in-
terest, and I think some respect. But why do I feel threatened? Is he a
little sinister?

Today, I look down on that scene from high above—I am a camera at
one corner of the ceiling. The uniformed young lions sit to eat in an Irish
country cottage. They ooze energy and good manners. The most distinctive of them, their crisp and powerful leader, has taken the chair at the
head of the table, directed there by Miss Begley.

On the table itself, the blue pitcher draws the eye to its point of color.
And this girl, this lively, inexhaustible girl in her mid-twenties, patrols
the fringes of this little feast; she's like a fixer, looking, checking, scruti-
nizing, and chattering.

Past them all, through the panes of the little window, the waters of the
ocean sparkle aquamarine, and under passing clouds some of the rocks
are purple again.

16

I'm not quite sure how the next development arose; no crude or obvious
moves occurred, therefore I must have missed the signals. Yet, when tea
had been taken, Miss Begley separated Mr. Miller from the others and
led him out of doors. His comrades remained at the table, asking polite
questions of the old lady.

My curiosity flared. I gave them some minutes, then I too moved out,
catching as I did so a frown from Mrs. Holst. Guessing that Miss Begley
would have led the officer down the path to see the view, I took an opposite direction, back down the lane, and turned inland to climb. Cutting across the higher slopes, I reached a point on the crag above and
behind the house where, if I lay forward on the heather, I could see all of
Lamb's Head and not be seen.

There they stood, far below me, on the slope that led down to the
jetty. Miller had taken up a position beside Miss Begley that spoke of re-

sponsibility, attention, respect. She, clearly telling him something in detail, laid a hand on his arm now and then; she moved in close, stepped back, moved in again. He in his olive green uniform, she in her yellow gingham checks—they looked like couples we've all seen so often in films. The wind tried to get fresh with her skirt, and in the distance below them, the sea kept coursing to the land, trying again and again to climb ashore.

Then, something changed. He turned from viewing the ocean and began to speak to her in a more direct, focused way. She took a large step back from him, as though startled. He followed, reached for her, took her arm, held it, and wouldn't let go. She subsided and listened with all her force. I didn't feel anything sinister—but I did sense an urgency.

In the months and years ahead, that picture came back to my mind so many times. *A couple on a cliff top, a more intense Heathcliff and Cathy:* That was one thought I had, and yet there was something disturbing there, something that alarmed her—and drew her to him. My mind filled up with questions: *He wants something from her? What is it? He matches her eagerness—why? Is he challenging her in some way?*

Time proved that I misinterpreted it all. He wasn't propositioning her with a soldier's wartime opportunism. Lewdness, crass advantage, sex, even the borrowing of money—I considered every possibility, but none had a part to play. Down there on the headland's edge, a more sinister matter was taking shape—a profound and dangerous transaction between those two people who had first met just an hour ago.

17

September 1943

The Sunday at Lamb's Head ended as I expected. Mr. Miller held out an arm, Miss Begley accepted it, and they toiled back up the crags. I slid backward, got to my feet, ran down to the lane, and was in my kitchen chair again before they reached the front door. Of a sudden, I had begun to feel angry, but I did my best to push the mood away.

With many thanks, words of appreciation, promises to write, all the trimmings of excellent manners, the visitors prepared to go. Miss Begley walked across to where I sat and murmured to me in a quick, low voice.

"Go with them and find out everything about him. I'll drop you a note to the post office at Valentia." I'd already told her my next port of call. She didn't have to specify Mr. Miller.

I watched with care how Miller took his leave of her, but I didn't watch nearly as closely as Mrs. Holst. The officer bent over Miss Begley's hand, bowing slightly from the waist, almost old-fashioned but not exaggerated. She, cool now, said how nice it had been and hoped they'd all come again. The grandmother circled, her eyes narrowing.

Outside in the sunshine came another urgent murmur from Miss Begley: "Can we make a bargain?"

I said, "Oh?"

She grabbed my arm. "You help me and I'll help you. All right?"

From that moment on, I felt it unnatural to refuse anything she asked.

In Killarney the Americans and I said our good-byes. From their map I advised their best route; they said they'd stay in Galway overnight. Exhorted to find out all I could about Mr. Miller, I wrote down his address.

"I hope we meet again," I said.

He said, "I never asked what it is you do." When I told him, he said, "That's so neat! I wish I could come with you sometime."

"If I'm in Derry," I said, "maybe we can go out to Donegal or somewhere, and you can hear some of the things I hear."

"Write me," he said, with another champion handshake, and at that moment the desire to like him was born in me. But how often it would be challenged! My postcard to Miss Begley, sent next morning from Killarney, read, "To use his own word—he's neat."

They drove off, I cycled away, each of us roaming the globe in his own fashion. I think that I had the greater affliction—because wanderlust is based on the homing instinct; we're always looking for the one place in which we'll feel safest. Miller already had such a place, on some big farm in a far continent.

As a stopgap for home, I liked bed-and-breakfast houses with older landladies; they know in their bones when a person wishes to eat in silence. In Killarney I kept returning to Mrs. Cooper, on account of her tact and her cooking. Also, I liked her, probably on the basis that we tend to like people who seem to like us. She knew some relatives of mine in County Limerick, and she had a gift of knowing exactly how much conversation to make about them or anything else. Furthermore, her husband had died in the previous war and, childless, she understood people who want to be left alone.

On the Sunday night, I stayed with her. Monday morning after breakfast, I waited for a shower to pass by, said good-bye to Mrs. Cooper, and set out for the long ride to Valentia Island. I hadn't yet decided where to stay for the coming night, but as usual I'd take steps to secure a roof before dark.

Clear of Killarney town, I was soon floating in long corridors of green, between hedges taller even than I on my bicycle, with an occasional glimpse of a field, cows, a farmhouse.

Those were wonderful moments, those long spinning rides through quiet country places. I had the open road to myself because few cars were able to get fuel in the middle of the Second World War. How fondly I think of those times, the hedges brushing me now and then, a bird screeching indignantly as her roadside nest was threatened by me, a tall marauder on his high contraption.

On those whirling days I saw things, images that to this day hang in my mind's gallery:

An old woman sitting outside her cottage, the sun giving impossible luster to her rusty black shawl. A serene farmer sitting on his cart, smoking his pipe, the blue plume curling in the air as his horse plods to the field. A muscled thatcher high on the ridge of a house, cutting the willow rod to the length of his arm, and then bunching golden straw under the willow rod to make the roof as bright as the sun itself. Barefoot children running alongside my bicycle, trying to keep up with me. The green weed smell of a roadside stream where I stopped to get a drink and found myself waist-deep in wild mint.

No war or rumors of war in these places, just scenes that could have been observed at any time in the previous hundred years in that part of Ireland. That's what I loved about my job—I traveled also in the past.

And so I went that morning, heading from Killarney down to Valentia Island, a place with nobody west of it, as they like to say, until the island of Manhattan.

Let me use this moment, as you ride along with me, to get something off my chest. Every story costs you something; as you tell it, you give it away—but that's all right; generosity comes with the storyteller's gift. In this case though, as my recollection will demonstrate, I've had to consider another element, very different from the impulse of generosity— I've had to weigh the anguish I'm reopening.

By telling the tale of Kate Begley and me, with its wide canvas, its wild swings of emotion, its heroes and villains, and its extraordinary conclusion, I'm opening old wounds to examine why I took the actions that I did, some of them terrible. Once more I'm hurting myself, and even though I long since traveled past all that, even though the life I've lived rewarded me acceptably, I'm still, as I write these words, having to calculate the control that I'll need merely to tell you.

It's discipline well expended, though; it's an effort worthwhile on many levels. Whatever my protests, I was enabled by Kate Begley and by the events in which she embroiled me, and by the people with whom she involved me—I was enabled to grow into a man I might never have become. I believe that the heights I reached were greater than the depths I plumbed, and if that isn't a recipe for a good life, what is?

By now you know, don't you, why my direct speech is addressed to the two of you, my delightful children. And as understanding as I feel you will be, you'll each forgive me a number of things—or so I ask.

Forgive the very indulgence of telling the tale; it's what old men do. And forgive me too a trait of mine, of which I think you may already be aware—my Digressions. It's a habit I picked up on the road. I spent most of my life listening to people telling me stories by their firesides, and those storytellers loved to digress; they wanted us to see not just the trees in the forest but the leaves on each tree.

I won't burden you with digressions as mighty as that. But if I wander, bear with me—I shall probably be doing so to ease the pain, and I'll always, I hope, take you to some interesting place. Indeed I can say now that however rambling they may seem, my Digressions will serve a purpose.

18

Apropos: The events of the next few days seem at first sight to have no bearing on the life story of Kate Begley—yet they do. My next appointment had been set for Valentia Island, where the transatlantic telegraph cable slid ashore from Heart's Content, Newfoundland, in 1866.

James Clare, my mentor in the Folklore Commission, the man of sublime character and salvational wisdom to whom I'd been so fortunately apprenticed, told me that he'd gathered stories from the islanders of the cable's great arrival—the mishaps on land and sea; the collapse of the first cable; the employment the telegraph company gave; and the general feelings of wonder that this great serpent could bring the voices of emigrants home from across the sea.

I, however, had a different reason for going there. Ever since reading *Treasure Island* as a boy I'd been interested in smuggling—the secretiveness, the atmosphere, the romance. Rudyard Kipling's poem jingled in my head:

If you wake at midnight, and hear a horse's feet,
Don't go drawing back the blind, or looking in the street,
Them that asks no questions isn't told a lie.
Watch the wall, my darling, while the Gentlemen go by!

Being an island country, and given our long hatred of authority, we must have had "gentlemen" by the thousand on our coasts. So I reasoned, and eventually a man told me of a family in Valentia.

"They're Buckleys," he said, "and there's eight generations of smugglers in their blood."

"Bawn" they called the man I met, the Irish word for *white*—Bawn Buckley, based not on the iron gray of his hair when I met him, but on the Viking blond locks of his youth. My hand thought it might not survive his grip; years of hauling in the nets—and contraband—had made it hard as coal, and more powerful than he knew.

Though he's long dead, Bawn Buckley still inhabits my mind, principally because of his stillness—and our later adventures, which I'll presently describe. I grew up an only child, and my father, an endearingly noisy man, preserved no space around himself. Bawn Buckley did, and I've most seen this enviable calm in the men of the Atlantic seaboard. A lifetime of being wary; a well-founded fear of the ocean, which could choose any day to take them; the daring to wrangle their living from such a power—whatever has caused it, they have that separateness around them, even in a throng.

There's a force that goes with it, and Bawn Buckley had that too, simple and direct. Although lines of merriment crinkled around his eyes, and he seemed not to care how the world spun, he gave the impression of being in control of everything, this unlettered man who had left school at fourteen, and who had spent most of his life trying to drag food from the teeth of the sea. His face reminded me of brown wrapping paper that had been scrunched up into a ball and then smoothed out.

He rewarded my visit beyond my tallest hopes. His narratives became the early—and the most vivid—contributions to the folklore collection I've built on smuggling, an Irish art form if ever there were one. And his smuggler's tales contained one surprise—plus, when I looked back on it, a reassurance that I would soon need.

For many years, his boat partner had been a man who sounded heroic—a man of strength and quick wits. In his multiple tales—some of which went on for an hour and more—he'd talk of "Flor."

He'd say, "Flor lifted the coastguard officer by the hair," or "Flor dressed up like an old woman hunched over her walking stick," or "Flor jumped off the vessel that arrested him, and he swam the three miles to the rock and waited there 'til I could take him off."

"Your friend, Flor?" I asked finally. "Can I talk to him too?"

"You can't," he said. "For the Atlantic got him."

I asked, "What was his name?" because I needed it for my notes.

"I'll tell you now who he was—he was a man called Flor Begley. His little daughter is a matchmaker over there on Lamb's Head near Caherdaniel, and a pile of men from around here go out to her every Sunday looking for wives."

I said, "I know her. I was at her house on Sunday." After a moment's thought, I asked, "Does she look like her father?"

"More like the mother," Bawn Buckley said. "The mother was a small, dark-eyed girl, she was from over there in Kilgarvan, lovely looking, bright as a bird. The father, Flor—big fellow, six foot four, I'd say, the only man I ever saw who had yellow hair. And you couldn't say no to him, he wouldn't let you."

19

Prepare yourself now for the first brush with war.

I have found that, in times of great crisis, every occurrence takes on the power of myth. Down in the southwest that week, as I looked out to sea, I witnessed something that, at first glance, might have come from a legend.

James Clare taught me to examine every part of my life as though reading mythology.

"It's very healing," he said, "to tell yourself your own story as though you were reciting a myth."

This event that I saw would soon become part not only of folklore, but of the mythic jigsaw into which I was about to be pieced. Though its outcome would be tragic, it also helped to save my life when I fell into circumstances as tormenting as West Kerry was tranquil.

Ireland's neutrality had turned us from *famous* to *infamous*. People great and small accused us of cowardice and treachery—cowardice for not fighting, treachery for exercising diplomacy. Beneath the charges of Irish perfidy lay a hidden purpose. Stated crudely, Winston Churchill wanted to shelter his war fleet in Irish ports—because German aircraft didn't yet have the range to bomb that far west.

Our premier, Mr. de Valera, surmised that ere long the German aircraft engineers would fix that, especially if they had fat targets such as British warships. If that happened, thousands of Irish civilians would die in bombing raids. Furthermore, under the natural law "My enemy's friend is my enemy," the entire island would become a target.

So, neutral we stayed, and we practiced the core protocol of neutrality—

we treated each side equally. That isn't to say that the war didn't touch us—and in the downpours of West Kerry it touched me in person. I still wince from it.

One noontide, as I rode my bicycle through the washed and stony lands, the rain proved too much. The ocean winds had gathered behind it, and the elements were blinding me.

I idled in Ballymacadoyle and found a kind of shelter under the waving branches of a bent and skeletal tree. The rhythm of the gray waves that I gazed on and the slapping of the rain on my waterproof cape produced a lulling effect, and when two excited men waved and shouted, I had to shake myself alert. They beckoned from rocks down near the water; I parked my bicycle, scrambled down to the sands, and ran along in the rain. As I drew near them, I saw that they had fixed their focus on something out to sea.

In from the wide ocean lurched a creature, half-bent, staggering through the surf, dragging itself to land. In the slashed view through the mist and the slanting rain, it kept redefining its form as it heaved its body and flailed in the waves. It could have been a wounded sea-animal; it could have been Proteus himself, changing his shapes with each lick of spray.

The mystery lasted no more than a minute. Its image clarified as it drew nearer—a man, bending over as though in pain, dragging behind him a rubber dinghy that had half-collapsed. As he hauled, he turned now and then, trying to tip it, to get the water out of it. Not a big fellow, slight but fit, he trudged in, then dropped to an exhausted crouch in the smallest waves; he didn't let go of the dinghy's rope.

When the two local men and I went to help him, he all but fell into our arms. He didn't speak, too exhausted; he was about twenty-five years old, and he bore no evidence as to whence he came. His clothes, a singlet and light pants, offered no protection; he shivered in his blue skin. The older man led the stranger out of the surf; the younger and I dragged the ruined collapsible. We hauled as with a whale onto the upper shore and stomped on it to squeeze out any remaining water.

Soaked and ragged, the young stranger squatted on the sands, his head low. None of us understood a word that he said, and one after another we shook his hand.

He seemed astounded and close to tears. Both his trouser legs flapped loose with torn cloth, and through them his legs glistened dark with blood—massive scrapes inflicted, we assumed, by the reefs outside.

Yet he stood up, turned about, and strode back like a demon into the waves. I know what frantic searching looks like, so I helped him; I stood in water up to my waist, staring at him as though to ask, "What?" The father and son (as they were) joined in.

Our wave-lashed, windblown search lasted an hour. He gestured us up one way and down again; he tried to go farther out, but the waves drove him back. Soon, between fatigue and agitation, he gave up—and the rain came in heavier than ever. I put my arms around his shoulders and led him ashore.

By now, his speech had slowed and I recognized German sounds. The two men guided him to their home up on the headland. I manipulated the rubber dinghy to a safer, higher place and followed.

20

That evening, as we sat by the fire, the young German and I tried to communicate. He wrote down his name for me—B-E-K-K-E-R. I learned that he was twenty-four—he counted on his fingers; with a wife, Alina—he tapped his ring; and a baby, Nadia—he rocked his arms. The woman of the house fed him and made him a bed for the night, and when he retired we spent the rest of our time talking about him. I told the family that I'd inform the authorities in the morning, and I stayed too.

Next day, I awoke to a shout. The people along that coastline don't rise early, and this was only seven o'clock. Through the window, I saw the young German running in the direction of the sea. I went to the door to see what had excited him—he had gone to greet another creature stumbling in the waves.

That night in Ballymacadoyle, the locals held a little party for the pair. Nobody knew a word they were saying, but the handsome young Germans tapped their feet to the fiddlers and smiled at the girls.

Back in Dingle next day, I told the local police of the two young men and wondered if they'd heard anything of a shipwreck. They told me that they'd go "down that way in a couple of days," and they seemed neither suspicious nor concerned. That tells you a great deal about our neutrality and the state of "the Emergency."

What tells you a great deal about war, however, is the fact that, several months later, the slim and fit young bodies of those two German boys were found twenty miles along the coast in a disused shed. Their throats had been slit and their bodies bore the profane marks of torture.

21

Now, while those young men are still in my mind, I must reveal something about myself. It connects to one of them and I saved my own life with it, and I must write it now because I want to heal myself a little after that sad recollection.

During all the lonely years of searching, I had also been educating myself. Everywhere I went I carried books. (Had Miss Begley been aware of it she'd have said, "Books are the Storehouse of Wisdom"—or some such motto.)

In general the books sprang from Miss Dora Fay, a friend to me since I was a little boy. She and her twin brother (whom I will not discuss, as his name would pollute the page) often rented the cottage that my parents owned on the bank of the river flowing through Goldenfields.

I loved Miss Fay, her toothy, tortoiseshell-glasses awkwardness and her sweet nature. She gave me my first jigsaw; she introduced me to two of the most magical words in the English language, *William* and *Shakespeare.* From Miss Fay I learned how to make egg custard; and I learned how to tie my laces so that they lie flat across my footwear and never come undone.

And then came a day when I discovered that James Clare, my protector, also knew Miss Fay. In fact, although they never married, they belonged in heart and soul to each other, and when Venetia disappeared, they became my spiritual parents. They guarded me from myself, never asked a probing question, accepted my dumb grief, and took me on up into adulthood as safely as I would permit.

As part of this process, they gave me my first major reading list, and Miss Fay, with her teeth as ever in the way of her tongue, said, "Did you know that books can save your life?"

How I wish that she had met the soldier who proved my savior. But at least I was later able to tell her the story of the scrawny little fellow, and it gave her the pleasure of saying, "You see, Ben—books truly can save your life." Miss Fay loved to repeat herself.

She had also asked rhetorically by what other means I intended continuing to learn, and at the same dinner table James Clare reminded me that many a good book would fit into a pocket of my greatcoat. So I took on every writer whom they recommended, from Chaucer to Dickens and Hardy, from Franklin to Hawthorne and Thoreau, from Balzac to de Maupassant and Zola.

And then I went on to read ever more widely, finding all the while many new friends on the page. I read Plato and tried to understand what understanding is; I read Socrates and learned how to argue with myself; I read Ovid and wished that I had been the one to collect those legends.

More important, I grew a kind of new skin—meaning, I gave myself a private identity. A librarian in a town where I'd been staying for two weeks introduced me to the work of a woman from Belfast, Helen Waddell, who had translated Chinese poems, some of which were written twelve centuries before the birth of Christ.

Then, not long before I met Miss Begley, this Miss Waddell wrote the book that became my constant companion, *The Wandering Scholars:* "To the medieval scholar, with no sense of perspective, but with a strong sense of continuity, Virgil and Cicero are but the upper reaches of the river that flows past his door."

When I read that sentence I became a Wandering Scholar; I began to see myself as a latter-day member of that band of men who wandered through twelfth-century Europe, sprinkling their Latin verses on the ground and watching them grow into culture. Was I not learning everywhere I went? And by sharing what I learned from the people of the countryside, was I not teaching? And isn't that the true definition of a scholar?

"Mustn't a young man make of himself what he can?" Miss Fay had asked, and this Wandering Scholar image is what I chose—the river, I told myself, had now flowed down as far as me. But I kept it secret; I felt it was too fragile to put on show.

I came to enjoy this new view of myself very much, and I believe you would have liked me in that mode. And indeed it was only when I dropped it, or became detached from it, that I drank too much and got into trouble. When I sobered up, and when the remorse kicked in, books became again my main recourse, and through which I again built up my picture of myself as a learned and learning young man, wandering from town to village, finding out what people had to tell me and offering them my own gifts in return.

As this person, I often forgot my own misery. Sometimes, and for weeks at a time, I began to cease thinking about Venetia, and about death, and the day it would come to me, and I began to look in other directions for fresh things, a new life. But I couldn't sustain it for long. The pattern, from the height of medieval dreaming to the depth of drunkenness, and back up again to a calm and respectful view of myself—that usually had a rhythm of about six to eight weeks.

Soon, though, I began to identify it, and sometimes nipped it in the bud. But being able to avert the plunge depended upon the location in which the bad mood set in—and in some places I never got it under control.

Consider Galway, because I had married there, young and full of hard-earned hope. How could my heart not crash there?

Our momentum now increases, as Galway provides the next and very revealing stage in the story of Miss Begley—because from Galway we went onward with no way of stopping her.

22

They call it the City of the Tribes, because the de Burgos from Normandy—today's Burkes—conquered it, and invited in thirteen other families, Blakes, Joyces, Kirwans, Lynches, and others, who ruled the place for centuries like European fief lords. There's a moment as you enter Galway when the city seems to float on the water, like Venice or Oslo, as the River Corrib mates with the sea.

I went back there every year at the time of Venetia's disappearance, to see whether such things as ghosts exist—or, indeed, miracles. My routine didn't vary—a walk along the quays, inspecting every ship tied up at the dock; a searching look into every dinghy and longboat from the vessels that stood moored out there in the offing. I stopped people, showed them the photograph; I asked the same question, always the same: "Have you seen this lady?"

By now, I was receiving the answer, "Didn't you ask me that last year?" Or the year before? Or the year before? And yet I trudged on, not knowing whether I had hope or not.

That year, though, I added something to my Galway inquiries; now I asked the question that had come to me out of the blue outside the dance hall in Killarney when I was fired up with aggression: *Do you know a man name of Raymond Cody?*

In Galway, I had no takers. Nobody knew this Cody, this slimy monster, this slug-white thug.

Depressed, my mind's voice a wooden bell, I walked around the city center, until a woman's call, from a distance, roused me: "Ben! Hoi!"

She had written to me at the post office in Dingle, "Meet me in Galway"—not a coincidence; she remembered my itinerary. And how precise she was with time and place; as she said in her note, "Twelve noon outside the main post office."

Not many women in Ireland wore hats, except on a Sunday going to Mass, and they certainly didn't wear great straw creations big as a wheel, with false cherries bobbing at the brim. Miss Begley did, on a midweek afternoon, with ribbons flapping out behind her head like red and blue tails.

"What are you doing here?"

She said, "I'm expanding my business," and when I looked puzzled she added, "The Galway Races. Isn't that why you're here?"

I said, "Which race are you in?"

"The human race. You should try it sometime," she said.

"That was low," I said.

"So's your mood."

She put her arm in mine, and we swung along the street like honey-mooners. "Come on, Ben. Chin up."

"You're not here for the races," I said.

"Maybe I'll marry a jockey."

You have the height for it.

I wanted to ask her what she was planning now. Even on our short ac-quaintance I'd sensed that this girl always had something going on—a scheme, a stratagem different from her declared intent, and the moment I saw her in the big wide hat I said to myself, *Now what is she up to?*

Asking her would yield no fruit. She only replied to questions that she wanted to answer. I had learned to wait.

"I met a man who knew your father," I said. "A Mr. Buckley."

And she said, "I know," but didn't elaborate.

She led me to a stone wall overlooking the water.

"I have things to say to you," she said. Hiking herself up on the wall, she arranged her skirts, holding her hat at the same time. "And I have questions to ask you."

Did I quail? I did, but could do nothing about it—because I had al-ready let her in, something I hadn't allowed with anybody, not even James or Miss Fay. With them, the exchanges had remained brief and delicate, as though they feared to tread on the eggshells of my sorrow. That cover was now broken; this woman was able to raid me.

"First of all. Your parents. You don't talk about them."

Some resistance must have lingered, or I was trying to take back lost ground, because I said, "I never had any, I come from a far distant star."

"How come you never mention them?"

"They're unmentionable," I said.

"I bet they're not. Somebody brought you up well. I can see the traces. Brothers and sisters?"

"I'm an only child."

"Like myself. One of God's Special Angels, did you know that?"

I said, "It's not true. God told me 'twas a rumor."

She said, "Jesus was an only child."

"By Jesus, you're right."

"All right, Ben. Stop being disgraceful. No more jokes and gibes, please. Do your parents know that you have a wife?"

"Had."

"Right. So that's how you want to play it," she said.

When Miss Begley folded her hands and her lips at the same time she meant business.

"Tell me the truth. Did Venetia run away?"

"Sort of. Her family intervened—"

"Because they didn't want her married to somebody who drank?"

"I was eighteen," I said. "I'd never tasted liquor."

"Is she, is losing her, the reason you drink?"

I said, "What else is there?"

She raised a mighty eyebrow at me. "That's a shallow little pool of character."

I said, "You know nothing. You know nothing about searching. And I hope you never will."

(Hindsight, that mean-spirited spy, whispers to me now, *Well, wasn't that a neat irony in the making?*)

"And she left no trace?"

I said, "A suitcase full of her money. And her account books. And her clothes."

"Her clothes?"

I nodded.

"That's strange," she said.

Miss Begley had the habit of thinking openly—by which I mean that she took on the attitude of thought in a very deliberate way. If I tried to interrupt her, she'd flap a hand and say, "I'm thinking." As she did that day, and for what seemed about three minutes, which is a long time of silence between two people.

At last she said, "No woman walks away from all her clothes. Things have to be done."

That last was a phrase I came to recognize.

"What does that mean?"

She said, "It means that I intend to take action on your behalf."

I have no doubt that she intended it. Now I ask myself had she done it sooner, had she not put her own wants ahead of mine—would we, would I, have had to go through so much? I think not.

"Remember what I said to you about a bargain?"

"Yes." I quoted her: "If I help you—you'll help me."

"Where do you think your wife is?"

I said, "I've searched all sorts of places. For somebody living or dead. And now I think—if I'm meant to find her, I'll find her. Anyway, what's this bargain?"

The wind almost flipped her hat and she grabbed it.

"I have the gifts to find your wife. But you have to help me in any way I want. You have to come and go everywhere I ask you to—right? And no questions—right?"

I nodded.

"One more question," she said.

I knew what it would be, yet I said, "Ask."

"What happened to the suitcase full of money?"

I said, "There was a lot of it. I saved it and increased it with good investments. I more than trebled it. Now I have a good income from it—which I spend looking for her."

She looked at me. "Don't tell any girl about that money. Ever."

A gust of wind snatched at her hat. She jumped from the wall and her skirts blew everywhere. I couldn't avoid glimpsing more than she intended, and I feared that she might have been embarrassed. Instead she laughed and said, "You're seeing my true colors," and I was the one who blushed.

23

At breakfast next morning, I tried to divine what was going on behind her eyes. Excitement had welled up in her; she bubbled like a spring. Could it be the day ahead of us at the famous Galway Races? I felt it ran deeper than that, but I got no closer than her effervescence; I learned nothing beyond her intent to get to the racecourse early.

And there, in the midst of the crowds, Kate Begley pulled her fortune-telling trick. I'd had the impression that she used it only for matchmaking, but not at all—she made money with it. No stall, no stand; she walked about and opened conversations, mostly with women, read their palms and told them that she did this for a living but had to be "very discreet, because the bishop doesn't like it."

I stood nearby and watched. In her great hat with its fluttering ribbons, she caressed the ladies' hands back and forth, murmuring words that I couldn't quite hear from my distance. Farmers' wives and daughters, shopgirls and spinsters of the parish, she told them their future and their eyes grew rounder; with trusting faces they extended both palms, and at the end, in discretion as deep as the confessional, money changed hands.

When she wasn't soothsaying, we rambled among the stalls of home baking and farm wives; we ate, we drank—tea, nothing else and nothing stronger. We went to a bookie's stand four times, and each time she won money. Not by any arcane or challenging system; "I like the horse's name," she said; or, "The jockey is related to people I know in Derrynane." Now and then she'd break off from this tourism, alight on some woman, and reduce her to wonder with a soft-spoken destiny.

And all this time I felt—no, I knew—that something else was going on, something that had nothing to do with Galway or horses, something that Miss Begley had planned with care and depth, and she'd made me part of it.

That night, I discovered what it was—but I didn't have it confirmed until breakfast. In fact, I uncovered it from my own divinations and felt more than pleased with myself when proved right.

It emerged spontaneously as I wrote my notes of the day. After a long account of the crowds, the jockeys in their gaudy yet grand racing silks, and the shiny horses and the stern winning-post, I ended with these remarks:

Miss Begley wandered through the Galway Races today with no sign on her that she had come to match-make. Instead she seemed more intent on gathering money, which she did by betting on the horses, and telling people their fortunes. I believe that she collected a great deal of cash; she had four winners on the card, and she spoke to more than twenty women. Why does she want the cash? And, it seems, so ur-

gently? She seems to have a prosperous and safe living with her grand-mother.

And then I wrote,

Aha! I know! She's not going directly back to Lamb's Head—she's going elsewhere.

24

In the morning, Miss Begley, in a blue-and-white-striped dress (and still that planet of a hat), seemed furtive. I decided to ambush her; and she gave me reason, because she said with a glittering eye, "Did you go drinking last night after you left me?"

I said, "No, I went straight to bed, as I said I would."

"Are you sure?"

I said, "I'm perfectly sure. I wrote up my notes and I went to bed."

She said, "What did you write in your notes?"

"I wrote the word 'Aha!' "

"That's not a word, that's an exclamation."

"Meaning?"

She said, "What were you exclaiming?"

I said, "You don't exclaim *things,* you just exclaim."

"So?" She looked wary.

I said, "I wrote it because I'd just realized where you're going next."

When Miss Begley blushed, which wasn't often, she looked discon-certed.

"Why haven't you used that gift of perception on yourself?" she said, in a kind of counterpunch.

"But am I right?" When she nodded I felt angry—for no discernible reason.

"So we'd better go, then?" she said.

"We?"

She looked a little frightened. "The bargain we made?"

I said, "Do you know where to find him?"

Blushing deeper, she said, "I had a letter."

"Inviting you?"

"He thanked us. Nana and me."

"But did he invite you?"

She rose with a flounce. I knew flounces, but although my wife and her mother were actresses, they couldn't flounce like Miss Begley.

25

Traveling with somebody imposes intimacy; there's little refuge and, on Irish buses and trains in the 1940s, no escape. Overcrowding had grown nationwide due to wartime fuel shortages, and we were like India—luggage and bicycles sprawling from the roof of the bus, or the train jammed with people, some of whom slept standing up.

I'd never been north of the Irish border, where, by all accounts, they felt jumpy about folks from the South. Since its establishment in 1922, the North of Ireland, as we called it, or the Six Counties, had felt more and more like a huge ghetto, into which southerners like us weren't welcomed.

That impression prevailed from the moment of first contact. They stopped the train on the border, and hostile policemen in black uniforms squeezed along the packed corridors; they glared into every face at close quarters. I remember thinking, *Of course they're suspicious. Because they're in the war, and we're not. Because they're under British rule, and we're not.*

Miss Begley tried charm: "Hello. Are we in the North?"

The man in the black uniform looked at her—as she said later, "The way a butcher looks at a pig"—and made no reply. She tried again: "Are we near Derry?"

He snapped back. "The city's name is Londonderry. Make sure you remember that. Londonderry."

Her eager smile died at his force.

As I moved forward to challenge him, she put a hand on my arm. When he'd moved on she murmured, "What would you expect from a pig but a grunt?"

Miss Begley used a lot of pig similes, probably on account of her liking for bacon and pork.

Our boardinghouse proved friendlier; as the woman said, "We're not heathens"—meaning not Protestants, meaning Catholics; the fault lines of the city ran then, as now, between the two religions. Miss Begley and I ate a long and hearty dinner, but I couldn't get her to discuss—or even confirm—her forthcoming meeting.

Now I know that her diffidence represented fear—not that she might be rejected, not even that she might be used and discarded, but fear of the unknown, fear that her own gamble, the kind of risk to which she spent her life directing others, might backfire and not pay off. When I think back on it, I see her utter bravery. She had decided to break all the taboos that she knew and pursue a man for herself. Accustomed to doing it for other girls and women, when it came to her turn she had more nerves than a debutante.

I did the unthinkable, couldn't stop myself.

"Shouldn't he be the pursuer?" I asked.

She said, "Next you'll be telling me that I've hair on my head."

I asked, "What does that mean?"

"To state the painfully obvious is a sign of low intelligence." She forced a silence and left the dining room. When she came back she offered no eye contact.

I pressed again. "Tradition is against you," I said. "If this were a legend—isn't he the warrior and shouldn't you be the shy maiden?"

With that powerful sniff of hers, she looked away.

"Did you hear what I said?"

"If a man is worth having, he's worth chasing."

"Whoa-whoa," I said. "Slow down, slow down."

She didn't listen, and so the world threw its worst at her.

When she quit the table to go to bed, I sat there. *Does he know that she's arriving? Has she set up an arrangement to see him?* Unable to fall asleep, I made notes, including this one:

No strong drink now for four days, and I must concede this: If one's head is clear, it's much easier to note down events and conversations.

In the night, however, I woke up and couldn't get back to sleep. Trembling, and without explanation, I found myself desperate for Miss Begley's company. I climbed out of bed, dressed, and tiptoed along the corridor. Yet I couldn't bring myself to knock on her door.

26

I can tell you how his superiors viewed Charles Miller. They had made him, in every sense, a pathfinder. He belonged to a powerful division of the U.S. Army known as the Special Observation Group, which had been sent into western Europe, specifically London, when the war had first gone against the Allies. With France long fallen and England in retreat, American officers, unobtrusive yet backed by full military resources, led the regrouping.

In the summer of 1941, two years before we met him, Lieutenant Miller had left his temporary headquarters at the American embassy in London for northwestern Ireland, to open the pathway for Operation Rainbow; that was his "cover." Strategic billeting would hold at least 25,000 American troops in readiness for a possible entry by the United States into the European theater. Eventually the number reached close to 125,000.

Near the city of Derry, whose official name is still Londonderry, the Americans built a major navy base, with facilities for seaplanes, the now-famous flying boats. Though close to the Irish Republic, the base was built strictly in the United Kingdom; our neutrality had been observed, and, I recall thinking, when I'd grasped the extent of it, *Is this a prototype? Did Miller and his two comrades come south along the coast to find other potential bases in places such as Kerry? Safe places, if, say, London fell to Hitler?*

In time I found that I was right and I was wrong; he had indeed been looking for something in southern Ireland, but it didn't include possible bases. And that wasn't his only visit. All this is hindsight, of course, but his familiarity in the jeep with the map, his keen interest in the southwest of Ireland, his pointed questions, his unexpected depth of knowledge—every bit of it came back to me.

A long time afterward, I agreed with the officer who said that something in the tale didn't fit, something was wrong. He said it because Mr. Miller would have been more than a match for the unpardonable Sebastian Volunder. I said it because so much had always felt out of true. Time gave its answers, as it usually does—but it didn't give all of them.

I'll come to that, but for now I still ask myself: *Should I have been more alert? On behalf of this girl-woman, my new friend?* As you've seen, I had already tried to halt her gallop. What more could I have done? In my bones, and despite her gaiety, I knew something wasn't right, because secrecy always implies a threat, and Miss Begley had hired a driver to take us to a place whose location she had "been asked not to disclose." Why didn't that Klaxon blare louder in my ear?

In my own defense, I did try to get the exact picture—of anything— from her. She twisted and turned; she wasn't sure where we were going; she wasn't sure who'd be there; she wasn't sure she was expected. All of this was, I imagined, false.

"If we're to be friends," I said, "why do I get evasions from you?"

People from Kerry have a renown for answering one question with another. She did so less than most, and only when under pressure. Now she said, "Does everything need a direct answer?"

I said, "That isn't what we're discussing."

She said, "Can't I travel if I want to?"

"Just so I know," I said. "You're chasing this Mr. Miller, you're pursuing him. Is there any other word for it?"

"Well, wouldn't you want to meet a fellow like him again?" And she smiled like Mona Lisa.

27

As you're about to meet him again, it's time to explain why Mr. Miller seemed different. To begin with, he had one of life's greater gifts—the gift of being believed. When he spoke, he could not be doubted. His manner of speech helped, a slow, thoughtful delivery, and, coming from that open face, his words conveyed unchallengeable sincerity.

Also, he conducted himself well, not in that exaggerated way that some military men have, as though rank mattered to them more than anything else. I think what I'm saying is: In my dealings, I saw nothing of the bully in him.

Which isn't to say that he couldn't be as hard as a hammer. Months later, I watched as he questioned, with words of ice, a distinguished man, a doctor of no little eminence.

"Is that your considered opinion, Doctor?"

The man bridled. "By which you mean—?"

Miller cut him off: "Prove to me that you're competent to make such a statement," and he kept the doctor hanging. "No, do not answer until you have thought about it."

In a bluster, the man rose to his feet, but Miller raised a warning finger and forced a longer pause. The doctor hesitated, bowed, and said, "Sir, I spoke loosely, I will correct it"—and clicked his heels.

Charles Miller had no such frightening effect upon me. I found that I wanted to do things for him. In his company, I was the one who offered to fetch the drinks, the tea, whatever—even though he couldn't have been more gracious or attentive.

He also made me check my own standards. In the times to come, whenever I knew that I was about to meet him, I took extra care with my appearance. Also, I find now that I remember the details of our every meeting; standing on a slipway in West Kerry, or playing snooker in London, or pitching stones on Lamb's Head—and especially our heart-breaking last journey. And I recall in particularly sharp focus the moment when Kate Begley and I saw him that morning, on the shores of the Foyle estuary outside Derry. It was a day with air so clear that I wanted to fly.

28

At a quiet word from Miss Begley, a uniformed soldier raised a barrier at the entrance to a military site flying the Stars and Stripes, and we drove onto a long flat of wide beige strand. Charles Miller was sitting at a portable table on the sands, examining maps and charts with two other men, amid a scattering of half-erected buildings. In his khaki shorts and military shirt he looked like a nineteenth-century explorer on an archaeological dig.

Miss Begley said, "Come on, Ben. I need you now like I never needed anybody."

A hundred yards from the building site, we climbed out of the taxi-cab, and she set a sauntering pace over the foreshore. Did we look like two people out for a stroll? Of course not—and besides, we had entered a restricted property.

What I recall is the expression on Charles Miller's face when he looked up. *He's not so much pleased as satisfied,* I thought. *And that's odd.* His lack of surprise interested me equally; if delighted to see her, he wished it not known; and if not surprised that she appeared, he didn't want that visible either. But what was the satisfaction about?

That morning, ever the gentleman, he rose to his feet and gave a brief salute before grasping Miss Begley's hand. At least she had the good grace not to say, "What a surprise!" She said, "Very nice to meet you again."

Mr. Miller then turned to me and, shaking hands, said, "Ben. Hi."

I said a weak "Hallo," and I recall the thought, *What can I do to please this man?*

In my later researches, I discovered that he'd been identified as special from the day he enlisted. Sidetracked to a fast commission, he had always been taken up by his superior officers—no matter who they were—

and given significant duties. Out of this remote Irish corner, he would lead a small, fierce team into undercover operations in Europe.

It's so plain to me now when I look back: He was running a different war. Yes, he had natural reserve, but the need for secrecy intensified it. And yes, he had a shrewd way about him, but he was also gathering every useful scrap of European local knowledge.

It took me a long time to find out the deal that Miss Begley and he had made in their moment on Lamb's Head. When I did at last put it to her, she told me everything—but on that morning they hadn't yet moved beyond the earliest stages. So far, he was the one who wanted something from her. I doubt that he yet knew how much she wanted from him—but in her fearless way she would soon make it plain.

That morning, she played it all in such a low key. Beyond the folding table stood a wide tent. They'd erected plywood boards on easels, and to these they'd pinned drawings and blueprints.

"Now tell me," said Miss Begley, "what are you doing here? Or is it all a big secret?"

Mr. Miller said, "I can show you," and led her across the sand to the tent.

"Hundreds of people—from all around the place—they're working here. So there's not much chance of keeping it secret, is there?"

They both laughed.

"Careless talk costs lives," she said, repeating a wartime refrain that we'd all heard on the radio, and they laughed again.

I saw him look down at her and I also saw how easy they were together. These were my thoughts: *When they stood on the headland, and I lay on the heather looking at them, he startled her with something he said, and then when she was rocking off her guard, he asked her for something. Whatever he asked—it's big. And she's here for a second look at him before she agrees, before she strikes her side of the bargain.* And I reflected, *Is it a devil's pact or an angel's?* And then I reflected further, *In a war, who can tell the difference?*

29

We met them that night at a hotel for dinner. Tall John and little Hugh came along too—Tweedlehugh and Tweedlejohn, as Miss Begley called them, though not to their faces. We ate vile food—a soup thin and sticky as green drool, followed by something alleged to be beef. The green cabbage tasted raw as nettles. However, the Tweedles exulted, and declared this a meal of Ritz quality after army rations.

Lieutenant Miller said to Miss Begley, "I've been dreaming of your grandmother's baking."

"Oh," she said, "that was mine."

After dinner I discovered that the men had driven to meet us in separate transports—the Tweedles in a truck, Miller, alone, in a jeep. Which meant that he could stay as long as he liked—and he did. At two o'clock in the morning I looked out of my window and saw him on the street below. Turned sideways to face him, Miss Begley sat in the front seat of the jeep, as he squatted beside the open door. On a balmy summer night in the high northwest of Ireland, twilight lingers forever; the sun scarcely leaves the sky.

At breakfast next day I said, "What time did you get to bed?"

"A policeman wouldn't ask that question."

"You don't look tired."

She said, almost to herself, "You can't feel tired near that man."

"How important is he?"

"He's taking today off," she said, "and we're going for a drive out to Donegal, up onto the north coast. I want to see what happens to the Atlantic Ocean after it goes past my house."

"When will you be back?"

"You're coming with us."

Good, I thought, *because my anxiety is rising again.*

I sat in the rear of the jeep, and, to begin with, Miss Begley directed most of her attention back to me.

"Ben, you know this countryside, don't you?"

"Ben, is there any place in Ireland that you haven't visited?"

"Ben, how do you remember it all? You must have a huge brain."

"Ben, I like that shirt very much. I haven't seen that on you before."

Flattery, deference, respect, admiration—before long Mr. Miller began to cut in, as I presume she'd intended.

"Ben, have you traveled all along this coast?" she asked me, and Mr. Miller said, "I have. If you go due north from here, you'll see some of the biggest Atlantic breakers you ever saw. I never dreamed of anything like them, I come from nowhere near the sea, I come from a wide sky, and you can see for miles and miles and not a house anywhere"—and he launched into a description of how, in his boyhood, he measured in the family car the distance to the nearest neighbor. "Twenty-two miles, can you believe that?"

I asked, "When did you come to this side of the world?"

"London was the first place, I was there for eighteen months." By now he had made himself the focus.

"Just, you know, working," was how he answered a question she asked, and she pursued with "War work?"

"I'm a soldier. Soldiers do war work."

"Who's going to win the war?" she asked him.

"God Himself wouldn't answer that question."

"But isn't Germany winning?"

"Winning, losing—they kinda mean very different things in a war."

"Who do you think is winning?"

"It'd be good for nobody if Hitler won. Or Japan."

"What do you think about Ireland being neutral? A lot of people don't like it."

"Folks can always volunteer for the British. Or for us."

"Ben, do you want to be a soldier?" she asked me, and before I could answer Mr. Miller said, "I'd want you in my platoon, that's for sure, big fellow like you. Can you shoot?"

"Never tried," I said.

"We don't have many guns in Ireland," she said. "We don't need them anymore," and when he looked puzzled, she added, "Now that we have our freedom. We had wars here, too, that's why we're not fond of guns."

The jeep bumped us—or was it the roads? I sat back, letting the sun warm my head and face. Watching them I could see the mutual voltage—mostly I could feel the heat from her to him. He seemed unfazed by her force, and I thought, *This fellow could probably handle a live electricity cable with his bare hands.*

"How do you like Ireland?" she said.

Around us spread County Donegal, in that pale mauve light you get in the northwest. The houses sat scattered about the countryside then; they're more numerous today. Sheep dotted the hills, distant white blobs. A donkey in one field, a pony in another, low stone walls—Mr. Miller looked all around.

"Reminds me of northern Spain," he said.

"Where haven't you been?" she said.

We stopped at a pub in Clonmany. The proprietor grew excited at the American, and began to inquire about a job for his son at the new base. Lieutenant Miller undertook to see the young man himself—"Tell him to ask for me," and wrote out his name. Drinks came on the house. I drank lemonade. Mr. Miller tried Guinness and made a face.

I can freeze that afternoon in my mind. I can go straight back to the moment and see us there, sitting on high stools at a long dark bar, eating sandwiches thick as doorsteps, with old newspaper advertisements plastering the walls, and posters for local charities, announcements of cattle fairs, and boats to Scotland. The sun found a way through the filth on the windowpane to fling a few bars of light on the floor, and the glow caught the young American full in his golden face.

Any attention that our group received went to Miller. A chatty local gave him the day's newspaper. The proprietor's wife gave him the largest plate of food. The proprietor gave him and him alone a souvenir mug.

The proprietor knew James Clare—who didn't?—and, discovering my connection, began to tell me about a haunting on the shore at Malin Head, where the ghosts of two young fishermen kept coming back. They'd been drowned there in the middle of the nineteenth century and everybody had seen these ghosts. I took out my notebook to write it down and, from the corner of my eye, saw Miss Begley and Mr. Miller enter a deep conversation.

When it ended, I wondered whether Miss Begley too had seen a ghost, because, as she sat back, the sun that lit this young officer also showed a desperation in her face. And a sense of confusion. And, I thought, panic.

30

That Charles Miller enjoyed our company couldn't be denied. As Miss Begley fell into a long silence on the way back to Derry, he wanted to know everything about my work. That's when I told him about the two young Germans washed ashore at Ballymacadoyle, and in the urgency of his response he almost stood up behind the steering wheel.

How old? What did they wear? Were they armed? Did you see a boat? Could they have come from a submarine? Where are they now? He turned me inside out with questions.

When I had told the tale he subsided and held a silence for long minutes. What did I know in those days—oh, what did I know?

But we could have talked all day and all night, he and I. No wonder I came to admire him so—he showed such interest, not just in me, but in life generally.

"All our neighbors back home—they have old stories," he said. "Their parents came west, or their grandparents emigrated from Germany or Russia or China. I love those stories."

I missed him when we parted. He shook my hand and said, simple as a child, "We'll meet again, Ben. I know it."

Although I wanted to tell him about Venetia and my own life, the time proved too short. But I sensed that he was the kind of man who would have taken on the tale as a project, and he'd have approached it in a practical way as a difficulty to be solved. He might even have involved himself in the search. I thought, *Maybe I'll ask him. Maybe he'll help or have some ideas.*

That night, I said to her, "There was a time when you looked shocked today."

Sounding candid, she told me, "There's been intimacy with a girl back home. He says he must marry her."

"Is there a child?" I asked.

"I don't think so. He says it's a matter of honor."

"What are you going to do?" I said.

"He's asked me to do something for him. It's outlandish, but—"
She didn't finish the sentence.

"Can you tell me what it is?"

"Not just now, Ben. Sleep's gentle voice is calling me."

Next morning, Miss Begley and I set out for the South. She, grave and less garrulous than usual, nonetheless made heads turn as we boarded the bus, the straw of her hat as round and yellow as the sun. We had no conversation, not enough privacy, until we caught the train at Sligo, and sat in a compartment, just the two of us. By then something of her bounce had returned.

"Well, what d'you think of him?" she asked me.

"He likes you," I said. My inner voice said, *And I don't like that fact.*
She laughed. "I like him."

"What's going to happen?" I said.

Mona Lisa smiled again. "We made a deal."

I said, "Why are you always making deals?" *Because you don't know how not to.*

"And what's wrong with that?" she said.

Everything. Everything's wrong with it. But I said, "I suppose it brings people closer."

She smiled again—but told me nothing more.

We parted in Galway, and I gave her a rough sketch of my travels for the next few weeks. Earlier in the year I had at last regularized my own timetable. I wasn't so scattergun anymore; I moved through the provinces now in a kind of loose rotation. Therefore I could say where I might be reached close to any given time.

And so, in the third week of September, in Watergrasshill post office, I picked up a card from Miss Begley: *CM transferred back to London. Come to England with me. KB.*

PART TWO

The Swing of the Pendulum

31

October 1943

Adolf Hitler had red hair. So a woman in Dublin, a cabaret singer, told me. She saw him in Berlin in the late 1930s: Sitting on her father's shoulders, she watched him drive down the street they call Unter den Linden.

"He was small and red-haired," she said. "Common-looking. And the crowd went wild."

That was the kind of detail I loved. I had been following the war in the newspapers and on the radio, and when it reached a finger into Ireland, I wished to touch it. In other words, I wanted to visit three of the four places in Dublin where German bombs fell in 1941. By the time I got to one of them, the worst of the damage had been cleared. Thus, I hadn't been able to create the sensation I sought—how it might feel to stand on the earth as it rained bombs.

For some unknown reason, I told all this to Miss Begley on the boat from Dublin to Liverpool.

She said, "There's times, Ben, when I don't fully understand you. What did you want to know—what it's like to be hit by a bomb?"

I said, "Sort of."

"Ah, for God's sake, Ben." Not much stopped her in her tracks. "Why?" she said, groping to make sense.

"I'd have a better idea of what war is like."

She reflected on this, and up went that damn eyebrow again. "Aren't you afraid of the war?"

"Are you?"

She said, "Why would I be?" in that belligerent tone she used when she didn't want to be challenged. "Ours not to reason why, ours but to do or die."

I said, "There's a lot to fear."

"What do you expect we'll see?"

I said, "Ruined buildings."

"They'll be taking it badly," she said. "An Englishman's home is his castle."

"Some of it may hit us."

And she said, "No. I'm never in the wrong place at the wrong time."

Not, eventually, true—not true at all. But I've just remembered something Mother once told me: It's the mark of a gentleman not to remind people of foolish things they once said.

Miss Begley then admitted that, like me, she'd been expecting to travel through a country shredded by bomb damage. We'd seen the photographs and newsreels of the devastation that struck Dublin. If that had been caused by a lone German aircraft (possibly a navigation mistake, we were told), what on earth must England be like by now? They'd had four years of ruin from the air.

As we stepped from the dockside to the waiting train, I asked her, "Why exactly are we going to London? What precisely will we be doing there?"

She looked at me with an impatient purse of the lips and picked up the book she'd been reading; I gazed out of the train window.

England looked glorious. They were enjoying an Indian summer, long days of golden light falling on leopard-colored trees. The train took us through acres of aftergrass green beyond reason, and spiky deserts of fawn stubble. England had spent the season growing extra food as part of the war effort; now, fallow and spent, their duty done, the fields rested, as calm as a woman after giving birth.

At first I felt confused, because it looked no different from Ireland—pastoral, empty, and still. Yet in my pursuit of every war report I could find I'd seen the rumors that we might get invaded; so these were my thoughts: *If either side invades us, we'll be exactly the same as England—the wide quiet fields in one half of the equation, the ruined towns and cities in the other.*

By now I had brought under control my resistance to Miss Begley's pursuit of Charles Miller. At first I had taken the old-fashioned, hunter-gatherer position, and I announced it.

"You should stop it. It's unseemly. Men do the pursuing. Men court. Men woo."

She didn't reply—and then I shut up, because I recalled that Venetia had been the one who'd initiated our relationship. The day we first connected she did all the running, declared her feelings, said that we were meant to be together. I never questioned it; I just followed her lead.

Therefore I'd have been a hypocrite if I hadn't supported Miss Begley's focused drive on London. I knew that I'd help her if I could, but I also expected to do nothing more than stand by and watch. Of course I had no idea what I would be watching.

As if all this weren't enough, I found myself sleepless again, troubled by something else. The night before coming into Dublin to catch the boat, I'd stayed at a concertina player's home near the town of Kildare. I'd visited the family in the past, they'd heard my questions, seen Venetia's photograph, and guessed at my anguish.

This time, though, the woman of the house remarked, "I might have a bit of news for you," and said that her sister had worked as a cleaner at the Abbey Theatre in Dublin and had known Venetia. "They all loved her," she said.

I nodded.

"Well," said the woman, "my sister says that they heard at the Abbey that Miss Kelly—well, she's not well."

I galvanized. "Where? How do you mean, 'not well'?" But inside I was screaming, *You mean she might be alive?*

My outburst scared her; sometimes I don't know my own strength. She retreated, and I now believe that I destroyed any chance I had of acquiring her information.

"Oh, hold on, Mr. MacCarthy, hold on. I mean, the same woman, she told me something myself once, and wasn't it all a lie?"

My face, I know, went white, and I walked out into the night. This was the old, awful pattern: *Cleft in twain again. No farther along, no more healed or eased.*

And yet, I observed something. However scorching this woman found my reaction, I could sense that the flame of that particular lamp was running low on oil. And I surmised why: As she herself might have

put it, Kate Begley had marched right into the fields of my private anguish, pitched her tent there, and was now redirecting the soldiers of my
zeal. As a consequence, I was thinking more about her than about Venetia. For the first time, but not the last, I felt disloyal.

32

As I was having these thoughts, something ridiculous took place. The
train stopped at some junction, Crewe, I think, and took on passengers.
Up to then we'd been seated in a compartment, just the two of us, facing
each other, by the window. Now a woman opened the door and raised an
inquiring look.

To my annoyance, Miss Begley said, "Come in, there's only us." Before I could help, the woman hoisted a crimson suitcase up to the rack
and plonked herself down.

I understood the invitation. In the privacy of the compartment, our
conversation about what would happen in London had been cranking
up again. This newcomer's presence, though, meant that I couldn't press
anymore, couldn't ask yet again, "What exactly are we going to London
for?"

Now comes the silly part. Miss Begley engaged with the newcomer:
Where are you from? Are you going to London? Isn't it a lovely day? A short
time later, they'd reached fortune-telling, soothsaying, crystal gazing.

"I believe in it wholeheartedly," said the passenger. "Do you?"

"Well, I'd have to," said Miss Begley.

"Why is that?" said the passenger.

"Because," said Miss Begley, "I do a bit of it myself."

A hand to her mouth, the woman breathed, "Oh, you don't, do you?"

I thought, *Oh, God. She's going to drag this out all the way to London.*

And Miss Begley did. "I consider it a gift that I mustn't waste," she
said.

Another inward groan from me: *We're going to get the works here.*

The woman, a decent creature of fifty or so, undramatic except for

her crimson suitcase, said, "How much do you charge for telling a fortune?"

"Oh, I only charge if I'm set up, and if it's a working day." I concede
that Miss Begley's next remark may have come out of kindness; she said,
"Would you like me to tell your fortune? There won't be any charge,"
and she smiled like a beauty queen.

The woman said, "You don't know how much I need it."

Miss Begley slid along the leather seat, and the woman slid to meet
her halfway.

"Now. Which hand do you write with? Because that's the hand I want
to see first."

Here's the worst part; not only was the woman hooked—so was I.
I picked up my newspaper, shook it out, opened it, pretended to read—
and eavesdropped like a spy.

"H'm." Miss Begley mused. "H'm. I see. I see."

My mind shouted, *What is this rubbish?* But my next thought was,
Well, who can't believe in magic?

"You're widowed," said Miss Begley.

The woman said, "Yes. My husband was—" and Miss Begley interrupted: "No. Don't tell me."

The woman said a chastened, "Oh, I, I was—" and halted.

"Your husband was killed in the war. I'm very sorry for your loss," and
from the corner of my eye I saw Miss Begley raise her head, look at the
woman with full sympathy, and return to her head-bent task. "And
you're on your way to London, for two reasons. You want to continue the
inquiries about war widow compensation. And you're hoping to get a
job, I'd say in the clothing business."

The woman almost cried out. "How do you know?" she said. "How
do you know all this?"

Miss Begley said, "I'm afraid I don't know. Does an artist know why
he can paint?" And again she went, "H'm."

The woman said, "May I ask a question?"

"Yes, dear." Miss Begley sounded like an old lady.

"What's the difference between the two hands?"

Miss Begley answered like an expert. "It's different for many fortune-
tellers. For me, the left hand has all the character you received at birth.
And the life you've lived so far is in it too. Your right hand—that's what's

going to happen to you, that's what's ahead for you. Another way of putting it is—the left hand is what you got, the right hand is what you're going to do with it."

"How much can you tell about my life so far?" said the woman, thrusting her left hand forward.

Miss Begley took the hand as though it were a napkin of embroidered silk. She scrutinized the palm, caressed it, traced some lines.

"Well, you've had an interesting life, haven't you?"

The woman looked alarmed and pleased.

"May I ask—are you still keen on him?"

The woman said, "On whom?"

"On him. You know." Miss Begley somewhat lowered her voice. "You know who I mean?"

The woman blushed, and Miss Begley said, "Oh, my goodness. Let me see your right hand again. Well, well." She sounded so final. "Have you actually made arrangements?"

The woman, startled as a bird, said, "How do you know all this? I mean, how do you know?"

Not for the first time, I felt reduced. Day in, day out, I tried to keep some intellectual rigorousness in my work. I approached my note-taking with a hardworking conscience. Every report that I sent in met the required standard of high legibility and provenancing detail. I wrote in a clear and wide hand, used indelible black ink, in lined, stoutly bound notebooks.

Every person I interviewed was given the appropriate date, on both calendar and clock; the interview was timed and supported with an identification, often with a brief family tree; for instance, *Thomas Buckley, so-called "Bawn." Son of Michael John Buckley, and Hannah Fitzgerald, both of Portmagee, Valentia Island; married 1909, Margaret, so-called "Madge" Ahern of Castleisland; no children.*

If the tale or tradition I was collecting had echoes of something else within my knowledge, I footnoted it, so future generations of students had at least a search to pursue. I relished this requirement to be accurate and consistent; I told myself that I had little time for frippery—yet now here I was, traveling with, essentially, a walking box of low-rent hearts and tawdry flowers. But look, there must have been, there may still be, something intellectually low-rent about me because I'd also loved the shoddier parts of Venetia's road show.

And thus did the cheapness of the music drag me down. Despite my loftier intentions, I, the Wandering Scholar, couldn't get enough of this stuff, especially the fortune-telling. You can see, can't you, how it must have appealed to someone with my burdens? And you can guess my next thoughts, which would recur over and over: *How about reading your own palm, Miss B.? Or mine?*

33

A city at war teems with opposites. As walls fall and naked gables claw the sky, people rediscover purpose. And so they scurry here, they scurry there, like ants hoping to dodge a great human boot. That was my first experience of bombed streets. My parents knew London well, had often described it to me, and once brought back a book called *Wonderful London in Pictures.*

Our train arrived in the early afternoon. That day, and for many days beyond, I walked where buildings leaned against one another with broken shoulders—some of them little more than ghosts from that old book.

This was my third kind of war. From legends and mythologies, from Finn MacCool and his mighty Irish warriors, from the Red Branch Knights of the Ulster Cycle and the Twinkling Hoard, from Sparta, Thermopylae, *de Bello Gallico,* and all of Caesar's campaigns, from Hector and Hercules, I knew of valiant war, victors and vanquished, hand-to-hand heroes, swords, javelins, and spears.

At home in Goldenfields, I'd been a child during our Irish Civil War, a family struggle where every man brought a gun to breakfast. We'd had ambushes near our gates, torture in our fields; we'd known of brothers fighting each other, split to their blood by the political structures that prevail to this day.

For instance, Mother visited a family where the father had killed a man in a guerrilla action out in the hills, and he'd got back home just as the police brought in the body of the man he'd killed—his own son. However epic the scale, war was always personal. That was what I knew from my reading and from my childhood; and to my surprise, that was what I found in wartime London.

When you see a house where a room still hangs on the outside walls, and there's still some furniture, and the flowered wallpaper still glows, and there's a coatrack with garments still hanging from it, and the rest of the house has peeled away and fallen—that's personal.

And when you see a young woman standing on a pile of rubble and begging the police and fire workers, "Dig faster," and "Over here, I thought I heard something!" and they rush to her, and they tell you in an aside that her two children aged six and four are beneath the rubble, as is her officer husband, and that he'd had an arm blown off at Dunkirk a few years earlier—that's personal too.

We'd lost our way from the train and walked too far. Around midafternoon, we rounded a corner and saw the scenes I've just described (and as I noted them down that night). Miss Begley turned away from the distressed young woman and walked off a few yards, gasping. She put down her suitcase and stiffened her shoulders to establish some resolve. For myself, I have a delay mechanism on my emotions; this wouldn't hit me for several hours. If at all.

I walked to Miss Begley and said, "Come on. Let me take you away from here. I'll ask directions," and I turned to go back the way we'd come.

"No," she said. "We should see this, we should see it."

And so we walked right into the Second World War. An occasional hiatus notwithstanding, it would be a long time before we'd walk out again. The smell will still come back if I evoke it: plaster dust, sewage, leaking gas—the smell of death as I know it.

Bombs had taken out four houses along that street. Flanked by the other untouched buildings, they looked like gaps in a row of teeth. There hadn't been time to stretch cordons; London had suffered a heavy twenty-four hours. One of those freaks of compressed air that you'll find in all bomb blasts had blown the young mother out of the house onto the pavement while her children and their father lay beneath immeasurable weight.

We weren't in a poor area, and the woman spoke with an educated accent—war has no respect for social class. Miss Begley, as ever, found a job to do. She walked forward to take care of the grief-stricken woman.

We settled in at the small hotel that Miss Begley had booked, then walked out to find a meal before the light fled the sky. I had taken care to bring money with me, and to make banking arrangements, should we need them. Up to that moment she hadn't confided in me. Still, we had an agreement—"You help me and I'll help you"—and I'd gone along thus far. Although I was a little frustrated, it suited me; I was curious about the war and England's survival, and I'd established with James Clare that I could always work at collecting lore among the Irish in London.

Now, though, with my own emotions bruised again by word of Venetia, and stirred by the violence of war as we'd seen it, I needed some security.

"All right," I said. "No more evasions. How much are you going to tell me?"

Some of the fight had left her too and she said, "I don't know what to tell you. I think"—she paused and reflected—"I think I'm waiting just now."

"For what?"

She said, "All right," and unfolded the next phase.

Many of the American officers were billeted in the Ritz Hotel, she said, although "Mr. Miller," as she still called him, hadn't been staying there. Nor had he disclosed his address. She said, "This is all I know. He wants me to go to the Ritz Hotel at noon and meet a woman named Claudia."

34

I've been looking back over my account so far of Kate Begley and myself in that year, 1943. What hasn't come across yet is what I later called the "quicksilver" between us. By that I don't mean the verbal challenges, the benign sparks that we sometimes struck off each other. I mean that quicksilver is another name for mercury, one of the densest metals in the world, and it has a very narrow range from cold to hot—and back again.

We arrived at the Ritz so early that we had to dawdle in the park nearby. How different we looked—Miss Begley a tube of dark red serge in her trim jacket and mid-calf slim skirt, fashionable beyond the powers of Lamb's Head or Kenmare, and I like a half priest or young undertaker in my trademark black suit. I towered over Miss Begley. She claimed five feet four inches, but it always looked doubtful, especially when she stood beside me—or Mr. Miller.

At the Ritz reception desk, we asked for Claudia and our inquiry caused a stir. The clerk fluttered, and a senior figure overheard. The lady was, he said, "in residence and expecting two visitors," to which Miss Begley said, bright as a breeze, "That'll be us."

"I'll just call through, if I may," said the Ritz man.

Miss Begley whispered to me, "This Claudia must be some big shot."

No matter what we may claim, we don't anticipate most of the major events in life. Accidents, prizes, sudden betrayals—they crash into us. Or they break slowly over us, as in this case, where I had no inkling, no flicker of premonition. Nor did Miss Begley, no matter how fey she liked to be; months later, when I asked her, she admitted as much.

Yet, when the Ritz man escorted us down a long, thoughtful corridor, why did I offer to stand back and wait outside as he knocked on the door? Why did I, with a rush of urgency like blood to the head, think about getting out of there fast? The Ritz man, one of whose eyes was blank white, shook his head.

"You're very much included, sir."

———

Let me tell you about Claudia, who lived to the age of ninety-six. A very specific and elite grapevine knew her as "Claudia at the Ritz," and she found classy English wives for foreign men, including officers and diplomats. Up to the time we met her, she'd been having modest success, but felt that she should have been doing better—or so she told us.

You may now be saying to yourself, "Huh. Bombs falling everywhere and people matchmaking? Bit doubtful, if you ask me."

But I'm not asking you, I'm telling you. Not only that, Claudia wasn't alone—and she may even have copied the idea from a woman named Sylvia, well documented and mildly famous, who plied an identical trade over at London's other posh hotel, the Savoy. And although they called it "matchmaking," who can say whether other wartime services weren't on offer—but that only occurred to me many years later.

Through "army connections" (Mr. Miller, obviously), Claudia at the Ritz had heard of Miss Begley, and "perked up," as she said, at the idea of help from an expert. That was the story she gave us. It didn't feel improbable at the time, but it makes me laugh when I think of it, because Miss Begley never asked Claudia a question, or inquired as to how we got there. It took me months to grasp that both women knew the score all along, knew what the game was and who the players would be. I was the only one who didn't.

Claudia had sufficient height to look me in the eye. Long after these events, I said to her one day, "Why does such a tall woman need such high heels?"

She said, "Every little bit helps, darling."

As with much of what Claudia said, I never quite figured out what she meant.

"Goodness," she said, gazing down on Miss Begley at our first meeting, "the Management does get it right."

By "the Management," I would discover, she meant God; Claudia prayed often. When she shook my hand, I saw that she swallowed as though her mouth was dry, and I felt that she didn't like me. Claudia looked like a large, walking duchess in blue silk. In we went, to an office furnished with ormolu, inlay, and jade.

I felt uncomfortable. Claudia reminded me of my erstwhile mother-in-law, the actress Sarah Kelly. Also nearly as tall as I, elegant and groomed, Sarah hadn't one trustworthy bone in her body. Claudia felt equally dangerous, and in the beginning I wanted to shy away from her. Maybe it was the English upper-class accent, a sinister matter in Irish race memory. Within a short time, though, she behaved so warmly that Miss Begley and I moved toward her like swimmers to a shore. We must have sensed her abundant moral courage.

"I love the Irish," Claudia began, "though you have a million reasons not to love us. Frankly, if I were Irish, I'd find it difficult ever to talk to an Englishman, given what we've done to you."

"But you yourself, you didn't do it," said Miss Begley in a stout, courteous defense.

"India was my family's playground. I think we behaved ourselves out there. At least I hope we did."

Every time Claudia looked at me that day, she ran a hand through her hair and turned away. Perhaps she found me distasteful—but my father swore that English nostrils had a defect, that they smelled many things as rancid, which explained why they grew so many roses. My father aired a lot of doubtful theories.

I, on the other hand, couldn't take my eyes off Claudia; I have to admit that I quickened when I saw her—her superior air, her grooming. And I found myself fascinated to see how little, parochial Miss Begley— "Dear Kate" as Claudia began to call her—might change under the influence of such a cosmopolitan woman.

"Have you been traveling all night? Poor dears. Traveling's calamitous for the bowels," said Claudia. "Do you need a bathroom?"

Her desk shone with details of silver, brass, and copper; little carved swags of golden cord formed the handles on the drawers; pearl medallions glistened at the corners. She saw me looking at a large marquetry cartouche of a tiger in the center.

"Aren't the stripes hectic?" she said. "Hickory inlay, I believe."

She kicked off her shoes—she had impeccable hose, worth a fortune that year in that war.

"It's all right, my dears. My feet don't sweat," and she rested them (scarlet toenail polish peeping through the nylons) on a red lacquered footstool that was alive with dragons, trees, and waterfalls. I had the idle thought, *Will Miss B. read Claudia's palm?*

On the walls hung large mirrors, so that when Claudia turned her head in any direction she had a full reflection of herself. Her skin had the creamy sheen of old English money. Directly in front of her desk sat two wide, carved armchairs covered in turquoise velvet. On these Miss Begley and I sat, like a couple of children summoned before the head-mistress.

Claudia pushed back her hair, clutched her diamond earrings, and wiggled them free.

"You both have to learn French. Very quickly. Can you do that?"

Miss Begley said, *"Mais oui. Immédiatement."*

Claudia looked at her in delight and flung out several phrases; Miss Begley retaliated; back and forth they nattered like French monkeys; Claudia laughed.

"My dear! You need no more than a teeny-weeny little polish. And you, dear boy?" she asked me, and I said, *"Non.* Not a word."

Claudia pursed those red-velvet-bow lips. "Very well. Dear Kate, I'll move you straight into German. Then you'll help me here in the after-noons. I have some lovely eligible fellas and gels looking for partners, and I have some so stupid, heavens above, it's a wonder they know how to use the lavatory. And Ben, dear boy"—she turned her beam full on me—"you will learn the beginnings of French and German."

To which I said, "But I have work to do."

"Oh?"

I recall thinking, *What is this? Do these women stand in front of a mir-ror and rehearse their eyebrows? One at a time, then lift both together?* And note Claudia's assumptions: no "Will you?" Just said, "You will."

"I'm collecting stories from Irish immigrants working in London."

Claudia's manners were too good to allow her distaste to leak through—but the tongue touched the red lips. And I never did go into the Irish communities; had James Clare not been my mentor I'd have lost my job.

In her diary that night, Miss Begley wrote this entry for that first day in the Ritz:

> *I feel I was born to come here. CM did say he wanted me to do some-thing "very important" for him. Why did he ask me so many questions about poor Hans-Dieter? What was that about? Question to Myself:*

Will CM be decent and do the QPQ? At least I've said it to him, and he didn't flinch. He didn't say "no." He didn't say "yes" either. Did I use the right words? Should I have said, "I'll do this important thing if you'll do something for me"? Ben would have called that too blunt, too crude. Question really is: Will he write her a letter? Her name is Janie Sonnhalter. What kind of a name is that? He spelled it for me. Is intimacy all that important? After all, he is a Protestant, and they do the bold thing all the time. Maybe I'll ask. But he'll have to show me the letter when he's written it.

Had I seen that entry next morning, I wouldn't have understood a blind word of it. Hans-Dieter? Not a clue. Janie Sonnhalter? Must be the girl of the "intimacy" back in the States. "QPQ"? I couldn't translate it.

Here is the note I made that night:

London after dark, and not a light to be seen; this is what they call "the blackout," where every curtain is closed tight and every shade drawn down to within an inch of its life. Today at the Ritz Hotel, I met a lady name of Claudia who asked Miss Begley to become her assistant and "train her," as she put it, "in the arts of love." I will be allowed to sit and make notes. And I have to try to take on board some basic French and German. I'm going to love that, because it means I might one day get even closer to my "friends," the scholars, and know better Rahingus of Flavigny, Heriger of Mainz, and Froumund himself on the road outside Tegernsee.

35

In her jewel-box office, with its shining wood and profound velvet, Claudia asked us many questions.

"Now whence do you hail, my dears?"

"Schools? I believe the Irish are very well educated. I myself, I had a girl's education, I can't tell *B* from a bull's foot."

"One of you is married and the other isn't, I believe—yes?"

This jarred me. How much did she know about us, and how had she learned? More crucially, why? But I didn't have the moral strength to ask; everything so far intimidated me—the rich surroundings, Claudia's power, the startling incongruousness of being there at all. A week earlier, I had been down on my knees in the corner of a farmyard in County Monaghan, looking at a family's amulet, a curved stone with two "eyes" in it, which they rubbed against any beast that fell ill.

I did manage to say, "Given where we come from, I find all this very strange. Can you tell me why we're here?"

Miss Begley glared at me and looked uncomfortable. Claudia said, lighter than a butterfly, "My dear, there's a war on."

Which, I was given to understand, would embrace every possibility under the sun. And it did.

Now that I look back on it, I can see, plain as a white plate, the smoothness of the entire operation. Claudia was part of a machine that, like any good part of any good engine, was supposed to work without calling attention to itself. There she sat, large and pleasant, writing our answers in a red book. When she finished, she closed the book, raised her head, and tapped the leather cover.

"They'll want records," she said, "for when they're handing out the medals. Now." She stood and stretched; today I know enough to call it a display gesture; she looked like a very big pouter pigeon with a blue silk chest.

"I'm giving you lunch," she said, "and a friend or two may join us. Remind me not to eat something that would make me belch." Claudia could have sold that smile of hers to a toothpaste company.

We walked from her office to a large dining room overlooking the river. Uniforms shone all over the place, and every table seemed full. Was this some kind of joyous war? The far corner to which she led us had been set for five people, with two already there. One looked not unlike my father, that is to say, a tall, jovial-seeming man with bulging red hair. The other—no surprise—wore an American uniform.

"I believe you know Captain Miller," said Claudia.

"Oh, 'tis 'Captain' now, is it?" said Miss Begley.

"Last week," he said, beamed a great wide smile at her, and shook my hand like a pal: "My friends call me 'Chuck.' " He directed Miss Begley to the chair beside him.

The pair of them dominated lunch. Claudia said almost nothing. From time to time she wrote in her red book, which she now held on her knee. She had introduced the big, red-haired man as "Mr. Howard," who asked only one question: "Do the local people in Ireland feel more hostile to Britain or to Germany?"

Miss Begley and I looked at each other and she said, "Don't we want our side to win?"

Captain Miller laughed. "What I think Mr. Howard is asking is— which is your side?"

Miss Begley put it beyond argument or doubt. "Your crowd, of course. We're no friends with that Hitler fellow, although mind you, we've nothing against him."

"Isn't he a little toad?" said Claudia. "I should like to slap his bottom."

When Captain Miller asked how we felt about the Japanese, Miss Begley replied, "I don't know anybody from Japan," and I said, "No, I've never met anybody from Japan."

Miss Begley added, with a helpful air, "I was in *The Mikado* in school," which Mr. Howard seemed to find very amusing, as did Claudia.

"Tell me," said Captain Miller, "what does it feel like to be neutral?"

I think about that question often; it came to have such a personal resonance for me; yet, that day, Miss Begley and I shrugged and we said that it didn't really feel like anything.

Looking back at my notes, I find that I wrote:

Capt. Miller asked us about fishermen on the southwest of Ireland. I told him, with interjections from Miss Begley, about Bawn Buckley and the smuggling. Is he very interested in fishing? In Irish fishermen and how they work? I was able to answer most of his questions, even when he wandered into politics. As before, he seemed most interested in whether we thought Ireland would ever allow Mr. Churchill to use our ports for the British navy. I told him the theory that Mr. de Valera was playing the ports as a bargaining chip—if Mr. Churchill gave us back the six counties of Northern Ireland, then he could use our ports. Mr. Howard said, "I doubt that will happen." Miss Begley at lunch was happier than I've ever seen her. Excited and alert. Delightful. Claudia kept glancing at me. Is she afraid that I'll object to something?

After lunch, with Miss Begley flushed and a little out of true with adrenaline, Claudia led us through the labyrinthine Ritz to a door that somebody answered from within.

In the middle of a sitting room ripe with antique furniture and golden fabric, stood a large desk. Behind the desk, shuffling some papers and books, sat a woman with blue lipstick. Nothing else about her proved as startling; the lipstick shone like a violet on a stone, because she was herself otherwise gray—of hair, face, dress, and personality.

Claudia had never met her, and asked—in French—"Madame Samadey?"

The lipstick lady said, "Sama-dett."

She spoke English with almost no accent. For a moment I thought that she could have been Irish or American. This was the woman in whose company we would spend every morning for the next two and a half months, and many Saturdays and Sundays, Miss Begley honing what French and German she had, me studying afresh.

That first night, as we walked back to our little hotel to collect our luggage, I said to Miss Begley, "Did it worry you that Claudia mightn't have thought us sophisticated?"

She said, "I hope she didn't."

I said, "Why?"

"Look it up."

"Look up what?"

"The word *sophistication*."

"I can tell that you've looked it up."

"I didn't need to," she said, waving her hands like a princess. "I already knew."

Nobody could get attention like Miss Begley could.

I said, "So what does it mean?"

" 'A thin veneer of artificiality.' "

"What?"

"You heard me," she said. "And who'd want that?"

36

They gave us spending money in Ritz-crested envelopes; they gave us ad-joining rooms in the hotel, with a connecting door we never locked. We lived in circumstances opulent beyond our norms, and we should have defined it all by words such as *strange* and *weird*—because it was strange and weird, and I still think so.

Compare it to how remote, how small, how *local* was Miss Begley's home at Lamb's Head, a place that she had never left and where she could never have met upper-class English people of opaque purpose. Or an enigmatic American officer—who now came back into our lives with some emphasis.

One morning, when we had been studying with Madame Samadett for some days, we found a new student waiting—Captain Charles Miller, tawny and huge, had draped himself across the sofa like a lion.

As usual, we launched into our greeting ritual with Madame, in which she asked us how our evening had been, had we heard from our parents, how we had slept—all in French. As Madame spoke, Captain Miller tried to make us laugh from behind her back. He turned his eyes inward, stuck two fingers up his nostrils, then tweaked his ear like a key that made his tongue pop out and back in again. To round off this per-formance, he made a goofy, bucktoothed face with a drooping eyelid.

Unaware of this clowning, Madame almost warmed to what she saw as the exuberance and delight of our replies; it would have been her first smile. She introduced us, and said that Captain Miller would be taking part now and again, just to brush up his French. He behaved as though we'd never met before, asked Miss Begley her name twice.

"Miss Beggar? Miss Wiggly?"

Madame corrected him with wide elocution and made him practice.

"Begg. Lee. Begg. Lee."

Captain Miller made a meal of it, and then kept saying, "Kate. Begg. Lee. Kate. Begg. Lee."

When he came to my name, he said, "Bennnnnnn," drawing out the *n* like a note on a mouth harp. "Mak. Cart. Tea."

Madame, perhaps catching on, thanked him with severity, and our studies began.

So, I believe, did the actual courtship of Charles Miller and Kate Begley, once my two dear friends. They handled it with a mutual cunning. For instance, to make smooth their own path, they made Madame part of an evident attraction between the pair of them, so that she could watch, as it were, a relationship growing under her wing, and perhaps become their emotional sponsor.

They pulled little stunts that I now see were lovers' games. In our first conversation class, Captain Miller asked, "Madame, is it true that the French are more interested in love than in war?"

Miss Begley chipped in, also speaking her best French, "Who wouldn't be?"

Madame answered, "The French prize love above everything else."

Miss Begley said, "Not like the Americans."

This opened a debate, exactly what Madame had wanted, and she sat back as they discussed, with an occasional halting interjection from me—not much more than a *"Vraiment,"* or a *"Mais oui"* or a *"Bravo!"* Essentially this was flirtation; they knew it, Madame knew it, and I knew it. After the second or third day, it would indeed have appeared to any moderately astute watcher that a new relationship was forming.

And still Madame never smiled, though she blushed frequently, and began to steer the studies toward realms of romance and love. She asked Captain Miller to read a poem by Paul Verlaine:

You see we need to pardon everything,
That's the way we'll be happiest,
And if our lives have moments that sting,
At least we'll weep together and be blessed.

And, in a moment that I shall never forget, she asked Miss Begley to read that description of D'Artagnan when we first meet him in *The Three*

Musketeers. Miss Begley read it with an actressy passion, her Kerry accent driving the romance of the text: *He had an open and intelligent face, and a hooked but finely chiseled nose. An experienced eye might have taken him for a farmer's son upon a journey . . .*

I watched all this enthralled, and yet fighting down what the Musketeers would have called "harsh pulses" in myself. As I've told you elsewhere, my emotional metabolism has a governor on it: I seem to regulate the rise of my feelings to the surface, until I can cope with them. If I can. If I can't, that becomes a matter of grave difficulty.

37

Soon the three of us began to spend several evenings a week together outside the classroom, plus long weekend. We wandered London on foot, getting ourselves back to the Ritz in the small hours. Miller claimed that he was billeted somewhere else; he never specified.

For the first ten days of those two weeks, that is, before they moved her to a different room on a different corridor, Miss Begley would then fling open the door between our rooms, and, while undressing with an air of great relaxation as she walked up and down (she must have known that I'd never peep), talked nonstop through the open door about our adventures with the man she called "the Captain." She had much of which to sing—those were merry, merry nights.

Was our jollity intensified by the war? Yes, because the cliché is true: Everywhere we went, people seemed heightened in glee. Captain Miller in his uniform sometimes received applause if we walked into a restaurant; in pubs they served us the first round free.

In all this time I never touched a drop. Nor did I feel like a ticking bomb, as I had done once or twice since Miss Begley had imposed her drink controls on me. I think that I must have felt some sense of responsibility—because there's no doubt that I was the gooseberry, the willing chaperone. Before long, our trio felt like a duo—the unit of them and me.

They grew close at great speed. Perhaps it was accelerated by the war; perhaps it would have happened anyway. Neither took the lead; in that sense, they resembled Venetia and me. Each took care of the other, each demonstrated affection equally—and they never made me feel extra or spare.

We went out every night. No lights, remember; every building, every door, every window, every night had to be subject to blackout, to try to deny the German bombers. Yet Captain Miller always seemed to know where he was going; now and then he checked a piece of paper with his tiny flashlight, and when he eventually knocked on any door he was welcomed. Then, when we'd fluttered our way through the heavy curtains, fun greeted us—London was a party, it seemed, with people made newly reckless by the war, as though saying to the world, "This might be our last night on earth—let's enjoy it."

I wonder what they made of us, those laughing revelers. "Cheers, mate," the universal drinking greeting of the English, summed up how they seemed, and the young American cheered them up further. Here, now, I saw the true coupledom of Charles Miller and Kate Begley—not so much in how each introduced the other, but in a kind of joint proprietariness. The world could see that they were together, and they wanted the world to see it.

In the back of one pub one night stood several snooker tables.

"Are they shooting pool?" Captain Miller asked me, and I shook my head, not knowing what he meant. The three of us wandered over to watch and stopped next to two men, faces white under the long lamps, intense in their focus.

When they broke, they greeted us.

"Are you shooting pool?" said Captain Miller again.

"No, mate, we're shooting Germans. Just like you."

Everybody laughed, and they began to explain the game to him. One handed him a cue, the other explained the rudiments, then set up the white ball and a red. Captain Miller slotted the red into the farthest pocket and kept the white ball on the table convenient to the next red—which he then drilled into another corner. The men whistled.

"Clear it, Major," they said, and everybody laughed—and then he did clear the few reds left on the table, and attacked the colored balls, ending on the black. Led by the two Londoners, we all cheered.

"Kate, you try," he called, and she trotted over.

She couldn't line up the cue on the ball.

"I'm not tall enough," she said, and Captain Miller got behind her, lifted her, and held her so steadily that she was able to attempt a shot.

That, however, is not what I watched. I saw the expression on her face change. Up to then, I had been with them all the time they were together, and I had never seen anything other than a jocose punch or swipe, typically from her to him. Now, feeling his hands around her rib cage, she closed her eyes for a moment, and next I saw the blush that happened so rarely as to be recognizable at once.

Another night, we'd come out of a pub in Drury Lane, where the proprietor, to compensate for the closure of so many theaters, had arranged a concert of the most mixed bag you've ever seen—Mozart to juggling; it reminded me of Venetia's road show. The sirens whined, and Captain Miller knew—again—where to go. We raced to a station in the underground, and clumped down many, many flights of stairs with hundreds of Londoners.

Sleeping bags, blankets, old mattresses—we made ourselves comfortable, and, with Miss Begley snuggled between her two men, we watched the place fill up. I tried to listen for the outside world, but by now we had come down so deep that I couldn't hear the siren anymore. Soon, the crowd settled too, waiting for the all clear, which would be relayed to the platforms.

It took a long time. I dozed, so did Miss Begley. In fact, she awakened me, because she'd become restless. I felt her move away from me, and closer, closer to Captain Miller. He, for the first time, put his arm around her. Bit by bit, she heaved herself ever nearer to him, until she lay almost astride his thighs.

38

Claudia never told us—not me, anyway—why we were learning French. If I'd asked anybody they wouldn't have said anything more than "The pieces will fall into place."

As they did. In essence, Charles Miller had found Kate Begley, and Claudia had "cleared" both of us for the task ahead. Claudia was a kind of spymaster, working in circumstances that gave her unrivaled contact with all sorts of useful people. Few in wartime London had as deep an address book. Claudia reached her long, alabaster fingers into the highest levels of the English war cabinet; it did no harm that her father had been a close friend of Churchill since school.

Through Churchill's transatlantic connections—he'd had an American mother—Claudia was given the specific task of working as a deep liaison with the U.S. military long before President Roosevelt entered the war in Europe. She never said so, no matter how close we became, but I believe now that she prepared and trained spies for them.

Her "marriage market," as she called it privately, provided her cover. She'd been doing some unpaid publicity work for the hotel before the war, and now she decided that the Ritz could become even more famous as a glamorous venue. Through London came large numbers of interesting and exciting men of all nationalities, especially Americans and Canadians. The Poles came too—some of them had been aristocrats—and the Australians, and the Free French, and the Free Italians, and exotic Armenians and Hungarians. Thus, Claudia came to know every useful diplomat and soldier who passed through during the war.

As a kick start, she had taken one of the large suites one evening and held what she called the first of her "fifty-fifty" cocktail parties—fifty handpicked women from the top echelon of London and surrounding counties, and fifty even more carefully handpicked men, most of whom had packed their dress uniforms before being posted to Britain.

For the women, she'd had cards printed, like old-fashioned dance cards, which she'd distributed before the evening. On the card, ten blank lines invited the names of ten men they had met and would perhaps like to meet again. After the party, in the ladies' cloakrooms, they could grade the names in the order of preference, and Claudia would arrange for them to meet any or all of them.

War generates license, and when the romances got under way, her "girls," as she called them, reported back to Claudia all kinds of pillow talk.

"It took some juggling," she told Miss Begley. "It still does." She was talking about more than matchmaking.

39

December 1943

One morning, after ten and a half weeks with Madame Blue Lipstick Samadett, Captain Miller walked in. He'd been absent for a few days again, he wore his uniform, in which we hadn't seen him for weeks, and this man-boy now had a new and more threatening authority. He muttered to Madame, who half-bowed and quit the room; I think it crossed her mind to walk backward, so deferential did she seem.

He sat in Madame's chair behind the desk. Without a greeting he said to Miss Begley, "We think we've found him."

Miss Begley said, "So this is it?"

Captain Miller said, "The French know where he is. We want you to make sure."

Did I look mystified? If I did, nobody noticed—or cared.

He opened a map of France and pushed it to her. "Do your stuff."

Miss Begley looked at me in an almost disturbed, embarrassed way.

"Don't laugh," she said.

You may remember that I told you she had "one specific gift that I still can't fathom." From her handbag she took a small purse, and from the purse she took a needle and thread.

"Did you bring something?" she said to Captain Miller.

Out of his pocket Miller took a sock and handed it to her.

"You must have broken into his house?" She laughed, sunlight in her bead-brown eyes.

He replied, "We have friends everywhere," and he didn't laugh.

Miss Begley rubbed the needle through the wool of the sock.

"Concentrate on the coast," Miller said.

Her elbow on the desk, Miss Begley bent her hand over the map of France. The needle dangled just above the French coast. Without encroaching, I looked over her shoulder. Miller sat back. We heard only our own breathing.

Nothing happened. Down along the coast of France she moved her hand as carefully as a watchmaker, using her arm like a little crane. Back up she went again—Le Crotoy, Fort Mahon, Le Touquet, Boulogne, Calais, up as far as Ostend.

Without raising her head she said, "Nothing."

"Go inland an inch," Captain Miller said.

She moved the hanging needle over Abbeville and Montreuil, right up to Calais again: "Nothing."

"We know he's there somewhere," said Captain Miller. "Move in another inch."

She positioned the needle halfway between Calais and Dunkirk and lowered her hand slowly. And then I saw her neck stiffen, and she held herself tighter. She stopped moving her hand, and the needle swung over and across in a straight line.

"Saint-Omer," she said. "I think he's in that town."

"Make sure," said Miller.

She bent her head again and held herself still as a statue.

"Look at it," she said. "The pendulum doesn't tell lies."

The needle swung in a stronger, straighter line.

Captain Miller nodded. "That figures," he said.

We all straightened up and I asked, "What's going on here?"

He said, "What you see is what you see."

"I don't know what that means."

Miller said, "Have you ever been to France?"

I recoiled and began to walk away backward. Miss Begley called me back.

"You promised you'd come anywhere with me."

"Into France? In the middle of the war? Is that what you're asking?"

Miller said, "With good reason."

I turned back to her. "Spell it out for me." Neither of them said a word, and I pressed. "What. Is. Going. On?"

They looked at each other as though to say, *You tell him.*

Miller spoke. "Kate knows somebody crucial in the German war machine. He could provide crucial help."

"What?"

She said, "He's a German gentleman. Used to live near us. He still has a house—back at Derrynane."

"Oh, for Jesus' sake," I said to her. "What has this to do with you?"

"He knows me. I was his matchmaker."

"He trusts Kate," said Miller.

"Trusts her to do what?" They didn't answer. Sometimes I'm just quick enough on the uptake. "Trusts you enough to go back to Ireland with you?"

She looked sheepish; he was opaque.

"What's his name?" I asked.

"Hans-Dieter," she said. "I call him Hans."

"And what about Mrs. Dieter?" I said. I felt like a policeman.

"His name is Hans-Dieter Seefeld. Mrs. Seefeld died. Ann was her name. I was at school with her."

All of this scene—they'd expected it; they'd worked out everything; they'd anticipated my every squeak of indignation. This plan had been put through every wringer they could find. They were miles ahead of me and I felt livid with anger.

I said, "You've decided to do it anyway."

Miller spread his hands, and said, "So?"

"But this is a bad idea. We're Irish, we're neutral."

He said, "There's no such thing as neutral when you're facing evil."

"But we have to be neutral," I said. "We're weak. We're tiny. And what would happen to us—I mean—" By now I was running out of language as I tried to assess their plan. "Is this—?" I stopped, incredulous. "Is this kidnapping that you're talking about? Jesus! What books have you been reading?"

"It'll work. His wife died last year," said Kate. "She was a close friend of mine. He wants to be where their life was."

"But why kidnap him?"

Miller said, "I already told you. He can give us crucial help."

"How?"

Miller said, "I can't tell you that."

"You mean you don't know?"

Kate intervened. "No. It's kind of secret."

Miller added, "It's a lot secret."

"This is far past ridiculous," I said. "You're trying to kidnap some-body German from a country occupied by Germany and take him to a neutral country—have I got that right? I mean—have you ever heard the word *implications*?"

Miller felt my outrage; I could see it in his darkening eyes, and I didn't care. Apart from our personal safety, which he can't have cared too much about, did he have any idea how vulnerable we were to the gods of war? Our guerrillas might have forced a treaty out of Britain in 1921—but Europe wasn't a farmhand war. We'd have no kind of chance in a major conflict—and Miller knew it.

"If you're trying to draw us into the war," I said, "that's about as un-fair as you could be. Do you know how weak we are?"

"Yeah, you have six thousand soldiers," he said.

"I know two of them," said Miss Begley. "And they couldn't fire a cat-apult."

Miller added, "You have twenty-one armored vehicles, including a pair of tanks."

"Exactly," I said. "Call that an army? And our air force? Two dozen planes, and only four of them can work as fighters."

Captain Miller said, "I know—and I'm asking you to do something that will help protect your country."

I said, "Nobody will bother to attack us."

He shook his head. "You're wrong, Ben."

"Tell us, so," said Miss Begley, coming a pace or two to my side.

I know now, from the history of the period, from the government pa-pers long released, that the two great antagonists, Britain and Germany, had drawn up extensive plans to invade Ireland. It didn't matter that we were a mouse, an island smaller than some of the counties in American states—and certainly smaller than most of the states themselves. The Germans wanted to invade us because we sat a mere sixty miles from En-gland. And the British wanted to invade us to stop the Germans. Did they need an excuse? If they did, we now might give it to them, and I said as much.

Captain Miller said, "A gambler would take a bet."

Miss Begley said, "What kind of a bet?"

Miller said, "That one or the other will come in on top of you."

I asked, "But wouldn't you fellows stop it?"

He flashed like fire. "You could be sure to stop it now."

"Ah, go on out of that," she said. "Ben and me?"

"If he knew—"

"Who?" I said. "If *who* knew?"

"Hitler."

"If Hitler knew what?" I said; my combativeness surprised me and made him laugh.

"Calm down and listen," Charles Miller said. He had that most useful of gifts—command without force. "If Hitler knew that we knew his plans, he'd either change them or give them up altogether."

"And we'd be the ones to cause that?" I said, sarcastic and cold.

Miss Begley stepped forward another pace. "Do you know where your ludeen is?" she said to him.

My turn to laugh; the ludeen, an old word from the Irish language, means the little finger. But Charles Miller looked as startled as though she'd suggested something indecent. She alarmed him further; she reached forward, took his hand, and held it up, then closed his fingers, but tweaked out the pinkie.

"See this? This is your ludeen, and Ben is saying we'd have as much chance of doing anything useful in that war over there as this ludeen."

Her language often amused me. I've preserved as much of it as I can remember. She once said that a man she knew had a face "as shiny as a shark."

Charles Miller saw no fun in this new turn of phrase. Instead, he said, cold as the east, "Perhaps you should wait until you learn more."

I blurted, "I know enough. In among the Germans? Kidnap? Is that it? Kidnap one of their top men? Is that what you really want us to do?" My words now came out in chunks. "He's a German, whose home is in neutral Ireland. He'd be there if he wanted to be."

"No," said Miller. "Hitler won't let him. He's too useful. They need him too much."

That night, in the frantic anxiety this turn of events had caused, an obvious question came sidling up to me. It had a bitter taste: *Why hadn't she offered her "gift," her "pendulum," to me? To find Venetia?*

40

Next day, they sent us back to Ireland. Claudia gave us two official envelopes and said an affectionate good-bye; she kissed me on the lips. A silent gentleman in a black car took us to the train.

One envelope held a document that guaranteed passage through England, Scotland, and Wales. Its power astonished us. We were actually saluted by the policemen and soldiers who inspected us on the train. And our private compartment had a guard standing outside it for the seven-hour journey from London to Holyhead. On the boat to Dublin we were given adjoining cabins. A sentry stood outside.

With my knowledge of her now, from this distance in time, I can see that Kate Begley was manipulating me, managing me, waiting for me to calm down. On the train, she'd initiated no conversations—nor had I, which was the only way that I could fight back. Nor, on board ship, did she attempt to reach me from her cabin.

The second envelope held our Irish passports. We had had no visas of any kind to anywhere, nor had we ever applied, or filled in forms. The supplying of them confirmed that we'd crashed into something very substantial. Government must have spoken to government must have spoken to government—American, British, Irish.

As the boat began to dock, we stood on deck, and I asked the question that had been rolled up and down my mind.

"The needle. How did you do it?"

She said, "The man found himself. That's where he was."

"There's no logic to it," I said.

She replied, "There doesn't have to be logic to everything."

In Dublin, we shopped for clothes. Captain Miller had given us the money, told us what to buy. We then took the train—on which life was normal—to the southwest; I was to stay at Lamb's Head with Miss Begley and her grandmother until somebody came for us. It would be "some time," said Miller.

One night that week, I wrote this entry:

Back at Lamb's Head, awaiting instruction. Miss B. is completely serious about our "mission" to France. Should we be doing this "task" for him? Am I not more or less insane to be involved?

I can't get out now, CM told me, because I know too much. And I can't hope to persuade KB not to go—she catches fire when she's near him.

Today, she asked a hundred questions of a lady in Kenmare, a Mrs. W. She asked about her late daughter, and about the bereaved husband, this Hans-Dieter fellow—where he was, what he was like, was he a good man, was he a violent man? I saw how she did it: She gave the lady an impression that she might know a nice wife for the gentleman, and Mrs. W. said she was very fond of her son-in-law, who had said he'd come back from Germany and live here when the war was over.

She told us that she had a letter recently from her son-in-law, and that the police delivered it and then took it away when she had read it. She added that all the neighbors loved him, and that she had felt very lucky when he married her daughter; he was a man who "wouldn't hurt no one."

41

And so we waited. My ice began to melt on the long slog of a journey; from the moment we got to Lamb's Head, we talked and we talked.

That first night I asked her, "Did you know we were going to be asked to do this task, job, mission—whatever you call it?"

"I don't want to talk about it."

"You promised to be direct with me."

No answer.

I said, "All right. This is how we'll do it. If I'm wrong, say *no*. If I'm right, say nothing."

She looked at me with disgust.

I said, "This is what happened. He said to you, 'Would you do something for me? Something big,' and you asked him about his girl back home, didn't you?"

Not a word from her.

"Isn't that how this all came about?" I asked.

Not a word.

And I said, "So it was all set up in advance, wasn't it?"

She didn't speak and I had my answer.

I made one more effort. "That day he came here. He knew what he was coming for, didn't he? And when you and he were down there on the headland—he told you a lot of things that he had learned about you, didn't he? He startled you with his knowledge of you."

She said, "I'm going to bed."

42

I again failed to sleep. Being without alcohol was stretching me thin. I felt anxious, nervous all over, and I'd been reading too much in the newspapers about the war in Europe—massacres, burning villages, crowded trains to unknown oblivion. *Am I crazy?* I asked myself again and again. *Am I stone mad to thrust myself into the pit of it? And for what?*

Some time in the small hours, I rose, dressed, and went out of doors. Even if moonless, and in all seasons, the Atlantic seems to give off a light. On Lamb's Head, it glowed bright enough for me to pick out the cliffs. I traced the badges of white on the rocks, the white sashes that the ocean wears as she approaches the land, and I could hear her, I could hear her advancing and fading, a rising and falling *swish!* of her waves, and I thought, *She's the one speaking the words of the night; there's not a bird or an animal or a wind.*

But I was wrong—the ocean didn't own the only sound during that winter moment of mildness and calm. Miss Begley slept in a room beside the front door, and, in love with fresh air, she habitually kept her window thrown open. As I walked back across the little plateau that fronted the house, I heard her in her room. She was weeping as desperately as any child ever did, or any grown woman.

43

January 1944

If I may, I'll use this sojourn that was forced upon us to catch up with something. You may recall that I asked at the end of that first meeting with Miss Begley in July '43 if I might come back to observe her at work. Among the letters waiting when we returned from London, she found a postcard that read, "Dear Miss B., I'll say 'yes,' won't I, for, as you say, every chance of Love is a Gift from an Angel. Yours very faithfully, E. Mangan (Miss)."

Miss Begley showed me the card.

"I'm excited," she said. "When you start putting two people together, and you know they're ideal for each other—it's just a thrill. This girl needs a kind man. And that's certainly what she'll meet."

Next Sunday came the sound of that same "kind man" whistling like a blackbird: Neddy the Drover trundled up, as shining as the winter sun. His boots gleamed like black marble; he had a sober red tie on a white shirt and a suit of blue serge. I recognized the rig—somewhere in his life dwelt a returned emigrant. The water with which he had plastered down his hair had dried, and he was left with strands jutting all over his pointed head.

"Hello there, Miss. Ah, hello, sir, Mr. Ben! Howya doin'?"

I've rarely met a man so easy to like.

Miss Begley took Neddy aside and, as I learned, debated with him as to whether he objected to my presence at his wooing. He had no qualms—because, as I now think, he had no concept of boundaries. It would never have occurred to him that he had any personal rights, not even something as minimal as privacy. Still, I left them alone, went indoors, and found a dim place in a far corner of the long, friendly kitchen.

I could feel their buzz. They came in and sat on facing chairs. Neddy had his back to me. While she tutored him I made notes. Her face glowed with praise.

"You're nicely dressed, Edward. Well done." He nodded. "And you got the teeth?"

"My mother doesn't like them."

Miss Begley frowned. "Does your mother have teeth, Edward?"

"Thirty-one."

"You mean she only ever lost one tooth?"

"She broke it on the bone of a pork chop. My father has thirty. And my two brothers, they've thirty each. And my sisters, one has the whole thirty-two, one sister has a few gaps at the front. But she has twenty-six if you add up the total. Another of 'em has thirty-one. And the twins, they have thirty each." He grew animated. "Miss, there's two hundred and seventy teeth in our house."

"But you've none."

"I bring down the average." Neddy had raised his voice. "That Limerick man—I went back to him, the lease on the teeth was up, and he sold them to me."

"Good man, Edward. Now, tell me."

I thought, not for the first time, *Difficult to believe that this woman is in her twenties; she has the authority of a dowager.*

"Oh," Neddy said. "And my grandfather has all his own teeth, and he's ninety, like."

Miss Begley rubbed her hands together. "Good."

"And my grandmother, she had none at all, I take after her, I suppose."

Miss Begley seemed keen to skip away from things dental. She clapped her hands.

"Now, Edward, did you remember? Soap and water?"

"Miss, amn't I as clean as an infant?"

"And what are you to say to this girl when she arrives?"

Neddy sat up, straight as a spear. He groped for a reply.

"Will I tell her about my teeth like?"

"No. You're to say"—Miss Begley enumerated on her fingers—"first, 'How do you do? I've heard a lot about you.' Second, when she sits down, you start by saying to her that you know a family the same name in Ballybunion. Now do you remember her name?"

"Eileen Mangan."

"And what does she do for a living?"

"She works in the bakery in Kenmare."

"Good. And what else do you know about her?"

"A fellow disappointed her two years ago. And she mightn't be over it yet, but I'm not to say a word about it."

Miss Begley, when she'd met Neddy, recognized a man "with a good heart," she told me. Here's the note I made of her remarks.

In the scheme of things [one of her favorite phrases] Edward was never going to have a decent life—unless he had somebody to live it for. He's an intelligent fellow, caught in the middle of a raucous family where there's nobody married. The parents keep them all at home and take all their wages every week. He left school at the illegal age of eleven, but can read and write and do numbers. As my grandmother said, he has great promise, and he's a man who'll never let anybody down. Why, I asked, do you call him "Edward" and not "Neddy" and she said, "To give him his dignity."

Her behavior that afternoon illustrated her sense of respect, but didn't stop her from introducing some controls. If her hand didn't wag a finger, her voice did.

"Edward, it's a big responsibility to introduce a lady to a gentleman. I'm responsible for her well-being and yours. Now, you'll be spending time alone with her. Are you accustomed to spending time alone with young ladies?"

"I've my sisters, like."

"That's different, Edward. Now—I want you to know something. You're to behave to this young lady as though she were a kind of a princess. Better than a sister. Be nice to her, be kind to her. Smile at her."

Neddy interrupted. "And haven't I the teeth for it now, miss?"

"You have, Edward. You have indeed."

Although his back was turned to me, I could tell that Neddy smiled at Miss Begley, because she reached forward and patted him on the knee. "That's a lovely smile, Edward, lovely. Just do that, and all will be well."

He nodded, as earnest as a friar.

"When you go for a little walk with her, Edward, offer her your arm." He must have seemed bemused, because Miss Begley stood up and said, "Like this. Stand up." She took his hand, placed it in her curved arm, and escorted him up and down the kitchen. "Always let her walk through a doorway first. That's what a gentleman does."

"What about a gate, miss?"

"The same, Edward. A gate is a kind of door outside, isn't it?"

Up and down the long kitchen they walked, turning and walking back, turning and walking back.

"Not too fast, and not too slow, Edward, and always making sure that she doesn't step in a puddle. And don't walk so fast that you're dragging her along behind you. And don't be so slow that she's dragging you."

Miss Begley, diligent as a governess, gave demonstrations of both. It was difficult to be a silent witness; I so much wanted to help.

"One more thing, Edward. If you feel you want to kiss her—kiss her hand, or kiss her cheek. Kiss nothing else, d'you understand? Nothing else. Here, let me show you."

And she kissed Neddy's weathered, menial hand, a paw of brown leather that mostly handled the rumps of cattle; and she kissed his cheek, that mottled, red cheek reamed by winds from the world's four corners, and I shall never know to this day why Neddy's new teeth didn't at that moment fly in ecstasy across the room.

Mouth open as a bag, Neddy the Drover, who looked like an old shed with a new coat of paint, stood in the middle of the kitchen, as pretty Miss Begley, with her hair fluffed and curled, smiled her famous smile at him, and I thought he might swoon—until we all started at the swish of bicycle tires in the lane.

"Wait in here," said Miss Begley to Neddy the Drover. "And you can leave your envelope over there on the windowsill."

To me she said, "Go in there and keep the door open a little bit but don't let yourself be seen."

Neddy tiptoed with his envelope of cash to the broad white windowsill—and I heard Miss Mangan's opening gasps.

"Miss Begley, there you are, God save us all, and aren't I after seeing a man down there bathing in the sea and he naked as a pig, this time of the year an' all, is he a polar bear or what?"

"Come in, Miss Mangan, I've somebody who wants to meet you."

"Oh, Miss Begley, shouldn't I not for a few minutes? With the heat on my face, look at me, I'm as red as your door."

The women remained outside, chatting in voices too low for me to eavesdrop. Now and then from the kitchen came the scrape of a chair leg on the floor, or a creak of the chair itself—Neddy the Drover with cold feet. Of the grandmother I saw no sight; Miss Begley had taken over the stage.

The voices rose again as the women came in. Miss Mangan, well upholstered, with an embarrassed smile and Viking-blond hair, held back, then surged forward, and blurted, "Hello, very nice to meet you." To which Neddy the Drover replied, "How do you?"

Miss Begley, in my eye line, sent a hopeful glance to Neddy and mouthed the word, "Do," which Neddy repeated—"Do, like." Then he strung it together; "How do you—do?"

"Edward, this is Miss Mangan, and Miss Mangan, this is Edward Hannitty. Now I want the two of you to be friends, so we'll all sit down."

Their voices reached me clear as bells.

"You're very blondy altogether," said Neddy the Drover, to which Miss Mangan replied, "Miss Begley didn't say, did you, Miss Begley, that he was, that's you, I mean, Edward, you're as big, like, you're nearly a tree."

Miss Begley said, "There'll be tea now in a minute," and I knew that she had ears a-flap for every word, every nuance. It was like watching a great conductor getting the best out of two highly anxious musicians.

"D'you like the bakery work, so?" said Edward, as my notebook, I see, now began to call him. "I've a great fondness for cakes—"

He was interrupted by Miss Mangan saying, "What kind do you like? 'Cause if I'd known I'd have brought some."

At which Miss Begley offered a burst of enthusiasm, saying, "Do you know those, do you call them cream horns? They look like a small cornucopia, and they have cream and strawberry jam."

I had the sense that Neddy the Drover wouldn't have known a cornucopia if it licked his ear, and Miss Mangan had no greater understanding of the word, but she did appreciate the individual pastry, because she said, "Cream horns, yes, and for the little bit of variety, I sometimes puts in raspberry jam instead of the strawberry jam."

To which Neddy the Drover said with a sigh, "That's inspired, like."

Clinking brought tea and Miss Begley did the fussing.

"Now, I've to go and do a small job out in the yard," she said, "and I'll be back in a minute."

I saw her stride out through the front door—and within moments she tiptoed through the door behind me, a shushing finger to her lip, a hand cupped to her ear.

We stayed there, Miss Begley with her head cocked a little, me with pen and notebook, eavesdropping from our silent place. The trysters in the kitchen warmed to each other, and when we sensed that the eating and drinking had concluded, Miss Begley left my side, quit the room, retraced her steps, and bustled back in through her own front door.

"You were hungry people," she cried. "Will either of you have more?"

Miss Mangan and her cattle-droving swain made demurring sounds, and Miss Begley drew up her chair. I sensed importance.

"Now," she said. "I've a few words to say to the two of you. My grandmother has made over four hundred matches. And with the exception of a few bereavements, and one match where the pair of them were complete rogues, all those people are still together, happily married."

Miss Mangan made a pleased, gurgling sound. I fancied that I heard Neddy the Drover's rented teeth clash a little, but I may have imagined it. Miss Begley continued and I made more notes.

"I learned a lot from watching my grandmother, and I'm going to say to the two of you what she says to every couple she introduced. This is what she says: 'I hope the two of you get on well with each other, and I believe you will. But there's a rule you've to follow—and you have to follow it from this moment on, no matter what happens. Neither of you is ever—not ever, not even once—you're never, never deliberately to do anything that'd hurt the other, or make them feel low. If you do, you'll have to answer to me. D'you understand that and agree to it?' That's what my grandmother would say if she were the one making this match."

Neddy the Drover got there first. "Oh, miss, like, she's right, isn't she, without a doubt, why would a person do a bad thing like that?"

Miss Mangan followed by saying, "That's a very good rule. If more persons only obeyed such a rule."

As Miss Begley remarked to me later, "Miss Mangan is still carrying an injury to the heart. She's not over the fellow who ditched her. She was actually standing at the altar when he never arrived."

To the couple she offered some more words.

"You've plenty of time to practice, and what you should be practicing is how to hold your tongue. Most people's problems would never happen if they thought first and spoke later. Words aren't like chickens. You can't call them back once you've let them out."

Then she dispatched them. "Go and sit on the rocks and look at the sea, and talk to each other. And I'll see both of you back here in a couple of weeks."

When they had gone, Mrs. Holst appeared from the other wing of the long, low house where she too had been listening. I walked, blinking, into the kitchen.

"What do you think, Nana?" asked Miss Begley.

"That'll take," said the grandmother. "They'll be married before Lent."

44

As the afternoon's chemistry warmed the two departing hopefuls, I felt a familiar and loathsome chill return—my own sense of loss. Often at the moment when I thought I had it under control, it rose again like some sinister yeast, forced the lid off its box, and foamed down the sides. Whenever I encountered comfort and warm good feeling, I had to fight off tormenting images of Venetia. Mostly I lost the fight.

We stood for a moment at the cottage doorway, watching the couple depart. I took Miss Begley's arm and steered her out into the winter light, toward the steep cliff path. We halted at the place where she used to watch for what she called "the anxious fishermen" coming in search of wives. I blinked away the sudden rush of tears, for once able to track my own emotions and bring them under control.

Down to my left, I could see the white horses on the waves galloping miles and miles of ocean as they charged the rocky shores of Deenish and Scarriff and Derrynane, then retreated and charged once more. Darkness from the rocky shadows cloaked the pool behind the jetty, waters magical enough for sea creatures. The sounds of the day ran around us high and free, with, always, the ocean mumbling and grunting and roaring below, like a beast beneath the ground.

To take my mind off myself, I said, "You did that very well."

As I said it, I realized how rarely I'd paid her a compliment—because she blushed.

"Oh, do you think so?" and then asked, "What was it that I did particularly well?"

"You were gracious," I said, "and you were firm. You were their leader."

She looked out to sea and said nothing for a moment. Then she spoke, slowing her speech.

"Sometimes I hear them," she said. "The voices on the wind. Mama's voice, she was a lovely singer. And Dada laughing. Did you ever hear anything like that? Voices, I mean?"

I said, "Oh, God, yes."

She said, "They'll come back here someday, I know that." When she saw my anxious face she changed her mood and asked, "How am I going to help you with your loss?"

I said, "By not going to France."

She said, "Matchmaking gives me a special power. I know things. I learn things."

I have here in front of me the notes she wrote that night:

A successful day. I introduced Mr. E.H., a Cattle Drover from Clare, to Miss E.M., a Baker's Assistant from Kenmare. Each has something the other needs. She's a fearful girl since being jilted, and she wants a steady man who will be hers and hers alone. He's a greatly deprived and lonely fellow, with a very good nature, and he can't imagine that a woman would be interested in him, so his eye will never rove. She needs an audience for her cooking and housework. He, always on the roads, needs a dream to come home to—a warm fireplace with happy flames and a smell of baking. They'll fit physically; he's built like a house, she has hips as wide and soft as a bed. Receipts: 200 from him, 100 from her.

Their tryst was witnessed by my friend the folklore man, Ben MacCarthy, who sat behind the door in the spare room and made notes. I saw tears in his eyes as he listened to the conversation between the couple.

I was so slow in those days. Too slow to see what had already been unleashed between Miss Begley and "CM," too slow to understand how each was playing the other. And too slow to grasp that Kate Begley's life might have been sheltered out there on the edge of the ocean, but her mind wasn't.

45

March 1944

No parachutes, no tap on the window in the dead of night, no submarine surfacing off the headland. Instead, after weeks of uncertain waiting, we got Bawn Buckley. The old smuggler himself docked his boat one bright morning, climbed up the headland path, strode into the kitchen, and said, "Are ye ready, lads?"

And Mrs. Holst, face as sweet as a cake, smile as ready as a child's, never asked a question, never queried our departure. Did everybody know everything—except me?

If it's night, and I'm returning from one of the Irish islands, I always feel the mainland approaching. Perhaps it's because I have a sense of how long the journey should take. Or perhaps it's because great landmasses tell you when they're near. France did.

If we were stopped and boarded—by either side—we were neutral. That was the whole point. We'd be taken, we hoped, for a fishing boat from the southwest of Ireland who had been fouled by German apparatus and war debris, causing us to put into port at Le Crotoy, renowned for mending nets.

Miss Begley slept for much of the journey. When she did join us in the little wheelhouse, she seemed as calm as wool. Bawn Buckley whistled and sang; he was, Miss Begley told me, an outstanding navigator. If he said that he was going to find landfall at Le Crotoy, then he would. And he treated her with tender, grandfatherly regard.

We hung offshore waiting for the tide. Bawn Buckley said that the skies promised weeks of unseasonal good weather. The long, comforting shape of France hardened through the breaking light. Not a vessel did we see in that quiet dawn. We stayed outside for another hour, as though becalmed, and when a small fishing smack headed in past us, we followed and sauntered into the harbor.

There's not much to see in Le Crotoy, except massive expanses of beach. When the tide ebbs, the sands have almost a desert feeling. Hazes shimmer over them, even in cold weather, and mirages appear—of hills and dunes and silver pools that vanish as you near them. Miss Begley and I were to walk those sands for three days. We were expected, we discovered, in the tiny hotel; Bawn Buckley stayed on the boat.

Were we afraid? That's the question I asked her as we walked those wide sands, those long days. In the flat sunshine and air cold as frost, Miss Begley kept on a woolen hat, as close to her head as a helmet.

She said, "I don't know whether I'm excited or afraid."

But once again, Miss Begley knew far more than I did, because on our first walk she said, "We have to go north along the beach for an hour. Then we've to turn and walk back for an hour. Then out for another hour. Then back to the harbor café."

"How do you know all this?"

She said, "Just walk."

On the third day, midway through our first hour, with the tide far out, a galloping horse appeared. Far, far down the sands from us, its hooves sent up flights of spray. In the distance we could tell only that it was equine. No color discernible, or breed. We stopped to watch.

A bareback rider. We stared. The horse veered toward us. It increased its speed. A teenage girl—that was the rider. Draped low along the neck. Gripping the mane. She never looked at us. As she thundered past, ten yards away, a tiny package fell.

I retrieved it; an old ring box, glue-wrapped in strong blue paper. No indication whence it came. We opened it with Miss Begley's fingernails. Inside, we found a square packet of the same tough blue paper. Unfolded it had only the word *Larbaud.* We walked on.

When we returned to the café for lunch, Bawn Buckley joined us. He took the piece of paper, had a furtive look. After lunch we walked the sands again, and at the end of the day we wandered down to the men and women sewing the repairs in the nets.

Under Miss Begley's tuition, I had been practicing my newfound vocabulary on the locals. For instance, I ordered our food at each meal. Blinking in the late sun among the net menders, I now asked if the name "Larbaud" meant anything to them. A man complimented me on my French—*"Bravo! M'sieu d'Irlande,"* and a woman too.

Nobody answered the question. But there are ways of not answering a question so that the inquirer is not offended. We strolled away, into the little café for dinner. A waitress more or less marched us to the big sea-view window. Miss Buckley nudged me.

Parked outside stood a bright yellow van with the name *Cirque Valéry Larbaud.* Beside it, in the sunny evening, stood a man and a girl, juggling colored plates to each other—husband and much younger wife, we would discover. Both wore clown suits without the faces or red noses, though he had a conical hat with yellow pom-poms.

"Now what do we do?" I whispered.

Miss Begley murmured, "Why do you think they gave us this table?"

The landlord, lean as a greyhound, long, sallow face, one eyelid drooping, came over. He muttered, *"Très chaud,"* and opened the window beside the circus.

The jugglers now began to sing. In French, it had the weight and lilt of a folk song, and they sang it very slowly in time to the rhythm of the juggling.

Miss Begley looked at me, her cheeks reddening, and said, "I have it. The song. They'll pick us up tonight." She waited. "They're repeating it—two o'clock. Listen." And they sang the chorus over and over, *"Deux heures. Ici. Deux heures. Ici."*

The pair of clowns finished juggling and held out a hat. I dropped some coins through the open window, as did Miss Begley. And so did two men I hadn't seen until that moment—German officers, coarse yet starched young men who applauded and walked off. With tooting horns and rattling bells, the Larbaud circus pulled away from the café, and we heard it clang up the little streets of Le Crotoy.

Later that evening, we alerted Bawn Buckley to the fact that we might be missing for some time. When we returned from the boat, the landlord with the drooping eyelid handed me an alarm clock. It was set to 1:45 A.M.

46

There was no moon when we rose, yet the light seemed not to have left the sky. Shoals can cause this effect; a great movement of fish just beneath the surface will grant a light to the sea. That night I saw the gleam of Heaven in the water and the sky. I always associate the color silver with hope.

The drooping-eye landlord gave us mugs of hot chocolate. As we drank, he peered through the window. Soon, he snapped his fingers at us and opened the café door. Outside, a man appeared, the husband who had juggled. He said not a word, merely turned so that we followed the beam from his very weak flashlight.

We walked through short twists and turns, past the high dark bulk of a church. A steep lane took us down to a sheet of water. In a rowing boat, the juggling young wife waited. We stepped on board, and as she cast off she waved good-bye to her husband.

In all of this, nobody spoke. We did as bidden or as events indicated.

"Go where others lead; do as you're told," Captain Miller had said in London. My fear had been that we'd forget some of the instructions, but in the moment they were few, and they never amounted to more than, "Follow what happens."

The curly-haired wife rowed like an athlete—long, powerful strokes that disturbed little water. Within ten minutes or so, she nosed the boat into an inlet, a lagoon. She steered us under trailing branches and tied the boat to a ring on a wooden fence.

We followed her up a long staircase. Now we had almost no light, because trees surrounded the place and deep foliage hemmed in the walls. At the top of a long climb, she tapped on a door, and waited.

In the silence, I listened to the night. I heard almost nothing—perhaps a slight wash from the water below, perhaps a rustle of leaves. For that moment I had a sensation that recurs with me and is not uncomfortable— that there was no world and I didn't exist.

Our guide folded her arms in a patient attitude, and we took our cue from her. The waiting felt like three or four minutes, a long time on a sightless, soundless night. When the curly-haired woman's shape disappeared from the gloom, we followed her into deeper darkness. A presence beside us closed a door and drew a curtain; I heard the bolt rattling home.

Then light flooded, and we blinked inside a French farmhouse kitchen, of a kind that I've seen many times since. A woman stepped forward, dressed for a day out in the world, though the porcelain clock on the mantel now said a quarter past three in the morning. She welcomed us with friendly if unsmiling handshakes and indicated the room.

At a table sat four men. One of these was her husband, a farmer—the lady of the house, we would learn, was the local doctor. Of the other three, all very much younger, two belonged to the British and American forces. And one—who became and remains my friend—led the local maquis, the French Resistance. Hugo Barrive's name was on every wanted poster in every village in the north of France.

He spoke first, in perfect English, with a very slight accent: "May I have your names, please?" and when we'd answered without a hint of fear or reserve he said, "Sit down."

No drinks were offered, no informalities, and the curly-haired, juggling wife, Annette Larbaud, sat a little away from the table, as did the doctor, a frown on her face too.

"Thank you for coming here," said Barrive, "and we will now tell you the details of the assignment. We are most appreciative of your help, and Captain Miller has our gratitude."

"We have a question." When Miss Begley butted in on any situation,

her force of presence, and the clarity of her speech, and perhaps the unusual Irish accent, ensured that she was heard.

The *maquisard* and the three other men turned a little in their chairs.
Miss Begley said, "Will anybody be killed because of what we do?"
Barrive said, "This is war."

"We won't have anything to do with anything that gets somebody
killed," she said.

Hugo Barrive said, "But you will save a lot of lives."

"You don't know that." She was scolding him. "But you will know if
somebody gets killed. I only ever act on what I know, and I won't do
something if it's going to have a bad end. And I won't do something just
because somebody tells me it might have a good end. This gentleman
you're going after, he was my neighbor. He was married to my friend."

The *maquisard* surveyed Miss Begley as a man looks at a pretty girl in
a bar. He smiled and said, "A defined moral position, is that it?"

"I don't care what you call it." She spoke in a civilized way, with no
rudeness, but as direct as a knife.

"What do you need?" he said.

And she replied, "There's to be nobody killed in anything we do for
you."

"What do you think it is that we want you to do?"

"If I'm to fetch somebody—and that's what I was asked to do—he has
to live."

In French, the farmer spoke to the *maquisard,* and the Englishman
also said something—they both spoke so swiftly that I didn't catch any
of it. But Miss Begley did and said, "Oh, sure. Fine. Send us back if you
like. But that'd be your weakness, not ours. And anyway you can't do this
without us."

The *maquisard* smiled like a gracious host and said, "Why would we
kill him? He is wanted for what he knows."

Miss Begley subsided; he had charmed the passion out of her.

The briefing began. Nearby, in the town of Saint-Omer, the Germans
had established a major communications facility. It aimed to get as much
information as possible from across the English Channel. Along the
coast, teams of German listeners and French collaborators gathered such
radio signals as they could. They took them back to Saint-Omer, to the
German official in charge of deciphering and interpretation. A civilian,

he was considered one of the key operatives in the occupation of France and the monitoring of Allied intentions. He had been one of the many Germans who had first come to Ireland for the fishing, and then stayed, in love with the terrain.

And by now I realized how deep a reconnaissance Captain Miller had made.

"We know a lot about this man," Hugo Barrive said.

To which Miss Begley said, "Well, you'd have to, wouldn't you?"

A tussle developed between Barrive and Miss Begley, the Irish country girl who, in her way, had as much daring and originality as anybody in that room, and a great deal more than most.

"His wife was very nice. They had no children," said Miss Begley.

"He wants to marry again," said Barrive.

Miss Begley laughed and shook her head.

"Captain Miller is one smart fellow," she said, and we laughed with her.

"So you will do it?"

She said, "Describe exactly what you want?"

They told us the circumstances that existed and the scheme they had conceived. I was to pose as a writer, researching the travels of monks through Europe. Miss Begley was to pose as my cousin—we had our Irish passports—and we would stay in Saint-Omer and watch for Mr. Seefeld. They knew all his movements; they'd been tracking him for months.

"He's very German," said Barrive. "He does the same things every day at the same time. It will be easy to bump into him."

"I'd know him anywhere," she said. "Full head of hair. Big lips."

In the first meeting she was to reminisce with him and then arrange a drink or dinner, if possible for that evening. The rest of the operation would be handled by the men whom we'd just met in the farmhouse. They'd whisk him from Saint-Omer, and then we'd be taken back to the boat at Le Crotoy. They told us that Bawn Buckley knew to expect an extra passenger on his journey back to Ireland. Barrive thanked us and left the house with his companions.

Was I still afraid? I'm not sure. They had arranged it as a placid event, easy to accomplish—or so they'd claimed. When I look back, it seems both ordinary and preposterous—but so do many of the events in all our lives, and most of us have never lived inside a war.

47

No sleep; friendly talk in the farm kitchen; food. In the early light, we saw more clearly the steep wooden staircase that we'd climbed a few hours earlier. When we looked back from the water, the place seemed more like a house from a Chinese fable, with trailing willow branches masking the hidden corner of the lagoon. I wondered how many of the neighbors knew that the farm possessed this secret waterside entrance.

Madame Annette Larbaud of the curly hair took us to a different part of this inlet. Wooden steps led up to a roadway, and she told us that a few hundred yards to the right was the place where we must wait for the bus to Abbeville. Two other people waited there—an elderly man and a child who held his hand.

Something about the elderly man felt familiar but I couldn't place it and put it down to fancy. He and the child boarded the bus ahead of us and never looked in our direction. They sat in the seats just inside the door. It was, of course, Hugo himself; the child, his nephew, was the prop to his disguise.

Throughout this escapade, I was managing to keep the observer in me hard at work, and I watched Miss Begley closely. She was gliding through it all—and looked so determined that I could imagine nothing would distract her.

At Abbeville, we caught another bus. When we arrived in Saint-Omer, we found our hotel and checked in; once again we'd been expected. Then we went to the *bibliothèque* for the first of my fake research inquiries. Hugo had warned us that we'd be tracked by the occupying Germans, and we could expect questions from them—the library also had spies, he said, tasked with informing the authorities if new faces arrived.

And with true German efficiency, they showed up inside an hour—an officer and a female civilian assistant. They strode into the library and, without a glance in any other direction, marched to our table. The man was uniformed, armed, and nervous; the woman, much cooler, spoke English.

"Your names, please." A command, not a question, and we gave our names with smiles. She didn't soften and asked, "Do you have papers?"

Miss Begley, as briefed, looked mystified. I produced—forewarned—my passport and letter of employment from the Irish Folklore Commission, in effect the Irish government.

"Why are you here?"

I explained. "I'm tracing the footsteps of the Irish monks who came through France on their way to Rome and the Holy Land."

The German lady official said, "But don't you know there's a war?"

Miss Begley said, with some surprise, "We were told that in France the war is over. That Germany had won. And anyway Ireland is neutral."

The German lady translated for the officer, who looked as though he'd been praised. They went away with half-smiles, and we sat down to our "researches."

Some time later, Miss Begley tugged my sleeve and pointed to the tall window. On the street outside, a small group of soldiers had surrounded a man in dungarees, a farmer by the look of him, frightened hair the color of sawdust. They stood him back against the wall, his hands raised above his head; they reached into his pockets, took out papers, and perused them. They turned him around to face the wall, searched him—and found a handgun.

On an order, two soldiers—each under twenty years old—spread-eagled the man, face forward to the wall. Another soldier, and he was no older, produced a knife and cut away the man's dungarees, shirt, and undershirt until he was stripped to the waist. There he stood, helpless, half-naked, his nose against the faded red brick of northern France.

People drifted past, crossing the street to keep out of the way, yet hesitating, halting, watching. The officer ordered the members of his platoon to form a line. He directed them to shoot. The impromptu firing squad raised its guns and riddled the Frenchman's naked back. His flesh bumped in little spasms as each bullet hit, and he fell like a red sack of wet grain.

Miss Begley said, "We have to go now."

We didn't look across the street as we quit the library; we turned sharp right and walked hard. She moved stiff and quick beside me, and I had to keep my head raised to keep from throwing up. The skin under my clothes went from cold to hot to cold. A few minutes after I'd lain down on my bed, someone rapped hard outside. I jumped to my feet, opened the door—and Miss Begley flung herself at me, into my arms. In utter silence, she pressed her face into my chest and tightened her grip on me. It speaks to the horror of the occasion that I never thought of the only other woman I had held so close.

48

We ate a somber dinner. I drank a glass of wine, and when the *patron* came across to pour another, Miss Begley put a hand over my glass.

"If you were never to be sober again," she said, "I need you sober now."

I said, "You need me sober always."

To which she said, "My God, I do."

After a moment she asked, "Did you think me very forward today? When I threw myself into your arms?"

I said, "My worry is that I'll never get that poor man out of my mind."

She said, "Would you object if I was in your bed with you tonight?"

So, Miss Begley slept with me—but I stayed awake with her. She arrived, demure as a nun, in a long white nightgown.

"I'm ready, brushed and clean," she said. "Which side of the bed do you want?"

Growing up an only child had meant years of sleeping alone. My parents had given me the best room in the house, the biggest, the widest, with the most appealing view over the garden and out to the mountains. I loved my bed; it jingled when I jumped into it; it had brass quoits on the bedposts.

When Venetia and I first meshed, I never stopped to think about bed sharing and its necessary principles. In any case, we had usually become such a tangle by morning that nobody could tell who had started out where. Now, in France, despite all that was going on, I was fazed for a moment at how to conduct this unexpected arrangement. Within seconds I ceased to worry, because Miss Begley climbed into my bed and settled down as though for the rest of her life.

And she slept thus too; she didn't move, and she didn't kick me, didn't fling an arm in my direction—she couldn't have been more natural or unaffected; she even snored a little. I, however, in my self-imposed celibacy, and fearing being misinterpreted, took the greatest care not to lie too near her, lest a sleeping arm gone astray or a nudging leg in a dream might give a wrong impression.

But that's not to say I wasn't supernaturally aware of her. My heart flashed and my mind roared, yet I stretched there like a plank, sensing the body that lay inches away. It might have been a bomb. I could feel its radiated warmth, and I had enough light from the street outside to watch the rise and fall of her body as she breathed. And I listened, because Miss Begley muttered in her sleep, mumbled and sighed, and made little whispered announcements into the night.

Did I want her? What a question—but I asked it of myself: *Do you want her as you wanted Venetia?* I couldn't get a straight answer; vacillations, hesitancies, no clear voice came through. And I evaded the answer by returning to the awfulness of that day's street scene, and in its tragedy I associated it with my years of searching, my loneliness. Slowly, I shook off the blood images, tried to focus on the task ahead and keep my fear under control. And my desire.

Next morning, Miss Begley made one—and only one—reference to our having shared a bed.

"You're more peaceful than I thought," she said.

It never occurred to me to ask what she might have expected, and whether she had a scale of comparisons, and if so how she had acquired it. And she had no idea that I hadn't closed an eye.

49

Now began the most frightening phase thus far. Today, we all know that Miss Begley and I weren't alone in an action such as this—how many war stories have you heard about kidnappings of generals, or glamorous female spies? Back then, we knew none of that; as far as I was concerned, nobody had ever done this before. And although I knew that I was opening a door into the dark, I didn't think about it. Maybe that was a sign of my own damage. Or maybe that's simply a human condition—to leap into danger without measuring it in advance.

A long and muted breakfast helped us to recover from the street atrocity. Not until almost eleven o'clock did we feel able to stand or walk. I distinctly remember the sweetness of the church bell chiming the eleven strokes somewhere.

Miss Begley said, "I hope it'll wake up God."

Precisely at noon, Mr. Seefeld would leave his office. So they'd briefed us. He'd "amble" (their word) to his lunch. This would be the moment. Miss Begley would intercept him. She'd recognize and greet him. After that, luck owned the game.

At first it went as planned—the surprise didn't come until later. We ambled too, that was our decision: Stroll in Saint-Omer like tourists, pretend there isn't a war. Along the rue Gambetta we wandered. The locals stared at us, unable to believe that people would visit France at that time.

We found the basilica. I stood there, making notes. The bell rang twelve. Miss Begley whispered, "There he is." I turned to look. A large man came down the steps of a building on the far side of the street. Walking like a very big, fat bird, he turned in our direction.

She moved.

"Excuse me!" she called. As she crossed the empty street, I heard her say, "I know you!" This sad, awkward man stopped, and she speared him with his name—"Hans-Dieter!"

Heavy, his arms loose on their hinges, uncomfortable in his sham-
bling body—that's the man I saw. He had sleepy eyes and a mouth like a
snowman's. He peered at Miss Begley.

"Oh! Oh! Kate! What are you doing in Saint-Omer?!" He stood a little higher, burnished himself.

Perfect English, full idiom. Miss Begley rushed to him and held out
her hand: "I can ask you the same question!"

They laughed. Phase One was up and running.

"Great to see you, Hans. Let me look at you." She stepped back. She
reached in and straightened his tie. She patted him a little.

I viewed him as though I were his hangman. A part of me wished not
to, because I feared for him. I feared that I'd be the agent of his destruction, no matter what assurances we had received. He had the demeanor
of a sad and powerless professor, and he kept licking his bulbous lips.

"Have you come all the way from Kenmare?" he said.

Miss Begley said, "You never met Ben, did you? This is my cousin,
Ben MacCarthy. He's with the Irish Folklore Commission, and he's re-
searching the Irish monks of the Dark Ages, their path to the Holy
Land." She didn't show an iota of fear.

He said to me, "You need to go to Péronne."

"Tomorrow," I said.

To Miss Begley he said, "There was a resting place for pilgrims in medieval Péronne."

Miss Begley asked, "How are you? I'm so sorry for your loss."

His eyes filled with immediate tears.

"The anniversary was last week," he said. "It is so difficult."

"They'll all be delighted in Kenmare when I tell them I've met you,"
said Miss Begley. "Your mother-in-law especially."

"I'm on my way to lunch. Will you join me?"

Miss Begley—as directed—shook her head. "I'm afraid we can't. But
we could this evening."

"I have nothing to do this evening," he said. She gave him the name
of the restaurant that Hugo had chosen.

We parted. Miss Begley and I went into the basilica. We almost fell
into the silent pews under the pressure of the stress.

50

He had changed his clothes since midday—a white shirt, a plaid bow tie. His face was sometimes young as a boy's, and sometimes creased with mourning. The talking began well—Ireland and fishing. We all liked one another. I gleaned further knowledge of his late wife.

"She had the blackest hair you ever saw. I mean, when you looked into it very close. Black as black can be."

With his grief, his daily, hourly sense of loss—this man could become my friend.

I ventured to ask about the war.

"If we weren't Irish and neutral, what would have happened to us by now? Here in France?"

He looked around, to see whether anyone watched. A few people sat at tables in local clothes. He relaxed—and drew his hand across his throat.

Miss Begley took back the conversation. "If this is painful," she said, "say so, and I'll stop. But would you tell me a little about Ann's illness."

Once again his eyes became glassy. He gathered some composure and shook his head in refusal. With a smile, he asked her, "Are you still making 'matches,' as you call them?"

Miss Begley replied, "They even call me the Matchmaker of Kenmare now. My grandmother'll be thrilled to hear that I met you. She was very fond of Ann."

Mr. Seefeld put down his cutlery. He took Miss Begley's hand.

"And you are not married?" To me he said, "Are you in love with her? I know you're her cousin, but you could be in love with her."

Miss Begley said, "I'm not married. And I'm just about ready to marry somebody nice."

Mr. Seefeld looked at her the way a lush looks at a bottle—and I noted the ambiguity of her words.

"As nice as yourself?" he asked. Miss Begley laughed. He said, "But there's this damn war," and she said, "But that'll end one day."

I asked him, "Are you, in fact, a soldier? Even if you don't wear a uniform?"

"Civilians—we have the same rules. Very harsh."

In the chair beside mine, a change came over Miss Begley. Her body altered its place in the world. She sat higher and more rigid, two feet planted side by side. I came to see this feature of her being, her spirit of determination, again and again. She seemed to change everything that was going on inside herself—and brought about change in the moment's task.

Now she leaned forward and said, "We came over by boat and we're going back by boat. The nets are being mended out on the coast."

How shrewd she was that day. I had long known how it feels to need urgent change. Moments come in men's lives when we must alter everything or we feel we'll die. It happened to me, quite some time after Venetia's disappearance, and I did change everything. I took to the road. That's how I helped myself to survive. It's terrifying in some ways, but it's essential. We'd met Mr. Seefeld just as he'd reached that awful inner place—and she had sensed it in him. She knew that we could become—as he would see it—the agents of his urgently needed change. And she knew that we didn't have to kidnap him. That was the surprise I mentioned earlier. He wanted to come with us.

Later we agreed that we had both seen it happen. The quickening of the eye, the lifting of the head, the long glance all around, the dropping of the head again—they led to the confidential, unfinished remark: "How I'd love to . . . "

She laughed, and whispered, "Why don't you?"

"Can you tell me if I would be all right?"

Miss Begley whispered back, "If you're not all right, I won't be."

In the years ahead, he told me that when he saw us on the street that day outside the basilica, he knew that we'd come for him. Or so he'd hoped.

She reached for his hand, leaned closer, and said, "If you ask no more questions—we'll go now."

Hugo Barrive was waiting where he said he'd be—at the rear door of the restaurant. Miss Begley said to him, "Behave yourself."

In the darkness of the car, Mr. Seefeld sat between Miss Begley and me. She held his hand as though he were her child; from time to time she patted his forearm; he leaned his head on her shoulder. This was the saddest man I had ever seen, and I can claim to know something about sadness.

Hugo sat in front beside the driver. Even in the blackest of nights, even in that strange landscape, I could tell by the savage bumpings that we were taking roads few other people traveled. And still Miss Begley held Mr. Seefeld's hand. And still she patted his forearm. He continued to lean his head on her shoulder. With what feelings was he overcome? Remorse at his act of betrayal? Grief for his dead wife? Fear of the void that lay ahead?

He told me once, "Until that night I had forgotten how to feel more than one emotion."

The farmer and his doctor wife behaved with the utmost courtesy to Mr. Seefeld; they showed him none of the coldness they might have been assumed to feel. When they sat him in a comfortable armchair, Miss Begley sat on its arm. Hugo told us that we would not be going to Le Crotoy for another full day, because we might not get there now under cover of darkness. To all and any arrangements, Hans-Dieter Seefeld did no more than nod.

The doctor led the way upstairs; Mr. Seefeld and Miss Begley followed. When the doctor came back down, she looked around the kitchen, at her husband, at Hugo Barrive, and at me, and shrugged. Naively, I didn't understand that she meant the couple upstairs would share the room that night.

He didn't come down next day, and Miss Begley took up soup to him.

"He's feeling wretched. He's in a bad state," she whispered to me.

At dusk, in the quiet of the evening, I went outside and stood at the top of the wooden staircase. Home-going birds were calling, their cries long and thoughtful across the water. In forty-eight hours I had walked straight into violent danger and seen an atrocity that haunts me to this day. The others, the ravages I was yet to see, haunt me too—but the first remains the worst and the most brutalizing, the event that most sensitizes and desensitizes; perhaps that is always so.

Presently, I had a companion.

"Kate, tell me now, or never tell me. How did all this happen?"

"Not now."

"But there's a deal up and running, isn't there?"

She turned away, as she always did when unwilling to face something.

"Come on, Kate. This is too much for me."

She took my arms and shook me. "No, Ben. It isn't, it shouldn't be. You're capable of it."

"This is preposterous. You undertook a spying mission. You took us into the middle of the biggest war the world has ever seen."

"Is that how you see it?" she said.

"Why? Why did you do this? We could have been killed."

"But we weren't, were we?" she said, and closed down as only she could.

51

My daydreaming, of Asian willows, waterbirds, and the banal, black languor of casual brutalities, yielded to lapping sounds. Beneath me, the curly hair of our boatwoman appeared as she eased the rippling canoe to the mooring ring.

Annette Larbaud came up the wooden steps without a noise. She half-smiled at me, and then grimaced. A wave of her arm suggested the wider countryside, and inside she told Hugo that German soldiers were everywhere, urgent and searching.

In an hour, when twilight had become night, we led Hans-Dieter Seefeld down to the boat. Annette went in front of him, Miss Begley behind, her hand on his shoulder. He looked like a man who had been sick to his stomach. As a last thought, the doctor handed Hugo a rug that he spread around Mr. Seefeld's shoulders, but the stricken German, though wrapped up warm to his neck, continued to shiver.

What is the name of the ferryman in the Greek mythologies? He who rows the newly dead across the River Styx to Hades, the land of souls? Charon—that's his name, and if you don't pay him, you'll wander the shores of the afterworld for ever and ever, unrewarded, ill at ease. Our

Charon asked for no immortal coin in her palm; she hunched amidships, pulling at her oars with slow, arm-length strokes.

Miss Begley sat beside Mr. Seefeld, her arm in his. I faced them, and Hugo sat behind me, peering forward, twisting this way and that, on the lookout for searchlights and guns. We moved easily, silent and strong, out of the little river and down the long oxbow. Nobody spoke; we heard the dip and *splat!* of the oars; we heard night birds here and there, calling across the water with an *oordle-oordle* sound.

And then we heard an engine.

At first it could have been anything, anywhere—a truck on a nearby road; I assumed a large boat heading toward us, that huge mechanical roar. But it came up fast, and then very fast—an aircraft, not much above head height, in fact so close that we all ducked low. No lights; we saw nothing as it approached, but as it flew directly over us we saw fire. From the tail came flames, and I knew that the pilot had lost control, and he hit the bridge across to our right, the road bridge, fifty yards away, on the main road to Le Crotoy, and the flames went everywhere.

The fallen plane belonged to the Allies. We saw it sinking. Mr. Seefeld, shaking like palsy, pointed out the tail insignia of the Royal Air Force now lit by the flames, said, "This terrible war," and shuddered again. If he'd had any notion of changing his mind, he told me years later, that incident would have cured it.

We beat the patrols that night, as we would do at other times in the coming year, though in very different circumstances. Through the lanes of Le Crotoy, and the humps and lumps of its sand dunes, we stumbled and staggered, Mr. Seefeld doing his best. During one moment as I helped him—and he was too young to have needed help—I began to realize that he probably had asthma; he wheezed like a horse. Miss Begley never left his side.

At the boat, Bawn Buckley looked at Mr. Seefeld and said, "Are you coming fishing again?" And Mr. Seefeld laughed—they had known each other for years.

Out quietly on a two o'clock tide, we now had to fear only submarines, but they tended to leave fishing vessels alone. I stayed on deck and didn't inquire into any other arrangements on board.

The weather gave out curious little voltages, like an unsteady person's moods. A wind came up and died as quickly. In its wake, heavy splashing attacked the hull beneath where I stood, rocking the boat enough to make me grab a hold. Then a calm arrived, still and silent as the desert, and with it came a surge of almost warm air. And next, an hour or so later, came a cold breeze that blew in our faces for steady minutes, until it too died.

52

From Le Crotoy, we went north. I looked at the map. When level with Le Touquet, Bawn Buckley intended to turn to port—or "left," as I called it—and make straight across the English Channel, as though to dock at Eastbourne. From there, having turned to port again, we would hug the shore of England all the way to the Land's End in Cornwall. After what he called "the sprint" across the bottom of the Irish Sea, he then intended to hug the Irish shore all the way to Dingle.

"Once we hit Waterford we'll be all right."

We made steady knots. In general, when I turned my face to the stars, it felt benign, and when I went to the wheelhouse to ask Bawn Buckley about these little phenomena of changes in the weather and in the sea, he pointed to his right.

"There's your reason," he said. "We're close to the land. And isn't the land always giving the sea problems?"

I looked for sleepiness in myself and found none. The deck, the night, the opening dawn made me feel wonderful, and for the first time in a decade and more, I began to believe that my melancholy would one day evaporate. That is not the same as saying I had begun to cope with my loss. As you know by now, it certainly didn't mean that I had let go of Venetia, or of whatever child (or children, as I must now say) I had fathered.

What I am telling you is that my spirit had been changing. Can I call it reviving? I think so. Hope had a better chance in me now—though hope for what I couldn't yet say. I moved here and there on the cramped deck of the little trawler, looking now at the land and now at the open sea, and I sensed that I had begun to feel different, even if I couldn't put a name to it.

At around five o'clock in the morning, I went back into the wheel-house and was handed a mug of tea by Bawn Buckley, who murmured, "They're awake, they're talking."

He had cut the engine to half-speed, and I listened. From below I heard the rise and fall of talk. Then some vinegar began to flow in me, and my mind began to ask difficult questions: *What is their sleeping arrangement? How cramped is it down there? I know it's where the trawler-men sleep, so are they lying in two sleeping bags or one?*

53

We didn't land in Dingle Harbor. He took us to a little jetty a mile west, where stood Captain Miller, in a fawn trench coat, looking jaunty. He was flanked by four tough-looking men—American marines, I would learn. Behind them sat three cars, an unusual sight in Ireland during "the Emergency." Near the cars stood an elderly German couple—a retired doctor and his wife, it transpired—who lived not far from Dingle, and who had been contacted by Captain Miller. They waved toward us—and Mr. Seefeld waved back; they knew each other.

I went off the boat first. As soon as my feet touched the stones of the pier, I moved ahead and to one side—I wanted to observe the full scene. Miss Begley, alert as a bird, began to steer matters. And all the while, it rained.

First, she called forward the German doctor and his wife, who went down to the trawler and greeted Mr. Seefeld like the old friends they were. Then she and I walked up the jetty, and Captain Miller came to meet us. From the wheelhouse Bawn Buckley watched everything, a man to whom nothing under the sun was new, his wrinkled face more than ever like that of an old king.

Before Captain Miller could say a word, Miss Begley turned to me. "Ben, I need a witness."

She led the three of us up the jetty, away from everyone, as far as the parked cars.

"Now listen to me," she said, squaring herself to Miller. "I had a long chat with Hans on the boat. If you've ever been a man's matchmaker he'll tell you anything about himself. He doesn't have great health—but he has great mental strength. If you take him away from here he'll tell you nothing, he's been trained against torture. But if you agree to let me come with him, and then send him back to his own house in Kenmare, and live a quiet life, he'll tell you everything. And he knows everything."

Miller looked at her. "Okay. I agree."

"No harm will come to him, is that right?"

"Sure."

"Say it."

"Okay. No harm will come to him."

"Give me your word," she said.

"I give you my word, Kate."

Then she put a hand on his arm and said, "And you and me, Charles. We have a deal, don't we?"

He looked out to sea, he looked at the ground, then he looked at her. He had no answer for her that would have freed him from his obligation. He said, in a voice quiet as wool, "We have a deal, Kate, you and I."

She raised that eyebrow. "And?"

He said, "I always keep my word. Name the date."

54

I was too staggered, I think, to take it in at first. She had landed him. The Matchmaker had made her own match! When I did reflect on it, I wondered whether that was always her only prospect. After all, a man who needed a matchmaker would never have had the courage to take her on. I watched both of them. She, to my surprise, looked serene; he, the more animated of the two.

"Do you want to shake hands on it?" he said.

"You mean—the word of a gentleman?" she asked, only half joking.

"Or sealing the bargain," he said.

At that moment an expression crossed his face that bothered me. The words to describe it came to me instantly—"a seeming wish to devour." He looked wolfish.

I recoiled. Had Miss Begley hitched her wagon to *that*? Remember my training. I lived so much with legends that I saw important things in legendary form, and I tried to translate significant events into instant myth. That was James Clare's doing; he taught me that if you can tell yourself your own life story as though it were a legend, you can cure many of your own ills.

You'll remember too that I remarked how I liked physical manifestations—how in Dublin I'd gone looking for the accidental debris of war in order to make the carnage of Europe real. Well, when I first saw Captain Charles Miller at a distance that morning, by the dove-gray light of the Irish southwest, he looked different. It wasn't the civilian clothes—I'd seen him like that many times during our London capers, where he dressed like a half-dapper American. Nor was it the environment—remember I'd first met him on that same coastline. He was about to grab a prize, and therefore he looked greedy. And perhaps a little sinister. As I say, wolfish.

This thought jabbed me, and I looked away from him. But when I scrutinized Captain Miller's marine comrades, one of them actually had the appearance of a wolf—steady eyes in a bushy face. To crown it, the German doctor (I'll remember his name in a moment) also looked at least vulpine, if not downright lupine. His face seemed to funnel to a thick point that projected his long nose forward, and he had gray, placid features—a wolf elder, so to speak.

After the bombshell of what was, in essence, a proposal of marriage, driven by her, completed by him, Captain Miller smiled a kind smile at Miss Begley, followed by a laugh.

"Kate," he said. "You're some woman."

"I'm halfway to Kenmare," she said, "and I want to get home. So we might as well get started," and the three of us walked back down the jetty to join the others.

Dr. Manfred Hortig—*that* was his name—and his wife, Elisabeth, sat with Mr. Seefeld in Captain Miller's car. I joined two of the silent marines in one of the other military vehicles, and we convoyed to the Hortigs' house overlooking the sea near Castlemaine. When we arrived, Miss Begley jumped out and held open the door for Mr. Seefeld; Captain Miller stood back and watched; Dr. Hortig and his wife trotted to their doorstep, where they turned around and welcomed us all. For me, the Seefeld incident, keenly real and yet preposterous, had ended. For now.

55

How things happen. Next time I picked up my letters, James Clare had written, saying that he wanted to meet me in Donegal sometime, where he'd heard that "somebody has a great old story about a wolf and we've been trying to get it for aeons." Therefore, I mulled the subject of wolves for days. I didn't know then what a theme they would become in my life, and yet I must have had some inkling, because I couldn't banish wolfish images from my mind.

I dwelt on Dr. Hortig's face, on Captain Miller's face, and the bearded chops on one of his men, and I wonder now if that whole wolf thing wasn't a kind of pre-haunting—by a man more ravenous than even the most rabid wolf, though with none of the kindness wolves are said to possess, a man who, had there not been a war, would probably have mutated into a serial killer, a man whose trademark was the slicing of flesh from female bodies before he poisoned them over a period of several days.

He was born in Templehof, Berlin, on the twentieth of December, 1915, to an educated Prussian named Otto Volunder and a woman named Sophia Lieberstoldt.

This Otto Volunder had a proud background. He claimed that his family went back to the Teutonic Knights and the Hanseatic League. These were the men who had most felt the sting of Germany's Great War defeat; Otto, a cavalryman, had been "von" Volunder, but he dropped the nobleman's identifier in shame at Prussian failure. Sophia came of minor nobility, and she broke all the ranks of aristocratic German young women in her day by studying medicine. The couple met at a military soiree, fell for each other that night, married within six months, and had three children, two daughters and one adored son, Sebastian.

The boy was educated in Berlin, at the Goethe Oberrealschule, but he didn't, as the school and his parents expected, go on to become a scientist or a mathematician—he wanted to be a soldier. In fact he wanted to be a cavalryman like his father, and he took riding lessons early.

When he was eighteen, despite a modicum of parental reluctance—they were "old" Germany, after all—he joined the Hitler Youth. That was in March 1933; and six months later, on the seventeenth of October, 1933, there's his name, Sebastian Volunder, on the list of men at the very foundation of the SS cavalry. He had amber eyes—amber like a timber wolf's.

Sebastian Volunder had put his foot on a golden ladder. From that early cavalry intake, his superiors selected him and one other to join a company known as Leibstandarte SS Adolf Hitler—the Führer's personal bodyguard. He and his comrade (who later became his commanding officer) received their second lieutenant commissions on 20 April 1936, a day of added joy for them: It was Hitler's forty-seventh birthday.

Die Kreme des Korps, Sebastian Volunder called them. "We were the most superb of the elite," he said to his sister, and they had to conform to dictates laid down in Hitler's own handwriting: exceptional health and fitness; at least five feet nine inches tall; no teeth fillings. The body at the hip had to measure as close as possible to halfway; the leg had to measure "with equal felicity," he said, between thigh and knee—in other words, no physical disproportion anywhere. As to the essential "racial purity"—for officers, they required proof of ancestry going back to 1750; for soldiers, the year 1800.

Though something of a bantam cock, and thus barely making the five feet nine inches, Sebastian met all the other requirements. And more: He had become a profound admirer of Adolf Hitler and the German High Command, and when drinking with his comrades or his father, he continued to weep for the humiliations of the previous war.

The other young man chosen with him to join the Hitler elite became

more famous than Sebastian—infamous, rather—and he was the reason
I went to Dachau. You'll hear more of these two gentlemen later, because
Sebastian Volunder was the German equivalent of Charles Miller, his actual opposite number. The first time I met him, Volunder reached up,
caught my nose between thumb and forefinger, and tweaked until tears
came to my eyes.

56

I wasn't privy to the conversations that began when Captain Miller "debriefed," as he called it, Mr. Seefeld. Miss Begley sat in, and indeed typed
the notes, which then became classified as Top Secret. Day after day, they
huddled in the small back study usually occupied by Mrs. Hortig, a
renowned botanist specializing in ferns.

From my occasional glance as I walked by the window of their room,
it seemed that Mr. Seefeld just talked and talked, for hours and hours—
to Captain Miller's delight, I assumed.

With nothing to do, I went away the next day. In Killarney, I retrieved my bicycle and stayed a couple of nights at Mrs. Cooper's, so that
I might gather myself and work out my immediate future. I had no idea
what would happen next. As I was leaving, to be driven by Dr. Hortig,
they all said good-bye to me. Mr. Seefeld told me that I must come and
stay with him in Kenmare; and Captain Miller thanked me.

"When we've won this war, Ben," he murmured, "I'll see to it that
your courage is acknowledged."

Courage? I hadn't even known what I'd been doing.

Miss Begley took my arm and walked me to the car.

"I'll write to you at the post office in Tralee. Or is Limerick better?"
And I said Limerick, because I wanted to visit my parents in Goldenfields, thirty miles from there.

And then Miss Begley tugged hard on my arm and hissed, in one of
the fastest sentences I had yet heard her speak: "There wasn't any sin,

there was only comfort, body to body. Comfort and warmth. I did the same for you, remember."

What could I say? What should I have said? My mind yelled, *No, you didn't do it for me*—because, whatever she thought, that night in Saint-Omer when she slept in my bed had been for her and her alone.

During the time of the interrogation, Mr. Seefeld, furtive and anxious, looked to Miss Begley for more "comfort and warmth." She, fearing that Captain Miller might see, kept his desire as surreptitious as a conspiracy.

With equal discretion, she now pursued her own interest in Captain Miller as though she were the man and he the girl. Her clincher, her closer of the deal, took the form of a letter that she wrote, on the Hortigs' typewriter, one night late, many days into what Captain Miller called "the softest interrogation in the history of military intelligence." I have the letter in my possession.

> *Dear Charles,*
>
> *(I dislike "Chuck," it reminds me of a tug on a rope.) This is the time to conclude the preliminaries between us, so that we can become husband and wife. In the next day or so I want you to write to your "girl back home" as you persist in calling her—I've drafted the letter for you: "Dearest" (or whatever pet name you use), "I fear I have disappointing information for you. Here in Europe, I have met another whom I love more than anything in the world, and we are to be wed imminently. This, I know, will come as a blow, but do not be too despondent—you have lost to a remarkable woman, and I hope that she will become your friend one day. Yours sincerely, Charles Miller, Capt."*
>
> *Make sure that you show me the letter. I will seal the envelope, and I will make sure that the letter gets sent to May or Ellie (I've forgotten her name). I will then make our arrangements; I have papers, etc., to get from the parish priest in Kenmare, and I know that the army will tell you that you're free to marry. I have already checked with them.*
>
> *This is the most wonderful moment of my life—because you are the most wonderful man. Even though I don't know you very well,*

*I recognized you the moment I saw you as the person with whom I
want to spend all my days, and for whom I would give my own life
if asked. Marry me at our first opportunity, win this war, and take
me back to those thousands of acres that you told me about.*

With love. Kate.

She made Miller read it while she stood there. She made him hand-write the letter to the "girl back home." She sent it to the U.S.A. herself.

In some bizarre corner of my mind where warnings hang like shrouds, I think I knew that her pledge to him would be tested to the hilt. I think I knew that she was entering a risk of which she understood nothing. And I think I grasped that she would have to pay some price for commandeering his life in such a ruthless fashion—but I could never have guessed at how much she'd have to pay.

57

Let me tell you about my parents, your grandparents. In the decade after Venetia's disappearance I rarely went to see them. Cruel of me, I know, their only child, but I included them in the wide spread of my blame. I knew too that my father harbored a jealousy against me. To put it simply, when he ran away with Venetia, he jeopardizing my mother's life unthinkably, and even though he had come back to Goldenfields and become even more attentive to her than before, he never forgave me for shattering his dream.

And that's what I did. I went after him and brought him home, as Mother had implored me to do. Falling in love with Venetia had not been in my plan, nor had anybody anticipated that she would cleave so passionately to me and not my father.

Every visit to them had this cloud hanging over it. I'd never told them that Venetia and I had married, and they only learned of her disappearance from the newspaper reports of the police inquiries. When I did manage to go back for the first time, I found my spirit freaked with the black jet of bitterness, and I left earlier than I had intended. Subsequent visits dimmed this resentment only a little; at any moment I felt likely to lash out.

Now, though, and it must have been Kate Begley's influence, or perhaps the bizarre Seefeld experience, I found myself mellower toward them. For the first time, I even brought them gifts.

My father had sprained his ankle and was walking with a stick. I'd sent a telegram, they'd been expecting me, and he was leaning on the gate. After a flicker of initial awkwardness, he took my arm. We paced in step along the avenue, across the gravel, and into the porch.

I asked myself, *Is he older?* He didn't seem to be aging, and yet I could see that he wasn't as young as in the days when I'd followed him from venue to venue across the countryside and he'd been so embarrassed to see me.

The colors thrown on the floor by the stained-glass panels in the porch brighten my day often. I can enumerate many of my childhood's light patterns: the shadows of clouds on sunny mountains; that sudden candid gleam of a far-off lake; the dappling of leaves on my mother's face under the big beech tree when I was little and looking up at her; the evening sun turning all our western windows into flat panels of opaque gold; the yellow of the flames in our parlor when the fire has been lit but no lights have yet been turned on.

"Louise," my father called, effusive as ever, "come-come-come out and look at us. Harry MacCarthy and Ben MacCarthy. Get outa the way, Bing Crosby and Bob Hope."

He began to croon, "Toor-aloora-loora, that's an Irish lullaby," and since he had the worst voice in the Western Hemisphere, a larynx like a cracked plate, Mother came running.

"Anything to stop that noise," she said. "Oh, Ben. Look at you."

She took my hand. Her hair, never longer than a boy's, had more gray in it; the eyes had never lost that watchfulness that hadn't been there before what she used to call the Catastrophe. I loved, though, that she'd never lost her austerity, her lean efficiency, her reserve.

This time, I stayed two days and watched how they were in their lives about the place, toward each other, and toward me. Mother told me the stories she knew would entertain, such as the latest high jinks by our farmhand, Billy Moloney.

"He came into the yard," she said, "one day last week, back from the creamery, with a wheel on the cart leaning like the Tower of Pisa."

We had long referred to him as Billy Flock, because we couldn't quote him without using some form of euphemism, so profane was his language.

"So I see him coming, and out I go and I say to him, 'What happened, Billy?' and he said [Mother began to laugh, and almost couldn't finish]—he said, 'Ma'am, the flockin' flocker's flocked.' And I had to leave the yard and find your father."

I found them less tentative with me than before because, of course, I was less tentative with them. My father, as ever, wanted to talk politics and the war. I longed to tell him of the exploits in France, but knew I couldn't—I might as well have put it in the papers. I could see the headlines: HARRY MACCARTHY'S SON IS SPY HERO.

Mother, for most of the time, confined her inquiries to my folklore work, asking for stories, whether I had called upon So-and-So or Such-and-Such, did I have any great new tunes in my head, how were James Clare and Miss Dora Fay?

I hadn't been home in a year. By the fire one night as we sat talking, I reflected on these two people who had known such foolishly induced pain. In local gossip, he was still the farmer who had left his wife and run off with a young actress. That was how the world would always tell the story, an actress whose family had tried to swindle him, rob him of his farm, an actress whom Harry MacCarthy's son, his only child, had then married at the age of eighteen, "ousting his father," they said.

All that was over now, and would never rise again, and I felt proud of them for having recovered so well, but as usual I didn't have the words to say it. Nor did they, nor could they, would they, ever refer to those events—too painful, too intimate, too sore, and too tragic for me.

Except: When I was leaving, Mother walked with me to the gate, and my father waved from the doorstep.

"He looks well," I said, "apart from the sprain."

She said, "He has great spirit, you should have heard the commotion he made about the sprain, he made me laugh until I was sick. Said he'd have the leg amputated and collect a war pension. And sell the toes as holy relics, say they were Saint Patrick's toes."

And then, before I mounted my bicycle, she said, "Ben, I never ask. But did you ever hear? I mean—a word?"

I shook my head, and she continued, very slowly as though prepared to interrupt herself if she was saying too much.

"They say. That, ah'm. That she's in America. That the mother goes to see her. That, well, there's, we have, I mean: Look. If there is, if there actually is—a grandchild—well, it would always be welcome here," and she stopped, quavering a little, and asked, "What do you think, Ben? Do you think she's alive? D'you think there's a grandchild?"

If Mother knew how often I'd asked myself that question—every second of every minute of every hour of every day of every week of every month of every year. And therefore I felt able to say, "I think so. But I don't know."

And she said, as she did about many things, "Let Life fix it." She patted my shoulder. "Ben, you're so good, you're such a good fellow."

"How are you, yourself?" I asked.

"I'm fine," she said. "Most of me."

I couldn't bear to look back at her because I knew that she'd be standing there, angular as a coat hanger, simple as prayer, watching me out of sight, and I knowing that a day would come when she wouldn't be there to look at my back as I went away from her yet again.

58

May 1944

Two weeks later, after uneven times and mixed results in Kilkenny and Carlow (the west coast is still the richest in our lore), I took my bike on a train, went to the post office in Limerick, and opened a letter from Miss Begley: "Come down here and celebrate."

Had she married already?

In the house at Lamb's Head, I found all the excitement of a fable. The place teemed with women and girls—no marriage yet, but trousseau time, with plates of food and bells of laughter. When I loomed in the doorway, big as a black shadow, Miss Begley clapped her hands, ran to me, and said, "I clinched it."

And from a chair near the window the grandmother said, "She clinched it."

"Clinched what?"

"We have a date, for the wedding," said the grandmother.

"If we had a tune to that, we could sing it," said Miss Begley, "and from now on you have to call me 'Kate,' because I'm going to show you my trousseau, and therefore you'll know a lot about me that most men never will or should."

"Is he here?" I asked.

"Oh, good God, we'd have seven years of bad luck if he saw any of this! The wedding's in London. And you're coming."

Like a servant in a play, I folded my hands in front of me and nodded my head.

I said, "I have to get something from my bike," stepped out into that wild Atlantic wind, and tried to find a place where I could vomit without being seen. I didn't in fact throw up, but I was sick to the core. My heart was now harassing me every day because I was having difficulty in maintaining to myself that Venetia was still my world. But I had articulated none of this to myself; now I know that my body was the messenger.

You can tell, can't you, how it must have felt? I was betwixt and between, yet the loss of people past still lay coiled inside me like a snake, ever ready to hiss and strike.

The light had turned pewter across the bay, as a small rainstorm swept in, but the squall touched Lamb's Head not at all and the sun lit the sea between the rain and me. Taking great care, I edged down the steep path that leads to the jetty, which I had never seen. Awkward as a hobbled goat, I kept my body low to the ground, ready for a fall at any time. Until it breaks away to the left and onto a little plateau, any drop from the path will pitch a body straight down into the waves. I made it to the safe level and walked the rest.

Unseen from above, the jetty had substance. An oblong of rocks, selected for their natural fit to one another, had been cemented together.

Over the years, seaweed, kelp, barnacles, and other shore growth had added to the welding, and the gray-blackened stones looked as firm as a harbor wall. Not more than ten feet long, the pier had iron rings embedded on both sides; from one hoop waved strands of an old rope like a lock of hair.

I looked up behind me but could only see the chimney and part of the roof on the Begley house. And I imagined the men who came here, with their rough faces and rougher hands, and, perhaps roughest of all, their manners, but maybe with yearning in their hearts for a fireside companion.

Such thoughts led me straight to melancholy and could produce a mood that would last for weeks, ever sinking, ever worse. I fought with it by looking around, by dipping my fingers into the wonders of a rock pool, where a tiny crab scuttled away from the shadow of my hand. Periwinkles cropped everywhere, and I began to gather them, to boil them later and winkle out the meat with a pin.

And then I saw the plaque in the wall.

A flat stone had been inserted high on the pier, out nearest the harshest drag of the ocean. Every wave must pound that stone, every lip of a tide must suck at it. Yet the inscription, the deeply incised words, had held fast:

FOR JOAN AND FLORENCE BEGLEY

MAMA AND PAPA

THIS IS YOUR HOME

KATE

The sentiment should have felt crass and mushy; it didn't. I'd known of similar little monuments on the coast of Portugal—they're designed to beckon home the lost mariner—but I'd never seen it in Ireland, and I've never seen another. The sea washed in; I had to jump to keep my feet dry; the pewter light out in the bay began to spread in my direction.

I never viewed the trousseau—too many girls and women, too much squealing and ribaldry. That suited me fine, and I sat with the baleful grandmother, and I ate every bite of food that was offered to me—which is what I do under stress.

However, in my personal journal I have a sensational entry, made next day. Though I didn't want to, I stayed at Lamb's Head, and, late in the blue and smoky evening Miss Begley came to my room. Here's the note I made.

Last night, I was lying in the dark, fully clothed, trying not to think. My mind refused to let me plan my next journeys. I wanted to go to Donegal in search of wolves, I needed to go to Monaghan. My brain lacked the strength for sequential thought. I heard a scratching noise—the gentle screech of the uneven door as it scraped across the stone flags. Kate B. came in, a finger to her lips. My candle fluttered; I stood. She reached up, unbuttoned and removed my waistcoat, then did likewise with her cardigan. Next she indicated that I must take off my shirt, and she took off her blouse. Garment by garment, and like puppets whose strings she held, we took off our clothes and stood naked face-to-face. Led by her, lit by the candlelight we ran our hands all over each other. Her hands guided mine. When we lay down on the bed, everything became soothing, as I think and hope it was meant to be. We seemed to have nothing but thoughtfulness for each other, nothing but a wish to be calm and warm, nothing but a yearning to give comfort. And she seemed to need it as much as I did, although we didn't talk about it. I'm not saying that I didn't want more, oh my God, I did. But I buried my head between her breasts, and we left it at that. We fell asleep. In the morning she had gone, and I was tempted to think it all a dream.

It wasn't a dream. Next day, she raised the event with me. We were sitting on the long train from Killarney to Dublin. I had put my bicycle in the luggage van; on the racks above us sat her suitcases and her trunk; Miss Kate Begley was about to become a bride, and she had packed for it like a duchess.

As the sunlight flooded her eyes, she raised a shielding hand and said, "How shocked are you?"

I said, "If you mean last night—why does the word *shocked* come into it?"

"Well—what we did."

I wasn't certain what value she was trying to extract—praise or blame. So I said, "I felt used."

She didn't recoil. "Do you know why it happened?"

I bit off the words. "No. I don't know why it happened."

She said, "I have nobody but you to trust with the person I am. Myself."

"Aren't you about to marry someone for that reason?"

She ignored my remark and said, "You're my security, Ben, if everything goes wrong."

"Goes wrong?"

"If a girl comes back to me after her first walking out with a fellow, and she sits there and says she had a lovely time, but she's twisting her handkerchief until her fingers are blue, what kind of a time did she really have?"

"What on earth has that to do with you and me naked?"

She said, "I'm going forward into the unknown. You're what I know."

When she spoke like a novelette, it drove me crazy.

"You're not answering my question."

She said, "So—how shocked are you?"

"You made me look at you," I said. "You made me inspect you. You used me."

"You don't believe me," she said, "because you don't want to believe me. I watched you in France, I saw the way you looked after me, you were a kind of overseer. And I trust you so much that I want you to remember me as Kate Begley, not as Mrs. Charles Miller. I can never have that chance again. And I couldn't have done it if you'd never been married yourself."

"What the hell are you talking about?" I said.

"Don't be so cross. I need to know that there will always be one person in the world who knows me best of all."

"Outside of your new husband?" I said. She nodded, and I asked, "Then why didn't you go the whole hog? Why didn't we complete it?"

"I wanted to," she said. "But there was no sign that you did."

This was defeat; this was humiliation. I asked the feeble question. "Why me?"

"Because you're the safest person in the world."

I said, "Kate, you're so many things—how do I know what you are at any given moment?"

She said, "Well, I'll tell you what I am. I'm the Fourth Fate."

This is very grandiose, ran my hostile mind.

She went on. "You don't know, do you, who the Fates were?"

I said, trying not to sound tart or smart, "One spun the thread of life, one handed it out, and one cut it."

"And I draw two of those threads together," she said. "Two lives, and I knot them to each other. I'm the destiny that those two people harness."

Yes, she is being grandiose. I need Billy Moloney because this is flockin' irritatin'.

"You've seen those people who come to us. You've seen Edward Hannitty, the drover. You've seen Miss Mangan from the bakery. What kind of a hand is Destiny dealing them? They'd be nowhere without my intervention."

My mind yelled, *She'd better stop this soon. I can't take much more of it.*

"And my Charles?" she said with a flourish. "My captain? Wait and see."

Too much—too much at that moment; I stood up.

"I'll be back in a bit, just going to check my bike."

And she, that brown-eyed girl, said, "He'll be a general before the end of the war. Just you watch."

She should have consulted the other Fates.

59

And so I became a silent witness to the wedding in bombed London of Captain Charles Howard Miller and Miss Katherine Ann Begley. They married in the church run by the Jesuits on Farm Street. Tweedlehugh and Tweedlejohn must have believed that groomsmen should look like sentries, because they stood at rigid attention throughout.

A cousin of Miss Begley's wept as every bridesmaid must weep. Behind them, in the soft mahogany light, stood no more than twenty other people, including Claudia, gleaming in cream, beside the quiet gentleman from lunch, Mr. Howard, he of the bunched red hair. A number of polished uniforms, spangled with decorations, gleamed in the dim church.

We all walked down a cobbled lane to a pub that, bombs or no bombs, kept geraniums in its window boxes. Miss Begley clung to Captain Miller's arm as though fearing he might run away. He loomed over her, attentive and calm. Whatever deal they'd cut was up and running like a hare.

In a back room upstairs, the wedding party, such as it was, convened. Nobody sat down; we drank beer and ate cheese sandwiches. No speeches, and I recall thinking, *His colleagues seem so somber. They're not laughing or joking. The war, I suppose.*

When some of the guests had departed, Miss Begley (as she would always be to me) left her bridegroom's side for just a moment.

I asked her, "What happens now?"

"Tonight and tomorrow night I have him to myself, and then he's off somewhere."

Stress, the fear of losing his company while they should be on honeymoon, the power of marriage—something was making her frown, and she saw me register it.

"It won't always be like this," she said.

"You've never looked better," I said to her.

"After the war," she went on, "he'll be back, and we'll be together all the time." She held a small basket of violets, saw me looking at them, and said, "From Claudia. Will you wait and travel home with me?"

We agreed to meet two days later under the clock at Paddington Station.

It rained that night, and all the next day, and the next. I sat in my hotel room, my thoughts mixed and confused. The fact of her marriage, and the honeymoon scenes in my brain's theater, troubled me like bereavement, especially after that strange, naked night forty-eight hours earlier at Lamb's Head.

There's something else hidden that you should know about me—and it's not as benign as the Secret Life of Ben MacCarthy, Medieval Wandering

Scholar. I've already hinted at it and its shame; and, although by now I have it almost completely under control, it has created some dreadful times.

Here comes the confession: I suffer from intense fantasies of violence. In my mind, I see the person who injured me, and I set upon them. I swing a chain, wield a knife, brandish a scimitar—anything that will hack bloody, rubbery chunks from their flesh. Down on their heads I rain stones, hammer blows, kicks. I rake them with daggers and spikes, I bite them. I gouge their eyes, I slash off their ears, I make them whimper. And I walk away not caring what damage I've done, because they've so harmed me.

The accuracy of how badly or unfairly they've treated me has nothing to do with the fantasy—I merely have to imagine that they might sneer at or injure me. You should know this about me, and you're already mature enough to grasp that the mind goes to black thoughts as the tongue to a broken tooth.

What has this to do with events in London at the time of Miss Begley's marriage? As I say, I tried and tried to put out of my head random images of their wedding night in—where else?—the Ritz. *Did they have breakfast in bed?* I'd become friendly with so many of the staff, especially those from Ireland, who had met me with Miss Begley. And now of course my mind's eye could actually see, in naked reality, what Charles Miller was seeing all day and all night, for ever and ever, amen.

The rage began to kick in. Deep, terrible anger, with scenes in which I first imagined attacking him, and then, at worst, moving unspeakably to her. The fantasy seized me, until the pair of them lay weeping, curled and bloodied at my feet, and it took a long, long time to bring the fury under control. No sleep that night, no sleep at all.

Late on the morning of the second day of their marriage, when I had quit my hotel in anticipation of the night train to Liverpool, I walked out in the rain. Still roiling, I had a goal—I wanted to find them; in fact, I wanted to find them in their room.

Without effort, without asking directions, I found myself on Piccadilly, right across from the Ritz, looking up at the windows. During rain we felt safe in London because—or so we were told—the German bombers couldn't find their targets through the overcast. A deep archway sheltered me, an arcade; others came and went when the rain squalled harder.

In my hectic and edgy state, my arms hanging long, my eyes fixed on the gray building across the way, I felt something take my hand. I looked down and saw scarlet fingernails; I looked up and saw Claudia, wearing a rain hat that made her look like a trawlerman. She inclined her head toward the hotel and led me across the empty street.

As we walked to the door she dropped my hand and took off her amazing, transparent helmet. I followed her, striding to keep up. Nodding to the hotel staff as she passed, she marched me to a door that I'd never observed, and opened it for me to step into a corridor. Again she drove onward, to the foot of a staircase, and I followed those strong hips for three upward flights. Soon, we stood in a room. She closed the door behind us and shook herself like a dog coming out of a pond.

Ignoring me, and not saying a word, Claudia kicked off her shoes, shed her rain clothes and the jacket she wore underneath, arranged them around the room on hangers, then did likewise with my sodden coat and jacket. She dropped to her knees, undid the laces on my boots, and set them to dry by an elaborate gas fire that she'd turned on. Raindrops fell down my neck from my thick hair.

Claudia took my arms and wrapped them around her. Her arms around my neck, she rested her head on my shoulder, and we stood for long moments, never saying a word. The embrace told me that she had more flesh than she seemed to, with a soft body and a softer nature. I still couldn't tell her age—later I learned that she was in her late forties.

When she stepped back, she said, "I hope you don't mind."

I said, "Why would I?"

"We've both lost somebody," she said. "You've lost dear Kate, I saw the way you looked at her. And I've lost him. As I knew I would one day."

Bewilderment had been with me so long that I sometimes saw it approaching and could compose myself to meet it.

"Is that how all this came together?" I asked. I could feel my rage flying away from me like a shamed, embarrassed thing.

"He and I—Ben, you have no idea how close we've been. My husband died at Dunkirk."

"His girl back home—?" I began to ask, and she interrupted with a smile of forgiveness and said, "Sailors, soldiers—what's the difference?"

I asked, "Were you very close?"

Claudia answered, "He loved rain because I did, and he hated the north wind because I did."

She sent for food; we sat and talked; her kindness at that moment generated our lifelong friendship.

"And now they're married," I said. "And they're here somewhere, along these corridors, in one of these rooms, behind one of these doors."

"Not for the first time," said Claudia.

I know that I looked puzzled and said, "What are you saying? That they—?"

"Don't, Ben," she interrupted. "Just tell me you'll be my friend."

We sat in the chairs, saying nothing.

"This war," she said after a while. "How are we to have normal lives again?"

The angry conversation on the train with Miss Begley had distressed me. I wished that I'd behaved better. With Claudia I found a chance to make amends.

"You'll have a very good life," I said. I must have been sudden in my words, because she started.

"Oh, do you think so?"

From somewhere inside me, deep in there, past all the forests of moping self-absorption, I found a clearing, a glimmer of tenderness.

"You're a remarkable woman."

She flinched; I thought it was alarm, but it was surprise.

"Nobody has ever said that to me," she said.

"You're warm. You're kind. And you're very clever."

These words of praise—whence did they spring?

"Thank you, Ben," she said. "But you have to stop now or I'll weep."

"Maybe you should," I said. "Maybe you need to."

"I've now lost twice," she said. "My husband. And—this. But I knew I was losing him while you and she were staying here."

"Was it that early?" I asked.

"Hotels are like villages," Claudia said. "Gossip, gossip, gossip. Those last few weeks that you both were staying here, they were very difficult for me."

She clasped her hands in front of her and gazed into the limited mauve flame of the fire. And I recollected how Miss Begley had moved to a room that wasn't next door to mine.

I don't know how long we sat there in silence. An hour, maybe. Claudia nodded off in the chair, and in her sleep I could see the exhaustion in her face. I was the one to rise and gather my drying clothes. She heard me and apologized.

"Oh, dear, I'm not a very good hostess."

"What are friends for?" I said—and I sounded like Mrs. Charles Miller, though I never would and never could think of her under that name.

60

On the journey back to Ireland, Kate and I scarcely conversed. In the train compartment, as we left London, she set out to sleep. I draped my omnipresent black coat over her knees and made her as comfortable as I could.

As she nodded off, I said to her, "I want to apologize to you for my hard words when we were coming to London."

She looked at me in a drowsy and odd way, as though I sounded different. Which I did; I put a finger to my lips and said, "Shhh. You must rest." And she slept until we reached Liverpool, and I watched over her all the way as though she were my wife or child.

You can see, can't you, that this rising simplicity toward her was quite sudden in me? I can track when it happened. During the time with Claudia, I moved from anger to serenity, and then, during the train journey with Miss Begley, I understood something. I realized that I had been reflecting for days on what I consider the most important conversation I ever had with James Clare.

Let me tell you about it now, and you'll see how central this is to me and my spirit, and to the man I would try to become.

You know, I think, how old I am, and you know that I'm trying to tell this story while I maintain the strength and energy. I won't preempt anything by saying, from hindsight, that I was at that moment embarking on a crusade to change myself, to change my inner life; I would rather that you perceive it from my account of my own actions, my own life as I lived it. Did I succeed in becoming a good man? It's not for me to judge.

Given how many such talks I had with James, and how deep and wise they were, to call any one of them "the most important" is saying something. This teaching took the form of a story that he had collected. In a lovely irony, the story had always existed near me—it originated a few miles downriver from my home, and here's James's version, reproduced from the archives of the Irish Folklore Commission.

There was a man in Knockgraffon who had a hump. His name was Louis, and he was known locally as "Sour" Louis, because he was very bad-tempered—maybe on account of the hump. Now if you know Knockgraffon, you'll know that there's a moat there, a big, domed hill made of earth. That was built centuries and centuries ago by the Little People, the fairy folk, the followers of the goddess Dana, who were consigned to live underground when they lost the surface of Ireland to the Spanish invaders, in the clear, crystal years ten million days before Christ was born.

Sour Louis couldn't make a dog wag his tail, that's how grim he was, and the look on his face made people think he drank vinegar for his breakfast. But the world turns, and we turn with it, and late one summer night, when nobody could see him, Sour Louis dawdled along the road, out for a stroll under the eye of a warm and friendly moon.

As he passed by the Moat of Knockgraffon, he heard music. Not loud music, nor with many instruments—if indeed there were any. As it happens, what he heard was what we call mouth music, or puss music, the lilting and chanting of tunes that people do when they have no instruments, yet wish to dance.

Sour Louis sat down on the grassy mound, listened hard, and made out the words. Deep inside the moat and underneath it, many, many little voices were singing in a very sweet way, "Monday, Tuesday, Monday, Tuesday, Monday, Tuesday, Monday, Tuesday."

People didn't know it, but Sour Louis had a very fine singing voice, and he had an instinct for melody, and to his ear the tune seemed un-finished. So, when the singers next came to the end of a line, he sang in his fine baritone voice, "Monday, Tuesday, Monday, Tuesday, Mon-day, Tuesday—Wednesday." His musical instinct made the word and the note fit perfectly.

Silence fell. Then Sour Louis heard a big whoosh! *of air, and a brilliant light fell from the sky. It was the moon herself, perched on the Moat of Knockgraffon, and as Sour Louis sat there, silhouetted against her milk-and-silver light, you could see the shape of his poor hump on his back like a young elephant.*

Then he looked down, because he felt something tugging at his boot, and there on the ground, all around him, dancing and swaying, he saw thousands and thousands of the Little People, and they were now singing, "Monday, Tuesday, Monday, Tuesday, Monday, Tues-day—Wednesday." Sour Louis smiled—it was a smile broader than he had ever smiled before, and as he did, the Little People ended their singing and began to applaud him.

"Thank you," they cried, "thank you for making our song lovelier."

Next, they formed up in orderly lines and began to march into the Moat of Knockgraffon, whose grassy mound opened wide in a pair of huge doors to meet them. They kept looking back over their shoulders and beckoning to Sour Louis to follow them. He was a little hesi-tant—what man wants to go under the ground with a lot of people he's never met before, and who, in part anyway, don't have that good a reputation?

The moon decided to go back up to the sky, and she placed a moon-beam in Sour Louis's hand as a flashlight. She gave him a big smile, and he felt that she was telling him to follow the little silver, dancing people.

Such a welcome they gave him down there—it was wonderful. They fed him and feasted him, they drank toasts to him, they thanked him for the brilliant embellishment to their song, and said they would use it forever more. Then, in gratitude, sixteen men and sixteen women climbed on Sour Louis's shoulders and by magic tricks they re-moved his hump. They lifted it off, took it over to a great stone shelf, sat it there like a monument, and lit candles around it. In the mean-

time, ten of the most beautiful of the Little Women began to dress Sour Louis, and then one of the most handsome men wheeled out a tall looking-glass so that Louis could see himself.

Now he knew that he must be dreaming—because the dapper and handsome fellow in the mirror had Louis's face all right, but this didn't look anything like the Sour Louis whose angry jowls he shaved every bitter morning of his life. He thanked them profusely, they began again to dance and sing and sway in front of him, and suddenly they evaporated. Louis found himself out in the open air once more, sitting on the greensward of the Moat of Knockgraffon on a summer night.

He pinched himself, to make sure he was real. Sure enough, the pinch hurt, and yes, there was the moon up in the sky, and she seemed to be sailing along minding her own business. He stood up—and that's when he saw the difference. The clothes he was wearing were beautiful, not at all the shabby old sleaze that had covered him when he'd set out on his walk. And something more remarkable—he was upright, he had a broad chest, he was strong and fit. The hump was gone.

Naturally enough, when he got home, people asked questions, and Louis—no longer did they call him Sour Louis because he now smiled all the time—felt obliged to tell them the tale of the Moat of Knockgraffon. He knew that the Little People wouldn't mind.

Louis's story ran throughout the land like the fire on the stubble of an autumn wheat field. They marveled here, they wondered there—people up and down the country talked of little else for weeks and weeks because, you see, they'd always wanted to believe that the Little People could do good.

One day, to Louis's door came a lady on a pony, not a very salubrious mount either—the hooves wanted for some care. She said to Louis, "Are you the man who had the hump?" and he said he was.

After he had told her the full story, to which she listened like a child to a talking dog, she turned the pony around without a word and rode back the way she'd come.

Now, this woman was a widow, her name was Mrs. Madden, and she had a son, Jack, who had a hump, and he was sourer than Sour Louis had ever been. Jack Madden slouched around the house all day, moaning and cribbing, refusing to work—he wouldn't wash his own cup and saucer, he'd say his hump was hurting him. So Jack Madden's mother told him to get up on the pony, ride over to the Moat of Knockgraffon, and join in any song he heard.

With as many complaints as a wet hen, Jack Madden rode to Knockgraffon. He climbed down off the old pony and went to sit, as his mother had bidden him, on the grassy slope of the moat. Within moments, he heard the little silver song coming up out of the ground like a million tinkling bells. "Monday, Tuesday, Monday, Tuesday, Monday, Tuesday—Wednesday."

Now, Jack Madden had no singing voice whatsoever—he sounded like a crow with croup. But he knew, or thought he did, what the song now needed, and also he was impatient with the whole scheme—he just wanted his hump taken away. So instead of being sensitive to the needs of the little singers, he stood there and burst out in his raucous voice, "Ah, to hell with it—Thursday, Friday, Saturday, and Sunday, Thursday, Friday, Saturday, and Sunday."

Next thing, he too heard a great whoosh! of sound, and he too was surrounded by a white light, but it shone in his eyes and half-blinded him, and it was cold when it silhouetted him, and it didn't look like a halo. The moon was angry, and when the moon is angry she lets you feel her ice.

Hundreds of invisible hands then dragged him to the ground, pinned him facedown, and he felt something heavy and strange being loaded onto his back. Far from easing his burden, they gave him Sour Louis's old hump, and as they left him lying there, they sang at him, "Jack Madden, Jack Madden, you ugly big lump; If you ruin your music, then you'll have a hump. But Jack Madden, Jack Madden, you ugly big lump; Spoil the music that we have, we'll double your hump."

I recall James's face as he finished his tale. He liked to be in the open air when he talked to me about what he called "the fitness of things." He'd say, "We can't be overheard under the sky," and that day we sat on a bench in the lovely little town of Edenderry. (His handwriting, by the way, that black, elegant script, when you come across it in the archives, looks medieval in its control; he was what they called a "true scribe.")

"James, why did you tell me that story?"

"So that you'd think about it."

It had been almost two years since he told me, and now, on that train, the meaning began to filter through. How I must have been oppressing everybody with my grief; how I must have sought attention like a spoiled child. I had indeed traveled around the country weighted down with two humps. My grief made people recoil, and my mourning, though deeply valid, dignified nothing and nobody.

PART THREE

The Brave and the Fair

61

June 1944

We parted by the train that would take her back to the south. Miss Begley had to get to Lamb's Head, I to the road and my work. At no time on our journey back did we have a long conversation, and thus I said not a word about Claudia.

As we clasped hands, I ventured the question, "When do you expect to hear from him?"

"He has a week of leave to come soon, and then he has to go back to Derry."

"Where is he now?"

"God Himself doesn't know that."

"I'll think of you," I said.

"We'll be all right, Ben. Only the Brave deserve the Fair."

She turned away and I thought, *She's going to need more than hearts and flowers.*

And as we stood there, on a bright May morning, Charles Miller was at that exact moment stepping back into Europe, into an uncivil world, where no laws prevailed beyond the laws of life and death, where no ordinary decencies had a chance, where terror came from both earth and sky—a world that he, poor fellow, believed he could contain.

I've just recently discovered an entry that Miss Begley wrote at length in her diary on the day after she returned to Lamb's Head. Here it is:

This is my first letter to myself as "Mrs. Miller." I am "Mrs. Charles Miller." In the morning and at night I look at myself in the mirror and I say, "This is Mrs. Charles Miller." But have I made the greatest error of my life? Have I ruined the very thing I had hoped for— a chance at contentment that would keep me safe long after Nana has gone from me? And children, maybe? And a life with a steady daily round to it? Inside, I am shivering as though I have a fever. But I do have a fever—of the heart, of the soul. And I can share it with nobody, not Nana, nor faithful Ben.

I must keep up appearances, even though I am falling apart, because I, who have made so many happy marriages for others, have steered myself into a desperate channel of life. Here I am, having married a great man, of strong and wonderful character, and he feels the same passion for me. But now I have discovered what he does—he kills people.

Can I live with such a man? Doesn't he know his Gospels? "Then Jesus said unto him, Put up again thy sword into its place: for all they that take the sword shall perish by the sword." And, worse, here I am letting go of him, waving him off as he steps into circumstances that may take his own life.

In our two days together, we never ceased touching each other. I discovered that we breathe at the same pace. He didn't need to speak a word—I always knew what he was about to say. And even as we had intimacy over and over, I cried all the time. I cried in bed, I cried on the floor. His kindness alone held me up. And such kindness: I told him my past—I told him before we wed, lest my history offended him beyond the possibility of holy matrimony, and he laughed, and said that he hoped I didn't want to know about his past.

How can it be that this man who kills people makes me feel that I am better than I am, and makes me want to grow even better than that? And now I have let him go, I have let the war take him—as it will. I have married a ghost, I know it.

The entry for the next night contains more of the same confusion. Her pain sears the page, and her desperation comes across so strongly that one can forgive Miss Begley her Victorian sentimentality.

She talks about *Seeing his back, the square box of his shoulders, as he walked away;* and, *Did the last touch of his skin have to be no more than a handshake?* and, *I wish he hadn't smiled at me as he left. It wasn't what I was feeling.*

I suppose there is no irony in cheap music. Later that week, she describes her own actions, the steps she took to dampen down the anguish.

Half-past five in the morning. There's not a sound. I can't even hear the sea. I shall get up and walk.

When she returns, she writes the next entry:

Seven o'clock: the world is completely still. This beautiful weather taunts me. He should be here with me, we should be lying on the grass down there, amid the yellow loosestrife and the opening fuchsia. Where is he? The wind comes always from the west, but I want the wind to turn east and blow word of him from Europe. I had hoped that the seabirds and the breezes and the white clouds would ease the time away from him. But it gets worse.

On and on her diary goes, in the same anguished chant. The strength of her feelings isn't surprising, but her incapacity to get them under control shocks me. I also find it somewhat annoying because she had so often upbraided me for my "moping," as she called it. But even as I set down these words, I know that I'm being unfair—because she did keep her feelings under control, confiding only in her nightly journal.

I suppose I wished that she'd been mourning the loss of me, that she'd been reflecting a horrified angst that she'd made a wrong choice. That's how far down her road I had traveled, and I recall thinking that I wished I'd had the power to anguish her as profoundly as Miller did.

62

Odd that she mentioned the word *ghost*. That same month, May 1944, when I came back from London, I received a letter from James Clare asking me about the matchmaking inquiries. As ever, he told me what he himself was collecting—stories of "Famine Roads," those well-meaning but often pointless enterprises, roads to nowhere, undertaken during the years of the great potato famine in the mid-nineteenth century to give local employment. He'd recently, he said, been in the Caha Mountains (not too far from Miss Begley), where he'd found such a road, and he was attempting to establish why it had never been finished, why it went nowhere.

In his last paragraph, he wrote and asked me to "hang out a good ear for any ghost stories. I'm finding a preference in many houses for such tales. Sometimes they're invented, I suspect, rather than traditional."

That very month, I took down this brief tale told by a woman in County Longford:

> *A man coming home from a dance here in Edgeworthstown was given a lift in an old-fashioned carriage by two ladies, mother and daughter. He went with them to their house out near Clonbroney, had a drink, had another drink, ate some sandwiches they made for him, and then it was so late that he took up their invitation to stay the night. Woke up next morning, took breakfast with them—all very old-fashioned, thanked them, and continued his journey home. That's when he missed his wallet; he had taken it out of his pocket as he lay down to sleep.*
>
> *He went back to the house. Found the gate locked with a rusty iron chain; found a way in, went up the overgrown avenue. Same house, no question—but it looked very different, it looked old, unkempt, with all the windows shuttered, the gravel overgrown with weeds, and no sign of life. He had to force the front door and he called and called*

the names of the ladies, but there wasn't a soul in or near the house. Yet, in the hallway he found two sets of footprints, one going upstairs, the other down—his own boot marks. Dust sheets covered the furniture; he went upstairs, found his wallet on the mantelpiece of the bedroom.

On his way home, he inquired locally. The house had been closed for decades, ever since a widow and daughter who had lived there were killed when their horse bolted in a lightning storm and overturned their carriage. The accident happened on the same day that the woman's husband, i.e., the girl's father, was killed in the Crimean War.

Call it *weird* or *disturbed* or any term you like, but when I heard that story, I had this flash of thought: *Will I one day go to Lamb's Head and have a meal with Miss Begley and her grandmother—only to go back the following day and find the house boarded and shuttered, the inside covered in dust cloths?*

As I tell you this now, a shiver thrills me—although back in those days I didn't believe in premonition.

63

In the house where they told me of the ghosts of Clonbroney, I asked, without quite meaning to, my new habitual question: *Do you know a man by name of Raymond or Ray Cody?* This represented a failure, a slippage on my part, typical of my gift for inconsistency. Since London, I'd been trying to change, trying to stop myself asking about Venetia or that period of my life; I'd been trying to take James's advice and let Life take care of it. But some flicker of seizure, I suppose, took me over, and I fell back into old habits.

Irony kicked in too; the first time I felt hesitant in asking was the first time that I received help.

"Cody?" they said. "There's a Ray Cody around here, all right. Is he a skinny, pale-faced lug of a fellow?" and they laughed. They knew him and didn't like him. "That lad was born four miles away from here, over in Templebeg," they said, "and he never did anybody any good."

They told me how to find the place, that his brother now lived in the family home.

"You can't miss it—'tis the only house in Templebeg that has a blue door."

Easy to find—though nothing can be obscure in Templebeg: six houses, a church, and a garage. The Cody place, shabby and unmemorable, except for the blue door, had no light or sign of life. In the field across the road, a steep hill gave me a clear view, and I waited there, under a tree, for several chilly hours.

Once again, I fantasized that I would inveigle Cody to some quiet, undiscoverable place, an old quarry, a deep, abandoned pond, and torture him, drive nails through his hands and feet. I'd also daydreamed that I would then probably kill him—but I'd have to do that with even greater care and secrecy because I didn't want my life any further diminished by that greasy slug.

Consumed again by violence? Images of savagery, of assault? Ben, come on! In the cold morning, I shook myself. *So much for the good intentions. Am I going to be like an alcoholic who keeps having another drink?*

At just after ten o'clock I saw life. A woman answered the door, a woman with a foolish, moonish face.

"Dan, there's somebody here wanting Ray," she called—and then she shrank back from me, as though saying, *I don't like the look of you.* "Dan, come'ere, willya?" And to me she said again, "Whatch you want, anyway?"

I said, "Ray Cody."

"Dan!" she called again, and he shuffled into the frame of the doorway behind her.

"Whoizzit?" he said, and then, "Who're you?"

Dan, who much needed cleansing, tried to close the door.

I blocked it with my foot and asked, "What's wrong?"

"What're you lookin' for?"

"I'm looking for Ray."

"Ah, Ray don't live here no more."

"Where can I find him?"

"Ah, Ray's away, he's, ah'm—he's over in England."

"Where? Where in England? I've just been there."

"Ah, he never writes."

I stepped forward into the house, and the man said, "Stop, stop," and the woman behind him began to wail.

Miss Begley said to me, after the dance-hall fight in Killarney, that she'd slapped my face because she thought I was going to kill the man I had grabbed.

"You should have seen yourself, I was so frightened of you. And Charles says you should be a soldier, that's where to put all that anger, into a war."

"I'm not going to do anything wrong here," I said to Dan Cody. "Just tell me where your brother is."

"I'll find out, I'll find out for you."

"When?"

He said, "Ah, I don't know, I don't know, but I'll find out."

"Good. I'll be back soon."

In the following weeks, I played that morning like a film in my mind, asking over and over, *What made them so afraid?* I felt no malice toward that couple. For me they offered no more than a means to an end, and yet they had behaved as though I might bludgeon them both. No good conclusion suggested itself, and when one day I asked Ray Cody why his brother and his brother's wife had been so frightened of me, he shook his head and said not a word—even though at that moment it would have served him greatly to speak.

64

On the morning of Wednesday, 7 June 1944, I opened the *Irish Independent* newspaper and I read the following editorial:

"The long-expected 'Second Front' has finally materialized and the crisis of the war is upon us. The first point chosen was the obvious one, the short sea and air passage across the English Channel to the Seine Valley and the north of France. Parachutists and glider-borne troops, esti-mated by the Germans to number four divisions, opened the invasion about midnight on Monday night."

I stopped reading—to let the picture form in my mind, to let the neg-ative develop. Looking for focus, I glanced across the page. A film called *By Hook or by Crook* starred Red Skelton, Eleanor Powell, and the Jimmy Dorsey Orchestra. It was the feast of Saint Colman. *Uncle Vanya* was playing at the Gate Theatre in Dublin.

On the other side of the editorial, the newspaper carried General Eisenhower's Order of the Day to his troops. "The eyes of the world are upon you. The hopes and prayers of liberty-loving people everywhere march with you. In company with our brave Allies and brothers in arms on other fronts you will bring about the destruction of the German war machine, the elimination of Nazi tyranny over the oppressed peoples of Europe, and security for ourselves in a free world."

At last the photograph developed into a print. Mr. Seefeld had been trying to eavesdrop on the plans for an invasion that the Germans felt certain would take place. That's why Miller wanted him—to find out how much the Germans knew, how much code they had cracked.

I sent a telegram to Miss Begley, told her where I would be, and re-ceived a letter in return:

Dear Ben,

Isn't it all exciting?! And to think that I'm married to a man who is an important part of it all. No wonder he doesn't know when he'll get leave again. I intend to sit here and wait until I hear that Charles is fine, and that we've won the war. When will you be coming to see us again? Since the word got out that I'm a married woman, Nana and I have been so busy. Last Sunday we had eight callers to the house, all looking for spouses.

I hope you're taking care of yourself and not drinking.

Your loving friend,
Kate Miller, née Begley (couldn't resist it!)

P.S. What do you think is the plural noun of "spouse"? Should it be "spouses" or "spice"?

And then I remembered that she had taken the notes of the Seefeld debriefing, and that she therefore had known of all this in advance, and had never breathed a word to me, the man she said she trusted most in the world. In what other ways did she trust me—meaning, what else did she know that I didn't?

65

July 1944

I spent June and July of '44 as I'd always tried to do—helping farmers with their harvest. In their houses at night, I gathered so much material that I often filled a notebook in a week. And I went home again, where I was able to sleep more soundly than anywhere.

Mother's need for my company lifted my spirits, and my father seemed to compete with her for time spent with me. Evening after evening, morning after morning, the three of us dined and breakfasted together, and he, I was pleased to observe, paid her more attention than he'd ever done.

"No-no-no, let me pour that for you." And, "I-I-I'm always telling you—you should wear blue, look at how lovely you look."

He found a baby rabbit in the fields and brought it home to her, but Large Lily, our housekeeper (Billy Flock's wife), left the kitchen door open, and the little creature ran away.

That year—perhaps it was the summer weather—they seemed to have aged less than previously, and Mother had commandeered extra square yards of the garden for raspberry canes, from which she got a bulging crop. And she'd added another beehive.

The war provided our main topic of conversation and we began to take an extra newspaper every day. All three of us agreed on everything—especially the fact that more fighting was taking place in France than any of us had expected. I told them the story of Miss Begley and her life and her new bridegroom, and I might have been unwrapping gifts for them, such a keen interest did they take.

Mother whispered to me later that she'd thought of telling me to invite Miss Begley for a few days, but decided against it.

"I didn't want to risk it with your father," she said.

Meaning that she was never again going to take the chance of letting my father anywhere near an attractive young woman.

66

As the weeks shone ever brighter, and the war became bloodier, I kept wondering where Captain Miller was at work. Had he now become a warrior in uniform, like the massed regiments of Americans who had landed in France on D-Day? Or was he deep behind enemy lines, pretending to be a Belgian or a Frenchman or even a German? Or, indeed, was he still alive—a question Miss Begley too must have been asking herself? In early July she sent me another missive: "I'm lonely."

I'd hoped to be in Donegal, on the track of the wolf story. Yet, I found a means to justify the change of plans. I'd long promised myself a visit to the headland above Smerwick Harbor where I hoped—without much basis—to check a tale that I'd heard.

When the Spanish Armada foundered along that southwestern coast in 1588, the English soldiers were waiting, and they massacred the survivors who struggled ashore. As a child, I'd been told that the bodies lay in open graves, and I'd nursed the idea that I'd see the Spaniards in their armor, in those silver Cortés helmets and spiked halberds, lying faceup to the sky and the Atlantic clouds. And although I'd allowed for skeletons, my imagination refused to permit the armor to have rusted; I wanted it still shining and silver bright.

I never got to Smerwick. When I rolled up to Lamb's Head at around two o'clock in the afternoon, Miss Begley sat outside as though waiting for somebody. She ran to me like a rocket and heaved herself into my arms.

"He's here, he's here," she whispered, and I said, "Where?"

She pointed to the house and said, "Asleep. He's tired out."

"When did he arrive?" and she said, "Yesterday. Just after I sent for you. I had no warning."

"For how long?"

"If I can I'll kidnap him."

I said, "That'd probably be treason somewhere."

"Nana's not here. She went down to her friends in Kenmare. To give us a bit of space."

I said, "Stand here where I can see you." She stood like a child, and I tipped her face up to the light. The sun came out to look at her.

Something had changed. Had I known then of the anguish in her journal, I'd have named the change, identified its root.

She asked, "Do I look married?"

I said, "You look great. How is he?"

"Very silent. A lot on his mind. But—well, he's glorious, really."

67

Above the collar of his army shirt he wore a long, serious plaster on one side of his neck; a blue bruise lit the ridge over his right eye. Miss Begley hovered, maternal like many women when they're happy.

Captain Miller said, "Don't say it."

And I said, "What?"

"Everybody comes out with, 'Well, you've been in the wars,' and I say, 'Well, yessir, I have, that's what I do for a living.' "

And we laughed, and the ice was broken, and he shook hands with me like a president, even though I must have felt like an invasion.

He said, "Thanks so much, Ben."

She said, "He means for looking after me."

I flapped my arms, very like a duck, because I couldn't think of anything to say or anything else to do.

While Miss Begley prepared a meal, Captain Miller wandered out and I followed him. Standing a little behind him—although he knew that I was there—he murmured something.

"Excuse me?" I said, and stepped forward.

He continued to look at the sea. "I said—have you been intimate with Kate?"

I said, "No. God, no."

"Didn't you want to be?"

"Well, if I say 'no' you might ask me, 'Why, what's wrong with her?' and if I say 'yes,' you might feel you want to warn me off. She and I, we're close friends. That's all."

"What do you think of her?"

"Of Miss Begley?"

He said, "I love the way you still call her 'Miss Begley.' "

"It's how we started. What do I think of her? Well, I think she's— well, just delightful."

"Is she moody? I can't stand a woman who's moody."

I said, "She's very forthright. She knows what she doesn't like."

"What doesn't she like about you, Ben?"

"I used to drink too much."

"She has anger in her, doesn't she?" he said, and inside me I flared at the criticism of my friend. "And I think she may turn out to be a nagging wife."

"But she's remarkable," I said.

He jumped in with, "Oh, do you think so?" and went on to say, "I can't believe that I'm married."

My mind raced. *How do I counter this?*

"So many men wanted to marry her," I said.

It didn't work. He said, "But they were all Irishmen," and his tone implied, *That doesn't count.* "I wonder how she'll fit in back home," he said.

I replied, "You could always live here."

"I don't like the old lady," he said. "And she could live to be a hundred." Then he paused and asked the worst question: "Do you know any gossip about your Miss Begley?"

And still I didn't dislike him; I should have, out of loyalty, but I didn't.

"She has a stainless character," I said.

And he retorted, "Nobody has."

He bent down and picked up a stone. Ten yards away, one of the boulders displayed a white circular badge, an old lichen stain the size of a beer coaster. Charles Miller threw the stone and hit that mark so hard and squarely that the pebble's imprint on it can be seen to this day. Then he walked back into the house.

68

We ate bacon and cabbage, and a pile of new potatoes; they were round and white and innocent, and covered in melting butter and parsley. No beer; no liquor of any kind—we drank tall glasses of milk, and he had water from the Lamb's Head well and declared it as good as gin.

I had time and opportunity to look at him closer. He had damaged his left hand; a bandage wrapped two fingers together, and when I looked again at his neck and eyebrow, I began to take in all the other marks on his face, and the jocose words came back, "Yes, you have been in the wars."

I had a coughing fit. Over and over, I had tried to persuade myself that the experience of winning Venetia, and then of losing her, and the awful manner of the loss—all that must surely have insulated me against the more extreme swings of life. I was, of course, wrong. I coughed and coughed until I had to leave the table, step outside, and recover. When I came back in, Miss Begley was stooping by Captain Miller's chair, touching the long sticking-plaster on his neck and throat, and they stopped their conversation when they heard me.

After dinner, they disappeared into Miss Begley's room, and I didn't see them again that night. Next morning, not long after dawn, I heard an engine in the lane outside, and—almost in stealth—Captain Miller left. A great unnatural hush fell over the house. I waited, uncertain, but wide awake. In time, I arose, shaved with the chilling water of the washstand pitcher, dressed, and made my tentative way into the kitchen. No sign of life there.

I went out. No Miss Begley there either; a faint smell of car engine, oil, gasoline hung in the air. Down in the bay, a trawler much like Bawn Buckley's shuffled northwest between me and Deenish Island, probably heading around Hogs Head to Ballinskelligs or Waterville with fish for the day's hotel trade.

No life did I find in the atmosphere; no life in the cottage's mood. So completely inert did everything feel that I assumed Miss Begley had left with Captain Miller.

And once again I misjudged. Two hours and more later, as I sat drinking yet another cup of tea at the kitchen table, she shuffled red-eyed from her room, moving with all the heaviness of an old lady. Head down like a sad child, she made straight for me, clambered into my personal space, sat on my knee, and wrapped herself around my neck and shoulders.

"He's gone," she said, "and they'll kill him."

I said, "Shhh. Shhh."

She stayed like that, clinging to me.

"What in God's name will I do, Ben?"

I said, "You'd tell me to pull myself together. Not to mope. That's what you'd tell me."

"But I don't know how to stop it. It's like dying."

"Come on."

I dislodged her, led her by the hand out into the sunshine, and stood behind her, watching as she gazed out to sea. She wore a nightdress of white lawn, neither opaque nor transparent—but thin enough for me to see the outline of her hips through the fabric, light visible between her parted legs.

Now I felt the lunge again—a wild swing into erotic attraction, and a retreat back to fond affection. Lover or friend or—even—potential wife: The question attacked me like a vandal swinging a club. Not only had I seen her naked, I had lain body to body with her; and I had slept—or stayed awake—in the same bed. I knew that she spoke to me in a way she never spoke to any other, not even to Miller—and I wondered whether she would be my friend for life. Or one day my wife.

"Will you stay?" she said.

"I can't. I have to go."

"Come back soon, will you?"

What can you do when you look back on your life and appraise so many of your misjudgments? What's your consolation? That morning, I pitied Kate Begley for the error she had made—as I saw it. I felt that she was unequipped for the marriage, for the war, for the world.

She, though, as I would discover, didn't think like that. Whereas I viewed her as some sort of rustic folk maven, plying her vernacular skills out there in the wilds, she considered her matchmaking the opposite of confining. She saw it as something that had great potential, and varied application, something crucially useful and universal.

In short, I misjudged her, I was wrong to pity her, and it could have been fatal. I told her that I'd try to visit her every month until her husband came back. Or didn't—though of course I never said that.

69

August 1944

I kept my word. After some weeks of collecting tales about boglands and their strange and ancient treasures, back I went to watch over my friend. Autumn had sent in its first messenger—someone had started a fire somewhere, burning stubble or old wood. The smell of the smoke lifted my spirits as I stood on the pedals and toiled up the hill.

A packed suitcase waited inside the door.

"I took your postcard as a sign," she said. "It's all arranged."

I sighed: *Why am I not surprised?*

"If I planted a wall in your path," I said, "you'd go through it."

"I'm doing the right thing," she said.

"Do you know where you're going?" I asked.

"I found Hans-Dieter, didn't I?"

"But it's only a needle and thread hanging over a map," I said.

"You know better than that, Ben."

"Kate, there's a war on."

"There was a war on then."

Next morning, I heaved her case and hauled my bag down the reckless path to the little jetty. Bawn Buckley picked us up and we chugged off, heading for Le Crotoy. Again.

He said, "We'll be as open as anything. We'll be all right."

"Good," she said, and went to stand at the stern of the trawler, looking back at her coast.

"Do you have a name for where we're going?"

She had a sidelong glance that could always uncover my thoughts.

"You have no faith, Ben."

Here we go again. What is wrong with me? Those were my thoughts, but these were my words: "What are we going to do when we get there?"

I'd asked her the previous night. Hoping to recruit the old lady into my support, I'd spoken the question in the presence of her grandmother. Any effort, I suggested, to find anybody inside the war at that time—especially an American intelligence officer who by definition must remain invisible—that must be as futile an exercise as could be imagined. Whatever her "pendulum" told her, that arena must by now, I suggested, be teeming like an anthill. And the ants had guns.

The grandmother ambushed me with a hostile jab.

"If I had to back Kate's judgment over yours, that'd be an easy bet to win."

When I asked later if I'd given the old lady some offense, Miss Begley said, "No," and that was it. My guess still remained that the old lady would have agreed to any softener of her granddaughter's loneliness.

70

Wednesday, 16 August 1944: What beautiful weather we had, and what turmoil I felt. Bawn Buckley exacerbated it by telling me that the two young Germans whom I'd seen coming in out of the sea had been found dead out in the countryside, in some deserted old farm near Ballydavid. Their throats had been cut, he said, but he had no further details. And I had no response in me—actually I had, but I cut it off before it began, unable to fit it into my heart.

We sailed over the deepest part of the ocean off Ireland, and I recollected how the two young men had dragged themselves in from the waves. I wanted to contact young Bekker's wife, see his child.

That's what "neutral" means, I said to myself. *It means behaving kindly to everyone.* And then I thought, *My God, you're getting as shallow as Miss B.*

The crossing, almost devoid of other vessels, might have been that of a toy on a millpond. This time we hugged every shore again, along the two straight lines of Bawn Buckley's navigations. The first line took us along the coast of Ireland, and then along the English coast to Newhaven, the point at which he made a right-angled turn and bisected the English Channel.

"We're best to look like domestic sailors," he said, "and I want a straight run at the coast of France."

He inserted us into that flange of inlet halfway between Boulogne and Dieppe like a man sliding a cork into a bottle.

Onshore, we knew whom to ask; we knew where to go. In the little hotel at Le Crotoy, they welcomed us like heroes; nobody gossiped like the French Resistance, and they all knew about Mr. Seefeld and sang our praises.

They told us of the relief, of the sudden quiet that had descended on them. Every place, they said, the villages, the towns, had fallen silent. Yes, they were still under German occupation, but the presence seemed to have shrunk. They hadn't seen a Nazi in a week. And they added to the silence, they said, by holding their breath.

First had come the wild rumors, because the Allied vessels had been seen by fishermen working south of Le Crotoy at dawn. Wild with excitement, they'd come rushing home into the little harbor. Miles long, they said the flotilla was, and miles wide, great and gray, spearing through the dawn like a vast and mysterious horde toward Le Havre. Some said that they feared they'd been dreaming.

I set to work with pen and notebook—I could hold such valuable witness to such a great event. And at that moment too, I understood that this calling of mine would make me safe. Miss Begley had no such protection. I asked questions, made notes, wrote them up at night. To any inquiring soldier I was a war observer.

Once I'd made it clear that I hoped to gather some sort of record, peo-

ple came to see us. As before, we stayed in the little hotel, with the lanky
proprietor, and for a day and a half we listened to reminiscences.

Miss Begley and I had our own to add, specifically of the atrocity
that we'd seen in the streets of Saint-Omer, and the locals made us
feel that we'd shared in the war as suffered by all of France.

Here is a taste of my collecting—just a few brief examples, all from
people who lived in or near Le Crotoy.

*A middle-aged spinster was forced to accept ten German officers and
civilians as nonpaying lodgers. They lived there for two years and
bankrupted her because they insisted that she buy all the food. She received some money from the Occupation authorities in Saint-Omer
but never enough.*

*One woman asked that she tell her tale with nobody local present.
She said that the officer billeted in her house raped her night after
night for over a year. But she could not and would not take her story
to the authorities because she felt they wouldn't believe her. When she
did, the Kommandant in Saint-Omer court-martialed the officer and
had him executed.*

*A man and his wife tried to hide their fourteen-year-old son be-
cause he looked much older and would be taken away as slave labor.
The dog barked, giving away the boy's hiding place, and the soldiers
shot the boy and the dog.*

71

Although she listened with as much care as I did, Miss Begley had a different mission. She had two questions for every speaker: Have you heard
of an American officer name of Charles Miller? And, Do you know a
farmhouse between here and Saint-Omer with its back to the water? She
cracked the matter when she asked about the traveling circus and, in a
pattern that I know so well from country people, somebody sent for
somebody else to tell us the way.

Next day, they lent us bicycles. With the roasting hot day baking our shoulders, we set out to find the farmhouse. We left Le Crotoy by a small lane, and since some of the road signs had been removed, we needed written directions.

"Why are we doing this?"

"You'll see," she said.

On a deserted road we came to a bridge, a flat, inglorious span across a broad neck of water. I made us stop and get off the bicycles, and I walked to one side and then the other, looking for something that I couldn't name or define. If you travel, as I do, all around a countryside, you can't avoid déjà vu—and sometimes it's true. It can be an uncomfortable feeling, as it was when my search for Venetia took me on digging expeditions into woodlands and along seashores. But here? In rural France?

Miss Begley watched and said nothing. Standing beside a shattered pillar, I peered down into wide stands of reeds and sedges. If, all across my life, I could have mapped my own instincts, if I could have harnessed the unspoken in me, the barely conscious impulse that drives me to do the unusual, I'd have solved my problems a long time earlier. I had indeed been here before, without knowing where I was.

One side of the bridge bore the marks of extensive burning, and as the light refracted, I saw the metal in the stream. The British had built fighter planes smaller than I imagined, and the wingspan of this machine scarcely reached into the middle of the river.

I called Miss Begley, and we stood there looking down, in a silent requiem for the pilot.

"D'you think they found his body?" she asked.

I said, "My bet is that we're the first to see this."

As we lingered, another cyclist drifted onto the bridge, a woman in her fifties, gray hair cut with a sword, defensive, steel-rimmed spectacles.

"Bonjour, M'sieu-dame"—she spoke it like a prosecutor, and was about to ride by until we pointed. She halted and looked. From her handlebar basket she took a notebook, then told us that her husband, a local coroner, would look into it.

To Miss Begley she said in the tones of a scold, "France is not yet free. Why are you here?"

Miss Begley tried to engage her in conversation. The woman said that no French person would ever speak to a stranger again, and rode off. Miss Begley jumped on her bicycle, rode after her, and made her halt. In a conversation that seemed vigorous, the woman gestured, and Miss Begley rode back—with further and more explicit directions to the farmhouse.

Yet, we didn't set out. Instead, Miss Begley parked her bicycle against the parapet of the bridge and began to clamber down the bank to the submerged and rusting aircraft. I followed her, under a sun that promised to roast my neck.

"Don't look," she said, and began to strip.

I said, "I won't." But then, remembering our moments in the past, I said, "What does it matter?"

She replied, "You're right."

"What do you think you're doing?"

"If it was your brother in that plane," she said.

And I thought, *What you mean is—"If it was my husband."*

Stark naked, she slipped into the water and disappeared. A moment later, her head bobbed up, wearing a coronet of green slimy weed.

"There's a body in there," she said. "I can see him."

By now, though, she had churned up the mud, and I could no longer get a clear look at the downed plane.

"We haven't got the strength," I said. "Not even the two of us together," and she agreed.

I took off my shirt and helped to towel her dry. She found a piece of calm grass and stretched out naked, saying, "The sun will finish the job." A moment later, with eyes closed, she said, "I'm glad I couldn't see his face."

72

The farmhouse door stood wide open. We rode by and back again, and then down a lane at one side to ascertain that the building did stand with its back to the water. Nothing from the roadway suggested it, yet there we saw it—the finger of lagoon, trees overhanging. Miss Begley's cheeks flashed up the doll's red spots of excitement.

We knocked and we called. I think we were timid; Miss Begley suggested that they might be asleep. As ever she got it right—a warm afternoon, just after three o'clock.

"But the door is open?" I argued.

She said, "That's only their newfound freedom."

We moved back and sat on the grass of their perfect little lawn. From time to time one of us would rise and knock on the door again, wait for a moment—and then return to sit on the grass.

"Why are we here?" I asked.

"Charles was in this house last week."

"What?"

"I told you."

I said, "But how can you be so sure?"

"The woman on the bicycle confirmed it," she said. "She met Charles last week."

In an hour we heard the voices and we rose, called out, and knocked on the door. Husband and wife recognized us immediately with hugs and kisses and, in the husband's case, tears.

I had long feared for them. We sat in the same room as we had that first night, and again when we brought Herr Seefeld back. They asked about him—more kindly than I expected.

When we'd exhausted that topic, I asked about Hugo Barrive from the maquis. I did so to open a path for Miss Begley's inquiry, which she now made.

"He was here last week—full of energy and delight."

I asked, "Was he alone?"

Miss Begley butted in. "Was there was an American with him?"

They looked surprised. "How do you know?"

"If his name was Charles Miller—"

"We didn't hear his name."

"What did the American look like?"

We could have had no doubt.

"A big man," they said.

"A scar," they said.

"A wound healing on his neck," they said.

"How would we go about finding him?"

They shrugged. He is with the Americans, they said, or the British, they weren't sure. Hugo had said that they were going down to Étretat, south of Dieppe.

They invited us to stay for dinner, which in that part of France takes place around six o'clock in the evening. We ate some piquant stew. All the talk remained focused on the war—what happened to such-and-such a farm; who died and how; what became of the two Jewish families in Le Crotoy who were taken away one morning in a truck; they didn't know. Where did the local Resistance hide the German officer that they kidnapped last year and recently handed over to the Americans? In the priest's house, they said.

Miss Begley assisted my French as I asked if things seemed different since the Allies had invaded. Here, recorded by me, is the reply they gave interpreted by Miss Begley:

For many weeks we had bad turmoil. Guns and explosions day and night, and vehicles roaring past our gates. The dog almost died of fright. Now you can step outside our door any time and not hear a sound. It has been as if we are all holding our breath to see if the war truly has gone away. And the sleep—we all say how much we are sleeping. Our neighbors tell us they also sleep like drunken people, nothing would awaken us. That is why we think the war has gone away from here, and we hope it has gone forever. We hear that the fighting south of us is very bad. There will be bodies in the fields, and other places, you will be frightened and made sick, maybe. And be careful if you meet the Germans, they may think you are Americans or Canadians. We feel we are still not fully liberated.

All during these days, my mind was shouting at me. We've given too little thought to this journey; we've had no discussion; we didn't assess what it might be like. And that, so often, was Miss Begley's style. Did this woman, whom, as you know, I've already described as "relentlessly real"—have no fear?

I knew, for example, that I got to terror quicker than she did. In bombed London her feelings went to victims, not her own safety or mine. All through the Seefeld incident, while I quivered, expecting death or worse—for him, for all of us—she never showed a tremor. Now, in France, she seemed as eager as a schoolgirl, impatient, pressing forward, and unaware of the magnitude, the difficulty of the task she had begun—and with no thought to what might lie ahead.

73

We returned to Le Crotoy at nine o'clock, ahead of nightfall. Two people waited for us, and they of necessity depended upon each other—Bawn Buckley, who wished to know if we would be returning to Ireland, and the woman whose presence would keep us in France, Madame Larbaud, our juggler boatwoman with the curly hair.

She thought she knew where to find Hugo; he was working his way down the coast to be with the Canadians, she said, at Rouen. The battles were moving across the country toward the German border—or so she hoped, how could anybody be sure? Étretat, she said, was likely—or one of the inland towns, Goderville or Fauville.

Bawn Buckley said that he could catch a tide if he hastened. He wished us luck, but behind Miss Begley's back he shook his head in a worried fashion. With which I agreed.

We said our good-byes and made our arrangements. Madame Larbaud would pick us up in the morning and take us down the coast. An argument broke out, between Madame Larbaud and the owner of the little hotel, and despite the furious pace of their speech I gleaned enough to know that he too questioned the safety of our plan. The bombers, he said, still came over; the armies still faced each other at Dieppe, and all across northern France. In essence he was saying, *What do these two lunatics think they're doing?*

When I asked Miss Begley for a clearer version she said, "It didn't sound important."

I said, "But they seemed heated."

She said, "The French are very passionate—*l'amour, l'amour.*" Which had nothing to do with anything.

Next morning, she sat in front beside Madame Larbaud, and I sprawled in the back, among the Indian clubs, colored balls, and trampolines of the *Cirque Larbaud.*

The women talked nonstop, and Madame Larbaud seemed so moved by Miss Begley's words that I tried to listen closer and determine their content. It seemed that they discussed Captain Miller, and it soon became one of those conversations of an intimacy that men never achieve. Both wept, both waved their hands, both laughed, both giggled—and I rattled from side to side, jolting my shoulder against the edges of the van's metal stanchions.

Trying to hug the coast, attempting to get around Dieppe unnoticed, we ran into many bomb damage detours. But we saw no military— Madame Larbaud had achieved her objective. After what seemed much too long a journey given the distance on her map, she pronounced us clear of Dieppe and, heading south, took us back onto the coast again.

Not for long. With roads impassable from barbed wire, craters, or destroyed bridges, we had to turn inland. As all the historians have since told us, France didn't return to the Allies in a soft bundle. The German army fought like tigers, yielding no more than a square yard at a time. For the regiments who landed in Normandy on June's great D-Day, Berlin in August 1944 still remained thousands and thousands of bodies away.

The van lurched through villages. We skirted the masonry from buildings in ruins, their walls charred and still smoking. The number of dead animals astounded me—horses, cattle, goats. Churches with lopsided spires, houses with holes ripped clean through from back to front—you've long been familiar with these photographs, newsreels, and films. Yet no matter how factual or realistic those images, I've never seen anything that conveyed the force, the devastation, the depressed gloom as those animal corpses—a white pony sprawled in the road, his stomach burst like a rotten fruit; a headless black and white cow; three sheepdogs lying dead side by side on the street, as though they'd had a suicide pact.

Madame Larbaud continued to negotiate deep holes, fallen gables, splintered and leaning trees. She sometimes opened her window for a closer view of the road, and dreadful smells caught us.

In one last place, whose name I've never known because it had no signs or name posts, she halted the van and got out. She crossed the road—such as was left of it—and entered a lone house that no longer possessed a front door. When she came back, our jig was up, but we didn't grasp it.

Hugo, she said, was in a house at the far end of the village that lay just ahead. The Germans had barely gone, they were being pushed back, back all the time; they were shooting the dogs as they left. Madame Larbaud kissed us good-bye and turned her van back the way we'd come. I thought, *There goes our last chance of common sense.*

I took Miss Begley's valise, and we began to walk through the debris of war. At our feet, a series of craters on the roadway became deeper and wider, as though successive shells had exploded while the gunners found their range. How incongruous did we look—a couple of foreign tourists, one with her handbag, one carrying his luggage, walking in a war zone? My mind snarled: *ludicrous, ludicrous, ludicrous, LUDICROUS!*

Of the buildings up ahead, we could see little in detail. The nearest houses of the village stood a hundred yards away, with nothing behind us except the dusty winding road, the departing circus van, the autumn fields—and the safety we'd left.

Miss Begley said, "I suppose we'd better walk on," and I said, "Yes, I suppose so"—it was as banal as that. Fear began to pound through me like a regimental drummer; I couldn't breathe.

When we reached the first house in the village, a man stood at his ajar front door. We nodded friendly greetings, and he shouted. Miss Begley waved and we walked on. He made a contemptuous gesture with his hand.

"What was that about?" I asked.

"He called us crazy people."

"Why?"

She said, "That's all he said—'crazy people, crazy people.' He said it twice."

I said, "What does he know that we don't?"

Miss Begley shrugged and kept walking.

"Kate—do you truly believe you'll find Charles here? In this town?"

"We have to start somewhere."

"In God's name, Kate, think about this."

She said, "Ben, I know I'm going to be with Captain Charles Miller very soon. I'm going to be with my husband."

"I doubt if armies like wives turning up during combat."

She said, "He needs me."

Such a triangle, I thought. *She's doomed to him. He's doomed to this war. I'm doomed to them both.*

Now we began to hear the noise—far distant from us, on the other side of the town, but mighty. At first sound the word *thunder* crossed my mind, but soon the pattern told us that thunder never echoed like this— these rumbles were shorter and at once softer and harder.

"We might be walking into a battle," I said.

At the beginning of a street, the first building, an agricultural feed store, had all its windows boarded and showed no sign of life.

"Can we get some directions?" I said, and tried to open the door. It didn't open and nobody answered my knocking. In a wide yard beside the feed store stood a truck, and something about it seemed so bizarre that I went to look. From its tail to its headlights, a necklace of holes ran through it. And the same row of holes started far behind it in the ground and continued far beyond it. The truck had been machine-gunned from the air. I climbed up to look in at the driver's door; nobody inside.

Next, we reached empty houses. One had part of its roof drilled with the same pattern of holes as the truck. When I followed the perforations I could trace the path of the aircraft's gun, across the street, into the gardens and open spaces behind the house.

I thought not to draw Miss Begley's attention to this crazy sight, but she had watched me, and she picked up the line of holes too. Once you saw them, they became obvious.

"Which side did it, do you think?" she said.

I answered, "Does it matter?"

We walked on. I've seen towns empty because everybody is at Mass, at a local fair, or at a show of some kind. This wasn't that kind of empti-ness. Though clothes hung on backyard washing lines here, this had the deadly, empty pain of evacuation.

In the teeth of that loud, unfriendly silence, the crackle of war called us forward like fools. I would like to say that we felt as staunch as adventurers, but I had begun to look for shelter. Yet—what kind of shelter? And for what reason? And for how long? The premises on both sides of the street looked closed to the world. What excuse should we give to a person whom we asked for hospitality? That there was a war up ahead? But that was why we had come here. *And for how long will you be staying, sir?* Until the war is over.

A shock of memory made me shudder. I recognized this desperate mood. For some years after Venetia disappeared I'd had this feeling almost every day—acute emotional isolation while living in, and surrounded by, "normal" conditions. Time after time I snapped myself out of it by allowing anger to invade me, and I could feel it rise now.

"Kate, I'm asking you again. Why are we here?"

She didn't look at me, but she did reply.

"If you knew how tender this man is. If you knew his gifts of loving."

"Well, I don't and how could I?" I rapped back.

To this she said, without breaking step, "I'd be a fool not to come and look for him."

I said, "He's a soldier. Do you think he'll come with us if you find him?"

"I'll make him safe. I know how. And he knows that."

"This is madness."

"Ben, he can't survive. He lives by the sword. You mightn't believe it but a woman knows these things."

"Are you sure," I said, "that you have enough experience to judge?"

She continued to look straight ahead, her jaw as dogged as her steady footsteps. "I'm not the simple creature you think I am."

My mind said, *Stop. This debate has no future. You'll not change her view of herself. So just be kind.*

At that moment, I saw something so bizarre that it took up permanent residence in my mind.

I expect you have images that recur. I often see myself swinging like a monkey through the trees, and that leads to trapeze fantasies; I soar back and forth through the air, very high up, in a wonderful rhythm of freedom and blue sky. I also contemplate being a tumbler, an acrobat, turning a procession of cartwheels.

These are daydreams. I understand them. If alone at a table, I play the piano, even though I've never mastered an instrument. I play with both hands. My fingers describe arpeggios. I play powerful, cunning riffs.

Or I manage wild things that come at me. A bull charges, a great, black beast, with drool hanging from the red cave of his mouth; I grab his horns and wrestle him to the ground. Or a lion, all mane and open jaws, attacks. I run at him and he turns aside. Or a runaway horse tears down a street, and I grab the swinging reins and haul down his head.

This new sight, though, had never been in my mind's gallery before. How could it, when I didn't even know it existed?

It was a shell, an artillery shell, behind us, glinting in the air high, high above. Instinctively I knew that if I could see it as clearly as this, it must be coming to the end of its flying time. In seconds it will crash to earth and bring havoc.

My first thought was, *What's the point in flinging ourselves down if this thing's going to hit the same ground?*

I grabbed Miss Begley's hand. "Drop your bag and run like hell."

I led the way. Through a gap, into a field. The farms ran up to the backs of the houses. This field had a haystack. We call it a "pike," a dome of packed hay about seven feet at its tallest. As we rounded the haystack, the shell hit the street. We heard the tearing, cracking sound. Twenty yards or so behind where we'd been. Then we heard the secondary explosion. The collateral damage. The gas tank of the feed store blew up. Then we heard the new silence. Different from the general, weird stillness. And then we heard the cries.

Miss Begley looked in no direction. She leaned back into the hay, exhaling and repeating, "Oh, Jesus! Oh, Jesus!"

I watched her—for signs of collapse, distress, unhinging. Who could blame her if she caved? Instead, she merely sagged, pressing harder back on the hay.

"We'd better go and help," she said.

"We won't move. If there's been one shell on that trajectory, there may be others."

She closed her eyes.

We sat, recovering, yet I was dipping further into terror. A violent headache crashed across my forehead and died as quickly as it came—the effect of compressed air. She must have felt the same because she pressed her hands to her eyes.

The second shell came whining over. And the third. And the fourth and fifth and sixth. We saw them. We shuddered to them. We felt them in our bones. They all seemed to hit the same target, because the cries from the houses ended with no fading. As I began to understand that the gunners had overcalculated and thus overshot the town center, the words came rolling through my head, *I am in the war, I am in the war, I am in the war.*

When many minutes had passed in which no shells burst, we rose and looked out at the world again. A roof had folded. Some chimneys along the other houses had toppled sideways like little drunken people. I reckoned that the barrage had ended. Or at least had moved closer to the gunners' targets. We might be safe for the time being.

In no hurry we moved out of the field, hay wisps festooning us. Two tiny people in a huge war. Our bags stood in the middle of the roadway where we'd left them. They seemed unharmed—until Miss Begley saw leakages from her valise. A bottle of toilet water had exploded—had, in fact, been atomized: Not a shard of glass could be found; the air compression had left only the cork.

Moving the bags off the road, we turned back to see whether help could be rendered. Two direct hits had landed on the feed store—in which people had been working, even though nobody had answered. Beyond a ripped-out wall, the bodies of a man and boy lay side by side on an open, almost pristine area of plank floor; both had leg injuries and severe head wounds. As we stood wondering what to do, I heard cracking noises and the remains of the roof began to fall in. We had to go.

On the street, it grew worse. Gunfire began spitting flashes like small lightnings into the rooflines of the houses. Diagonally across from us, up the street, I saw an open and empty garage. I grabbed her hand. We ran. That was all we could do. I know that I ducked my head. And I know that I felt more ridiculous than I'd ever felt. There's another feeling that war promotes alongside fear—stupidity.

We got there.

"My bag," she said.

"When things calm down," I said.

I closed the garage door behind us. Stiff, it stuck; I had to slam it. A hail of bullets hit it; two dribbled through. Then a heavier torrent began to rip it apart. We squeezed into the farthest-away corner. The metal door held the bullets back far enough to stop them reaching us.

More shells exploded, some nearby. The garage shook and so did we. A new noise came in—an aircraft with a powerful droning sound. I heard the stuttering thuds everywhere, metal *chings,* glass breaking, and the earthbound gunfire too, and loud, wild shouts. All of a sudden the war had moved full force into the street on which we'd been walking. The nausea that hit me was unlike any other. Bullets now began to penetrate the door at will.

I lay on top of Miss Begley, covering her body completely. No recollection of having done so comes back to me—I have searched and searched my memory; it must have been instinctive. Beneath me, she vomited, her body convulsing with each retch.

They blew the garage to bits. The walls, the roof, the stout metal door that had resisted so much—they shattered it. After the first grenade took the door off the hinges, they found us on the floor, deep in the farthest corner.

Silence. Boots rang on the concrete floor. Words. I didn't know who or what they were. They came closer. Words in English. I flapped up a hand.

"We're neutral. We're neutral."

"Neutral?" They turned the word over and over. "Neutral?" How they laughed!

Canadians, they were, "Canucks," they said, en route to take Abbeville in the next week or so. One said that his mother came from Scotland and wasn't that the same thing as being Irish? And Miss Begley said it was. They reached out their hands to steady us when we clambered to our feet.

Lowering their guns, they walked us out into the sunshine, and that's when they turned back and finished off the garage with a couple of grenades. What the heck, they said; the government will provide a new one. They walked us up the street and calmed us down. To our surprise I saw our bags standing where we'd left them. But my legs didn't work and a Canadian sergeant fetched the luggage.

Neutral? They kept shaking their heads and laughing.

That afternoon's battle had been an encounter with a German rear-guard pocket, who had fought, said the Canadians, like champions. A U.S. Air Force plane had finally taken them out. They had seen the garage door open and thought we were German soldiers looking for a hiding place. The war had now moved on from here, they said, and they handed us over to the Americans.

In the town's biggest building, a church hall, an American sergeant, perhaps ten years younger than I, looked at us as though we'd lost our minds.

Miss Begley said, "We're looking for Captain Charles Miller."

He said, "There's no Captain Miller in this post, ma'am."

"Where would I find him?"

At first I thought that she had no grasp of the war's magnitude, but she told me later that she knew exactly what she was doing. "An innocent question often takes you farther than you expect, Ben."

"What's his platoon, ma'am?"

"I don't know."

"Ma'am, what kind of soldier is he?"

"A very brave one, and he's very important."

The young sergeant looked at me, and, cowardly of me, I looked away.

"Ma'am, do you know how many troops came into France?"

And Miss Begley said, "A lot, I suppose."

And he said, "One hundred thousand, ma'am, and probably many more than that."

"Where should I ask?"

He, with infinite courtesy in the face of what he could fairly have called two idiots, said, "Let me make some inquiries. Where are you staying?"

She said, "I don't know yet. Do you know a Frenchman called Hugo Barrive?"

The sergeant shook his head. "No, ma'am." Smart as green paint, he then said to me, "Sir, this is a military post. We have to search you, I'm afraid."

He beckoned me into a back room and whispered, "Sir?" with a squeak of agitation.

"He's her husband," I said. "He works in military intelligence, that's all we know."

"A Special Ops guy?" he asked. "Nobody will find him. If he's still alive."

"What's Special Ops?" I asked.

He said, "They raid places, they work with the local underground, they kill high-ranking enemy one at a time."

What had Miss Begley said in her journal? *He kills people.*

I said, "The French up the coast told us to come down here."

The sergeant disappeared and I returned to join Miss Begley. When the sergeant came back, he said, "My inquiries will take some time. But we need you out of here." He wanted to rid himself of the problem every soldier fears—an officer's wife.

74

They put Miss Begley in the care of two women in uniform, who led her away, with her valise. I was given coffee, and then some food. Later they led us to a requisitioned house across the road where they had thrown sleeping bags everywhere. Before she lay down for the night I took Miss Begley in my arms, gave her a big, slow hug, and said, "It'll all work out. You'll see."

"But, Ben, how do you know?" She shook from head to foot.

I said, "I've just heard the news. Paris has been liberated. Everybody's celebrating."

Let me recap, because the sequence of events has some importance. We had set out to make contact with the maquis, with whom Miller might or might not have been working at that time. First, Madame Larbaud dropped us from the van in the little town where she assumed him to be, but bomb damage prevented her from taking us further. Then we walked straight into the war, ran hotfoot from bursting shells, and hid from fusillades of bullets. Rescued, we retrieved our shattered minds in a temporary American base, where Miss Begley went to bed at nine o'clock in the evening. I sat on the floor by a camp bed and wrote a long entry in my journal that tells what you've just been reading.

That was my second taste of war. If by any chance you do not yet understand why I became a devout pacifist, you soon will.

That night, something happened that I can't explain and can only describe. As I understood it, I had a dream in which, still on edge, I walked out of doors again, to listen to the night, to reassure myself that the war had left this town at least. The waning moon held lingering power, and I could see the street ahead, shadowy with the ribs of its shattered buildings.

I found a promising lane into the open fields behind the town and I wandered along, breathing easily for the first time in days. Not a sound to be heard, not a night bird, not an engine, not a gun.

The lane petered out and, ahead of me, the largest field ended at a dramatic outcrop of whitened rock. Generally bleak, some acres long and wide, it had hostile scrub and a handful of feeble pine trees. It seemed geographically out of true with the general neighborhood. I learned that it was born to a rogue seam of limestone, a geological erratic that shot straight as an arrow across the countryside for about ten miles.

The seam broke ground in this place alone. I stood on its edge, on a small plateau almost like a pavement, and looked up its sloping height. It reached a hundred feet or so, and I thought of Donegal and its mountainside faces of scree and bleached, blank stone, and County Clare's moonscape, the white tundra of the Burren. The sparse thorny brush, the famous maquis whence the Resistance got their name—from guerrillamen who hid in this nationwide scrub—spread up to the hapless few pine trees tilting near the crown.

A calm night. Yes, the war had moved on. And I was beginning to feel that I was, at last, maturing into a fully grown man. A half-moon radiated white where it stroked the stone of the plateau.

As I stood there in a bright twilight, something moved behind the scrub. A creature emerged. It took some steps forward, halted, and stood looking at me, quite composed, unalarmed. I knew at once what it was—a wolf. Taller than a dog, grayer than I knew wolves could be—not that I'd ever seen one, except in photographs.

Fear arrived first. *Am I to be devoured? And if I turn and run—can't it outpace me? And is there a pack?*

I did nothing. Through indecision, fear, and cowardice I made no move. Nor did the wolf. It sank onto its haunches and continued to look at me as though I were the curiosity here.

No wind, clear sky, no odors in the night—a welcome change after the day's smell of death. No clouds either; the moon continued to hand down her cool, bathing light.

I have no weapon. If it attacks, what can I do? It can outrun me. What will I do if a pack appears?

The wolf stood up. It stretched, yawned, lowered its head, and sniffed the forward air. My blood turned to water, which began to run warm down my leg. The options roared through my brain like rockets. If I run—he'll get the back of my neck. If I stand—he'll get my throat. If I lie down—he'll simply chew my flesh. The last rocket burned the brightest—I had only one choice.

I attacked. Ran at the wolf. Shrieking at fever height. Arms flailing, fists pumping, I ran like a focused dervish.

The wolf looked surprised. The expression on its face, big, wide, and scarfed with fur, said, slightly pained, "Oh, well, if that's how you feel." It turned its back on me calmly and loped away, contemptuous in its relaxed speed.

By then I had reached halfway up the rocks, and from a vantage point I saw the wolf heading away through the open fields, out across the night. No trace of any kind did it leave, no smell, no spoor. I stopped agitating. My shoulders sagged. I know a great deal more about wolves now than I did then.

Next morning, the vision of the wolf dominated my mind. I rose from my sleeping bag, left the house, and followed my dream footsteps. I found that there was indeed a lane, and there was an outcrop of white rock several acres long and deep, and there was harsh scrub topped by exhausted pine trees with deep brush behind.

Even today, I have difficulty sometimes separating my dreams from my realities.

75

Here are two excerpts from Miss Begley's private journals for those few days. They're important as guides to what lay ahead. I believe she must have written them on pieces of paper that she then copied into her diary when she came back.

August 1944: We are in France, Ben and I. Nearer to my bridegroom Charles, whom I have come here to find. I have lost track of the date, but that is not important because I have been seized with a premonition too strong to resist, a feeling that Charles needs me as he has never needed anybody in his life. This is not me making myself important— this is me relying on feelings that in the past have been important and useful. They're the same feelings I had all that Sunday when I was little, when they didn't come back from the wedding. I don't want that to happen in my life again, but if I want Charles to come back, I'll have to find him for myself and bring him home. If he's ill, meaning wounded, I'll be allowed to bring him back home.

These are terrible times. We have heard awful things. I have listened to many tales of what has happened to people in this war, and I do not know how they have survived. In Le Crotoy, the sadness that hangs over people must, I think, be the same that hangs over all of the countries where people have been dying—and that's most of Europe. We're lucky to have been neutral, and so are Spain and Portugal and Switzerland.

And I am lucky to have Ben with me. What if I had met him when he was in better condition, as he is now? Would I have fallen for him as I did for Charles? Who can tell? I know that he thinks me irresponsible to have come here, but it says a lot about him that even though he is afraid (and I can see it), he came here with me, to help and protect me. When I have found Charles then I will devote all my energy to finding Ben's missing wife. Or her mortal remains. Ben is so often sad. I see him when he isn't aware that I am watching, and he stands as though completely alone.

Nana still doesn't like him. Before we began our search for Charles she tried again to warn me. She said I shouldn't let him go with me, that he's dangerous, and God knows what he'll do under pressure, that he might turn on me. But I don't think so (at least I hope not!), and anyway I have to be practical: How can I search for Charles alone?

I carry in my bag a little square of calico, from a shop in Kenmare. It's green and white check and when I saw it, I thought it might make a nice summer dress, so I brought the sample to show it to Charles. If he likes it I will make the dress.

Her second entry disturbed me less in one way and more in another. Less because it contained no criticisms of me; more because I hadn't known how the evidence of war had so disturbed Miss Begley.

Today (again I don't know the exact date), we found ourselves right in the middle of the war. I feel so ill, I feel worse than I have done at any time in my life. Today I suffered insult to all my five senses; seeing— I saw the works of Satan, with bodies torn apart as though he had ravaged them at the gates of Hell; hearing—I heard the screams of people in pain at their loss; smelling—I smelled the sulfur of a thousand infernos; tasting—tasted the dust of war, the filth of carnage on dust borne by the wind; and as for touch—I stepped on something, a woman's corpse, barely recognizable. Terrible, the squelching sound my foot made.

My stomach is in turmoil, I can retain no food, I have severe pain in my back, and my head is splitting with headaches. But I must let nobody see any of this; as Nana always taught me, I must show no weakness. I know what's causing the pains—I'm thinking of Charles and I can't help worrying about him. That gash on his neck and throat was awful, and he wouldn't explain to me how he got it. It looked to me like a knife wound, but I know nothing of what a soldier has to do; it definitely wasn't a bullet wound, and I thought they only fought with guns. I'm thinking of going back to praying, to see if it will do any good, if it will bring him back to me.

As she experienced physical pain and discomfort, so did I—a permanent headache for months if not years. More revealingly, she focused on the injury to Captain Miller's neck. I understood that kind of focus. When the initial search for Venetia yielded no fruit, I began to envisage how they might have killed her. I saw bullet holes and stab wounds and decapitations. Miss Begley's pain seemed to gush from a similar fountain.

When I came back from my mystifying walk on the little white tundra of the wolf, none of war's mighty sounds boomed or thumped, though strange odors floated everywhere.

I heard laughter as I walked through the door of the American billet. It came from the kitchen, where I found a rejuvenated Miss Begley holding court among the two women who had taken care of her the previous night, and several men. I listened outside the open door for some minutes, as she told stories of marriages that she had made or attempted to clinch.

"We had one man my grandmother wouldn't handle at all. She gave him over to me, and I said, 'Oh, thanks very much, Nana'—because although he had plenty of money and insisted on paying us a fee every time we met him, he was impossible. And d'you know why he was impossible? He wouldn't speak. Instead of opening his mouth and saying something, he winked."

One of the women asked, "Winked?"

Miss Begley gave a cartoon wink, head ducking to one side.

"I'd say to him, 'Now I have a very nice girl for you to meet.' He'd wink. 'She has her own hairdressing business over in Killarney.' Wink. 'And her mother is dead so there'd be no mother-in-law to deal with, and there'd be a second income. Would you like to meet her?' And he'd produce an almighty wink."

Her listeners laughed. I laughed.

"And after the wink," she said, "he'd slide this envelope full of money across the table at me. And he'd wink again."

"What did the wink mean?" asked one of the men.

"I never found out," said Miss Begley, and everybody laughed.

A footstep clattered beside me on the tiled floor and I started. Sudden noise, sudden movements: I thought their power would have diminished in a war. An older man in uniform came and stood beside me, looking in.

"Hi," he murmured to me, looking in at her. "You're the two Irish folk?"

I said, "Yes."

"Crazy guys, right?"

I smiled my wryest.

Inside the kitchen, Miss Begley said, "And that was bad enough but I did get him a date with a girl. A nice girl. She was thirty-five, all her own teeth. Understood about corsets—you know, an intelligent girl. And her father died and left her a small farm of land. She walked out with my Wink, and then she reported back to me. 'Oh, my God, Kate Begley,' she said. 'What kind of men do you know?' And I asked her why, and she said, 'I asked him would he like to go for a walk and he winked at me. I asked him would he like to sit down, and he winked at me. I told him I had go to the toilet and he winked at me. I said to him that we should have a drink and he winked at me. And the more he drank the more he winked, until his eyelid was flapping up and down like a signaling lamp.' "

They roared with laughter, and one of the women asked, "Will you come out to the States and get husbands for us?"

Miss Begley said, "Indeed, I may be going to the States anyway because I'm married to one of your comrades."

They chorused the question, "Who?"

The officer at my elbow eyebrowed an inquiry at me. I nodded and whispered, "Listen."

"I'm sure many of you know him," said Miss Begley. "He's a captain. His name is Charles Miller. I came out here to be with him."

In the kitchen (and I hadn't yet shown my face) they looked at one another but shook their heads.

Miss Begley said, "He's in something called Special Operations."

One of the men said, "We never get to know those guys."

And one of the women said, "Where did you meet? Was it very romantic?"

As Miss Begley launched into the epic of her romance, the officer beside me stepped away and beckoned me to follow.

Outside, he asked, "Is that true?"

I said, "Every word."

"How did you get here?"

I told him the story in brief. He walked me back across the street, saying, "There's something off the rails here."

We walked into a building and down a corridor.

"How well did you know Miller?" he asked.

I said, "I like him. A lot."

We reached a small room, where two uniformed men sorted papers that looked like official documents.

"Guys, get me everything you can on where Miller is." Then he turned to me and said, "He was here two days ago. With two French guys and an Englishman—they met here."

When the men left the room, he said, "I know Miller." He took a pause. "Killer Miller."

I must have looked shocked, because he said, "It's okay—he's on our side. What's your name, by the way?" and when I told him he said, "I'm Mike Morrigan." And we shook hands. "Grandfather was Irish."

"Probably County Mayo," I said, "with a name like that. How long have you known Captain Miller?"

He took this in and lit a cigarette.

"First time I saw Killer Miller," he resumed, "we were all in this hangar for a lecture on Special Ops. Or as much as they wanted to tell us about it. Long bitch of a place with the wind coming through. Scraping the faces off us. Doors are open wide, there isn't a thing to be seen, we're near Tacoma, out in the country. Empty building, bigger'n a football field. We're sitting there, looking out across the open sky, not a house in sight, we're called together for a briefing, a whole bunch of us, and waiting and getting raucous. This was a place they built aircraft, and it had long, wide-open spaces."

He stopped and looked at me. "Are you the one I should be telling this to?"

"Look," I said. "I think Miller is one of the best fellows I ever met."

"Yeah," he said, doubt hanging from his tone. "We'll talk about that. Anyway, I'm sitting there with all these other guys, some brass, some grunts—that's officers and men. I'm looking out the wide-open, non-existent doors, and way off in the distance I see this dot. It's just a dot—but it's a moving dot and it's moving toward us. The word goes around, and suddenly we're all staring at this goddamn dot. There's chitchat and shouts, Hey Mack, it's your missus, she's found where you are, and Hey Bud, it's your mother. And worse."

Mike Morrigan sat down at what I presumed to be his desk.

"So we're sitting there, and slowly we all get quiet. The place gets to be a mortuary, it's so quiet. And all because of this dot, because we can tell that it's coming straight at us, and by now we've figured that it's a man. And we've also figured that he's coming for us, in fact so determined is his walk he looks like he's coming *at* us. As if he's gonna take on the whole three hundred of us. I can't take my eyes offa him. And he gets nearer and nearer, and goddamn it, this guy isn't walking, he's marching. He's marching like he's on a forced march, and by now the silence is really crazy, I mean crazy deep. We're like mutes the way we sit there, and I don't know about the others but my head has already cottoned on to the rhythm of his steps and they're like a march tune in my brain, and I can tell that he's marching fast. Now if you count the distance he was when he started from us, he must have marched a straight mile."

Morrigan stopped, looked away into the distance, and shook his large, shaved head. He took a long pause and wound himself up to finish his tale (which I, that same night, wrote down in another notebook—not my war journal, because Miss Begley sometimes read that).

"Now he's a hundred yards away and we can see him, and we can see that the uniform is perfect, the creases in the pants are like he was wearing swords inside them, the tunic is as fitted as a glove, the boots shine like lamps. And now he's fifty yards from us, and my first sight of him is accompanied by the thought, 'Does this son of a bitch ever sweat?' Because his face is as dry as flour, and he must have been walking at twenty miles an hour. He comes closer and closer, and now he's in the doorway, the wide-open space where a door should be, and we're looking at him and still he's coming at us, and at the middle chair of the top row he stops and says, in a voice cold as the friggin' Arctic, 'Stand up, gentlemen,' and we stand up like we were shot in the ass. That's how I first saw Miller. And he briefed us like we were donkeys. Like he was a genius and we were dumb-ass. That's Killer Miller."

I've written that exactly as I heard it. Imagine, now, what it was like for me to try to digest it.

"But where is he?" I asked.

Morrigan shrugged and spread his hands.

"That's what I hope my guys will tell you. Word was that Hitler had a price on Miller's head."

At that moment, one of the men returned with a note that he handed to Morrigan, who then dismissed him. When we were alone again, Morrigan said, "Well, we have your answer."

He looked at me, made his hand like a cleaver, and whipped it across his throat.

I gasped. "What? Jesus!"

"That's the scuttlebutt."

"Are you certain?"

He held up the piece of paper. "Why would you use the word *certain* in a war?"

"Are we talking about Captain Charles Miller, an intelligence officer, who was based in London for a while and in Ireland, and then went into France? He's from Kansas originally?"

"Killer Miller. I told you. And he's not from Kansas, he's from Pennsylvania, and he could have been based in Kalama-freakin'-zoo, for all I know. But in my book there's only one Captain Charles Miller. Or there was."

"When was he killed? And where?"

Morrigan stretched like an athlete. "Christ, this war doesn't half make you tense. Okay. Word is he was in a sanitarium near Fauville that got infiltrated."

"How do you mean?"

"That's the kick of the freakin' thing. He was killed by some Nazi doing for them the kind of job Miller did for us." He squinted. "Want me to put in an inquiry on behalf of the widow?"

76

In a clanking jeep, the Americans took us to Dieppe—or what was left of it. As though we were prisoners of war they handed us over to the Canadians, who had liberated the port. We had a rough crossing to England in a troopship. *And how will they stop the torpedoes?* I asked myself. From there we were escorted to a series of trains. Two armed soldiers sat with us all the way—and they finally supervised our embarkation on the Dublin boat at Liverpool.

"Stay neutral," cracked the corporal.

Miss Begley didn't speak once, not to me, not to anybody. She looked forty-five, not twenty-five, a face pitted with shock, the black light of despair in her eyes, hands listless as dead flowers in her lap. I've ransacked my memory for the truth of those two days (we had a night crossing to Dublin), and no matter what nets I trawl across my mind, I can't haul in a single word that she spoke.

And I? Remember that metabolic device that I mentioned, the control valve, which, over the years, I had attached to my emotions? It had kicked on some days earlier. It's useful; it delays an impact until I can digest it, until I can release it slowly into my system, examine it, and cope with the feelings. Yes, it holds up the pleasure in good news, but it mostly stops bad news from ambushing me—unless I've been drinking, and thanks to Miss Begley's eagle glare I hadn't touched anything beyond a drop of wine in months.

In Dublin, I took over the rest of the journey. I went to the bank, drew out enough money to book two adjoining hotel rooms, and sequestered Kate in deep comfort for four days and four nights. She ate not at all the first day—no breakfast, slept through lunch (I kept a duplicate key to her room), and refused dinner.

On the second morning, she drank some tea. I sat by her bed, eating the breakfast that she hadn't touched. She didn't look at me, kept her head down, her unwashed hair falling in a lank mask over her face. She had slept in her clothes. I warmed a face towel in the bathroom and held it to her forehead, her cheeks, her neck. And I said not a word, just waited—and waited.

An hour later, I rose to go, saying, "I'll look in soon."

She blurted, "I don't believe he's dead."

"Shhh. Take it easy."

"He's not dead."

"Kate, what are you saying?"

She said, "I asked the Americans. At that place."

"Asked them what?"

"I said, Do you know a Captain Miller, an intelligence officer?"

"Kate, I heard you. I was listening at the door. But they didn't seem to know."

She said, "Others came and told me. A senior officer."

I asked, "What did he look like? Was he as bald as an egg, was that the man?"

"Yes, and he said Charles was dead."

"Sometimes they give details."

"He said, in a hospital. It was bombed."

I said, "You can't be sure of anything in a war."

She said, "Charles is very famous in the American army. Everybody knows his name."

"Why don't you believe them?" I asked.

Words burst out of her with a wail. "Because the force in that man would spin the world. He's alive, Ben. I want to bring him back to Kenmare. I want to look after him."

"Get yourself up and about," I said. "You'll feel better."

"He's. Not. Dead. I know these things," she said.

I walked away then, wanting so much to agree with her.

77

Back in my own room, I waited for her to knock on my door. Through the wall I could hear her running a bath and clattering about. *Good!* I thought. *Energy is what we need in her.* And then came the dry caution, *What in God's name will she do with new energy?*

I read my newspaper, keen to follow in print the events we had just survived. Even though Dieppe and Le Crotoy and Étretat received no mention—the Allies had, after all, pressed on by now—my heart still jumped. Reduced by the wartime paper shortages, the *Irish Independent* stretched to only four pages. Inside, under a heading, THE WAR PASSED THIS WAY, they ran a photograph captioned, "A general view of the devastation at Rouen. In the background can be seen the spire of Rouen Cathedral. The edifice escaped damage."

We'd been close to Rouen, I thought. *And all over Ireland this morning they'll be breathing the word* miracle *because the cathedral didn't get hit.* I laughed, almost out loud, when my inner voice said, *They know nothing.*

It took Miss Begley two and a half hours, but when she knocked on my door she had pulled herself together.

"I need some clothes," she said.

I replied, "So do I."

And she said, "You always need clothes, you just don't buy any."

I said, "I buy them all right, but two days later they look old."

She patted me on the arm. "We'll fix that."

Some recovery had begun.

Separately, we shopped in a single department store, and she made straight for the ladies' underwear department.

Ha! said my silent mocker. *Wish you could be with her?*

I hadn't heard from my inner gentleman in weeks. When I went looking for him in France and on the way home, I couldn't hear him. I could only hear screams of fear from that quarter of my mind, and I preferred to ignore them in order to survive.

Now, though, he was back and with a subtle change—not so much mockery as challenge. Yes, he would continue to make sarcastic remarks when I felt under pressure, but thanks to his voice, that is the moment to which I date full acknowledgment that my feelings were, indeed, changing. It was as though I'd had too much respect for Captain Miller to let my thoughts roam.

Therefore, that is the moment when I ceased denying. That is the moment when my friendship with Kate Begley deepened and strengthened. And that is the moment I have had such cause to regret.

78

In the disjointed hours that followed, our emotions flailed all over the place, racing up and down different scales like the mercury in a demented thermometer.

Shopping done, we walked back to the hotel. As we climbed the stairs, Miss Begley said, in a voice that didn't sound insincerely gay, "Would you like to see the clothes that I bought?"

In her room she staged a little fashion show for me. To do so she had, naturally, to remove her outer garments—which meant that much of the time she stood, or pranced, in her underwear.

She posed this way and that. She showed me dresses, shoes, a hat. She laughed, paraded—and burst into tears. With me holding her hands, she'd pull herself together and say, "Oh, I've got something else to show you," and resume the mannequin act. She'd then weep again, as helplessly as any young widow.

I stayed and stayed—and stayed until she had cried herself out. Then I laid her down, as she was, in her new underwear, drew a sheet over her, and sent her to sleep. Tiptoeing around the room, I picked up the clothes where she'd dropped them, folded or hung them, set the room to rights, and sat to watch over her—all night, if need be.

Does great and savage experience eclipse previous emotions? In France's war zones I had scarcely thought of Venetia. Now she came back to my mind with force.

Those days in the house down at Charleville—we called them our honeymoon, because they were. Our journeys into the countryside, incensed with fierce heat, bathing in cool lakes, walking in fields of deep grass, and the nights that became mornings, and the force and the flavor—we called that our new, true life.

And now, long bereft of that exquisite, incomparable bride, I found myself in a hotel room with a woman who had become, one way and another, almost my permanent companion, who was from moment to mo-

ment appearing in provocative clothing (she'd also modeled the underwear she'd bought), and whom I was helping through that most binding
of experiences: dismayed bereavement.

No wonder I became confused. As ever, I reached for a practical
thought, something that I could bite into in order to fight the pain, like
the bullet they give a soldier during battlefield surgery. That night, I
found my bullet; I decided that, no matter what happened, I would write
Kate Begley's "biography," or at least get down on paper everything I
could record of her. In a sense what I'm actually saying is: That was the
night I first saw how entwined she and I had become.

79

Next day, Kate had recovered some more energy, sufficient to lead me by
the nose and unprepared to the American embassy. I should have known
that she was up to something—by the set of her jaw at breakfast; by the
speed of her walk as we left the hotel; by the clown's red spots of excitement on her cheeks; by the heightened agitation. She wouldn't tell me
where we were heading; I sighed with inevitability when I saw the building; and once we had been granted entry, she startled me again with her
opening salvo.

"Where can I apply for compassionate overseas leave for my husband?"

The official to whom we were referred reacted with the tools used by
all diplomats—a slow, carefully worded response, and a face without expression.

"Leave from where, ma'am?"

"Captain Miller," she said. "He's serving with the U.S. Army in
France, and he's not well."

The official, seeking to kick away anything that came at him, as all
bureaucrats are born to do, said, "There'll be a lot of Millers in the U.S.
forces, ma'am."

"Charles. Sometimes called Chuck, which I've never liked," said Miss Begley.

"The name Charles is often turned into Chuck in the United States, ma'am."

"I still don't like it," she said.

"If I'm guessing right, you're not a U.S. national, ma'am."

"Irish."

This looked like a different Miss Begley—crisp, no charm on show (as yet), and her technique sought to create entitlement. She wore one of the new dresses, the green with big yellow polka dots, and she gleamed like a sunburst—no trace of widow's weeds there.

"Ma'am, do you know if your husband registered your marriage with us here in the embassy? He doesn't need to, but some U.S. nationals have done so if they married Irish people, because it makes the later paper-work easier." He was as patient as a gardener.

"We married in London. Here's the certificate."

The official took the paper and dipped into his toolbox for another distancing stratagem. He said, "I'll just refer some of these papers to an-other department, if I may," and disappeared.

Half an hour later, he came back and sat down, and as he opened his mouth to speak, Miss Begley said, "Well? Can I?"

"Can you what, ma'am?"

Poor fellow. He had no idea of the force confronting him.

She ignored his question. "And did you get the forms?" she said.

"Forms?" I saw the first variation of his repertoire—a frown. "What forms, ma'am?"

"To apply for compassionate leave. He was wounded. Here." She reached across and tapped the diplomat on the neck, and he recoiled as though from a viper. "A long wound. I helped to dress it when he was last home."

"So he's already had some leave?" The diplomat clutched at the straw.

"But he went straight back on duty. That's the kind of man my hus-band is. You should be proud of him."

"Ma'am, we're proud of all our soldiers."

"He's an officer. Doubly proud, I'd say."

"Now where was he stationed?"

"I believe he was part of the Allied landings, or had a lot to do with them."

"Ma'am, do you know how many men landed—"

She interrupted. "I know nothing. My husband would never betray a secret. He's in military intelligence."

The diplomat brightened. "In that case, ma'am, I can't help you. Officially we don't even know he exists, if you understand me."

Miss Begley held out her hand. "But this is my wedding ring. And I was with him last month."

"If he's on active duty," said the diplomat. He might have thought that he was getting free, but she interrupted again.

"He never wants to take leave. That's why I thought that if I asked officially, the army would order him home."

Which energy was going to win this battle? The official's training or Miss Begley's emotional strength?

She said, "I'm more than happy to go back to France and bring him home myself."

"Ma'am, I don't think the U.S. Army will want that. And the U.S. government can't interfere—the army's fighting a war."

"I wish you'd seen it," she said. "We actually watched, didn't we, Ben? This is my cousin, Ben MacCarthy, he's a war reporter—we actually saw the shells falling and exploding beside us."

The term *war reporter* introduced the next facial expression in the diplomat's repertoire, and I'd have characterized it as a mixture of mild panic and great caution. Like a cloud's shadow crossing a hillside I saw the resolve creep across his face—he'd decided that he'd try to close this down.

"Let me understand you, ma'am. You want the U.S. government, through this embassy, to ask the U.S. Army—right?"

Miss Begley nodded. "Very good so far."

"To ask the U.S. Army to grant your husband—"

She interrupted again: "Captain Charles Miller. He's from Kansas. They might know him as Chuck Miller. He was stationed in London for a while. And in the north of Ireland too."

"To grant your husband compassionate leave on the basis of a wound that you have observed."

"And dressed," Miss Begley said, "but I'm not a nurse, of course."

The diplomat sat back. "I just wanted to understand it, ma'am. But as you can imagine, in the war and all that, it may take some time."

"Do you want me to sign something?" said Miss Begley.

"In due course you'll definitely have to sign something," the diplomat said.

"Shall I wait?" she asked.

"No, ma'am, but we'll need your address." The trained skill had trumped the emotional cunning. "Where was Captain Miller last seen on duty?" The diplomat flourished his pen above his pad; he was on the home straight now and he knew it.

"Near Dieppe in France," said Miss Begley, who saw that she'd been outsmarted. She almost crumpled, caught herself just in time. Then, as I watched her face, I saw her decide to harness that emotion and show some of it to the diplomat.

Voice breaking a little, she said, "You have no idea what a fine man he is."

She had such force—such compelling force.

"I'll do all I can," said the diplomat, and I think that he meant it. And I was left to speculate, *How will he handle this when he discovers Captain Miller's name on the dead-and-missing list out of France? Will he write her a tidy, compassionate letter? And get the ambassador to sign it?*

We walked from the embassy, our heels ringing in the sunny, empty city, and I said, "What do we do now?"

She said, "It's four o'clock and I want a cup of tea."

In Bewley's on Grafton Street, with the smell of the coffee making me wish that I were on the move again, I said, "We have some thinking to do."

"Do you know what Charles and I talked about those nights he came to Lamb's Head?"

I said, "Kate, we have to go deeper into things. This is getting very complicated."

She took no notice. "We talked about being together. That's all we talked about. Here's what we agreed. If he can be sure of getting a letter to me, he'll write and tell me where he is, and where he's going next. Though it mightn't get past the censor."

Now my heart began to weigh heavier. She was never going to accept that he wasn't coming back.

"And if the war starts cleaning up France and Belgium—it'll be safe to meet him there. He was thrilled that I was prepared to go and see him, because he can't always get to Kenmare. And you'll come with me, Ben, won't you?"

She had a shine to her as she said this, a glow not unlike somebody in a prayer ecstasy, and when she put it to me like that, I saw my own full picture—which told me that I'd have gone anywhere with her, done anything for her.

She had one last thing to say.

"And we agreed something wonderful, Charles and me. You saw how chaotic things can get. So, if by any chance the war cuts us off from each other, I'm to wait at home in Kenmare. Then, when the troops are returning to the United States, I'm to go and meet him at the boat. If I miss him there, it'll probably be because he's maybe wounded or tied up on official business or something. So I'm to find the very center of America, which is in the state of Kansas, and wait for him. He told me it's a place named Lebanon. God fits the back for the Burden."

80

That evening, over dinner, much of her vivacity had returned. She played with me, and grew serious with me, and played with me again.

I would like to argue that I saw desperation in this behavior, an artificial gaiety—but I can't say that. By a swing of mood as wide as the sun's crossing of the sky, she had become again the woman I'd first met on her knees keeping ants out of her kitchen. She didn't look like somebody grappling with a dreadful loss. Nor had she let the glue of mourning cling to her. Above all, this did not look like a young widow who needed more bravery than she knew was to be had in the world.

Alone in my room later, I tried to make sense of it. If a colonel among our American custodians could insist—and from, it seemed, official knowledge—that Captain Miller had been assassinated by a German infiltrator in a sanitarium at—what was the town? Fauville?—how could that not be true? He'd been handed a report. He'd have seen lists. And he seemed to own the information, be convinced of it. Not only that, he knew Miller, disliked him even. "Killer Miller," he'd called him. How could he, Colonel Mike Morrigan, have got it wrong?

Also, and this troubled me almost more, Morrigan questioned Miller's origins. "He's not from Kansas." How much of Miller's story, his identity even, might be false? I reasoned, *He must have had to give his real name for the wedding ceremony, show some papers. Although in wartime anything goes, doesn't it?*

I came down to one conclusive thought: *This is over. Miss Begley, when she's been back at Lamb's Head a few weeks, or maybe months, she'll receive one of those awful telegrams. Or a letter from her new friend at the embassy. Can I be there to cushion her blow? I need advice.*

81

James Clare, in his long black coat, had infinite wisdom and country-wide renown. His Folklore Commission reports became famous, a national treasure. He used a particular type of pen, the kind favored by nineteenth-century schoolmasters, and a black ink more commonly seen in music notation.

Every corner of the country, and each one of the islands, had seen James Clare, with his bicycle and his gleaming black leather document cases. In all weathers, he journeyed to all parishes, following a regimen as organized as a military campaign, yet seemingly as relaxed as a gentleman.

"I have only one clock," he liked to say, "that smiling man up in the sky," and indeed he lived by the sun—and the moon, and the stars, and the rotation of the earth, every tremor of which I'm certain he felt. His was the kind of character that I most admire; he was a generous and steady man.

He tried to make me steady too. Whatever his declared reliance on the orbits of the solar system (and I suspect that it was somewhat pretended, uttered more for the poetry than the veracity), he insisted that I note down my daily rising and retiring times. I also had to keep a record of the weather, the food I consumed, and the times of my meals, the mileage covered, the number of days spent in a neighborhood, the enthusiasm of the people for the tales they told me, their general health, the mood of the house, and the level of their comfort.

Not only did he instruct me in building the content of my daily record, he drilled into me the necessity of pristine form.

"You can always tell a good craftsman," he used to say, "by the way he keeps his tools. They'll be neat and clean and always near to hand. A drudgy fellow will scatter them all over the place."

And he supervised me by inspecting my notebooks, my pens, my erasers. He taught me the system of taking down the original site notes in pencil, then transcribing and expanding them in ink. When I asked the obvious question, he answered, "Because you'll have made a deliberate effort to establish something permanent."

To hear James recount one of the thousands of stories he had collected amounted to a theatrical experience. He had a deep open voice, and the broad simple accent of west County Clare.

I asked him once, "James, what's the shortest tale you ever collected?"

Not for a second did he have to pause.

"A man in Clifden told me how dolphins came about. You know how sweet they are, with a kind nature and always ready to help or play. Well, this man's great-great-great-great-granduncle, gentle of temperament and playful of nature, fell in love with a female seal back at Rosses Point. He'd go down to the water every day, and the girl seal would swim closer. One day she seemed very lonely, and when he spoke to her, he found that he could interpret her barks, and she was asking him, this young man, to come and live with her people.

"So he said good-bye to all his family—who had always considered him a bit strange—returned to the shore, and threw himself into the ocean. As he hit the water, hundreds of seals popped up their little heads, and with big smiles they surrounded him, and he swam with them out to sea and never came back. And when, some years later, people along that coast saw dolphins for the first time, they recognized this boy's gentle smile, and they knew what had happened. He had married his seal and the dolphins were their children."

I believed every word, as did anybody who listened to James.

He was a wonderful man. I could ask James any question, and I'd get a decent attempt at a useful answer.

James, I met a man in Ballinrobe, and I think he's making up the stories he's telling me.

And James said, "Record the tale anyway, but make a note that it might be an invention rather than an inheritance. In its own time it'll belong to the literature of the country. Because that man had to get it from somewhere. Maybe the wind told it to him. Or he heard a whisper from the river."

James, there's a widow in County Monaghan who keeps asking me to come and stay in her house, and she wants to buy me clothes and give me money. What'll I do?

And James said, "Treat her with the utmost kindness and the good manners of a gentleman, and that behavior will give you the distance you need to keep from her."

James, do you think that Venetia—and you knew her, and you liked her so much, and you were so kind to her—do you think she's still alive?

And James said, "Let the world tell you that. Let Time bring you that information. And be sure of this—whatever it turns out to be, you'll not guess the circumstances accurately."

Now I wondered what he'd say when I asked him, *James, I want to help my friend, even though I'm sure her husband is dead, but I'm afraid that if she goes looking for him, she'll be killed or maimed. And so might I.*

The Folklore Commission confirmed for me that James was indeed staying in Dublin; his respiratory problems had cut him down again. That, however, meant that I got two birds with one stone—he was without question staying with my beloved friend, Miss Dora Fay. She, a woman of great intellect and learning, taught me—among so many things—generosity of spirit, and how to identify people worth valuing.

When the Disappearance first caved in on me, when I didn't know whether it was Tuesday or Easter, Miss Fay rescued me, kept me in her house, gave me absorbing tasks to do—saved me. She knew when to let me weep and when not; she knew when to feed me and to leave me alone. Where and how she herself acquired those gifts I cannot say.

———

The two of them had been expecting me; they always seemed to know when I was arriving. James was more ill than I wished to see, but I also knew his resilience. Miss Fay had been making (and tasting) black-berry jam, and had a purple halo around her mouth that made her look Egyptian—doubly bizarre in a woman with very prominent teeth, and who never wore cosmetics of any color. With her high steps she looked more than ever like a heron or an emu as she walked back and forth across the kitchen floor.

I told them what amounts to the story I've written for you so far. They applauded Neddy the Drover and his rented teeth, and they worried whether Miss Mangan would bully him. They marveled at Claudia, the matchmaker of the Ritz Hotel—and they hushed like rapt children when I talked about Miss Begley.

James had known her father.

"Has she brown eyes?" he asked me.

I said, "She surely has."

"And is she as brave as a charioteer?"—one of his favorite expressions; I'd heard him use it many times, but never had it fitted so well.

"That's exactly what she's like," I said. "She thrusts forward into the world without fear—but I know she's afraid to her stomach."

"Her father's name was Florence or Flor Begley, and he was the most mourned man to die on that coast in a century," said James. "Everybody loved him. And the mother was by all accounts a beauty."

Miss Fay, who, for all her perfect English, loved slang, said, "I want to zero in on Captain Miller. What's he like? If the present tense still applies."

I told them my fears—the Kansas and Pennsylvania contradiction, the neck wound, the kidnapping of poor Herr Seefeld, and the terrifying nickname, "Killer" Miller.

They fell silent. Not a word. I, as they had taught me to do, let the silence hang. The wisdom would descend with their first remarks.

Miss Fay said, "You must of course help your dear friend."

And James Clare said, "Take care, if you can, to get killed rather than maimed. But be sure to fill in your journal as much as possible."

Thus was I committed; that was my "interlude." I told James of my intentions, and he agreed to arrange my time off with the Folklore Commission. I also told him of my interest in the wolf legend, and he promised to try to locate the tale's teller for me.

And so, after two days with my spiritual parents, and then ten days with my blood parents—during which I again told them nothing of my adventures—I returned to the world of Miss Begley.

82

October 1944

What did I find? If I expected water, I found blood. If I expected a soft breath, I found a gale. If I expected a mourner, I found a dervish.

I had sent her a telegram. A wind off the sea made my face fresh. She, sharp as ever, heard me come up the lane and rushed out. Her embrace contained as much relief as affection.

"Come in, I'm alone. You're so good. I knew you'd do this."

"How are you, Kate?"

"Look, Ben," she said. She grabbed my hand and dragged me through the doorway. "This is what I've been doing."

"Where's your grandmother?"

"She goes away this time every year. Friends in Cork."

Standing at the kitchen wall, she showed me her work. Against cold winds some of those old houses had rough wainscoting that reached almost up to the roof. To these planks she'd pinned a series of newspaper headlines, culled from many sources, detailing the progress of the Allies through France.

On the table beneath sat a pile of newspaper and magazine clippings, again from many sources; and on the floor stood a high stack of books—military history, war strategies, campaigns.

"I'm acquainting myself with everything that's going on," she said. "And I have a good idea of where Charles might be."

In a grave in Normandy, I thought. *Or a plain pine box, awaiting burial with all the other thousands of fallen men.*

"Oh, and I've heard from the American embassy. They've put out an inquiry to see if they can locate him, and they promise to come back to me."

I held up my hands, as though to ward off things. "Kate—what's going on?"

She retreated a little. "I knew you'd jib."

"You're planning to go and look for him, aren't you? Are you a lunatic?"

Tears came to her eyes. She turned away, and I watched her shoulders make the effort to gain composure. When she was ready, she turned back.

"I didn't tell you this," she said. "Charles and I made a pact."

"What kind of pact? Another of your deals?"

"He told me." She stopped, in difficulty, then forged on again. "He told me—that I'd hear all kinds of things about him. He told me to ignore each and every thing I heard. He said, 'You and I, we're a team now, Kate. You're my platoon leader. Of the rest of my life. No matter what you hear—come looking for me. Think about it carefully, take your time, and come for me. You'll find me. I know you will.' And that's what I'm doing, Ben."

I never saw such force. And she saw my slump of acquiescence.

Refreshed by her confession, she grew as enthused as a good teacher. "I'm up and running here. We'll have to do this ourselves. Given the special nature of Charles's duties, I figured that they're never going to tell me where he is."

On the train to Killarney, on the bus to Kenmare, on the long ride to Lamb's Head, I'd been reflecting. *I must become the safety net, the great mattress, that gives her a soft landing when the truth brings her down.*

Now, though, because she had invoked the pact they'd made, her denial of his death had set in stone. Only if the U.S. Army brought Captain Charles Miller's corpse to the red door of that cottage and asked her to identify the body—only then would she believe him dead. Fingers in the wounds of his feet; a hand in the gash at his side—Doubting Thomas was gullible compared to Mrs. Charles Miller.

So I worked out my own strategy—go along with her belief, never challenge it, and when the blow came, my arms would be held out to catch her when she fell.

She, though, steamed on. "So," she concluded, "I've been analyzing how war works."

And how does war work, my dear? said my keeper and guardian, and out of kindness to my friend I stifled him. I didn't need to say a word.

"This is what will have happened," she said, and like a general briefing his officers she pointed to the wall, and the newspaper clippings and the maps. "With the Allied gains in Normandy, they'll have begun the push toward the German border." She had even begun to sound military. "Now Charles will—this is my guess—have gone ahead, and he'll have crossed from France into either Germany or Belgium. I've asked the American embassy to confirm whether such a move would be typical of their Special Operations people in this war, and I'm expecting their reply any day now."

Oh, yes, and you'll surely get an answer to that little inquiry.

I had a question; I dreaded to ask it, but couldn't avoid doing so. "Have you tried your pendulum?"

She said, "Come with me," and marched me to her bedroom.

On the little table beside her bed sat her pincushion; on the floor lay a great map of Europe.

"Every morning when I get up, I concentrate on this."

Her zeal reminded me of a missionary whom I'd once seen in County Donegal. A firebrand Presbyterian, he'd ventured across the border and was preaching gospels at the people in the street of Ballybay like a vandal hurling stones.

"Have you had any result?" I asked.

She shook her head. "Nothing yet. That usually means somebody is traveling."

Or dead, I thought.

"But I may not have looked widely enough," she said. "It's a huge area."

There and then I did something that I've tried to train myself not to do—I embarked upon an act of potential self-destruction.

"One day perhaps," I said, and I sounded a little tentative, "you might use your pendulum on my behalf."

"Oh!" She clapped her hands. "I forgot. I meant to. I'll do it now. It'll let me pay you back. All you do for me. Ben, of course I will. Do you have something that"—she paused, seeking the delicate phrase—"that was touched?"

"I have a lock of her hair," I said. As I'd always had, from the first night we spent together, a night that I'd so often replayed—with all the others—like a film that only I could see.

Straightaway, I regretted what I'd done. Miss Begley took the little silk purse from me. Soft as a cat's paw, she drew out the lock of hair. I tried not to look, but couldn't manage that.

"My God above in Heaven," said Miss Begley. "Did she wear the whole moon on her head?"

In truth I had forgotten that glowing light, that silver blond color, and it had been a long time since I'd opened the purse.

"I suppose we should begin with Ireland," Miss Begley said.

She spread the atlas on the bed and found the appropriate page. The room grew so still that I could hear the sea beneath us. So hushed I could hear the distant call of the kittiwake, a bird that frequents those coasts. So quiet that I heard the peat shift in the kitchen fire.

Using her very slow and simple up-and-down method, Miss Begley scanned the map of Ireland, from Donegal down to the tip of west Kerry, from the coast of north Antrim down to the Saltee Islands off the Wexford coast in the southeast. Along those lines and at no point in between did the pendulum once halt or quiver.

"She's not in this country," she murmured, so softly that I had to ask what she'd said.

Now she turned to Europe. She began with Scandinavia; no surprises; I hadn't expected any.

"Avoid the war," I suggested, and we covered Spain and Portugal. The fruitlessness, the deadness of the needle, began to bore into my brain.

"Europe is the least likely," I said. "There's nowhere she'd have felt safe. What about America?"

I'd been told that Sarah Kelly, my mother-in-law, had boarded a liner for the United States not long after Venetia's disappearance. My own mother had mentioned America—not exactly a pinpoint; and some other gossip had long ago said Florida. Did I dare suggest Florida? No. I lay back, then stood and walked around.

"Do I want to go on with this?" I asked myself, and didn't realize that I'd spoken aloud.

Miss Begley said, "A pain endured is an inch grown."

I spun around to look at her—because she hadn't spoken claptrap for such a long time.

She climbed from the bed and walked to me. I, stretching, had my hands on my head, and she wrapped her arms around my body so tight that I could think of nothing.

I said, "We'll drop it."

"Whatever you like, Ben." She gave me an extra squeeze and turned to putting all her maps away.

We ate supper. For long intervals we said nothing. She played with her hair a great deal, and every time we caught each other's eye she smiled at me as though I were the most important man in the world.

83

Next morning, I joined forces with her in earnest. Together we set out a list of information that we needed, and its possible sources. I rode my bicycle down into Kenmare and returned with every newspaper that I could buy. At the library I searched for any and every book about war that she hadn't already taken out.

Were we crazy? I thought so—but what was the alternative? Faced with her drive, I had to either help or go away. I tried to think my position through—I was assisting in the search for somebody whom I believed dead, and I had a strong belief that all the inquiries Miss Begley was making, or was about to make, would either confirm that fact or lead her down long roads to nowhere.

A thought ran through my mind like one of those songs that you can't shake off: *Who could be better qualified for such a task? Haven't I spent a dozen years searching?*

We approached it in a disciplined way. At my suggestion, we entered in a large notebook various snippets of information about the fighting in France. I, the eater of newspapers, tracked every paragraph on the Allied advance.

Four sessions of three hours, fifteen-minute breaks—we worked from eight o'clock in the morning until ten o'clock at night. In the last effort of every day we compared notes, and then tried to assess whether we'd advanced our knowledge of the war to any purpose.

But we were amateurs, butterflies alighting on this vast burning tree. I joined in her assumptions—that Captain Miller had worked forward from Fauville in the Allied push. We agreed that he could have gone anywhere; up northwest to the Belgian border or due east to wait for the American troops slamming up from the south of France. If fit enough, he might even, in disguise, have reached Berlin by now, to run some kind of deadly work there. Who knew?

Actually—one man might. And I suggested his name.

Miss Begley "eyebrowed" me, that "lawyer's look," as I called it, and I said, in something of a hurry, "Why don't I go and talk to him?"

"I'll do it," she said.

"Let me."

She frowned. "Why do you think I shouldn't?"

"He might be afraid of Charles."

She said, "But Charles is a sweetheart."

"I still think," I said, "that it might be better if you let me do it."

"Ben, it's my husband we're looking for."

"But suppose you learn something about the kind of work Charles does in the army?" I was training myself to remain in the present tense.

"You mean that he's an assassin? Oh, he told me that ages ago."

"Will you tell Mr. Seefeld that you're married?"

And she said, airy as a sprite, "I'll tell him I've found a wife for Charles."

"Then he'll want to marry you," I said.

She replied, "I can handle Mr. Seefeld."

As you did before, I thought, and surprised myself at the bitterness of my jealousy.

84

By mid-October, the Allies had liberated much of France—but the German armies had shocked the world with the ferocity of their retreat. Initially, as the *maquisards* had done in the south, the Germans used the terrain to their advantage. The rich farms along the coast of northern France had been fenced for centuries by tall, tough hedgerows, and the Allied troops found these medieval bocages unfamiliar and impenetrable.

When the fighting moved inland, the Germans, directed from Berlin, and led by some of the best soldiers the world had ever seen, defended as though attacking. The Allies experienced many, many days in which they took two steps forward and one step back. And often one and a half steps back. And sometimes two. And days came when they took three steps back, thrown into reverse by massive German infantry and air bombardments. That's what we'd run into in the little town near Dieppe.

Viewed from neutral Ireland all of this might as well have been a drama of the silver screen. The newsreels in the cities, though, didn't make it to the country towns for weeks. In Killarney they showed the Normandy landings two months after the event. Those who watched the newsreels felt pleasantly knowledgeable, as though they were viewing the confirmation of what they had already ascertained from their reading. The Irish newspapers, generally up-to-date, also seemed to tell the war from the German point of view, too. Neutrality might yet be our guide.

85

Mr. Seefeld beamed at us like the moon. Miss Begley pretended to be
checking on his health and general well-being; I behaved as though collecting his lore. I'd written him a postcard, giving dates. On the second
of those, we called on him—a Sunday, at Miss Begley's suggestion: "He
has no religion."

"Kate, will you find me a wife on Lamb's Head?"

She laughed and said, "There's only my grandmother and myself."

He said, "It is not a grandmother that I wish to marry."

By now he had recovered so much that he almost had a twinkle. She
laughed again—but kept him charmed, and on a leash.

After sipping the elderberry wine that he'd made, and admiring the
four cats, and marveling at the weather, I chose to dive in.

"If you were looking for an officer in the middle of this war, where
would you look?"

He laughed. "Ben, my friend, what tricks are you doing now?"

My mind called up the picture of how frail he'd looked walking up
the jetty that morning, or standing beside me on the trawler's deck. How
had he recovered so well? Not only had he been through the trauma of
kidnapping that we'd inflicted on him, he'd been grieving for his wife—
and God knows I was familiar with that feeling.

"No tricks," I said. "There's somebody we need to find."

He asked, still smiling, "Your side or mine?"

I said, "It's somebody you know."

He knew whom I meant, and said, his face growing cold, "Don't look
for him. Let the war take him."

I saw Miss Begley wince—but only I, who knew her so well, could
have caught it. She braved the moment.

"It's kind of urgent," she said. "A girl, a local girl—she's very worried
about him."

"What do you know," I asked, "about the term *Special Operations*? That's what he does."

Mr. Seefeld looked at us. "It means that he's a bad man."

Miss Begley was about to challenge that; my glance stopped her, and I asked, "What's the equivalent in your army?"

He said, "Our problem was that we didn't have enough of them. Where we did—it worked perfectly."

"Explain," I said, and he settled to the task.

"In many places all over Europe, especially at the beginning of the war, when we feared great local opposition, we sent in officers dressed as businessmen or clergy or whatever might be acceptable. They went into a local community and organized support for us."

Miss Begley asked, "How efficiently did that work?"

"We fomented attacks against the police in France. We assassinated local leaders who might have led resistance to us."

I said, "Is that what Captain Miller does?"

Mr. Seefeld reflected. "I'd say—no. If I were to guess, I'd say he's deep behind our lines, German lines, that is."

"As far as Berlin?" I asked.

"No, not that far." And all the while my brain is saying to me, *He's in a war cemetery in France, not far from the city of Rouen, that's the fact.* Followed by the thought: *But we're not dealing with real facts, are we? We're handling blind faith.*

Miss Begley said, "How much do you know about the kind of work Captain Miller is doing?"

"We used to call our fellows 'the wolves,' " said Mr. Seefeld. "But Miller doesn't belong in a pack."

I said, my mind in a shudder, "Why wolves?"

"The fear. Everybody fears wolves. They're silent. They kill."

I was about to say, "That isn't always true," but Mr. Seefeld continued. "I asked Miller about his work. Do you know what he said? Nothing. He said nothing. When I asked him what his work was, he just laughed and did this." Mr. Seefeld clutched his hand to his throat and made strangling noises.

Miss Begley pressed. "Where would you search for him?"

"In Hell," said Mr. Seefeld.

I, laughing to reduce the sting, said, "No—where would one look seriously?"

He left the room and came back with a map of Europe; it bore all kinds of marks; he'd been following the war as closely as we had.

"Look here," he said, and drew with his finger a line that ran northeast, from Paris to Berlin. He circled Liège, in Belgium.

"That's where the worst fighting will be," he said, "my country's last stand." He shuddered. "I don't know why any of this happened. I don't know. I don't know anything," and he began to cry, a man still in shock.

Miss Begley jumped from her chair. "Hans!"

Now he flooded, boo-hooing like a boy. I had no idea what to do.

"Come on," she said. "You and me'll go for a little walk," and she eyebrowed me behind his back.

I sat and talked to the cats. And looked at his map. And retraced his line. And that part of me in which I'd been holding on to some doubts or hopes filled up with the deadweight of premonition, because I knew what was going to happen—we would soon be traveling.

That night, she took out her pendulum—as I'd expected she would do. She concentrated on Liège. It took some time, and after a faint tremor the needle began to swing over an area southeast of Liège, close to the German border. It didn't pinpoint any one place to her satisfaction, and she said that she'd try again.

We spent another week at Lamb's Head. From my next visit to the library I returned with travel guides to northern Germany and Belgium. On their walk together, Miss Begley had elicited advice from Mr. Seefeld.

He told her, "Mirror what he's doing. Go behind the lines of my armies. The people you will meet are friendly to the Irish. He will be among them, or they will know or suspect something. He will be meeting German resistance, they are under very deep cover, or he will be trying to connect with the German forces by pretending to be a sympathizer."

"With his accent?" she queried

Mr. Seefeld replied, "He will have said that he lived in America for some years. His false papers will show that."

When she told me this, I said, "But if we're captured?"

She said, "He told me to ask the Americans for protection."

"But we're not going in with the Allies?" I said, my mind's voice a shriek.

This was just getting worse and worse. I prayed for the KILLED IN ACTION telegram to arrive, and then felt guilty. She sensed my anguish and appeased it by agreeing to go back to the American embassy. *That's where the truth will catch up with her,* I thought. Followed by the realization, *But will she show any regard for it?*

86

In the second week of November, we waved good-bye to Mrs. Holst— who approved every step her granddaughter was taking. Her only disaffection showed when she saw or listened to me. We didn't have a confrontation; no matter how she goaded me, I played for peace; I had enough friction going on in my head.

When Mrs. Holst had come back from Cork, she'd announced a curious development in her life—a proposal of marriage. It seemed preposterous to me; she was, after all, in her seventies, therefore ancient to someone my age.

Miss Begley danced at the news. "The matchmaker matched," she cried, and danced again. And I thought, *Poor bastard doesn't know what's going to hit him.*

He, the swain, was the brother of Mrs. Holst's Cork friend, and he'd also returned from the States, but quite recently. She'd never met him until a few weeks earlier; and, by all her accounts, love had swept in at first sight. *You can always sell to a salesman,* was my thought.

She said that she'd be leaving Lamb's Head "at some stage in the not-too-distant future." Mrs. Holst spoke like a strict official.

"Good news all around," sang Miss Begley. "Imagine? Two brides out of this house in one year!"

And one already a widow, I thought.

Our plan had been worked out elaborately. First Dublin, and the embassy once more. Then London, a visit to Claudia at the Ritz. And then—and this staggered me—the small port of Hull in the east of England where, through a contact of Mr. Seefeld, we could get to south Denmark or Kiel in northern Germany.

That was the day I discovered that Miss Begley kept a detailed journal. We had spent hours working out a schedule, and I said to her, "I'm going to bring a notebook and try to keep some kind of record."

She said, "I'll do the same. I can't lug my diary with me."

"What?"

She laughed at my surprise. "Of course I keep a diary. Look at the interesting things that happen to me. I might let you read it one day."

"When do you write it?"

"Like you," she said. "At night. I'm not always as diligent as you. And when we're old and gray, and you come to visit me and Charles, we'll look back over our notebooks," she said, "and wonder that we had such adventures."

At my age today, I delight myself with my own emotional vigor. When I reach into my memory, I can recall so much, down to the details of my own thoughts at any given moment, and, almost more important, my own mood. It's always been my burden—and my pleasure—to take my mood from those around me. I think it comes from having been an only child, when I couldn't help but observe my parents at very close quarters and be affected by them.

And I believe that it explains why I went along with such aplomb every time Kate Begley proposed an outlandish scheme. I picked up her energy, her vivacity, her life force—and I needed all those to help me stay alive.

That is how I went into that horrible war a third and final time. I even found in myself noble feelings about it—principally because James Clare had told me once, "In all great legends, the important things happen three times."

87

Yet, I know that we faked the lightness in our hearts. There were even moments when I tried to seem like a holidaymaker. We'd hired a hackney car with a good pony, and he took us to Killarney—where we shopped for some personal needs. A chemist who knew Miss Begley kindly gave me extra razor blades, and apologized to us for the quality of the rationed soap.

I went to the bank and inquired about money. They raised eyebrows when I said I wanted German marks. An order was placed that I would collect in Dublin. "Take some American dollars," they told me. "That's what the international financiers are saying."

We stayed at Mrs. Cooper's; she and Miss Begley liked each other, and mutually knew wide circles of people. Much of the later evening was spent in trying to render our luggage as efficient as possible. We had so overpacked that we had to leave a suitcase—containing possessions from both of us—in Mrs. Cooper's care. I joked to her that if we never came back she could sell the things and go on a spree. I don't think the joke went down well with Miss Begley.

Here's the first entry from Kate's new notebook, made that night.

12 November 1944: Ben usually lodges in this house when coming through Killarney. I think she's the Mrs. Cooper whose husband got drunk, and staggered into no-man's-land during the last war, and was shot. Nana told me that story. I'm so excited that Nana's getting married. Charles will be delighted too—he loves her. I know that Ben's trying to tell me we have tough days ahead and I respect him for that. But my excitement will carry me through, and I'll try not to worry as to Charles's health.

And here's my own earliest note from that last, awful foray, during which all my views about life, liberty, the pursuit of happiness, and every other damn thing in the world were scuttled.

13 November 1944: The morning train was empty, and the guard joked about whether we'd have enough fuel to get us to Dublin. Miss B. doesn't like jokes that threaten our plans. People who see us together assume that we're married. Miss Begley, showing no tact toward me, corrected a lady, "No, I'm the one who's married." And I thought with a huge sadness, "Oh, but I am married." And then asked myself, "But am I? What an irony is all this. She's searching for somebody I know is dead and I'm searching for—what?" I can't actually say, because I can't actually put down on paper what I believe about Venetia anymore.

88

While I think of it, I'll include here a selection of entries from our separate journals (with commentary now and then from me) because I believe that they have the value of greater immediacy than my simple reminiscence. So that you know what to expect, they take the story right up to the moment when circumstances prevented us from taking notes.

You'll ask yourself as you read them, "How in the name of God did they preserve those diaries?" Well, I'll take the credit for that. No matter what happens in a war, people on the move have to have clothes, and there came a moment when I took over the custody of the notebooks. When, eventually, I told James this, he smiled and said, "I trained you well."

13 November 1944: I love train journeys. Ben is a good traveling companion. He's such a peaceful man to be with. And I like to be seen with him, given the way girls look at him. If I hadn't met Charles— would I have wanted to marry Ben? Maybe, provided I could knock the sadness out of him. He's a lot better now. He doesn't mope as much. Why doesn't Nana like him? And she surely doesn't! She keeps nagging me about him, says that there's a volcano in him. Tonight, we're in the Wicklow Hotel and tomorrow we go to the embassy again.

14 November 1944: In the Wicklow Hotel. I'm exhausted. How does KB do it? How does she produce so much energy? And the charm that goes with it? That man in the embassy would do anything for her. We weren't supposed to hear a fraction of what he told us—he seemed to have forgotten war censorship. I'm too tired to write up in detail what happened today.

14 November 1944: Ben was so startled to wake up and find me in his bed! I wanted him to have company in the night. He looked so scared when they told us at the embassy that we can become part of the American war effort. They'll let Ben drive an ambulance in France. I can be his assistant. This is the best news. I don't think Ben can face it, but I can give him the courage, I know that. He's brave in himself, he just doesn't know it. Tomorrow night we leave on the boat for England. I'm looking forward to seeing Claudia again. Sent Nana a card. I think Bob (Nana's man-friend) will call to see her, now that he knows I'm not there.

Thursday morning, 16 November 1944: Slept badly, but was able to catch up on the newspapers. KB is singing in the room next door while mighty battles are being fought in eastern France. I hadn't imagined that the Americans could drive up from Italy so fast. If the little maps in the newspapers are right, they'll be in Germany within a week or two. Wouldn't that be our best policy—to wait until that happens? Then we could have the best of both worlds—be safe with the Americans, yet able to ask questions of the ordinary German people? She won't agree. I wish I knew what to do.

Later (Thursday afternoon): Miss B. is shopping; I'm waiting for her in the lounge of the hotel. We sail tonight, and I'm not too comfortable now with our plan. To judge from the news reports, Europe is going through awful turmoil, and we have no business going into that kind of scene. We've already been near shells and machine guns, and it got us nowhere. This is a wild-goose chase—to find a dead man.

Thursday, 16 November 1944: Night on the boat from Dublin; the sea is calm. Ben isn't. I don't think he's speaking to me. He says he has no faith in this mission. I've told him that to be a friend you must have faith. He got very cross with me and wanted not to get on the boat. He says that he will only come as far as London. He says that we have to go—"have to" emphatically—to the American embassy in London. I say, "Why?" And he says, "Because." I say, "Because what?" And he says, "Just—because" (which is no sort of grown-up answer). Now I'm the one who's afraid. But I'm not going to let him see that.

Thursday, 16 November 1944: The Irish Sea is v. rough; I'm feeling sick. Not a bother on KB. She sails blithely on. I'm going to confront her; I have to. I'm going to say, Look, Charles isn't with the American forces, and he's not behind enemy lines. Charles was assassinated in Fauville. When will I do it? On the train? Or should I do it before we disembark so that we can just stay on the boat and go back home?

Later: 4 A.M. I knew she wasn't sleeping either, so I suggested (an hour ago) that we stand on the deck and enjoy the air. Stars everywhere, and a whipping breeze that would scrub the face of the moon. I said my say. "Charles will not come back," I said. "They told me in France that they had no doubt. Why don't we go home and leave it at that? Have a Mass said for him. Pray for him." I thought that would soften the blow. It needed to—literally. She slapped me on the face. The few other people taking the night air looked around. She walked away.

Thursday, 16 November 1944—or is it now Friday morning?: A beautiful night. Lots of stars. A pleasant breeze. Ben has been very agitated. And stupid. He's behaving as though I don't know what went on in France, what the Americans said. What he doesn't know is the strength of my instinct. And it tells me that Charles is not only alive but well. I've given Ben a good talking-to.

Saturday, 18 November 1944: KB still not speaking to me. Claudia not at Ritz Hotel, won't be back until Monday. Are we waiting until then? KB won't say. She seems distressed, won't answer my questions.

89

In London on that November Sunday, as you may suspect from the journal entries, we saw nothing of each other. Around lunchtime I knocked at her door and waited; she slid a note out underneath; it rustled at my toe cap: GO AWAY.

I turned the note around and scrawled on the back of it, "I will. I'm going back home." Then I left the hotel and walked for miles, utterly confused about everything. In the weeks to come I would recall that walk as peaceful, a haven, a small paradise.

Of course I didn't go back home, because I'd given my word. As I walked, I brought myself around to catch the breeze of optimism, despite the ruined streets. A curious note in the newspapers over lunch triggered it: MANY IRISHMEN NOW ENLISTING IN BRITISH FORCES. What was their thinking? To get in at the end because victory must soon come?

My own *war effort*—I used the term mockingly—didn't seem nearly as grave as the sacrifice they were making. Or, second thoughts, was it a sacrifice at all? An army in retreat attracts increasing enmity—everybody wants to kick the dying man.

Not that you could tell the Germans felt weak. Their military spokesman, General Dittmar, had been quoted as preparing to counterattack in Holland and Belgium.

"We stand at the interval between the stage of thinly manned fronts and a new phase of the war. The outlook remains hopeful in view of the means of war, some of which are already in use and some in preparation."

By "already in use" he meant, I assumed, the V1 and V2 rockets that had been falling on England, and which therefore might now kill us in London.

I read General Dittmar's statement with further confusion. He was the official spokesman for the German High Command. Whom can one believe? Are "we" winning? Certainly the maps show the German fall-back—and now I learned on the same page that the Allies had taken the town of Metz, close to the German border. Also, Stalin, coming in from the east, was at the gates of Budapest.

When I folded the newspaper and went to finish my mug of tea, I found my hands shaking. Oddly, our neutrality calmed me. I began to focus on the word and think what it meant. The political fact of our Irish leaders not wanting us to get bombed had little to do with this idiotic es-capade on which I had embarked. Or had it? If I grew "neutral" about it, if I became less emotional, might I be of greater service? Might it not be kinder?

But oh, what a thing is a demon! Could I honestly call my feelings toward Kate Begley "neutral"? Thus ran the argument in my mind. But at least I had begun a useful debate with myself, and one based on kind-ness. It didn't do me much good.

90

Monday, 20 November 1944: Lovely to see Claudia again. She was so helpful, and gave me a letter of introduction to General Montgomery, who's with the English army in Holland, and may be moving into Belgium and would love a soldier like Charles. I said, "Wasn't he born in Ireland?" Claudia laughed and said, "Please don't mention that to him."

Claudia and I had a long talk. She told me many things about the war. Her great friend is the American ambassador in London, and she sent a letter to him while I was with her to get me introductions inside the U.S. Army too. She also showed me a report (I don't think she should have shown it to me) about Charles and his unit.

I think that Claudia has been much more involved in the war than I guessed. Ben always said that she was probably part of a secret network; Ben may be right. I wish that boy would take more credit for his cleverness. I went to the ladies' room and when I came back, Claudia was standing in front of Ben and holding both his hands.

Monday night, 20 November 1944: Hull, a town in the east of England: We are stuck in this damp hotel, to which we stumbled from the train in the pouring rain. What a day! Very early, KB dragged me to see Claudia at the Ritz Hotel, and Claudia behaved as though we were her long-lost children.

When she heard of our "mission," as she called it, she took us away from her office to a much more private set of rooms and began to talk to us. I didn't get the impression that she thought Captain Miller was dead, but, as she said, How would she know where he might be? She tried and tried to dissuade us, but no argument worked with Miss B.

I asked her how safe we would be if we found ourselves behind the German lines, and she said that we should spend time "out in the countryside among the people"—exactly the same advice as Mr. Seefeld. She said that being Irish and neutral would probably help, but if we'd like to think about it, we could also be very useful. She was going to "send some messages." I knew what that meant, and I didn't like the sound of it at all.

KB went for everything gleefully. I wonder if, deep down, she suspects that Captain Miller is dead, and wants us—or herself—to die too. Death wishes are strange things; the sanest of people can have them. And, with her rampaging sentimentality, she may want us to die in battle—but I'm not ready for that sort of sacrifice. I don't want to be here, and I don't want to go there.

Claudia asked me to come and stay with her on our way back if we're coming through London again. She believes that the war will end very soon, and perhaps after that I might like to visit her in her country home.

Tuesday, 21 November 1944: The night is as dark as can be. If I look out my window I can't see as much as a glimmer. Ben is in the next room sulking. I haven't told him about today's telegram; we are to sail on tomorrow's second tide to Bremerhaven.

Claudia has suggested that I get to a village "southwest of Bonn," she said, "because that's where the Allies will be breaking through," and she thinks it "possible that Charles would likely be working around there." I've looked at the map.

Ben is going to say, "How in the name of God are we going to get down that far?" Claudia has assured me that we will be "handed on," she calls it, "from person to person. You may have to carry some things, but it will be all right." She is such a decent woman. We'll become good friends. I've changed my mind about the English, and I now begin to like them a lot more.

PART FOUR

A Time of Wolves

91

November 1944

In the hold of the ship, I couldn't see my hand in front of my face. Then somebody clicked something and a light swung like a lantern from a legend. Great stacks of cargo in sacking permitted only narrow corridors; we walked sideways, heads low. This might have been a passage grave. *Perhaps it will become one,* I thought.

Aft, embedded in the stern, two false stacks had been built. Into one of these they fitted Miss Begley; the other took me. I had room to stand, crouch, and sit. They gave me a flashlight. Under the door they slid a white sheet of paper. As long as that stayed there, we could leave our stowaway place and walk around every two hours.

A Dutch sailor with a fantastic mustache said, "God will protect you. Our cargo is Bibles." He laughed at his own sarcasm. They had been carrying Bibles all through the war, into Holland and Germany and Scandinavia; they're printed in the east of England. I now know that the Bibles contained messages for resistance groups all over Europe.

We sailed on Wednesday afternoon. As instructed, we remained in our "lockers," they called them, until we heard three quick toots on the ship's foghorn. I was first out—and regretted it. Within minutes, my forehead went clammy and my eyes began to swim.

Seasickness was invented by Satan's teacher. I went above to heave over the rail. The Able-Bodied Mustache ran at me. "No-no. Nobody knows, nobody knows you're here." The mustache made him hiss like a gander.

He took me back below. "Use the bilges," he said. "If you fear the smell, use the aft bilges. This ship is modern, we have bilges in the holds too, they drain out here."

At that moment, the ship heaved as though struck. I almost screamed. She heaved again, and took what I thought a heavy blow on the hull near where I stood.

"Sandbanks," said Able-Bodied Mustache. "Rough here."

The night blew up into a catastrophe of weather, pounding waves, and seasickness. Miss Begley emerged once or twice, hale as day and mildly impatient.

"I can't write my notebook," she said—her first words to me in several days. "But Liberty in every blow, let us Do or Die. Things will soon be easier."

I returned to my locker and, some undetermined time later, woke up amazed that I had slept. It took a moment or two to understand that the ship wasn't moving. The white paper had gone from beneath the door. Not a light to be seen; not a sound in the hold.

Above, heavy boots trod. Were we being boarded? Would men with prods and guns come down looking for nefarious matter?

I learned later that we'd met no trouble; the pilot had come aboard.

92

On the corner stood a tobacco shop, a large window on each side, one of which carried handwritten cards, local notices, advertisements, funny drawings of a brass band. In the other window stood tall ceramic jars from exotic lands beside racks of pipes, some beautiful, some carved with ugly, jocose faces. I went in, not to buy tobacco (though I asked for a box of matches), but to take the temperature of Bremen.

The tobacconist, tall as a flagpole, and not a blade of hair, asked something in German. I held out a gesture of incompetence. He switched to English.

"You are Scottish?"

When I disabused him, he smiled and said, "Ah, the Irish. Many jokes. And big, *big*"—he made a drinking gesture.

I admired his shop. He reached under the counter into an unseen drawer and drew out a gorgeous, mahogany box.

"See?"

He opened the lid like a man at a ceremony. Resting on burgundy velvet cushions sat two curved pipes, as creamy as wealth.

"Meerschaum," he said. "The very best." Like bleached little pigs they spooned up to each other, their amber collars catching the light. "I do not want them bombed. This war"—and he cut loose.

"If only the generals would listen to our Führer. But they won't. The Führer, he would not have us in the pickle we are now."

I said, "Who do you think is winning?"

He said, "We've been taking the bad times. But the Führer, he knows what to do."

"You yourself—have you fought?"

"I lost the leg," he said, tapping his right hip. "In the last war. I didn't want to lose the other. Or anything else off me."

"Herr Hitler—what kind of man is he?"

The tobacconist looked down at me; he must have been six foot six. Not so much a flagpole as a lighthouse, with his bald shiny head and the beam of his green, watery eyes.

"He is being the savior. They cheat us at the last war. We would won. And they take everything from us. We are treated the dirt. Even though we are stronger. When the war goes away—*pouf*! All we had—it is all the dirt. The Führer, he have us get back what we owned, have us get back our pride. He is the God. There is no other."

"A powerful leader. We have one too in Ireland."

He showed no interest. "But—" He waxed. "The leaders with him. They are such men too. They are handsome. And great. Poor Heydrich, the genius of them all, and the anarchist kill him. And we have Herr Rommel, my own very the hero. Their wonderful uniforms."

"Is Germany safe now? I mean, safe to travel."

"For you, *mein Herr*—we love Irish. Is your papers good?"

I showed him my passport; he scrutinized it like a balance sheet. Then he stood to attention like the old soldier that he was.

"*Mein Herr,* it is our honor that you visit us. To come here in war, that tells you like us."

He refused payment for the matches; he gave me two boxes—in wartime, a singular compliment.

Monday, 27 November 1944: Noon; I sit at the kitchen table in this little house in some German village somewhere; KB prowls, restless. I haven't seen her so anxious for some time. A man came to the door; we leave here at three.

Monday, 27 November 1944: Later we go south, and I know, I know that I draw nearer to Charles. Ben reports that the streets are quiet and ordinary. He met a German gentleman who gave him a different view of the war. Our driver will be here in one hour. I am packed and ready to go.

Tuesday, 28 November 1944: Late night; not a roadblock yesterday or today. Not a trace of war. We saw planes once, flying east. In a village, ten military trucks stood parked by the railroad station. And that was all. We stayed last night in a small town called Visbek. Nobody met us. Food waited on the kitchen table. The beds upstairs felt surprisingly dry in such a cold house. The rooms contain almost no furniture. To-morrow, we will be picked up at eight and taken to the next staging post. It's to be a very long drive, "more than all day," the man told KB. She gets more and more excited.

93

December 1944

On a quiet road somewhere, as we stretched our legs and relieved our-selves in the woodland, a new driver took over, the strong, silent type; he wore blue dungarees. Many hours south of there, another driver in an-other van took over from him, a man old as my father.

He tried to give me a gun: I handed it back. He froze me for a moment. I thought he might attack, but he laughed.

When they finally put us down, we'd come to a village deep in farming country, where a furtive man met us. Our "cover," he told us, in excellent English, was that of my job; I would take notes of German rural life in time of war. The local authorities had been informed by the university at Bonn that I was there under a grant from them, in association with the Folklore Commission back in Dublin.

Somebody, somewhere, had been working hard. I suspected Claudia. Had I been the German police, I would have found it all very far-fetched. But the furtive man told us, "The authorities are very stupid."

Not so stupid. They wasted no time. Midafternoon, we heard the engine outside. Three men walked to the door, one in uniform, all in their fifties. *The younger ones are all at war,* I thought, as they hammered the door knocker.

Nothing friendly; they demanded our papers. One spoke perfect English; all came from the local police station.

After no more than a few minutes of questions and answers, they directed us to the large gray car outside. I had to sit beside the uniformed one, the driver; the two plainclothes detectives flanked Miss Begley; we drove with not a word.

Our journey lasted three minutes, perhaps less. We halted outside the village police station, white as a wooden church. No defensive installations of any kind could I see. *They expect to win this war,* I thought.

Grim, not discourteous, yet intent, they separated us. I saw Miss Begley disappear down a corridor; they took me to a windowless room and left me alone.

In time, the English speaker returned. He brandished my Irish passport.

"Are you a spy?"

"For whom?" I said, more reaction than answer.

"You are an official of the Irish government?" He must have lived in England, or gone to school there; he spoke better English than I did.

"I'm a folklore collector."

"So you say." This man was not holding a slack rope.

"Yes, that's what I am."

"But not in Germany? You don't even speak German."

"Miss Begley does. She's my cousin and my interpreter."

"She's married to an American officer."

I all but swallowed my tongue—how did they know that?

"Not now."

He looked at me, angry. "Eh?"

I said, "He's dead."

"How do you know?"

"She won't tell you that. I'm the one who's telling you."

"Please explain." He was one of those men who seem intelligent, sound intelligent, and are in part intelligent, but the part doesn't spread very wide or go very deep.

"I'm writing a report on matchmaking in rural communities. I'll compare it with Ireland. I made her travel. She'll do some matchmaking here, and I'll observe her."

He repeated himself with the obstinacy of all limited people. "Her husband is an American officer."

"One of your special operatives killed him," I said. "Check up on it."

"I will. Give me the details," and he pulled out his notebook, and yes, he had a little stub of a pencil, just like the Irish police.

He certainly had some knowledge because he spelled the word *Fauville* without hesitation. Twice he left the room, and on each occasion came back with documents in files, and German newspapers. Soon, he showed some relaxation with me, and said that although he would have to wait "for direct knowledge of events in Fauville," he did grasp that I couldn't otherwise have known.

I said, "She doesn't believe that her husband is dead."

He looked at me. "Haven't you told her?"

I said, being careful, "And the American embassy in Dublin gave her no comfort. None."

"So why is she here?"

"I've persuaded her—her German and French are good enough—to try her hand at matchmaking here. It will give me excellent notes. And she has this idea that if the war ends soon, she may meet her husband over here in Germany."

People who have partial intelligence will always climb on the bandwagon of a theory. Even if—perhaps especially if—it's cockeyed and half-baked.

He said, "We have a winter fair on Sunday. In the village. Your friend could set up a booth."

I nodded, rubbed my hands. "Good idea. And you will be able to see us at work. We are real," I said to him.

Nothing convinces dim people more than a bald statement of one's own authenticity.

They took us back and placed us under a kind of house arrest—but at least we could talk. Kate fretted; they'd asked her at great length about her husband; she'd answered as though he would at any moment leap through a hedge and take over the village. Somehow our two stories worked—hers the real version, and mine the fake. *What's the lesson in that?* I wondered.

And on Sunday afternoon, they took us to the village hall. We had no choice; our English-speaking detective arrived to lead us there. The detective's wife, all braids and bonhomie, would be Miss Begley's interpreter when she needed one. And I, notebook poised, would sit by, ready to make copious notes in my performance as a traveling folklore collector.

Earlier on Sunday, with a man in uniform never far behind, I took a walk through the village, past the houses of brick walls and white wood, so neat, so ordered. Policed or not, I loved being there; my mind ran free. A light sun was breaking through the overcast; the villagers had cleared pathways through the snow.

This was the land of logical thought, of measured rhythm, of people who descend from Teutonic legends—the country of Wagner and Beethoven, and of my beloved wandering men, all Latin rhymes and medieval passions, whose words so often gave me such hope. *Come sweetheart, come, dear as my heart to me, come to the room that I have made lovely for thee.*

Followed by a man who would shoot me without a second thought; watched by village eyes from behind lace curtains; voices whispering *There he is, the Irishman, the spy*—I didn't care. One of the things I learned about war is, there will come a time when nothing much seems to matter.

94

The hall seemed far too large for such a small village. Whatever its recent economy, this place had once had a rich hinterland. At the end of an aisle stood a small medieval pavilion, the kind they used in King Arthur's jousting fields. Its patched red and yellow canvas walls made a grand splash of color in the dimly lit building. How improbable could this get?

A great deal more, I felt—because I'd already seen the face of war and I knew that if their armies retreated across these fields, drawing the Allies in pursuit, the people talking and laughing in this village hall would soon undergo the same shattering kind of experience that we'd known in France. Until that occurred, they wanted to get on with their normal lives, holding their annual pre-Christmas fair. They had sideshows, and a stilt walker, and a band. "Normal life" was what they needed now, and my guess was that they wouldn't have it for long more.

The faces around us had a medieval look, some noses red with the cold, others lumpy as potatoes. We could have been in a painting by Brueghel or Averkamp. Wide smiles didn't always show perfect teeth; some hair braids shone so yellow that they might have been painted; many wore clogs.

The two detectives had collected us at the house and walked us to the lamp-lit hall. Some women saw us, detached themselves from the edge of the crowd, and came to look. They, like so many others, carried lanterns into which candles had been irretrievably fixed. And these swinging lights, all through the gathering, shone on their faces from beneath.

A man shouted something, and one of the women who came to welcome us translated for Kate, who murmured to me, "She said we've to be careful. He's telling everyone that we're spies."

I wanted to say, *Well, we certainly have been.*

The friendly woman led us here and there. Someone put in my hand a mug bearing a carved face. Hot to the touch, it smelled of apple drink, and it tasted heavenly. I hadn't tasted decent food in days. The stab of comfort and delight told me how generally frightened I'd been and how responsible I felt for the safety of my headstrong friend.

Long wooden trestles stretched down the middle of the hall. Our ladies escorted us to seats at the end of one table, and they sat by us, smiling and warm. In the distance, watching from a place by the door, stood the two detectives—and four armed men.

The women began to interrogate Kate—who told me later what she'd been asked: questions about marriage, questions about matchmaking in Ireland, questions about her grandmother, questions about the couples she'd introduced, questions about whether Irishmen made good husbands.

After perhaps fifteen minutes of this, one of the women rose from the table. Sensing a purpose to her, I watched her as best I could. She walked to the door, and I saw her talk to two of the detectives. They nodded a great deal, looked in our direction—and they left. The armed, uniformed men stayed.

Food now came to our section of the table, mountains of dumplings with potatoes, gallons of dense local beer. I drank some and my tongue felt looser.

Kate began to shine like a star. Women and girls and a few playful men came to where she sat and engaged with her. And when the beer began to kick in, the war faded from my view. But the war arrived, at first quietly and then with dreadful force.

I've long since verified everything, gone back to that village, met the survivors, asked the careful questions, and satisfied myself that what transpired at that lantern-lit feast was a true bill.

Throughout dinner, people rambled about the hall, talking to neighbors, laughing, embracing, snacking from one another's plates. A band played. Great brass sounds oompahed; light bounced on the bell of the tuba; and the band members came and went on the little stage as each took his turn to eat and drink.

When the heavy chocolate cakes began to arrive, new musicians took over, and soon we had waltzes and quicksteps. All sorts of people took to the floor, heavy with age, light on their feet. Happy with beer, I asked Kate to dance.

She whispered, "I can't. I promised Charles that I wouldn't dance with anybody until he and I had danced. And we haven't danced yet. Anyway, I have to work."

The thorough Germans: They brought her six people, three men and three women. My notebook became more than a theatrical prop, my note-taking went beyond acting; and in the interruption that you're about to see, it became a war reporter; here are the entries from that Sunday night:

I'm in a small German village not far from Bonn, not far from the Belgian border. Land not very unlike Ireland, richer, perhaps; late on a Sunday afternoon, a few weeks before Christmas 1944. Miss B. is matchmaking; but not as she does at home—here she's advising people who are looking for partners.

First Woman: Ilse—nervous, heavy; late thirties—not shy; Miss Begley and she talk; only the interpreter (whose name is Trudi) and I are permitted to listen. This exercise is, I think, to prove that we are who we claim to be.

Miss B. as ever is both expert and compassionate with Ilse. She asks Ilse, "Have you ever been in love?" and Ilse blushes; "With the schoolmaster, but that was when I was little." And Miss B. asks if Ilse has ever been in love with a man who knew she was in love with him.

Ilse says no. Nein. *Very definite about it. I look up. The detectives have come back. From a distance, they look at us—and they've brought with them a man who is obviously superior.*

Miss Begley: What kind of man do you want?

Ilse: A kind man. Who will be nice to me. Who will not speak harshly.

The police stood their distance, peering with suspicion into the little ragged pavilion. I wrote with more industry than I knew I possessed. And as I wrote, I began to observe something. I had seen traces—or so I thought—that Miss Begley had begun to grow a little wild.

Now, as I watched, she pushed her hair back with more power. The shoulders tautened. Her feet kept shifting; one moment she would tap her toes to the music of the distant band; another time, she would dig both her toe caps into the floor. Or rock her feet back and forth, heel to toe.

Most of all the hand gestures caught me; I had first seen them two nights ago—a movement from wrist to fingertip, a washing of one hand by the other—over every square inch of her skin. She did this with no great drama—quiet and slow movements, repeated and repeated. In the night I had heard her groaning, and I knew that she was doing so in her sleep. I wanted to go into her drab little room (mine was worse) and hold her as tight to me as I'd ever held Venetia.

Here's my note of what happened next.

Where there had been two chairs, now we had four. I sat a little distance away.

Miss Begley: Now, Ilse, do you know anything about two people being married to each other?

Ilse shakes her heads; Ilse giggles.

Miss Begley: It is the gold standard of life—do you know that?

Ilse looks solemn; Trudi translates, and is now melting. Miss Begley, who now has her two longest fingertips pressed like the points of spears to the temples of her forehead.

Miss Begley: I can vouch for marriage. Trudi has a little difficulty translating the word vouch. *Miss Begley waits.*

At that moment we hear a mighty roar overhead and people everywhere that I can see from the little pavilion shake their fists at the sky—the roar dies as the aircraft travel on, deep over Germany.

Miss Begley: It would be strange, wouldn't it, if I were telling you to marry, and how wonderful marriage is if I weren't married.

Ilse smiles. As does Trudi. Several yards away, the police scowl and the superior man looks at his watch. I feel a stab of fear and my stomach heaves.

Miss Begley: I met my husband one sunny afternoon when he came to my house to ask my grandmother find him a wife.

Ilse: Where is he now?

Miss Begley, smiling like an angel: Waiting for me. Would you like to hear how we met?

No surprise that Ilse—and Trudi—nodded.

Miss Begley: He came up the lane to our house—we live on a cliff

overlooking the Atlantic. The roses were in bloom beside the front
door. My grandmother was sitting outside making lace.

From overhead came another roar, longer this time, nearer, and
with greater shouting from inside the hall, wilder brandishing of fists.
Trudi spun in her chair as her husband and his colleagues advanced to
the pavilion. They too—I watch them—look upward and shake fists.
Trudi holds up her hands, palms flat out to ward off the advancing po-
licemen. They indicate that they've come for Miss Begley and me. Nat-
urally they ignore—

My report ends there—because it was then that Hell arrived. A bomb fell
near enough to the hall to shake the building and bring down part of the
roof. Twenty feet from us, dust and debris, roof tiles, beams, wall sidings
cascaded upon the people sitting and standing and eating and dancing.

How shocking it is to discover that the human body amounts to little
more than a sack of soft materials that scatter apart when torn by something of great force traveling at speed. A siding plank became a spear and
ripped open a grandmother in a black and white dress. She—or what she
had become—fell to the ground and burst open.

And how shocking are the multiple and myriad ways in which people
react to being bombed. They weep; men, women, and children weep
rivers, they weep tides. No surprise with the children; they haven't yet
learned the management of feelings. And the women have learned the
uses of tears, the positive and healing effects of crying, and they do so in
war, and seem the stronger for it. To me, though, the men's had the greatest eloquence—a rage of high, irascible wailing, and no care whatever as
to who witnessed such unmanning.

But I know why they did it—they wept at being denied the opportunity to guard and protect their loved ones. They wept because they'd
been made subject to forces so great that they had no chance of coming
to any terms. They wept because in that fell and disgraceful moment,
they had been staring into their own graves.

We don't know what dust we harbor in secret. It piles up in walls,
around the stones with which our houses are built, in the woodwork, on
the tops of closets too high too reach. When a bomb causes a building to
burst open, the dust comes billowing out like some foreign, secret cloud
that has been accumulating in there all along.

In the first billow that night it looked, from my distance, to be no more than a great puff that rose, and in a minute or so seemed to dissipate. But as I walked—I ran, I leapt—to find survivors or pull bodies from the wreckage, the dust was waiting for me, waiting to invade my thorax, to stick in my pores, to clog my hair, even my eyebrows. I found its residue billowing forth a second time next morning when I sneezed.

I never gave any help. Not a survivor did I find. They stopped me—three men stood in front of me and shooed me back. I ran and put my arms around Kate. The uniformed policemen raced to help the victims, as did one of the detectives. Their superior officer left and the remaining detective came for us. He beckoned us from the little pavilion, and then led us from the hall, never saying a word. I didn't know what to expect.

He drove us to the house in which we'd lodged.

"Collect your belongings," said the man; his glasses were speckled with dust.

Kate, her eyes flashing, said, "Can you give me until tomorrow?"

"No."

"Do you have a map of Germany that I can borrow?" Miss Begley asked.

He said, "Europe would be better."

I can't tell the name of the place to which he took us, and I've never been able to find it. He took us from that house, and that village—where another bomb fell as we were leaving—and he loaded us into the back of a large truck, where he covered us with tarpaulins and sacking and told us not to say a word. And then somebody slammed a foot down, revved the engine like a lunatic, and drove us forever.

95

I fell asleep. When I woke, nothing had changed—it was still dark. I heard Miss Begley next to me, and put out a hand to find her. Lying on her side, her back turned to me, she took my arm and wrapped it around her waist.

Soon after that, the truck stopped. We heard voices. Something outside slammed the metal just above my head. More voices. All in German, not clear enough for me to pick up a word. We drove on.

Five minutes later, the truck changed gear and slowed down. Within moments, after hefty bumping, it stopped again.

Somebody opened the rear doors. No daylight; I had lost all track of time. No flashlight either. Legs climbed in and clambered beside us. Hands pulled back the tarpaulin.

"*Raus,*" said a strange voice. I didn't know what it meant, I just followed Miss Begley's lead. Now they put us in a car, in the backseat of a luxury sedan. From outside, somebody gave us rugs and flask tops of hot coffee.

Four people in the car, and the girl beside the driver turned to look at us. "We will soon be somewhere more comfortable."

Dawn began to break; it would be a cloudless day. The car took us slowly past farmhouses, and farmyards, over postcard-perfect little bridges, up high country roads where frost glistened in pools like leftover glass. Under the rugs, Miss Begley reached for my hand.

Outside a high, red-roofed village, the car turned in to a massive gateway, where two armed men opened the tall wrought-iron gates. At the end of a dipping and swooping avenue stood a mansion with more turrets than Walt Disney ever conceived. Inside a man and woman met us without a word, took our ragged bags, and walked up the wide staircase.

The girl from the car came with us.

"Where are we?" I asked.

"Hitler did his worst here some time ago."

I said, "Eh?"

"The couple who met you. They own this house, and one of the Nazi Party commandeered it in 1938. When the owners objected, he had their tongues cut out."

I said, "Why are we here?"

"Somebody talked," said the girl.

"About us?"

"Trudi and her husband were shot yesterday. He was the detective who led you from the hall. They knew when they saw the Kommandant that there had been betrayal. Trudi's instructions were to make you safe. You were smuggled away."

"But the policeman?" I asked. "Trudi's husband?"

"Our greatest hero," she said. "He had enough dirt on everybody to blackmail the entire village and he was our leader."

On my journey of discovery years afterward, I learned the details of how the village had worked its quiet resistance to Hitler. I'm telling you now so that you can understand, while you are still relatively young, the power of ordinary people. You will, I hope, conclude that there may be no such thing as an ordinary person.

Most of those villagers did nothing dramatic, nothing showy—they paid their taxes, they lived their daily lives. If coerced into attending a Nazi Party meeting, the unbelievers sat without a word. Inside this quiet existence, they ran an undercover transport system, part of a chain bringing secrets and operatives across Europe, and inserting them behind German lines.

Until they shot Trudi and her husband in front of the white church next morning—with all the village press-ganged into witnessing the execution—they'd had no difficulty of any kind. Not even Charles Miller, who had passed through months earlier, had caused anything like the trouble we brought them.

96

The tongue-less man and his wife, silent as robots, came back and took us to bedrooms, and the girl said that she would see us later. I slept like a man who had died. Only when I awoke many undetermined hours later did I have the strength to observe the grandeur. From the window I could see distant mountains—but, before them, rolling lands with excellent fencing.

Nothing gave any clue as to ownership. I tried most of the books on the tall, ornate bookshelves; not only could I not read German with any useful competence, all of these had been printed in a kind of Teutonic that I'd heard of but never seen.

The room had a bathroom en suite, with a toilet, ancient shower, deep tub, and, by the basin, a pile of fresh clothing for me. I'd read of such things happening in the adventure stories of my boyhood; here I was, living them.

From the texture of the sunlight it felt like three o'clock in the afternoon. I went downstairs and found Kate sitting in the hallway; she too had been given fresh clothes.

However, she had no good mood to offer. In the car, nobody had mentioned our next step; I guessed that we'd have to wait until somebody led us. Kate had no such feeling.

"They're arranging to get us back home," she said. "She told me yesterday." I thought she was about to scream.

"Do you have any idea where we are?"

My abiding thought was, *Where's the fighting? I hope it's not coming closer to us. Are we out of the bombing pathways?*

"I'm restless," she said. "I want to get to Charles."

I said, "And I'm as hungry as I've ever been in my whole life."

After a breakfast of omelets and coffee, it became a strange and shadowy day, with the tongue-less man and woman ghosting about the house, continuing to pay attention to our every need, and never saying a word—not a grunt, not a whisper, not a cough. They had eyes like marbles. I found a deck of cards and played solitaire until I thought I'd go blind.

97

That night Kate called me to her room. On the bed she'd spread the map of Europe, and she'd taken out the needle and the handkerchief.

"I'm going to start right here," she said, "because I have a hunch, a feeling, that Charles isn't far away."

"Do you know where we are?"

She said, "The girl told me that we're well south of Bonn, very near the Belgian border."

She stood by the bed, smoothing her skirt over and over. She fiddled with her hair. She pressed her fingertips to her temples again, and her face glowed red.

"I couldn't do this without you," she said. She took my hand, led me around to the other side of the bed, smoothed the quilt, sat me down, and walked back to her needle and handkerchief. Sprawled across from me, on this great, sagging old bed, she rubbed the needle slowly through Charles Miller's handkerchief.

It took no more than a few minutes. When she dragged the needle across the border in the direction of Liège, it began to quiver, and when she held it over some hills, it swung, firm and confident, from side to side.

She stopped, raised her head, and looked at me like a lamp.

"I found him. He's near a place called Saint-Vith. That's where we're going." She began to cry. "I knew it. I knew he wouldn't die on me. I knew it." Her fists dug holes in the soft bed. "He wouldn't do that to me, he wouldn't. I knew it. God bless you, Charles, God bless you."

At that moment, I saw what she would look like when old—a little Irish countrywoman, with a dimpled and wrinkled face, and still the dynamite smile.

"Let me get you a cup of tea from downstairs," I said, using her own tactic of escaping from tough moments.

She cut in. "No. Hug me first."

She did the hugging; she clung to me the way a baby monkey clings to an adult.

"Thank you, Ben. Thank you, thank you, thank you," and her voice could scarcely make itself understood above the noise of her weeping typhoon, and I thought, *Jesus God, what is she going to do when she gets to the true end of all this?*

I didn't make the tea. We both went downstairs, and in slow German she asked the robots for tea and toast—and they made perfect, thick-ish slabs of cream-colored, bready toast, dense with melting butter.

Keeping my voice light, I said, "How does that needle work?"

"Blessed if I know," she said, "but it's always worked for me."

"Never wrong?"

She said, "Sometimes you get a false start. Remember that murder case I told you about at home? Well, at first they found only a coat. And when they took the coat away and I did the pendulum again—the body was in a completely different place."

I dropped a piece of toast—naturally it fell on the buttered side—and said, "You mean it found the missing person's coat before it found the actual person?"

She said, "It does that sometimes, but it always comes out right."

Heart in mouth, I said, "Shouldn't you go on looking?"

And she said with a laugh, "You don't know Charles. There's no chance he'd ever lose a coat."

98

Next morning the girl arrived, and I intercepted her.

"Are you trying to get us back to Ireland?"

"That is a fact." And she smiled.

"She"—meaning Kate—"won't see the joke."

"We're hiding you here until we get a boat out of Bremerhaven. The way you came in. There's no place else to go. Getting you to the American lines would be too difficult."

I said, "She's talking about a place named Saint-Vith."

"Why does she want to go to Saint-Vith?"

I said, "Did you ever hear of a thing called a pendulum? For finding people?"

She said, "My grandmother did it."

"But isn't it mere witchcraft? Or old wives' tales? I mean, there's no rationale in it."

"I believe in the possible," she said. "I'm from Belgium."

"Come on. How can you find somebody by rubbing a needle through a possession of theirs, and then holding the needle over a map? Ridiculous."

"Why do the police use it? They don't believe in magic, would you say?"

I said, "It makes no sense. On any level."

The girl cut in, with a measure of sarcasm. "I can tell that you don't want to find him alive, do you?"

I said, "She will ask me now every hour of every day—she'll get up in the middle of the night and knock on my door to ask me—when can we go?"

And every hour of the past two days, Kate had indeed asked, referred to it, made some allusion, pleaded, begged, entreated—find all the synonyms in the English language for the word *demand,* then find all the synonyms for the word *supplication.*

Now she trotted out to the steps on which we stood.

"How far are we from Saint-Vith? Has Ben told you the good news? When can we go?"

The girl led her away from me, to the far edge of the terrace, where they stood and talked, animated like negotiators. I hoped that she was telling Kate of the plans to take us back to Bremerhaven. But it has been one of the trials of my life that I so often confuse what I hope for with what I should expect; too much of what I forecast comes from wishful thinking, and I didn't anticipate that the Belgian girl would support Kate's belief in the pendulum.

Looking back on it now, how could I have won? Any woman, no matter how pragmatic, would always have sympathy with another woman searching the battlefields for an adored husband.

Next morning we climbed into another van, this time heavy with police insignia, and driven by a man with recklessly thick glasses. In equally dense French he told Miss Begley that he would take us to the Belgian border not far from Saint-Vith. He lectured us all the way, sour and obscene, ridiculing us for getting into an area so near the war, and now he was going to pitch us farther in and he didn't care what happened to us.

To Kate, he made appalling remarks, too crude to repeat, and largely to do with having shared the bed of an American officer. I thought, when he finally let us out of the car, that he might kick us into Belgium. To the guard on the German side of the border he described us as "a couple of Irish fools, whose country is so small and backward they don't know what's happening in the rest of the world."

Of course, as I discovered, both the driver and the border guard had been part of the Belgian girl's strategy. When I went back after the war, I met them both—and I might as well reveal that I went back as much to apologize to the villagers, whose neighbors had been shot because of us, as to pick up the story of Charles Miller, which still had so many baffling parts.

"What did you think of us that morning?" I said to the man with the thick glasses. He had prospered after the war, owning a chain of accountancy offices and a coat with a fur collar.

He said, "I told you that day: a pair of idiots. I thought she was leading you around by the nose—or some other organ."

99

We walked into Belgium, Kate Begley and I, into war-torn Belgium, a country ripped open and bleeding, and the blood was all flowing in our direction, only we didn't know it yet. Neither did I know that I was entering the worst period of my life—although I did suspect and fear so. No matter what had gone before, nothing could compare to what lay ahead.

By now, my resolve to keep a journal had failed, and I felt disinclined to write at all. When I simply had to keep a record—and it can be a compulsion—I did my best, but it never lasted for long.

Miss Begley didn't do so well either, probably because I had fallen back in my resolve; or perhaps on account of the severe tension she must have been feeling. Yet she made one entry, a passage of her journal that I later found so valuable. She wrote it the morning after the pendulum had danced over the village of Saint-Vith and the town of Liège.

I knew it! Charles is alive. Thank you, God! Alive! He is in Belgium, near the village of St.-Vith. My pendulum told me, and that is where we shall go next. I don't know whether I can get him to come back into Germany with me, and from there we'll go home to Ireland, or perhaps get to Paris.

If I had read that journal entry while still in Europe in December 1944, I think that I'd have found a doctor and had Kate Begley taken into some sort of care in order to get her back to Ireland. Those can't have been the thoughts or reactions of a sane woman. And yet, other than some tics and twitches, I hadn't seen any serious hints of derangement—unless that intense focus of hers amounted to some kind of instability. In fact, with the women of the village in Germany, she seemed very like the girl I'd seen at Lamb's Head.

So what can she have been thinking? Did she know anything concrete of her husband's style of soldiering? What had he told her? That he got behind enemy lines undercover, and hid all day? And at night, like some werewolf, he came out and slit the necks of German officers?

That's what I assumed he did, and that's what had been hinted to me—Killer Miller. Even if she hadn't known, how did she assume—and she knew that we were going behind German lines—how did she assume that he could just walk away from the war, as though he were a member of some wandering troupe of performers?

My guess is that it belonged in the same kind of thinking that she developed when she was four years old. By refusing to accept that her parents had drowned, she'd built and maintained a kind of shield around herself. Otherwise courageous, she had granted herself one area of life in which she never had to face reality.

100

Our first challenge arrived within minutes. Once the border point disappeared behind us, not a soul did we see. We walked along a country road, and a steep hill rose ahead. Loose trees stood like soldiers across the heights. We climbed to the hilltop and saw a long farmland valley below. A small sign pointing left said, SCHONBERG—8KM. Since the previous day, my heart had begun to pound so loud that I could hear it.

Kate scrutinized a piece of paper and hummed a tune. She had written out, she told me, the name of every town and village that we were likely to see, and she began to recite them: "Bütgenbach, Stavelot, Büllingen—"

A roaring sound overwhelmed her voice. Above the treetops, with the suddenness of panic, came an aircraft. It aimed itself down at us. What could the pilot see? Two small people on a country road. Each carried a not very large valise. They looked hesitant.

He banked, turned, and came back. From the side this time, and lower, he had plenty of room to get down near us. The road amounted to no more than a ribbon in this huge furrow of the forest. Trees didn't begin for hundreds of yards on either side. A squadron of planes could have flown down this corridor, wingtip to wingtip.

We could smell the fuel he came so low. A small, fast plane, black cross on the wings. He went right over our heads. Peeled off up into the sky. How can an engine snarl and whine at the same time? I had never seen anything move that fast.

Back he came, straight at us. I saw him, face masked with goggles. He was so low that we ducked. Miss Begley's hair flew up and back. She looked at me, said nothing. I didn't look behind. She said, "He's gone."

Once again, she was mistaken. I heard him whine and snarl in a circle. Around the trees he went, over the hilltop and down the valley, a long way down the valley. And then he climbed, high, high, into the clear frosty sky—and turned.

I watched him. Down he came. His steep trajectory aimed him straight at us. And then I saw the puffs. Little fast-rising pouts of dust, a chain of them on the road. A line of white puffs was racing up the hill toward us.

Déjà vu. Of course we knew what they were. For once, Kate did the right thing—she flung her arms out like a crucifix and threw her head back. Her entire posture cried, "Shoot me! Shoot me!" So did her voice. She didn't scream the words, she didn't shriek them, she called them out.

"Shoot me," she cried a third time.

The little road explosions veered away because the pilot did. A few yards into the no-man's-land open roadside the machine-gun stuttering stopped. Miss Begley stood there in open air, head back, arms out, lepidopterized like a pinned butterfly.

And once more the pilot flew away down the valley and once more he came back, only this time his trajectory was not angled down, it was level and would take him a hundred feet above our heads, and as we looked up, he waggled his wings three or four times, and, as jaunty as a school-boy, he flew away across the hills to his Fatherland.

"Some joke," I said. "Are you all right?"

"Ben, don't you understand? We're under some kind of protection. And I know who's providing it." Her face shone with the zeal of an evangelist.

"We must walk on," I said.

I see it so often in my mind—that road, that wide woodland corridor. The climb had required all our breath; the descent was a slow and pleasant relief. Near the bottom of that long hill, a village began to slope up toward us. The houses had been built by somebody who painted Christmas cards. We walked in, along the only street we could see—but there was an intersection.

Not a soul appeared as we walked past the first few doors. We reached a small bar and café on the corner of the junction. Neither of us saw the vehicles down the side street—nobody can see around corners.

"Tea or coffee?" I joked, and Kate smiled. Not a trace of nerves or re-action did she show to the fighter plane experience; she might have been going to visit an aunt. In fact I thought of Little Red Riding Hood and the woods, and that brought back thoughts of wolves, and as we walked into the café, there they stood, the wolves, all gray coats and danger.

Kate might have thought that they smiled when they saw her; I knew better—they were baring their fangs. In a pack, too—six of them, and their shiny black paws, and their fierce eyes, and the end of my life, as I thought.

From that moment on, in that little Belgian café, my view of the word *neutral,* and the emotional and intellectual condition it describes, began to change. How could it not? In aura, in attitude, in the capacity to strike terror into human hearts, I was confronted by a hunting pack of wolves—six officers of the Waffen SS, the worst of the worst, who had come for a briefing in the village. We never got to Saint-Vith.

101

When, long after the war, I went back on that journey I've mentioned, to trace what had happened to us, to attempt a clearer recollection in tranquillity, I found my expectations disturbed. Have you ever had the experience of visiting a house you'd lived in as a child? And did you observe how much smaller it was than you'd remembered?

I still hold as one of my biggest surprises how tiny was that little theater of the war. Those towns, those villages, those places of battle, Baugnez, Elsenborn, Malmédy—they stand no more than a few miles from each other; they're local places, not epic plains over which mighty wars should be fought. That morning, we'd crossed the border east of a hamlet whose name, the border guard told us, was Andler; the wolves took us northeast to Losheim.

I didn't know, because I hadn't been told, that Miss Begley carried in her possessions a letter from the American embassy in Dublin, saying that she was the "wife of the American Officer, Captain Charles Miller," and she was to be "shown every courtesy." Presumably the embassy official wrote it in order to get rid of Kate, but no wonder the wolves howled—with laughter—when one of them found this, and handed it to another, who translated it into German.

They took me in the leading car, and I couldn't turn my head to see Kate in the car behind. I can still feel my panic. They didn't manhandle us. In fact, their behavior to her came straight from an officers' manual on good manners—slight bow, clicked heels, courtesy. No doubt, though, as to their firmness; their black leather gloves touched neither of us—not an arm grip or a clutch on the shoulder; when they walked, we walked.

I saw her face one last time as she climbed into the rear of the car behind. She looked at me in such a stricken way. I had identified the English speaker among them. He was in my trio of captors, and I asked if I might travel with her. He didn't bother to answer.

And in that car on that morning, I first heard the name Peiper. The wolves mentioned it several times; he was their alpha.

102

Tanks, armored carriers, guns, lines of soldiers; some moved in the direction whence we had come, some the way we were going, some never moved, merely hung around as though awaiting orders. No longer were we behind the German lines, we were in them.

I have to confess my fascination. Although the events in France had appalled me, and had forever annihilated any notion of war's "romance," I still stared with great visual hunger at the troops. And then, past a signpost that read MANDERFELD 2, I stared with greater appetite—and shock.

Now I found myself looking at American troops, in tanks and other vehicles with American markings. The officers, in our Mercedes with its German livery, laughed, smiled, and waved at them as our cars inched between them on the narrow roads. Active troops, these Americans were, full of vigor, alert, sharp, and without question on active duty—and respectful as could be to the SS officers in the two cars.

Speculations came at me like arrows. That the German army along here had surrendered? And the Americans hadn't yet caught up with the ones whom we had driven past earlier? No, that couldn't be, because we'd been taken by German officers, who were still in some sort of command. That these Americans had been captured? No; they didn't look like defeated men. That the Germans and the Allies had joined forces? But who could have been the common enemy? A horrid thought struck me: *Could the American troops have surrendered—or worse, deserted?* They seemed on such friendly terms with our wolves.

Not even thinkable. My speculation went nowhere.

When the wolves saw my intense interest, they muttered amused remarks to one another. Addressing the English speaker, I said, "Has there been a surrender?"

How they laughed—long and out loud.

"No," said my co-linguist, "no, no, no." And as he ran out of breath from laughing, the other wolves in the front said in a chorus, *"Nein, nein, nein."*

I can still recapture the perturbation that I felt: disoriented, puzzled, confused. Sitting in the backseat of that plush car, with its black leather shiny as fear itself, I ran it through my mind: *Yes, these are Americans. Look at the military insignia, the star inside a circle; look at the stenciling, the numbers. Look at the uniforms. Those are American tanks.*

It took us several minutes to get through these American lines, and nobody shot at us, or halted us, or took any hostile action. What was going on? In fact, the Americans cleared the roads for us, and waved us through, and the wolves waved back with their gloved paws. And I reflected, "This is a very gentlemanly war that's being fought here. Or is it?"

I also contemplated what might be taking place in the car behind us. Soon, I would learn that, as they drove past the American tanks and uniforms, they encouraged Miss Begley to take heart. They told her that her husband had been here, and that in fact he'd left some of his clothes behind, and they would soon give them to her.

Alas! Once again she said, "I knew it. Nobody would listen to me, but I knew it."

And how they laughed.

The American troops gave way to more German soldiery, and I confirmed their identity with my own eyes: the black cross, the different lettering in the stencils. I could have no doubt in my mind—I had just seen hundreds if not thousands of American troops between two similarly large contingents of the German army.

103

Our car swung down a side road. In the wing mirror I glimpsed the following car do the same. Do they mean to keep us together? Are they going to hand us over to the Americans? If so, why didn't we stop earlier?

In a field by a farmhouse, rows and rows of tents had been erected. Troops kept up constant movement—repairing vehicles, hauling crates, pushing handcarts in this mud-deep anthill of gray uniforms. Two armed and unsmiling soldiers sentried the farmhouse from the steps of the porch. Neither flinched as our cars drove almost to their toe caps.

Directed by the wolves, I climbed out. Nobody moved from the car behind. I could see only the two men in the front—not even the silhouette of Miss Begley's head. The light was leaving the sky, and thick rain had begun to fall. Escorted by the wolves, I trotted up the steps.

One of the sentries opened the door—he moved like a robot. The leading wolf strode into the house. I followed, with the other two behind me, their leather coats creaking. Ahead, as I waited in the hall, I heard the "stand-to-attention" stamp of feet. The wolf pack leader yapped out something respectful in German.

From inside came an excited little shout, and a noise of boots scrabbling on a wooden floor. Heavy steps came toward me and through the doorway into the hall stepped two men. One became famous, not least by his manner of dying long after the war—Joachim or Jochen Peiper. Short of height, he had smart blond hair and the crispest uniform I had yet seen—impeccable. As I look back at him now, down the tunnel of my memory, I can best describe him by saying that he should have been playing German officers in Hollywood—that's how perfect he was.

He looked up at me. For a second or two I thought he had stood on tiptoe to do so. He turned to the wolf who had led me in and said something in German. The man nodded. Peiper asked some questions—he looked, I felt, many years older than I, instead of a year younger, as I would discover.

The wolf provided answers; I didn't catch a word. Peiper directed him to bring me into the room from which he had come. They maneuvered me to stand to one side of the fireplace, where logs burned. So far, the man beside Peiper, who was almost exactly the same height, said not a word; he took up a position on the other side of the fire, looking at me as though at a curio.

Through the window of the house, I could see the cars parked outside. Now the rear doors of the second car opened, and its trio of wolves escorted Kate to the porch as they had accompanied me—firm and brisk, not touching shoulders, arms, anything.

Before she reached the house, Peiper sat down behind the dining table that he had commandeered as a desk. *He's nervous,* I thought. *He's an efficient man, and he's tough. And who is the fellow on the other side of the fireplace?*

This one hadn't yet spoken, had a mark on his right temple, a blue star, an unserious bruise. If Peiper did indeed have the vanity that his personal appearance suggested, he must have felt rivalrous with this fellow—who also wore an impeccable uniform; at his neck he had a cream scarf of a silk so dense it must have been brought back to Europe by Marco Polo.

On his right hand he wore a ring whose dial, a perfect circle, was studded with tiny turquoises and diamonds—capped, so to speak, by a larger diamond in the center. From his left cuff hung the edges of a silk handkerchief in black and cream polka dots.

This fellow had a humorous face; he'd been half-smiling since they'd walked me into this house. As Peiper indicated that I step forward and stand in front of his desk, the other man stood aside to make room for me and gestured in a gentlemanly way. I stood in the space provided, like a clerk in front of his boss.

Peiper looked down at his desk, searching for something. He found it—a photograph of Kate, Charles Miller, and myself taken on a day of winter sunshine in London. I hadn't known that such a picture existed. He held it up to me and smiled, with his head cocked slightly to one side, in the manner of a wordless question.

I bent forward to peer a little closer, then I nodded and said, "Yes, that's me," and straightened up again. The man with the polka-dot handkerchief, the impeccable man, with the head of an aristocrat and a profile from an ancient coin, stepped over, reached up, grabbed my nose between thumb and forefinger, and tweaked harder than a man turning a key in a heavy lock.

And now you know—that man was Sebastian Volunder.

Volunder? *Volunder?* It wasn't that the name was familiar—but the word was. Even so, it wouldn't come. When somebody opened the door to the room, Volunder walked across. He limped.

Watchful as a predator, he stood there while they brought in Kate. Her eyes were red-rimmed. Furious, my mind racing to ask, *What's this?* I began to move toward her when Peiper said, "*Nein.* No."

He barked something at one of the wolves, who came over and forced me aside, to a point behind Kate.

She stood before Peiper's desk. He looked her up and down as candidly as if buying her. By now, I knew every move she had. I knew when she was stubborn or malleable, when she was in full command or merely hopeful, when she was trying to take over or just going along with things. The squaring back of her shoulders, the quick settling of the feet on the floor told me that she had composed herself and was returning Peiper's direct look.

Peiper held out one immaculate hand to his officers as though calling for something. One of the wolves came forward, taking the embassy letter from his tunic. The wolf began to read, translating into German as he went along, until Peiper held up a hand and the wolf stopped the reading.

"The wife," Peiper said, and repeated it. "The wife."

To Kate, Peiper said something in German and she answered him in English. "I don't know."

Peiper came back at her in English. "But you must know. Why are you here?"

Kate answered, "We weren't coming here. Your fellows brought us."

Peiper frowned. I looked at the wolves that I could see. They winced when Peiper frowned. One shifted his feet—just a tiny bit, but a shift nonetheless. Peiper's frown didn't go away.

"Why are we here?" said Kate. "We're not fighting you."

"Where did you think you were going?" said Peiper.

"To see if we could find my husband. He hasn't been well."

Peiper looked at the others, and he had no expression on his face, nor did they.

104

Let me tell you about Peiper. I hope that the way I tell you will constitute an objective view—yet I also feel obliged to include what would be the more common opinion of him as expressed by the Allies, history being written by the winners.

Anybody who traveled those fields and forests, during or after the war, would have to say, "Peiper? Oh, he was a piece of work." An Allied observer at his trial in Dachau would say, "Well, of course he was responsible for war crimes."

From the German perspective, Joachim Peiper comes across as a brilliant soldier, a magnificent commander who almost turned the course of the war. He, as much as any other German in uniform, caused the Bulge that created the Battle—and he almost won. And when he didn't succeed, he still led his men out of the Allies' trap, and, through sheer leadership and grit, got them back to his own lines by means of a forced march of breathtaking endurance in deep snow.

None of that takes away from his coldness, his ruthlessness, in those Belgian villages. He may have insisted that he didn't order nearly a hundred American soldiers to be shot where they stood, captured and helpless, in a field at a crossroads—but because they were prisoners of war, protected by the Geneva convention, Peiper knew that he should have prevented any such atrocity from ever taking place. In fact, as he drove past them standing there, hours before they were massacred, he shouted, "It's a long way to Tipperary," the famous old Allies' song from the previous war.

And, by way of one last piece of balance—to point out that he was human, after his forced march, after his failure at the Battle of the Bulge, Peiper disappeared, and it's thought that he had a nervous breakdown. When he resurfaced, he faced the horrors of the Eastern Front.

105

Peiper handed Kate Begley the photograph that he'd shown to me. He watched her reaction.

She said, "It's not a good likeness. My husband's handsomer than that."

Peiper held his hand out to take back the photograph.

Kate said, "Do you mind if I keep it?" and slid it into her pocket.

Peiper looked at her, almost not believing. He said something in rapid speech to one of the wolves, who acknowledged with a formal salute and left the room at a clip. Peiper turned again to Kate, whose legs I could see trembling—yet she held firm. I coughed, knowing that she would recognize the sound and knowing that she would turn her head.

When she did, I nodded and half-smiled, as much as to say, "I'm here. I'll do what I can."

Peiper said, "So you have a husband and a lover?"

"I have a husband. Ben's my friend."

He shook his head; he had charm to burn.

"But you travel with your 'friend.' I call that opportunity."

Kate shook her head. "Ask him."

Peiper said, "I don't need to. I'm much more interested in why you crossed the border when and where you did. Who told you that your husband was in this region?"

Kate said, "I just knew."

Peiper said, "You believe in instinct?"

Kate said, "It doesn't lie."

"Perhaps *you're* lying."

"Not me."

Peiper said, "Of course you're lying. How in a war so huge and complex can you come straight to the place you think your husband has been? Did he marry you because you're an American spy? How old-fashioned."

She said, "Where is he?"

"Captain Charles Miller. Special Operations, U.S. Army. A wife in Ireland. Married her last May." Peiper spoke as if reading from a document.

Kate said what I was thinking—indeed, she turned and said it to me. "So he didn't die in France?"

To my left, Sebastian Volunder, who had listened to all this with great interest and a smile, stirred and half-moved forward, and said, "Yes, he did. He tried to kill me there."

"I'm sure that was his job," said Kate. "All's fair in love and war."

The wolf to whom Peiper had given an order returned, carrying a cloth bundle, which he placed on the long, gleaming table.

Peiper nodded at the bundle and said to Kate, "Do you recognize this?" Using his fingers as delicate tongs, he held up, and then shook out, the bundle. "You recognize it?"

Kate said, "It's an American soldier's jacket."

"But don't you recognize it?"

"I do—I've seen thousands of them."

"Well, maybe you recognize the blood," said Peiper, and pointed out a great dark stain on the shoulder and arm.

Although Kate's legs trembled as with chills, she kept her voice steady. "We've no way of knowing whose blood that is. If it is blood."

Peiper said, "Touch it and tell me."

"Gladly," said Kate.

I thought, *Where's she finding this courage?*

The wolf handed her the jacket. Kate held it up to the light, turned it this way and that as a tailoress might have done, fingered the large stain, and then—to, I think, everyone's surprise—held the jacket to her face. It told her something. I knew by the way her back stiffened. But she didn't say what that message might have been.

She said, "I can't tell."

Peiper said, "It's your husband's tunic. A souvenir."

He repeated it in German, and his wolves laughed at the sarcasm.

"May I keep this?" Kate asked.

Peiper shrugged. "It'll make a shroud."

"Are you going to kill us?"

"You're a couple of American spies behind our lines—what do you think?"

I spoke. "But we're neutral."

Peiper looked at me. "Is that how you also describe your relationship with Frau Miller?"

When, in crucial times, people don't quite know what to do or what's going to happen next, the world often introduces a peculiar silence. Such a stillness now fell over that room. Peiper sat at his "desk," on which lay a folded map, two books, and a large black leather folio.

Kate stood before him, the bloodied tunic pressed to her cheek, her feet square on the ground. I, to her right, but farther back, could see most of her face. Sebastian Volunder stared at me. And the wolves pawed the ground, so to speak.

Peiper next said, "You know you're going to die, don't you?"

Kate said, "One day. That's what the Lord says."

Peiper said, "No. Not one day. Today. That's what *I* say."

"What harm are we to you?" she asked, and still I saw not a flinch from her.

"Do you know my nickname, Madam?" Peiper looked at one of the wolves. "Tell her what they call me."

The wolf barked, in German, and Miss Begley said, "My German isn't that good."

Peiper said, "I'll translate. They call me 'Blowtorch.' If somebody fights or resists me . . . That's how I got the name."

Again, the silence floated in; I have so often been so grateful to the world for providing that little phenomenon.

Kate broke it. "Well. Kill us."

Peiper stood, and I had two thoughts: *She doesn't want to stay alive, she wants to die in the same war as her husband.* And, *He's not going to kill us. He's not going to kill us because he can't kill somebody who asks him to.*

As though he'd read my mind, Peiper said, "On the other hand, I've just thought of a way you can be useful. We're going to put you on the front line." To one of the wolves he said, "Kampfgruppe? Scherff?"

The wolves laughed.

Peiper explained to us how he intended to use us, and thereby answered the puzzle of the American troops we had seen on our way to Losheim. He would put us in one of his three battle groups—X, Y, or Z.

By now, you'll need some explanations, so let me tell you what I learned after the war. We had landed right in the middle of one of the more unusual military developments, and we were therefore, for Peiper, perfect. Hitler's armies fought rearguard actions all the way back to Germany. Through the Ardennes, in the forests, under the trees, in the clearings, in the villages, on the hillsides, they battled while going backward. Now and then they turned defense into attack and created some massive thrusts forward in a planned, fully engineered counteroffensive.

This measure had one centralized aim, and every German officer and soldier knew it: Stop the Americans and their friends from crossing the River Meuse by taking key bridges. If the Allies did cross, they'd have their toes on the German border, a dozen miles from where we stood.

In the most far-fetched thinking of the plan, the Axis would counter-attack. They'd pierce the Allied lines advancing on the Meuse and make it to Antwerp, perhaps Rotterdam too, take back those ports, defend a long stretch of the Dutch coast, and argue for a peace treaty. That way, if he got any kind of terms, Hitler could hold Belgium and Holland and perhaps part—or all—of France.

As his generals on the ground described the hefty Allied troop movements coming at them, Hitler sent for one of his officers, Otto Skorzeny. Skorzeny had a reputation for imaginativeness beyond the battle-field. Now he got fresh orders: Form a special brigade, dress it in captured American uniforms, staff it with officers and men who can speak English—especially, he insisted, American slang—and sow confusion in the approaching enemy ranks.

They called it Panzer Brigade 150. Peiper, though not part of it, knew its three companies; battle group X, commanded by a man named Willi Hardieck; Y by the man whose name Peiper mentioned to us, Scherff; and Z led by—and I smiled when I heard it—Oberstleutnant Wolf.

As you know, we'd seen their uniforms and their green, American-liveried vehicles. When Peiper explained it to us, my heart sank—here was confusion on a grand scale; who would know who was fighting whom? And how were we to help?

Peiper told us, "We do not have enough speakers of English. We need more. You will join those companies and teach the men English. In return you take your chances. If you refuse you will be shot now."

"You're very persuasive, sir," said Kate, and even Peiper laughed at her dry tone.

As he dismissed us, I recalled the police case in Ireland where, Kate said, her pendulum had found the coat in one place—but the body in another.

106

They took us away from that house, took us far down the row of tents in that muddy field. On field chairs we sat, beneath leaking canvas, in the freezing cold. They even gave us back our travel bags. Mine had by now begun to fall apart, and such clothing as I'd had inside had been reduced to dreadful condition. Only my beloved *Wandering Scholars* remained in any kind of shape.

Two soldiers with guns sat nearby. They had been given orders that we mustn't speak. Kate kept her bag on her knee, and even began to repack it. I was reminded of a squirrel arranging a nest of nuts. She took out every object, one at a time, reorganized it, and put it back in the bag in a different way. Blouses, underwear, cosmetics—the repacked bag looked as though it might have been handled by a trained maid or valet.

Straining in the dim yellow light of the hurricane lamp, I read from my book. Neither soldier showed any interest in what we did—although they did steal glances when Kate redistributed her underwear. I can see us now; a large picture of that moment, clear as day, hangs in the gallery of my recollection.

Kate Begley's navy serge coat had some mud stains on the hem; they had dried but she hadn't yet noticed them. Her hair had been washed that morning in the tongue-less house and had retained its body. The bright red nail polish shone like the defiance of glamour in that umbrageous tent, the darkness heightening my gloom.

I wore—as ever—my long black coat and wished that I had gloves. My hands shook with the terrible cold, and I was glad of the book's anchor. An hour passed; then another hour—or was it five minutes, and then another five? A large man, with oil-black sideburns, brought food and mugs of beverage to the soldiers; nothing to us.

As the darkness fell in earnest, a young officer walked into the tent, eager and nervous.

"You are to come with me," he said to Kate. When she rose, he moved to take her bag and then seemed—I guessed—to remind himself that she was his prisoner, and he checked. Over her shoulder he said to me, "I'm the one who speaks English here, I will come back for you."

I saw that he looked at the book in my hand.

Within minutes he strode back into the tent and gestured like a boss. He turned and I followed him, down the sodden and muddy path to a smaller tent, in which sat three soldiers, one an officer.

"We need to speak English better," he said. "Can you speak with an American accent, do you know American slang? Speak to us."

Saying to somebody "Speak to us" poses a challenge that it's oddly hard to meet. Say what? What shall I speak? Recite verse?

"I've never tried to imitate an American accent," I said. "But I come from Ireland, and the Irish are renowned for speaking good English."

One of the men said, in a thick German tone (Heaven help him if they wanted to pass him off as American), "Tell us story."

"A story?" I echoed, and the young earnest officer said, "Tell us the story of your family. In Ireland. Tell us slow, and explain words."

And so I told them the story of my father and his farming, of Mother and her bookkeeping and beekeeping. And I told them the story of Venetia Kelly, who had been my wife for no longer than a matter of weeks, and how the ship's captain who married us had said to me, "If she were my bride I'd smile every time I looked at her."

And I told them of Blarney, her ventriloquism dummy, who was harsh and irascible and satirical and sometimes even funny, and how I never allowed myself to think that his vile sentiments and foul attitudes were coming out of the mouth of this glorious woman.

And I told them how somebody—evil people—came for this tall and lovely creature in the middle of the night, and how she had left all her money behind, and how they had decapitated the dummy, Blarney, and left his head in the street outside the front door of our house.

And finally I told them how I had, ever since, roamed the roads of Ireland, gathering stories, yes, and collecting songs and tunes, but in truth looking for my dear, lost wife, and how I asked everywhere, and I showed them the photograph of Venetia.

In that little German tent, on that rainy, cold evening dark with threat, with those young German boys, that's all they were, boys, each one younger than I, listening, listening to the sad story of a young Irish-man—the war stopped for just a few minutes.

As they left, each soldier patted me on the arm or shook my hand, and I knew we weren't enemies and never would be, these boys and I. Enemies are natural creatures, like friends or lovers or couples.

107

Into my minuscule sector of the war, that soggy and wind-scoured tent where I sat, unguarded, on a folding chair, crept one more positive force.

Half an hour or so after the soldiers had left, the young officer came back, accompanied by an orderly, or a soldier at a menial level, who carried food—a tin bowl with some meat and potatoes, and a mug of hot and sticky coffee. When I'd found a way of managing all this on my chair, the menial was ordered back to his supply wagon or wherever he'd been.

The young officer said, "May I ask about the book you have been reading?"

I said, "It's my most treasured possession," and I handed it to him.

"Who are *Wandering Scholars*?" he said.

"Probably among your ancestors," I replied. "Men who wandered through the European countryside, writing poems and reading them to people."

He handled the book as a priest handles a chalice.

"Homer is my hero," he said. "I have not seen a book for close to a year."

"Please have that," I said. "As my gift."

He recoiled and thrust the book at me. "I cannot do that. I cannot. No, I cannot."

"Please. As a gift from one reader to another."

"No, I mustn't. But if I give you my name and address, will you write after the war? And we may meet and speak of Homer?"

"And Virgil," I said.

"And Dante. Do you know Dante, Dante is also my hero? I do not know Virgil."

"Then you can teach me about Dante, and I can teach you about Virgil," I said.

"And *Wandering Scholars?*" he said. He scribbled his name and postal address on the inside rear cover of my book.

"Yes," I said. "Always *Wandering Scholars.* Perhaps you will come to Ireland and travel with me."

He stepped back farther and, to my shock, saluted.

I said, "I'm not an officer, I'm not even a soldier."

He replied, "My father was an officer in the last war, and he taught me that we must salute gentlemen as well as officers."

As he ducked through the flap, he half-turned and said, "Your friend, she will be all right. I promise."

When he had gone, I looked at the name in the book: "Stefan Bekker." In Ireland, as in all villages, everybody knows everybody else. My father—and mother, even though she's more withdrawn—always tried to make connections.

"Now what O'Connors are they?" my father would ask regarding a new family, and I'd heard that kind of inquiry almost every day of my life. Thus, no matter how vast the country, I was conditioned to assume that people were related to each other.

Now I saw the name "Bekker" and remembered the young man who came from the sea that morning of rain and gray mist.

That night, I thought I would freeze and drown. Nobody came to guard me; they reasoned that I wouldn't get far in this weather—and that I would make no attempt to escape on account of Kate. They gave me a sleeping bag, allegedly waterproof, which it wasn't. The wind whipped the rain into the tent, and the rain turned to sleet and cut into my face, no matter which way I turned.

Believe it or not, I did sleep. It took a long time, principally because of Kate, about whom I worried with the same throb of desperation I'd had when Venetia disappeared. My young officer had promised to take care of her, but was he even in the camp anymore? All sorts of possibilities, from Peiper down, flooded my mind: *The wife of an American officer—what finer plaything could they have found?*

In the interests of chronology, I include now Kate's account of what happened to her when they took us separately away. She had managed to get herself into much more salubrious circumstances, a local house managed by Belgian women, who had been commandeered to look after the senior officers while Peiper was billeted there.

From all the evidence, Kate seems not to have believed Peiper. Here is her—surprisingly calm—journal for that night, scribbled on pages from a school homework jotter that one of the women gave her.

Now I know why we need faith. Why we need forces greater than us and more mysterious. They sustain us. But what is my faith tonight? Since my marriage I've discovered that much of my faith comes from my own self. I pray, God knows I pray (that's quite funny, I now see), but it's not the praying, it's the belief. That's what has sustained me. My belief may come from the wind, for all I know.

I am sitting in a nice bedroom, in a house near a village in Belgium, not far from the German border. It doesn't feel as if I'm a prisoner, but I am. So, this is what has happened to me, and I'm trying to understand it. When I met Charles I said to myself, "This is your fate."

Is this war a lesson to me? Is it saying I must understand that I intrude into people's lives? And that from now on I must do it more sincerely, more responsibly? I forced myself into Charles's life, and more or less forced him to marry me. Then I forced myself into his work, which is how I came to be here. And look at what I've done to Ben—the kindest, most loyal friend in the world. If I get out of here alive, I will do penance.

The women who look after me here have been nicer than I expected. One speaks French and a little English. A young officer came to the house twice and asked the women if everything was all right. He saluted me very formally, and he told me the name of the man in charge today, Jochen Peiper, who is like a colonel or something, not a general. I can tell that he's a very competent man, but he's also frightening. Do I believe that Charles tried to kill him? Do I believe that he has had Charles killed? I don't know what to believe.

*I've been coaching the women on how to make marriages, and they
are very interested. And I have read their palms, and told them that
they will all be safe.*

108

Next morning, I heard artillery, and Stefan Bekker came to the tent.

"You must come with me now. I have orders."

Through the mud we ran. I had no bag; I had time only to make sure
that I had my book and notebook in my pocket. We made it to the Peiper
house without falling into the mud, but I could tell as we climbed the little steps to the porch that Peiper had gone—that's how much force he had.

Kate stood inside.

"They wouldn't let me bring my bag," she said.

Stefan Bekker asked, "In the house?" and when Kate nodded, he ran.
Within minutes he came back with the bag. "Tell nobody I did this," he
said.

The three of us stood there as soldiers raced in and out. Then one of
the wolves appeared in the hallway and spoke in a hard voice to Stefan
Bekker. Kate told me later that he said, "You are to shoot the spies."

An argument broke out—very brief; I saw the wolf leave, his long
leather coat darkening with rain spots, and Stefan Bekker said, "We have
to go."

We stood in the front doorway, stepping aside now and then out of
the way of men bringing out files, clothing, and equipment.

One of the cars that brought us there the previous day drew up.

"We get in," said Stefan Bekker.

Inside, I asked, "Can you tell us where we're going?"

He turned from the front seat and looked at me, shaking his head very
slightly, and in a voice more unfriendly than his face said, "Please do not ask.
You are prisoners of the Reich. You are being taken to the train station."

I understood his circumspectness in front of the driver.

Neither Kate nor I knew the implications of the train, and wouldn't know—like everybody else in the West—until long after the war, when the news broke of the cattle wagons to the concentration camps. But Stefan Bekker knew.

I said to him, on an impulse, "Do you have a brother serving also?"

He almost broke his neck, so hard did he swivel his head.

"What are you asking?"

"Do you have a brother? In the navy? With a little daughter? Nadia?"

"His name is Frederik. How do you know?"

How often has this happened to me? How often have I encountered coincidences so unlikely, so preposterous, that would have seemed and sounded ridiculous had they happened to someone else? I used to think it only occurred in my life; now I know it's universal.

I told him—the full story. No matter how many years have passed, I can still reach out and touch the sadness that I felt when I discovered what had befallen his brother. It still grieves me—especially after that morning in the mud.

We eased out of the lane that led from the house and joined a line of military traffic. It moved at about ten miles per hour, hemmed in by lines of marching soldiers. Ahead, two of the half-tracks had left the road and gone into the woods, following a tank. Along that stretch, the trees stood wide enough apart to let the tanks and troop carriers through.

Our driver spurted, and we caught up with the vehicles in front. As we turned a bend, we could see through the rain a steep hill rising ahead. The road, axle-deep in mud, slowed us down so much that the marching soldiers passed us by. It took an hour to get close to the summit of that hill, which was flanked by dense woods.

I looked back. We had become the last vehicle in the long convoy. Those behind us must have peeled off into the trees. The last of the soldiers had also trudged past us.

We stopped completely. The rain turned to heavy snow. Stefan Bekker said something to the driver, who climbed out and went forward. We saw him walk to a truck five or six vehicles ahead, and as he engaged somebody in conversation, Stefan Bekker turned to us.

"Go now." So urgent.

"Where?" said Kate.

"Into the trees. Keep going west." Even more urgent.

"But we'll get shot."

He smiled at her. "No. The Americans are near. Go west." He wagged a pointing hand. "West. Go!"

He climbed out of the car, ran in the opposite direction, and disappeared into the snow and the trees.

I never saw Stefan Bekker again. After the war, I wrote to the address that he had written in my book—somewhere near Limburg; I wrote three, four times, but I never heard from him. I've been tempted to try to find him through war records, but I fear that he died, and anyway I think that I'd rather be accompanied by the Stefan Bekker I'd met with my *Wandering Scholars.*

Kate dragged her bag from the car and I grabbed it from her. I can't say that we ran. Nobody could. The mud massaged our ankles. Cold speared my throat.

She said, "Oh, Jesus. Jesus God."

The trees, tall and cold, offered no welcome. They hid us, though. Behind, I heard shouting and gunshots. The driver had come back— I could see him. He didn't know where to look and fired his gun into the woods on the other side of the road. A flurry of snow, driven by the wind, forced his arms to his face. Now he looked in our direction. He couldn't see us, not in that dense dark.

But I could see him, clearly across the snow. As he looked around, not knowing where to fire, somebody called him from up the hill— Sebastian Volunder, who began limping down to our car. He had dressed in the white uniform of Alpine soldiers.

As I watched, he turned, called, and beckoned to the troops behind him. One, two, four, eight soldiers walked down to where he stood and inspected our footprints on the slope above the road.

109

With Kate's damn bag heavy in my hand, we began to run. The forest loomed toward us; we crashed into it. She kept up. Despite the clothes, the hair, the shoes, she ran like a goat. She jumped. She swerved. She danced. And now, in the deep trees, it was dark enough to lose us. And wild enough to stop us. And cold enough to kill us.

All of this I knew as we ran like blinded animals.

"West," Stefan Bekker had said, and "West," I said to Kate Begley, and she said, "Who knows where west is?"

I reckoned that we had three hours before the night fell on top of us; the darkness would multiply the chances of freezing death.

"We'll just keep going," I said.

And she said, "We're due some luck."

To which I said nothing.

Here, in order that you grasp the essence of what we went through, I'll tell you what I learned after the war about Volunder. Then you'll appreciate the pack that followed on our heels.

After Peiper and Volunder came up together through the ranks of the German cavalry, they contrived to stay close together. All through the 1930s, Peiper kept rising in rank above Volunder, who was considered unstable—a reputation that didn't prevent him being part of Hitler's ceremonial guard at the 1936 Olympics.

As the appetite for war surged, Peiper became known to Himmler—to whom he then introduced Volunder. Himmler, a chicken farmer before the war, had always longed for what he couldn't have—the air of an aristocrat. So he took it vicariously from Volunder, and from the even more cosmopolitan Peiper, whose fluency in English and French had enhanced his standing as a man of style.

When Peiper joined Himmler's staff, he had no difficulty bringing Volunder with him. On 29 June 1939, Peiper married Himmler's secretary, with Volunder as best man. On 3 September, the two men went by train into Poland to inspect labor camps. (In one of war's more striking ironies, Peiper once inspected the camp at Dachau, where he would later be tried as a war criminal.)

Now Volunder began to come into his own standing. In January 1940, he went with Himmler deeper into Poland. Leaving Peiper behind on purely military matters, Volunder watched Himmler carry out a symbolic execution of a Polish intellectual—and then took over.

Some people he killed quickly, with a gun. He slit the throats of others. And some he killed slowly, especially the women, the wives of the professors and the doctors and the teachers.

In which case, why had he been Peiper's friend, Peiper the consummate soldier, Peiper the remarkable commander? Who can say? Nothing makes stranger bedfellows than a uniform. Especially in war.

110

For ten minutes, ten surging, running minutes—and maybe more—we ran and scrambled and stumbled through that forest in the Ardennes. I had a dilemma: Should I lead and make smooth a path—insofar as I could—or should I follow and protect Kate's back? I compromised—we went side by side. I held her bag; she held my other hand. Hansel and Gretel. Running from Death.

We made progress. The terrain proved less difficult, more level than I'd expected, and this wood hadn't been recently planted—the trees had been there thirty years and more.

She stopped, to draw breath. I tried to look behind, but could see no more than maybe twenty yards. And I shuddered at how clear a trail we'd left in the deep snow. How far behind could they be?

Not far. Not "they." Him. One man. No others. Do I want to say that he had a limp? And that he wore a black-and-cream silk polka-dot handkerchief in his white uniform cuff? Yes, I do want to say that, but I can't—or to be more truthful, I don't know.

I do know that when I looked back I saw something. Something that moved. Not a branch, not a black tree, not a deer or some animal sliding down the deep snow. This was quicker. And it stopped. Kate saw it too. She struck my arm with hers. By now the cold was once again limiting the use of her hands. She used them to balance, her arms held out. A stumble might mean a ravine we hadn't seen. This was a foot, maybe two, of old snow.

The object moved again. I knew what it was, and I gestured her toward a wide tree. She went to it and stood there, somewhat obscured by its huge trunk from the direction in which we'd seen the movement.

It moved again—a man. Impossible to define him in the snow, a ghost against a sheet. One tiny definer—his white headgear had a black something on it. He saw Kate's movement. He changed his trajectory until he could see her better.

I stood beside her. She whispered, "We must move." I heard her teeth rattle, iced castanets. With my finger to my lips I went in front of her. Not beside her; I wanted to keep looking toward danger. Was it danger? Oh, God it was.

Not a sound could I hear in that sparser part of the forest. Not even one of those far-off sounds that epitomize countryside atmosphere. No barking dog. No comforting owl. And not even a war.

Since the wind had dropped, the branches made no noise. Or else I had shut out everything in my concentration on this distant white figure. Who could tell in that depth of snow if somebody were limping? The white figure seemed to disappear, into the trees, walking laterally, but not toward us.

I didn't move us forward; I said we'd wait to make sure that the figure in white had gone away. After too many minutes I heard a sound. *What was that?* said Miss Begley's eyebrows. I shook my head, said nothing.

What was it? The sound of a deep—a deep something? A deep what? A deep crunch? Just once. I took the finger from my lips, put it tight on hers. Telling her silently, *Not a sound.* Don't. Even. Breathe.

I turned my head forty-five degrees to the left and listened. Another. Yes, a crunch. A second crunch. Then another silence. Then a third crunch, nearer—not by much, but nearer. *Identify it! Identify it!* In crisis I've often found that my mind's voice becomes unexpectedly articulate. It didn't say, "What is it?"—it screamed, "Identify it!"

And I did. It was a "something" stepping toward where we hid behind the great wide tree. A human? Must be. Taking one great step at a time. Listening between steps. That was the identification I made. There! A fourth crunch. Getting nearer.

Crucial to know which side of the tree. Had it—had he—seen us? *Well, of course he has!* screamed my mind. *Why do you think he's crunching his way toward us?*

Much closer now. *Awful.* The crunching stopped. Stopped completely. *He's ten yards away, and he's puzzled because he can see nothing. Neither can I.* He crunched again. One-crunch. Two-crunch. Three-crunch. Four-crunch. Nearer. Nearer. Nearer. Nearer. Now he's at the other side of the tree.

111

I saw him before he saw me. The insignia, that's what I saw first, the black cross on the helmet's forehead. And the black gun. He brought up his right arm as he steadied himself for the next deep step forward in the crunching snow. It was, I now know, a Luger, long slender barrel.

Another step forward once more. With his snow mask and goggles I never saw his face, only his hand with the gun. Pointed straight at my head. And he stepped forward with a much harder crunch now. I held my hands out. Cruciform. He stepped away to one side of me.

Christ! What has she done? Kate stepped out from behind the tree. Four feet from me, seven feet from him. *What is she doing?* She spread her arms in her own crucifix.

He said something. I didn't know what it was. She said later it was, *"Was ist?"* How could I know? I didn't even know for sure whether it was Volunder. I still don't know.

"Nein," she said, a gasp in her voice. *"Nein, nein."*

"Ireland," I said. *"Irlande. Irlanda."*

"Nein, nein, nein," she said, in the voice of a woman about to go crazy.

"No, no," she said, and I said, "No!"

Such bizarre thoughts as we get. *My parents didn't prepare me for meeting a man with a gun in a snowy forest during a war.* I can't remember any other thought.

He raised the gun a little higher. Still pointed it at me. Straight at my face now.

He flapped a hand at her, beckoned her forward. It must have been Volunder—he'd kill me and take her back with him. *Come here and stand beside me,* beckoned the hand. He stepped forward. So concentrated. So focused on my face. And I couldn't even see his eyes.

How did I do it? Height and reach. I have long arms. I hit him with my right fist. Where was his strength? Military rations, perhaps? As he staggered he fired. Kate fell with a grunt.

I was on him. On him, on him, on him. I stamped on the gun hand. Stamped and stamped. He didn't let go, he fought me off. On his knees he fired again. This shot, not a loud crack, a strange, dull sound, a metal grunt, whistled past me.

I kicked him as he rose. Kicked him in the face. Kicked him with every ounce of my six-foot-four bulk. He went down, he dropped the gun, I picked it up, I knelt over him, and I shot him in the head. Twice. With the two bullets he had left, and if the gun had held two hundred and two bullets I'd have fired every one.

On the nights that I can't sleep, the all-white snow outfit of a German soldier haunts me. If it wasn't Volunder, did he have a wife? Did he have children? And a pleasant house with a staircase and pine banisters? And I killed him.

It's right that I should care. I should wake at nights. I should be hurt. Even if he was Sebastian Volunder. But I didn't look. Only a rose of black blood above his ear—that's all I saw. One perfect rose.

At that moment I had but a single thought. Kate was sitting on top of the snow like a doll.

"I fell," she said. "Ben, Death is God's Remedy for All Ills. For All Ills, Ben." She was losing her composure again. "Ben, I miss my father, did I ever tell you that?"

"Are you hurt?"

She shook her head. I lifted her to her feet. She was as limp as a glove. She didn't look toward the dead man. I figured that she must have dropped to the snow in shock.

"Go," I said. "Go!"

She moved. I picked up the damn bag and followed her, forward through the snow, and now I was the one making the deep and huge crunches—but in my soul, I was now and forever brutalized. I was in some part of me a dog of war.

No words can discuss the act of killing somebody. Nothing I can say will take me forward into a place of comfort on that topic. I can compartmentalize it, put it under the heading of "An Act Necessary to Stay Alive." But I can't sanction it. God, it hurts.

Through the goggles, I saw into his eyes; I tried not to, but I saw them, and snow-mad or not, he knew what was going to happen. He knew that he was about to lose his life, that his corpse would lie there in the snow, covered over and preserved until the spring, and some farmer or hunter or band of soldiers coming along these woods would find him as the snows thawed and he would be tagged and carried to some military graveyard, and if lucky he still had legible papers on him so that his family could be told in order to permit them to mourn him.

Other than that he would become a name listed as MIA, missing in action, and his family would forever wonder what had happened to him. How had he died? they'd ask themselves. And his wife, now alone with her body in bed at night, might console herself that her husband was the nameless hero in the tomb of the Unknown Soldier.

Even if he was Sebastian Volunder.

He had stiffened almost the moment the life left his body. I had been as tidy in the killing of him as I am with my notebooks and pens, the tools of my trade, but I didn't know I was being tidy. One shot, then two—oh, dear Christ, do I still hear those dull echoes in the nights? And why is it always—this is some irony—why is it always the case that I most hear them in the balmy, twilight deeps of Irish summer nights?

112

We moved through the snow, trying to be steady, but near to destruction. I felt certain that I had broken my own heart. At one moment, we halted because I heard in the distance behind us a long fusillade of shots. Rifle fire—my God, I could now tell the difference between guns! It lasted for long minutes.

If I had known that I was overhearing one of the foulest atrocities of World War II, the massacre of American prisoners of war at the crossroads of Malmédy—for which Jochen Peiper stood trial at Dachau—

would it have healed my remorse at the killing I had just done? I doubt it. I was born to live life, not take it. Or was I? Would I, like so many, kill again?

"The woods can't get deeper than this," she said. Her tone had strengthened again. Whence came that girl's resilience?

I said, "Listen!"

We listened. The gunfire ended.

For some moments we stood, exhaling, looking for some more recovery, listening for the next noises. It took some time for their pattern to soak into our minds.

A deep wood can sound like a sailing ship. It creaks. Things flap and fall. Or crash. I retraced five or six yards—no sound of pursuit, but they could be stalking us, waiting for us to tire. Finger still held to my lips, I went back to Kate—and again felt astonished; she seemed to have reenergized. She clapped her hands to keep them warm, she shook her head to clear her brain. Her energy, her composure—so rewarding, such a lesson.

We held hands again, and as we moved on we heard a new sound. Running water—hard, fast, running water, meaning that in this climate, in that season, something was big enough and tough enough not to be frozen over by the weather.

Rivers have to go somewhere. We went forward, found it, and surrendered to its leadership. This stream, powerful as a lateral cataract, had enough size and importance to need a destiny. We had no idea where we were. Belgium, yes, and therefore this river wasn't going to the sea, yet it surely must lead us somewhere.

But did it have shallows? I had no idea of its depth at the middle. Could we cover our tracks by walking in the actual water? I calculated that if we stayed as close to the bank as possible, we'd be stepping in six inches of water, which would then erase our tracks.

The riverbank gave us easy passage down to the stream, which measured maybe six, eight yards across, and it flowed high, rough and fast, white spume everywhere. I made Kate stand in the shallow water, and I stepped into the middle. The water came to my waist, then my chest, then down to my waist again.

I made it to the far bank, where I created two sets of footprints up the slope and into the trees. Putting my feet carefully into one set, I came back down and crossed the river again. Now it looked as though we'd gone deeper into the forest on the far side.

We walked in the shallows of that stream for what seemed like an hour. The miracle of circulation kept our feet alive—and the river erased our footprints almost as soon as we'd made them. Were this a legend that I'd collected in, say, Donegal, or Mayo, the myth would have been, "The river spoke, and the god of the stream came to their aid."

Kate walked ahead of me, and the shallows, little mudflats, continued; the river must have carved out a deep furrow over the centuries. And then—it vanished. It went underground, and Kate, in better spirits than I could have expected, said, "Now we're high and dry."

"Look up," the god of the river said, "look up and see how the trees are thinner here. This means that you may be coming to an edge of the wood. And now look ahead and see brighter light."

I did indeed look up, and ahead saw brighter light. The snow had ceased falling, or else we'd gone in so deep that the branches had kept it from us. In some places, it lay three or four inches high, and we couldn't guess where the drifts might be; in other, denser stretches of the forest, the ground lay bare. To those patches we kept, leaving as little spoor as possible.

Following this brightening light, we found ourselves almost in open ground again. We had come to the innermost border of a huge U-shaped plantation that spread for miles and miles over the booming hills.

I guessed the time at around one o'clock in the afternoon. We'd walked about three hours. Clouds somewhere thinned a little, and a weak sunlight strengthened—not by much, but by enough to let us see that we must have come far away from the roads and the troop movements. As though to confirm, we heard, from a great distance off to our left, the sound of heavy guns. I looked up, found the sun, and said to Kate, "Whether we knew it or not, we've been going west." We stood on the top left-hand spur of the U, the eastern side.

Over her shoulder I saw something. I walked past her, to the very edge of the wood, to a sign on a tree. It said, amid smudges, DIR. BAUGNEZ, but no arrows, nothing else, nothing to give us direction. From behind a tree I looked out across the U and saw nobody, nothing but a wide, white, silent plain of thin snow. Looking back, I heard no sound of pursuit.

We agreed to stay just within the trees and pursue the forest line to take ourselves west. What choice did we have? We needed to stay as concealed as possible. Side by side this time, we set off along one leg of the ∪, more conscious now of how wet we were, and how cold, and how incongruous we would look to anybody who found us. And the wind was coming up, whistling here, sighing there.

After an endless, stumbling trudge, and just as I began to panic about my freezing clothes, Kate stopped.

"What's that?" She pointed—a hut, twenty yards inside the tree line, a not insubstantial hut. We had reached the belly of the ∪—and the center of this legend that our lives had become.

Neither of us could read the language on the door notice, and in alarm we wondered again where in God's name we had been traveling. (Later, when my mind came back to me, I reasoned that it had been printed in one of the Belgian dialects.)

The hut, closed but with no lock, contained nothing. Worst of all, it had no fireplace. And no lighting of any kind, not even a window. In fact, it seemed to have no purpose that we could define, and there we stood, in a wooden building, measuring about twelve feet by ten, with four walls, a roof, a moist dirt floor, and nothing else.

Its builder, however, had made it windproof. I held my hands to the walls here and there, and not a draft could I feel. And so soundproof; we cocked our heads and listened and heard nothing. We could hardly see each other in the gloom.

Everything I wore had become as wet as the sea.

Kate said, "I'm soaked too. To the skin."

We had no materials to light a fire. We had no means of drying or changing our clothes. We had nothing on which to sit. All we could do was look at each other and shrug.

I opened the door, then shut it fast. The howling of the wind made us appreciate the shelter.

"There must," I said, "be a purpose to this hut."

"A woodsman? A forester?" She walked around touching the walls. "It's very dry."

"Except for the floor," I said.

"My belly is touching my backbone I'm so hungry," she said.

"We should probably stay here until morning," I said.

"And anyway, if we had a fire"—she looked up at the planked ceiling—"we wouldn't be able to see each other for smoke."

I opened the door again, not quite knowing why, and asked out loud, "What is it used for? What's the point of it?" Something was arresting me. "There must be a purpose." I stepped out into the wind; a branch somewhere cracked, and I jumped. "I'm going to look around," I said.

Hugging the walls, I walked down one side to the rear, where loose branches almost tripped me. Looking into the woods, I saw extraordinary effects—some trees waving like crowds, the rest tranquil and still. In the clearing, snow began to fall again, whipped by the wind. Treetops waved, and white scuds flew from them. I worried about animals, predators; I worried about soldiers. For any of them we made a fine prize, and easy to catch.

By now I knew that I was searching for something—perhaps a toolbox, where foresters stored axes; perhaps another shed, more fitted for habitation. Looking down, I saw no footprints—and yet somebody had spread broken and heavy branches at the rear wall of the hut; I could see white fangs of wood where they'd been cut from their trees. I bent and lifted two of the branches—and found the unknown thing for which I'd searched, a wooden trapdoor, as in a fairy tale or a pirate's yarn; it even had an iron ring with which to open it.

113

With the trapdoor open, I could see nothing, other than a small ladder, down which I climbed. A flashlight hung from a rung halfway down. When I shone the beam, I saw that the underground room ran the length of the hut and underneath it. It had recently been inhabited. No stove here either, no fireplace, but masses of blankets and clothing, enough for a dozen people. It felt safe. I ran back up, fetched a shivering Kate, and when she had descended I closed the trapdoor on her. Snow had begun to fall, powerful and thick.

As I feared, the ring almost shone, the planks of the trapdoor looked inviting; how could I camouflage that? I must have spent two or three min-utes pulling branches so that they covered most of the trapdoor in a nat-ural sort of way. When I squeezed myself down, I kept the trapdoor opening as narrow as possible. I hoped that the angle at which I'd left some of the branches would jerk them across to cover the trapdoor if I took it down fast. On the ladder I heard the branches fall over; I pushed up gin-gerly and felt that sufficient weight had fallen; the snow would do the rest.

Now everything felt still—and unexpectedly warmer. I soon discov-ered the reason for the warmth—double walls, a thick wooden floor, a dense ceiling. Whoever had designed this place meant people to stay in it for long periods, or in terrible weather.

With the flashlight I explored, found another flashlight and a carbide lamp. Now we had light, and we inspected the place. We found bone-dry clothing for men, women, and children, and we began to change. Some-body had even supplied rough towels, and I could hear Kate's teeth chat-tering as she undressed from her sodden clothes.

With her back to me, she began to towel herself dry, and then she turned and said, "No. You do it. And I'll do it for you."

We might have been husband and wife, so tenderly but naturally did we dry each other.

No food; we found empty tins, but nothing edible. I spread blankets thick on the floor, and, more warm and comfortable than I'd ever ex-pected to be, we lay down, side by side but not touching.

I guessed it was four or five o'clock, with night falling headlong out-side. Kate fell asleep immediately. I lay awake, attempting to think a way forward. Before long, I also fell asleep.

How can you tell the time when you're beneath the ground? And have no watch or clock? It might have been midnight. It might have been only an hour later. I woke to a noise above. Yes, a noise.

I listened. Then I sat up. And crept in my new and awkward clothes. Across the pitch-black floor. I listened again. A tapping. Strong tapping. With something sharp. On the trapdoor right above my head. Not rhythmic. Nor calculated. More an irregular thumping.

And now snuffling. An animal. Without doubt. A deer, probably. I climbed the ladder. To press upward on the door. Above my head the tapping stopped. I heard the big snuffle, and then the sound of a little gallop away.

Followed by a shot. Muffled, but a shot. No doubt about it. Then three more shots. Then men talking. Laughing.

Wide-eyed, Kate sat up. I lit and shaded the flashlight to see her face, then shone it on mine, then crawled to her.

"Shhhhhh."

"They missed."

I whispered, "What?"

"They fired at a deer and missed."

"How do you know?"

"They're teasing each other," she whispered.

Above our heads, boots stomped. They were in the hut. I switched off the flashlight. One, two, three, four, five, six pairs of boots. Or so it felt. A few feet above our heads. The aroma of cigarette smoke reached us.

We sat as though paralyzed. She took my arm and wrapped it around her. I tightened my grip. Five, then, fifteen minutes—or hours, how could we tell? They had a radio of some kind; I heard the unmistakable static.

"They're moving on. The snow is heavy. They think they're near us," she said. "And that anyway we won't survive. But they know it's us they're following."

Neither one of us moved a muscle. When we did, I couldn't flex my arms or legs. They had gone. We waited and waited—yes, they'd gone.

She slept first; I kept watch. In the darkness I could almost see her face; I never took my eyes off it.

My next passage of sleep took me close to oblivion. I have no knowledge or feeling of how long I slept. When I awoke, Kate was sitting on a camp stool, the carbide lamp beside her, just looking at me. She held out a book, a small, green book with a Star of David on the leather cover. Now that the war is long over, we know the truth about that underground hiding place—and it saved our lives too.

114

For a moment, I couldn't raise the trapdoor. And then I remembered: snow. I pushed harder and opened it an inch. At least a foot of snow had fallen. The wind had died, and the sun shone into my eyes. But I was facing west, and that meant another night in the woodland cellar. I put the time at around three o'clock.

We'd slept a great deal. In retrospect, we'd been shrewd because we'd needed the sleep. And this time we both slept at the same time, and this time nothing disturbed us. Our bodies adjusted. We were dehydrated, but because we'd had no food, we needed no toilet facilities, and hadn't since we'd begun our escape.

Morning, bright and cold, would energize us as much as it could. We stretched, yawned, checked our clothing. Most of it had dried a good deal, though our coats remained damp. We decided to continue in the clothes we had found, although I retrieved my black coat. Miss Begley wore a dress of brown serge that came down below her knees; I had corduroy pants, a heavy woolen shirt, and a thick vest with pockets. Our shoes had to continue; we found none.

With something close to pleasure, I recalled that we were still near the verge of the wood and could, today at any rate, see where we were going. When we came out to the forest's rim, the light almost blinded us. In the long hollow of the forest's U shape, new, deep snow lay higher than before and stretched as far as the horizon.

Not a living creature could we see—not a bird, not a deer. The snow had also obliterated the tracks of our pursuers.

We talked through a simple plan—to walk along that forest edge until we came to some manageable terrain. And we'd stay just inside the trees, so that we couldn't be seen, yet we could see anybody coming up through the open spaces of the U. If military, we would have to be careful—who would they be? German? Allies?

Five or six hours we walked, on relatively easy ground, and Kate's bag seemed not as heavy. Babes in the Wood, we were, and I recalled the lines from a childhood poem that used to make me cry. *And when they were dead, the robins so red, brought strawberry leaves, and over them spread.* No strawberry leaves now, but dying remained a significant possibility.

Kate remained silent while walking. When I asked her, for the third anxious time, "Are you all right?" she nodded.

"I'm conserving my breath," she said.

What was she thinking? I couldn't read her mood. All I could sense about her may be summarized by the word *determination.* At one moment, on the crest of a sharp little slope, when we stopped to rest, I reached over and hugged her and held her.

We walked all day. How we kept going I can't say. In the midafternoon, she began talking to herself, loud enough for me to hear.

"Constant Occupation Prevents Dreadful Temptation" was the first thing she said.

"What?"

She answered with, "Exercise Patience in one moment of Anger and you'll escape many hours of Regret."

"Are you keeping your spirits up?" I asked.

"Lose the saddle, not the horse," she said, but didn't mean it as a reply.

"Kate—stop," I said, and pulled her to a standstill. Her face had turned blue.

"One today is worth two tomorrow."

"Kate!" She looked up at my face but didn't see me. The brown eyes had begun to cloud over with a heavy glaze, almost like a gray film. She was babbling, and light saliva frosted her mouth.

"Poverty waits at the Gates of Idleness," she said. "Error Clouds the Windows of the Mind," and she began to weep, as though the clouds in her eyes had turned to rain.

I inspected her. Feet bleeding. Shoes had leather strips flittering from them. One shin with a horrible gash. A thin stripe of blood drew a dark line down one cheek where a tree branch thin as a fingernail had reached down and scraped her. Nose and eyes blue, eyes blinking all the time against the glare.

What could I do? I wrapped her inside my arms. I rocked her from side to side, and rocked her again. She began to feel limp. I picked her up, got her onto my shoulders, and carried her through the wood, one hand gripping her legs to stabilize her, the other carrying her bag.

115

Did I feel her weight? No. And when I go searching my memory now to try for a more accurate answer to the question, I still can't feel it. She either fell asleep on my shoulders or she passed out. Lifting my feet high above the snow, I set a deliberate pace. I reconciled myself to one thought: If the soldiers come, we can't escape. And it had begun to snow again, the same heavy, drifting flakes, intent on covering the world.

Traveling inside the tree line proved too difficult. Staggering with tiredness and freight, I bumped into trees, and I feared that I might hit her head off something. I opted for the open skies, and took a little comfort from the fact that nobody could see me in this snow. The slope helped too, not too steep, not too rocky—in fact by now the older snow had frozen so hard that I almost had a firm base beneath my boots.

Down the hillside I went, trying to keeping my stumbles to a minimum. If I fell forward, I had no means of protecting her head—and perhaps not the strength to get up again and lift her onto my shoulders. The world had by now turned entirely white—the sky, the land, the two beset human beings.

116

Kate Begley had gods on her team of Life—because, with such daylight as still glimmered through the white veils beginning to quit the sky, I hit level ground—and a gate. From there, a secluded lane appeared, so shaded by trees that it had almost no snow. Under this thick canopy, the lane petered to the edge of the wood where I walked—but from where? It seemed respectable enough to be worth following—and I had no options. The gate had no catch; easy as a door, it swung open, and I applauded the smoothness of the track.

What's this? A mirage? Must be. No. But—how had that got here?

Even now, as I look back on it, it would have felt more at home in a Paris or Berlin suburb; and it still looks like that. I stood and stared— a cube of white with rough walls and acres of glass. As I drew closer, and by now the snow had reduced itself to light whipping flurries, I could see a pair of doors as white as the walls, and all but camouflaged in the way they had been inserted.

Lights shone inside. Suddenly breaking down, I staggered to the door at the side; judging from the unshoveled snow, nobody had come out of this building in the past twenty-four hours.

I knocked—and it wasn't a dream or a mirage: Somebody inside opened the door. A tall woman, severe as a teacher, looked at us, and said in English, "Well, hello there!"

She reached down and tried to take Miss Begley's bag—my fingers had frozen to the handle.

"Max," she called.

A dog appeared, a big clumber spaniel. Too lazy to have barked when we knocked, he looked up at us without even a whit of curiosity, sort of wagged his tail, and ambled back to his place in front of the fire. He wasn't Max, his name was Shambles.

A man appeared, twenty years younger than the woman, handsome as groomed leather.

"I'm Max Jackson," he said. I couldn't place the accent. "This is my wife, Joan."

Between them they got us into the house. When, hours later, they asked about our journey, I, accustomed to countryside travel, could give them a good description. Between then and the previous day, they reckoned, with their knowledge of the area, that we had traveled about seventy miles.

"In this weather?" they said.

Architects, both Australian, they became friends of mine after the war, and I've visited them, and they've visited me here on this mountainside, and every time we meet, they ask me again to tell them (and their guests, if I'm in their house) the story that I've described so far. I always leave out the killing.

That night, when they saw our condition, they became our nursemaids. Only much later did I surmise—and they've never confirmed or denied—that they had done this often. Their skill seemed too practiced, their surprise too mild. For instance, they wouldn't give us much food, they said, not until next day.

Together they lifted Kate from my shoulders and carried her to a couch. I leaned against the wall and then sat on the floor.

Warm flannels, hot towels, a dab of brandy on her lips—Kate had indeed passed out and had escaped frostbite by less than an hour, they said. They carried her upstairs, where they laid her on a bed and covered her with blankets, taking off only her outer clothes. Max lit a fire in her room; an hour or two later, Joan revived her and helped her into a hot bath. I sort of passed out on the sofa downstairs.

Not for long; I took some brandy, and perked up enough to want a bath too. With every fiber of my body a burning pain, I lowered myself slowly into the water—where I almost passed out again.

Next afternoon, when we had grown lucid, and when they had taken into account all our details, they made our next plans for us. We would stay with them until, as Max put it, "the right information" reached him as to the safest place to go. He told us that we had walked through the forests above the village of Büllingen, and that he'd heard of German troops heading west through there that very morning.

I asked, "Are we safe here?"

He said, "What's safe? Tanks. Allied or German. They could get down this road."

I said, "Nothing to stop them, I suppose."

Max said, "But you're in from the weather here."

They'd seen almost nothing of the war. Max had an office across the border, in Germany.

"I think I'm on some kind of safe list," and he laughed. "I wasn't part of the Bauhaus group, so I'm not suspect. And I used to work for Albert Speer—so maybe he's protecting me." He laughed again.

I was too tired to check the references.

Our few days there felt like a vacation. And it snowed, and it snowed, and it snowed. On Saturday morning, a plow arrived and cleared their path and the lane. The driver, a neighbor, brought news of the war. He said that the Germans were pushing back. Hoping to take Liège.

Max said, "They're crazy."

Joan said, "They've already captured a number of Allied forces."

And the snowplow driver said, "But the Americans have almost surrounded them. And they're at Elsenborn."

I think that we all play games in our minds with words and language. Even in dire conditions, we dally with little runs of word sounds and phrases that ring like small bells or bounce around like toys. This is the phrase that danced in my head in that house: "scared and scoured." My mind went, *We are scared and scoured. Scoured and scared. Scared-scoured, scoured-scared. Scared. And. Scoured.*

No need to explain *scared*—you can tell whence that came. But we never found Captain Miller in those Belgian villages, and the failure to fulfill my dear friend's dream left me whitened and empty inside, like a shed that has been stripped of everything but its walls, roof, and floor, and all of those whitewashed. In some places, the gray shows through the rubbed white. That's what the inside of my mind felt like: blank; bleak; brittle—scoured.

117

Max's snowplow driver got us almost to Elsenborn. Almost. A Walloon who spoke perfect German, Ernst knew every road in his region. We drove through people's yards, we drove along the banks of rivers and across frozen streams, we drove into the woods again; the little truck must have been made of the greatest steel. In the rear sat three of the driver's friends—with hunting rifles across their knees, their faces masked against the cold.

We stopped multiple times—to hide, to stretch our legs, or to wait while Ernst could go forward and look down a hill or around a corner. In one village (it may have been Saint-Vith), he stopped beside an army truck—a German army truck.

Ernst joked with the soldiers in German, smoked a cigarette with them, told them that he worked undercover locally for them, and said he'd return and help them. He said that we were a young Walloon couple with a pregnancy that was going wrong early, and he was trying to get through to the hospital in Liège. They told him not to go near Elsenborn, that the Americans now controlled that side of the forest.

From that village, Ernst headed east. As I was about to inquire why, he turned hard right and hard right again on a series of lanes and now we were heading west. I saw a sign for Malmédy, and we went down that road.

On the sharp crest of a hill, Ernst made an error. He stopped so hard that Kate and I, sitting beside him on the bench seat, almost cracked our faces on the windshield. Ernst began to back up—but too late: We'd been seen. Down the hill, at a crossroads, gathered a thick agglomeration of German troops—it seemed almost an army unto itself.

They saw us—they saw our sudden stop, our urgent backing up. No more than a hundred yards or so from us, they opened fire. Nothing hit us, but they began to follow. Ernst revved and revved; the wheels stuck and whizzed—no purchase on the iced mud of the little road.

The three men in the rear jumped out and opened fire down the hill. Two of them continued the fire and the third, with me helping, and Ernst at the wheel, pushed the truck out of the mud. The gunmen jumped back in, and away we went. Two miles on, Ernst turned down another hill and pointed ahead.

"You're safe."

118

In the American camp at Elsenborn, a wide and deep scattering of tents and vehicles under the loosest trees of the forest, the nurses sedated Kate and put her to bed. They had to. When she walked into the medical tent, her feet in six inches of mud, she pitched forward into the arms of the first nurse she saw.

I stood by, as though to make sure that they laid her down carefully, tenderly. "Her husband," I told them, "is an American officer—Captain Charles Miller. We believe he's here somewhere. We're searching for him."

The second nurse pointed through the door of the tent and whispered, "Go and ask over there."

And still I lingered. When she and the first nurse had wrapped Kate like a baby and put her gently to bed, her face the shade of blue chalk, only then did I leave. I walked from the tent and, in the mud outside, bent forward and threw up everything that I'd eaten in the last ten years—or so it felt like.

This thought I remember: *The difference between a friend and an enemy is friendliness.* I had come that low—into banality, into wary thought, into nonstop fear. A bright, heavily uniformed young man with beetling eyebrows said, "Can I help you, sir?" and he smiled.

"This is who I am," and I told him. "This is what I'm doing here," and I told him.

"Dunno if I can help," he said, but he certainly tried. He gave me coffee and a chair to sit on, went off to make inquiries, and returned maybe ten minutes later or maybe an hour later, that's how stunned I was—with a senior man.

At this officer's request I repeated my name and my mission and pointed to the tent where Kate lay asleep.

"In the name of Christ," said this new officer, "what were you guys thinking of?"

"Don't ask me," I said.

"I will ask you. You're here. Middle of a damn war."

Billy Moloney, where were you when I needed you? You recall that Mother—that's your grandmother—and I, in order to report his hilarious speech accurately, had agreed years ago to substitute the word *flock* for every second word Billy spoke?

"Don't flocking ask me," I said, not knowing that I was yelling. "Just flocking don't. Don't flocking order me, just flock off and leave me flocking alone."

"Hey, hey," said the senior officer, who had slightly bulging eyes. "Nobody's threatening you."

Was he the kindest man I've ever known? Perhaps. And he knew how to handle men; he stood close to me, put his hands on my shoulders, and said, "You're okay. Take it easy, take it easy. What have you been up to?"

I told him—about the woods, the hiding place, the Messerschmitt and its trigger-happy pilot, the German camp, and he said, staggered by my story, "You need more coffee, sir." I didn't tell him about the killing.

The "sir" did it. I started to weep and couldn't stop. He never let go of my shoulders and he just looked at me and said, "It's okay, it's okay."

The beetle-browed young man fetched a second chair and more coffee, and this senior officer and I sat down. We drained our tin mugs, not at all battered, shiny new in fact. And we looked down at the muddy ground.

"I met a fellow called Peiper," I said. "He has American troops."

"Peiper's a tough egg. Him and his gang—ravenous."

My mood frightful, my spirits destroyed, my intellect a sputtering candle, I nonetheless noted the word. *Ravenous.* A ravening wolf. If nothing else works in the world—legend does. It steadies us, it restores us, it tells us who we are and what we do. That was James Clare's thesis. He would have latched on to the word *ravenous.* And I, his earnest student in legend and life, took comfort from the fact that the word had been used, and I had noted it.

119

Kate went back to Lamb's Head, and I home to Goldenfields. Before that, we had been debriefed at the embassy in Dublin. They didn't try to tell her that her husband was dead; they saw her passion; nobody could stand close to that fire. It will take a long time, they said, to "sift the results of the war."

Such diplomatic language—but it was good enough for her. She asked them to tell her when the soldiers were going home from Europe; by now we knew who was going to win the war.

And by then we looked like refugees; each of us had lost a great deal of weight; I could afford it, she couldn't. And yet she put out so much energy at the embassy that they all but summoned the ambassador himself. She paced up and down, she spread her hands in powerful gestures; she spoke in emphasis strong as a preacher.

"When you know something—when you know that you know it. Deep in here"—she stabbed a finger into her chest—"you have to believe it. Life is a River with Stepping-stones of Belief."

Those officials, those decent men—I knew they'd never seen anybody like Kate. They couldn't calm her because she wasn't hysterical. They couldn't deflect her because she was so focused. They couldn't deny her because she wouldn't allow it. Her pact with Miller was as powerful as any fuel the world has ever found.

"What will you say to me," she asked them, "when he comes home from the war and I'm waiting for him?"

They had no answer. Neither did I.

Whatever her show of bravery, she still trembled; on the train south, she failed to keep her hands from shaking; she spilled tea. I had offered—indeed, tried to insist—that I go to Kenmare with her, but she refused, so I climbed from the train at Dundrum and, to my profound astonishment, found Mother and my father waiting. I had sent them a telegram: IS IT ALL RIGHT IF I COME HOME TOMORROW? They'd seen that it came from Dublin the previous day, and they had gone to meet both trains.

No embrace; neither took my arm. I had no luggage, just my battered, shattered journal, my *Wandering Scholars,* and my long black coat, and I was still wearing the clothes that I'd found in that cellar in the forest. We walked together, three abreast, each of them close by me, down the platform to the car.

As we sat inside, Mother reached a hand back and patted my knee, and my father said, "You-you-you're all right now. All right." How did they know what I'd been through? His little stammer used to irritate and embarrass me; not then, not ever again. We drove home in silence. My irrepressible father broke the silence just once.

"John-John-John Casey's wife makes him sleep with the horses these days, since he's so fond of them, she says."

In the house, Mother beckoned me upstairs. Without a word she showed me the new bathroom, and in moments the steam rose.

"Come on down when you're ready," she said. Huge towels lay on shelves, and when I looked in the mirror I wondered whose face I saw.

Almost an hour later, I walked down the back stairs to the kitchen and found nobody there. I heard Mother call; they had a fire lighting in the parlor, the room where I had first sat and listened to Venetia as she told me the story of my father and herself, of their one-sided love affair. A tray sat there, of ham and onion sandwiches, my favorite food on this earth, and two large pots of tea, and an apple pie as big as a wheel.

"Sit-sit-sit down now," said my father. He didn't offer me a drink, he never offered me a drink, and when he died I asked Mother why not?

"He didn't believe that a parent should encourage their children to drink," she said.

That was my father in trumps, in all his uneven and cross-eyed philosophies. He thought it all right to down tools and quit his farm— forever, as he thought—to run away with an actress, imperiling everybody left behind, and the farm they lived on, their livelihood and their future, but he wouldn't pour a glass of whiskey for his only child. I laughed. What else could I do?

"You-you-you've been through the mill," he said. When I nodded, he continued, "You can tell us about it or not, as the case may be. Now or any time you like."

I had a mouthful of food. When I'd chewed it, I said, "This isn't irrelevant, but do you think the Policy of Neutrality has been the right thing?"

"Ah, the old fox," he said, meaning our premier, Mr. de Valera, whom I had seen on the campaign trail, whom I had met, and whose politics I'd been watching every day of my life before Kate Begley blew me off course.

"He kept us safe," said Mother. "He kept us out of the war. They can say what they like about him, but he kept us safe."

"This-this-this is what he did," said my father. "He played Churchill off against the Yanks, and against the Protestants in the North. He told Churchill to give us back the six counties in the North, and he could use our ports, and when Churchill threatened to invade us anyway, and take the ports by force, Dev welcomed the German ambassador to lunch, 'twas in all the papers. And the Protestants—they're calling themselves 'Northern Ireland' now, by the way—when they heard the bargain that Churchill might make, there was blue murder. 'Ulster will fight and Ulster will be right'—same old threat. They say it over and over."

Naturally, I never told my parents the true reason for asking their opinion on neutrality. In Germany, and at Lamb's Head, and in the forests of Belgium, in the little hotel at Saint-Omer, even in the white house of Max the architect, I had shared a bed with Kate Begley—and would soon do so again. Her presence, her arms, her sleepy warmth, I knew and loved and relished them all—but never her body in full. On the ship coming back from Europe to Liverpool, I pointed this out to her. She listened with that grave child's face that so endeared her to me.

When I had finished she said, "Call it neutrality, Ben," and she shrugged as she always did when she had no more to offer. In her exhaustion—and mine—I pressed no further.

120

My parents told me next day that I fell asleep in mid-sentence. I had been asking for news of neighbors, of Billy Flock and his wife, Lily, of little Ned Ryan who helped look after our animals, whose son had enlisted in the British army and had been killed in the retreat from Dunkirk— and I simply stopped and fell asleep.

Mother said that she took the cup and saucer from my hand. They covered me with a blanket and left me there all night.

"Your father went down three or four times to put logs on the fire," she said next morning as I woke up. "He told me that he never saw anyone so deep asleep."

I had nothing to say, and Mother, with whom I had been through so much when my father ran off with Venetia, looked at me, ran her hand across my hair, and said, "Ben, what desperate things you must have seen."

In our language, words often had skewed and sometimes more effective uses. *Desperate* didn't always mean "without hope" or "driven by the disappearance of hope"—it also meant "dreadful." So I answered Mother.

"Desperate," I said, "in every sense of the word."

"Are you all right?"

I said, "I think I'm numb."

"Numb is the best thing," she said. "It'll help you to hold on until you recover." And then she delivered a chide that I never saw coming. "You should have come home here too when the other thing happened."

"The other thing." Meaning the Disappearance of Venetia—Venetia whom I had wrested from my father, and whom I had married a matter of weeks later.

"Mother, how could I have come home then?" I said. "In all the circumstances."

She said, "But where's more flexible than your own home?"

So I stayed in that flexible home for many, many weeks. I had days in which I did nothing but sit and look into the fire. I had days when I walked—down through our woods, so benign and safe and gray after the black and terrifying Belgian trees. I had days when I read—every poem in *Palgrave's Golden Treasury,* every stanza in Yeats's version of *The Oxford Book of English Verse*—my father brought it back from Cork one day; I'd been wanting it for years.

Unable yet to revisit my beloved *Wandering Scholars,* because the landscapes of Europe still terrified me, I read the newspaper from cover to cover. And I had days when I wrote down as much as I could bear of the events and incidents that I've been describing here.

I also wrote letters—to Kate, to Miss Fay, and to James Clare. By way of response, Miss Fay and James arrived one Sunday and I'll come to that in a moment. I didn't hear from Kate—but her grandmother, Mrs. Holst, wrote me this single page.

Dear Ben,

Kate will not be replying to your letter. She is unwell and is in the hospital in Killarney, under observation for exhaustion, and perhaps rheumatic fever. Please do not try to contact her. What in the world did you put her through on your travels? A gentleman would at least have tried to look after her, and I'm sure her husband will have things to say to you when he comes home.

Yours in disappointment,
Delia Holst

Too much; too unjust; I didn't have the energy to sum up a reply. One day I might, but I couldn't do it at that moment—which is how I came to keep the letter and not throw it on the fire.

Miss Fay had purchased a car—an Austin Ten, with a tall shiny nose between two huge-bug headlamp eyes and two chrome wing-mirror ears.

My father, whom she adored, said to her, "Where-where-where in the name of God did you manage to buy a car in the middle of the Emergency?"

"Half-price," she said. "The garage was going out of business"—as so many did during the war.

James described her as the best driver they'd seen on the road that day, and Miss Fay discounted the compliment, saying that they'd encountered only one other car during the three-hour journey from Dublin. "It was easy to avoid," she said. "It was parked."

Both fussed over me less than usual—tact in the presence of my parents. And both said that they longed to read my journals. Then James and I took a walk down to the river, and he told me to submit a report to the Folklore Commission.

"They're expecting something from you," he said.

"I have a lot of stuff from France. And Germany."

"They'll love you for that," James said. "They'll have their arms open for you."

"I may not want to go back," I said.

This stopped James in his tracks. "With your gift of listening?" he said.

"There's unfinished business," I said. "And I don't know how long it will take."

"Do you want to say what it is?" James asked.

How could I? How could I tell him that I had fallen under Kate Begley's spell, that I was mesmerized by her gift of belief, and that the thing had to play itself out?

"Let me write up my report," I said.

James, kinder than the best teacher in the world, said, "I'll be waiting with delighted anticipation. And then, Ben—I'll have a gift for you."

He had such good timing. I knew what he meant.

I said, "Has he agreed?"

"We'll go there together. He'll talk to me, but you'll write it down."

"In France one night," I said, "I think I saw a wolf."

James looked at me, those shrewd eyes in a face made of old stone.

"Ben, I'd say you saw more than one wolf."

Easter came, as early in April as it could be, with that cold east wind the Italians call the *tramontana*. When it blew, I dug out our big old atlas. There wasn't much by way of shelter between us and the Ural Mountains. In Berlin, Hitler was feeling an even colder wind, as Stalin sent his millions down the wide avenues into the city; and Eisenhower delayed at the gates, not wanting his armies to lose too many men.

In what seemed to me the first of the final cracks in the war, the *Irish Independent* reported,

> *No German is permitted to abandon his post or evacuate his home without express orders from Herr Hitler himself, according to a proclamation issued last night by the Chief of the National Socialist Party Central Office quoted by German radio. The proclamation said that after the collapse of 1918, "We dedicated our lives entirely to fight for the right to life of our people. Now the hour of the supreme test has come and the danger of a new slavery which is threatening our people demands our supreme exertion. From now on this is the order—the fight against the enemy who has penetrated into the Reich has to be waged everywhere and with the utmost determination and ruthlessness."*

For a moment I was back in Bremen, talking to the tall, passionate tobacconist who had lost a leg and his pride in the previous war.

My father developed a fresh bout of car fever. Miss Fay's Austin Ten had ignited him and he began to scour the country for bargains. He found an Armstrong Siddeley and gave me the Morris Eight, which he'd had for six years and which I loved.

With limited fuel (siphoned in part from his tank), I began to take short trips here and there—old castles and abbeys, river walks, mountain views, childhood haunts. I avoided two places: Charleville, where I'd lived with Venetia and whence she had vanished, and Kenmare.

Which made no difference. On 10 May 1945, days after Victory Europe, I received a telegram.

PART FIVE

Travels with a Giraffe

121

1945

Today, were I to go to New York, I could walk to the exact spot, the two square yards of concreted ground where I stood with Kate Begley for weeks, finally months. From May 1945 to April 1946, Kate and I lived in Manhattan.

Such a curious life: We had jobs of a kind; we shared a room, because people believed us a married couple, but we spent the bulk of our time standing in the same place many, many hours a day, watching ships dock and American soldiers disembark. Often in the lee of my big shoulders while a wind cut in from the Hudson River, she scanned every gray vessel, every face. As I had once promised, I again stood with her.

I helped her to write the innumerable letters to the military authorities, asking them for any trace of any kind of Captain Charles Miller. By now, she had acquired from the embassy in Dublin his serial number and the description of his most recent regimental attachment. They replied; they always replied; the reply was always the same, with variations. "Errors happen in war. Especially with commonplace names."

And by now she had almost allowed herself to believe that Peiper had been telling her the truth. I know this because she asked me his name a number of times.

"Ben, that general we met, or was he a colonel or what? Can you remember his name?"

And I'd say, "Peiper. Joachim Peiper."

She would take it in with a nod and say no more.

Yet, just as she had believed for many years that her parents would one day return from the waters of Ballinskelligs Bay, she also believed—whatever her saner moments of doubt and inquiry—that Captain Charles Miller, her bridegroom, with whom she had spent fewer than seven days of married life, would one day come home from the war. Holding two conflicting beliefs with equal strength of faith—I think only the Irish do that.

On my worst days, I feared for her sanity in the years up ahead; on my better days, I visualized marrying her, settling down with her, and in time healing the accident to her heart. During such moments, I scarcely thought of Venetia—and at other times, I missed Venetia with a pain deeper than ever, a sense of loss that cut me as never before.

I should have paid closer attention to those two feelings, especially as they were now so unprecedented in their acuteness and freshly identifiable in their poignancy.

From the room we rented, up the slopes from the river, we could hear the music of New York harbor. Some of the arriving troopships sounded their horns, a deep noise that to me will ever become associated with the word *promise*. Hearing this deep voice that boomed like a metal hippopotamus, Kate would turn her head, cock an ear, and say, "Another promise!"

By this she meant what she called "the promise of good things," and now, if I'm in a port town anywhere, in Ireland or in Europe, and I hear this sound in the night, or in the dreaming swirls of a northern fog, I replay the moment in my head.

Within minutes of hearing the ship's horn, we'd quit the room and walk at an athlete's pace to the docks. As we rounded the corner of the block, depending on the time of day, on the incoming ship or ships, and on the expectations that had been raised by military information, we'd then join myriad other people walking fast. On our first day there, the lines and lines of war brides already stood by the water, as pretty and multicolored as an aviary.

One morning, in late August 1945, will serve as an example for all our other such days. The apartment was so small that we shared a bed, Kate and I; we shared it with modesty but affection, and this enabled me to watch out for her during the night, to keep an eye on her moods, and to calm her if she grew distressed in her sleep.

Did I wish that matters could proceed beyond such a platonic and fraternal status? Of course I did, but I knew not to try just yet, and I also knew that long thoughts and patience must surely serve me best.

When we heard the foghorn's boom, and she said, "Another promise!" and we hurried from the building, and we saw the others on the street taking the same direction, the life of that day began. By this I mean that all other events—our jobs such as they were, she in a laundry, me in a bar and then a retail store, and then multiple other places—existed only to serve this scurry to the banks of the Hudson.

The New York authorities had set up an area where the waiting people could stand and watch the disembarking soldiers. Sometimes, using barriers, they moved this "waiting pen" up or down the docklands, and, for half a morning or so, people wandered around confused. But always someone stood on hand to help in that fraught place of high expectations and higher emotions.

On the calmer days, when the waiting pen had been in the same place for weeks, and people knew where to go, I always surveyed the throng— which, of course, grew thinner as more and more troops came home.

Women comprised almost all the waiting crowds. Many of the wives looked a good deal younger than thirty years old, especially the G.I. brides whom the military had brought in from countries such as France, England—and Ireland. They had applied, had been given tickets of passage from their countries of origin, and by and large had an indication of the dates when they could expect their husbands home.

Mothers stood there too, and sisters, and sweethearts, and fathers and brothers; I have never been in a place of greater collective expectation, and then release.

That morning, so typical, three distinctive small groups disembarked early from the gray troopship. First came the stretchers, and if I ever think of the New York docks these days, I automatically see the Red Cross symbol. Like the briefest of telegrams, it told those of us watching that all was not well, that for the loved ones of those accompanied by people wearing that Red Cross, life would be different from now on, and generally not easy.

Their appearance reduced that gathering—often several hundred people—to a silence, a stony and fear-filled quiet, in which I often heard only the slap of the river's wash against the hull of the ship.

As the stretchers came up the dockside toward the waiting pen, and thus closer to being recognized, the cries began. They began as sobs, a loud catching of breath, then turned into small screams—and it has to be said that some of the people thought to turn away instead of going forward.

After the stretchers came the men on crutches or walking sticks, sometimes accompanied by a helper carrying their knapsacks and duffels. Many had lost a limb; their formerly young faces had developed new muscles to accommodate the grimaces they had been making, as they accustomed themselves to their new physical conditions.

In among them, also accompanied by the Red Cross nurses, walked the men who had neither crutch nor walking stick, but whose faces wore bandages. These great white hoardings sometimes obscured most of the face, sometimes covered an eye or merely bandaged a heroic forehead. At the sight of these walking wounded, these slow, hurt young creatures, even the cries faded for a moment, and the waiting pen grew as respectful as a funeral.

Then the babble arose once more, as those waiting rushed forward to their new lives and trepidations. They couldn't yet reach the men to hug them, and I couldn't say which side of the barriers witnessed the greater distress. Directly in front of me that morning, I saw a young man who had lost several fingers and still wore a vast dressing on his right hand; and I heard him say to his wife, in all her colored print skirt, her white blouse, her yellow frizzy hair, and her earnest, welcoming, anxious, excited face, "Honey, I lost three fingers. I'm sorry."

There is nothing—and I mean nothing, zero, nil—that you can say when you hear something like that, especially when you've known and have experienced some of the context.

As the waiting people greeted these walking wounded, I watched for the next batch to stomp down the gangway. That morning too, I saw something that many ignored, or saw but didn't perceive. Still accompanied by the Red Cross in all its squared, crimson, and starched reassurance, came a separate, quiet group of men. About thirty of them appeared that day; I had seen their kind before; some people called them "the Silent Ones."

They never spoke. They didn't look anywhere for anyone. They walked straight ahead, without marching formation, without military clip of any kind, faces mostly cast down or, if not, eyes so inward in mood that they might have been closed.

These were the men whose wounds didn't show, who typically—as on that morning—carried no physical marks, yet might never recover. They had suffered shell shock, the feared "war strain" that had first been identified as an actual syndrome in the ghastly massiveness of the previous European hell.

Today we call it "post-traumatic stress disorder." It amounts to a horrible dis-anchoring of the soul, a dismembering of the power of rational thought and response. Many of these men coming down those gangways heard voices, they saw again the awful sights of war that unhinged them in the first place; they whimpered in their minds by the minute. For them, each day was forever night.

Most were taken from the dockside in transports or ambulances to clinics and rehabilitation centers scattered across the states nearest New York. For weeks and months and maybe years, they would live there, vacant in their minds and spirits, staring at the ceiling, or out of an unseen window, bursting into unexplained and inexplicable tears, unknowingly waiting for a day when their senses might return, and they could stop trembling and find new thoughts and hopes coming to them like birds returning in springtime.

Every morning, I watched these men with extra attention. From what I'd gleaned about the kind of soldier Charles Miller had had to be, and the things he must have had to do, I didn't see how he could have escaped severe damage to his soul. He was, after all, a man so capable of tender intimacy that Kate Begley searched deep inside a war to find it again. If he hadn't been wounded physically, what must have happened to his mind?

About this kind of experience I knew a great deal. On the night they took Venetia from me, my heart broke away from its moorings inside my chest. I felt it come loose, I felt it work free of the veins and arteries that held it, and I felt it rattle around inside me, as hollow as a stone in a tin can.

It took years for it to reattach itself to any tissue whatsoever, and that, I knew, is what had happened to these men, too. I hadn't seen invisible things—but I had heard Venetia's voice, over and over. Whether in my bed or on the shore or deep in the fields digging a ditch, she spoke to me, and that's how I knew and recognized the Silent Ones.

When they had passed, I turned to watch for the final disembarkation—those soldiers, still able-bodied, who trudged down the gangplank and, in march time, turned their exhausted bodies up toward the bright city and the eager waiting faces.

Kate Begley looked to these and to these only. She never sent a glance in the direction of the three previous groups, the stretchers, the crutches, the opaque. I felt bothered by this. Surely it might have occurred to her that an injury might have caused the delay in which she so believed.

Were psychology as advanced in those days, I should have known what to call her avoidance of them—another denial. Or maybe her faith in Miller's survival simply overwhelmed her. I can vouch for the fact that she never tried to communicate with any of the men in the first three troop sections, and yet she tapped so many passing arms in the main group of soldiers and in a voice of cellophane asked her question. "Was there a Captain Miller on your ship?"

Once again, I could hear my heart cracking, drifting loose, this time in pain for her. Every day, we did the same things. She dressed like an American war bride—merry patterns, bright colors, a welcome as pleasant as a summer morning for her man coming home from the war. She did her hair. She bought bobby pins, Kirby grips—I know the terms only because she told me. She painted on lipstick, tried several shades of red, and she was indeed the fairest of them all.

And every day she came away disappointed—but you'd never know it to look at her, unless you knew her well enough to know where to look.

And every night, at some moment, I would feel her heave a sigh, and then I would feel the trembling in her body beside me, in its long white chaste nightdress, as she began to cry like a child that misses her father. Sooner or later, she would turn to me without a word, take one of my arms, wrap it around her shoulder, and press her face into my chest.

My habit of insomnia returned in those New York months, as I helped Kate Begley breathe life into the dream of the man she had married, even though I was the only person in New York who knew and acknowledged what had happened to him.

122

September replaced August; the fall replaced the summer; winter replaced the fall, and we stood there every day, until we learned from the port authorities that the schedule of troopships had been so reduced they would now remove the waiting pen.

This brought us closer to the very point where the returning heroes first stepped on American soil, only now they arrived not on troopships but on ordinary vessels—ocean liners, and even freighters, and they arrived not in thousands or hundreds, but in tens and fives, sometimes in ones and twos.

Likewise, the waiting lines thinned, to around a hundred, and then fewer and then fewer still. Came a day when no more than a dozen people stood there; and came a day, New Year's Eve 1945, with 1946 about to dawn, when Kate and I stood alone, waiting for a liberty ship, as they were called.

It arrived as promised and scheduled, but it contained only refugees from Germany and the Low Countries, many of them Jewish, hoping to reunite with their relatives who had been lucky enough to get to the United States before the war. Or had come in from Spain during hostilities.

The weather that day proved too inclement for anyone to wait long or at all; nevertheless, Kate and I stood there until every last person—passenger and crew—had come ashore. Still bright and still breezy, she turned us for home and another night of dreadful hope. On Monday we went back to our jobs, in hotels or factories or bars or wherever we were working that week—or day.

Months later, on Easter Sunday, she and I planned to walk down and greet a new ship. She had not shared with me whence came her information. I believed that she had a contact in some military authority office attached to or under the aegis of the City of New York. We woke early, she in the path of the sun in that wide flat bed. I heard her stir and watched her. She sat upright and stared at the window, the sunlight all over her face and hair, which had now returned to its loveliest; after the depredations of Europe she'd had it all shorn off.

As I watched, she shook herself, a dog's shudder, and she hunched her shoulders as though swept by a sudden cold wind. She closed her eyes, and I knew that she hadn't closed them against the sun—she loved the early light, loved it more than I did; it didn't sting her eyes as it did mine.

Watching from my pillow, I waited for the mood to pass, and when I saw her shoulders go soft again, I said, "Good morning."

She turned, smiled, and tugged my hair a little.

"Sleepyhead."

"The sun's up," I said, and she said, "It's Easter Sunday and we never saw it dance."

"Never have," I said. "Have you?"

She said, "Oh, millions of times."

"Liar," I said.

An Irish legend, attributed to some monk somewhere, said that ever since Christ's resurrection the sun danced just after dawn on Easter morning, danced across the sky, then back into its slot again, and continued to climb.

"How would you know?" she said. "You've never been awake early enough. But those of us who work for a living . . ." She left the sentence unfinished. "Come on. The boat's in at nine."

"From?" I'd forgotten the port of origin, didn't need to remember, Kate knew every one, and the embarkation times there, and the disembarkations in New York.

"Hamburg," she said. "And this one's a full troopship."

She began to stretch, her body now restored to the greater roundness she'd had before Germany and Belgium.

I said, "Kate?"

"What?"

"How many ships, how many times—"

"I don't want to hear," she said. "Ben, I don't want to hear."

"But—" and she interrupted.

"Ben, are you my friend or are you not?"

I said, "I am your friend, Kate."

"Are you my dear friend?"

"That's not the point. It's because you're my friend that I'm asking—"

She jumped from the bed. "You're not coming with me today. You just are not. I'm not going to let you."

Without a brush to her hair, without washing her face in the tiny corner vanity, she grabbed clothes and disappeared.

How did I spend the day? Without my constant companion? New York felt as festive as a carnival. Bells rang everywhere; every church had a service of joy—the first Easter after the war had ended and things were settling down. Stores had stuffed their windows with merchandise; this spring, more than the earth was awakening—the soul of Man was coming back to life.

I lingered outside churches and watched the congregations emerge with the young soldiers in their uniforms being welcomed, thanked, and applauded. If there had been a band playing, the people would have danced in the streets.

Back in the apartment, and still alone, I listened to the radio and heard a news announcer mention the names "Malmédy" and "Peiper" and "Dachau." As I remember it, my note to Kate told her, "I'll be gone for a while."

123

May 1946

The Malmédy Massacre, as it's now known, became one of the most infamous atrocities of war. Neither side, Allies or German, consisted wholly of angels, but in the age-old systems of conflict, "our" atrocities are better known than any of the incidents "they" suffered.

We had indeed heard the massacre, Kate and I. At least I'd heard it—I don't know if she was hearing anything at that moment, except the blood rushing through her own brain and the roaring of her life in her ears.

I knew that something awful had happened. First, a shout echoed up to us. A harsh voice smashed the high air. A gunshot came next; the single middleweight crack echoed. Another shout, a second shot. Then silence. Next, a scream. Then, gunfire stuttered for longer than I want to tell, death with a metal stammer.

My groin tightened into a knot. Kate stared. At me. Not down the valley. Too afraid.

The machine gun stopped. And now it got worse. For the next five, ten, fifteen minutes, the old folds of the Ardennes echo to pistol shots. One at a time.

I remember a mental image, an impression—that a stream of slime and liquid filth had been poured on my head and had begun to slide down my bare face and naked body like a veil. Was I wearing clothes in this vision? I can't tell and it doesn't matter. My ears were telling me that I was listening to something particularly revolting, and that's how my imagination responded.

Everybody knows the facts of Malmédy—how Peiper's colleagues took hundreds of American prisoners of war. The deliberate confusion of authenticity had done some work, and the Allied soldiers weren't quite sure what was going on, who was American and who wasn't.

Before we got there, Peiper's soldiers, the ones we'd been with, saw what turned out to be a small unit of an American artillery battalion, which, carrying only small arms, was trying to link up with a large U.S. division coming through from the River Meuse. The Germans opened fire, took out the vehicles at the front and the rear of the American column, and the Americans surrendered.

By then, Peiper himself (it was said in his defense) had moved on, just as his officers herded their newly taken prisoners into a field, where they joined other American servicemen who had been captured a few hours before.

In the freezing cold, the Americans stood there, unaccustomed in any way—militarily, culturally, emotionally—to defeat or prisoner-of-war status. One of them made a run for it. A German soldier shot him down. Disturbance bordering on panic spread through the American boys, and in their movements they gave the impression that they were all about to make a run for it. The Germans opened fire.

Most of the Americans went down under heavy machine-gun fire from close quarters. A few individuals escaped through the woods—they told their story when they got through the enemy lines to their own camps.

Eighty or so men had been in the group shot at close quarters; not all died, some played possum, trying to look dead in the snow. When the heavy firing died down, individual German officers and soldiers moved through the prone bodies and put a bullet into every head.

That night, the heaviest snow of the winter came in, to a height of some feet, and covered all the bodies. As you've seen, I know about that snow. But I can still hear the shots and when I first read of the massacre at Malmédy, I was able to reconstruct the pattern of gunfire in my head. That awful music still played in my brain when I went to Peiper's trial at Dachau in May 1946.

I didn't go into the carnage yards of the camp itself; I couldn't, didn't have the emotional muscle at that moment. Besides—and this is the excuse I made to myself—the cleanup gangs were still working there. Instead, I did what I had come to do—I went and sat in those spiritless rooms where they held the military courts.

An officer outside the door asked me why I had come to Dachau.

I said, "I'm trying to find out what happened to a friend." When he asked if my friend had been an American serviceman, I replied, "One of the best."

Later, I reflected that I'd spoken without thinking, and I've always had a belief that what I say spontaneously is what I truly believe.

I asked the officer, "What's your role?"

"Back home I'm a lawyer. So I'm assisting one of the defenders here."

The room felt damp and dark, despite the tall windows and the hot day outside, despite the spheres of lights, despite the vast and glowing American flag above the judges' bench. Damp and dark? Maybe I was thinking of the word *dank,* and had confused it with the language, because all around me I heard the word *danke* spoken over and over; German for "thank you." Danke: a dank room. That must be it.

"Danke," said the prosecutor's translator. *"Danke,"* said Colonel Willis Everett Jr., the appointed defense counsel. *"Danke,"* said a prisoner against whom the evidence didn't stack up. *"Danke,"* murmured my wolf.

I looked at him again, the man I'd come to see. He looked different now from the rainy, cold morning when he terrified me, though he still had his composure. His name still puzzled me: The Germans called him "Jochen," the Americans said "Joachim," and sometimes not even that, because for the purposes of the trial, the number around his neck had become his name: "Forty-two."

Did he, I challenged myself, look like a wolf? If he continued to let that beard and mustache grow he would have a trimmed oval of hair around his mouth and chin; he'd look like an Austrian doctor. I suspected that he would maintain the beard beautifully, because I could see how he kept his strong hair parted and firm, a neat man of, I could guess, significant personal discipline.

That first time I saw him, I remarked to myself on how pristine he kept his uniform despite all the mud and weather. How old was he? A year younger than I, I would learn, born 1915, aged thirty-one. Dear God! And the things he had done—or they said that he had done. No marks of torture on him, though, no matter what the chatter has been.

I must answer my own question. Did he look like a wolf? No. Would he look lupine if and when that beard grew? Maybe. He didn't have to look like a wolf, though; I'd already seen him in action and now had my impressions vindicated by the word CRIMES on the great banner above the entrance.

124

It had taken me almost four weeks to get to Dachau, but I'd felt that it was the least I could do. The proceedings had already begun, with rows of accused men seated in such an orderly fashion that my mind began to play with the words *arranged* and *arraigned*.

Other neat ranks of chairs overflowed with members of the public. In the later weeks, they ceased to come and listen in on a matter that had happened eighteen months earlier, and many hundreds of miles north, in the Belgian countryside.

"May I make notes?" I asked my officer.

"Where are you from?" he whispered, and when I told him he said, "My mother's from Limerick."

He held the door open and urged me to keep edging back along the crowded passageway; he then went to his table and sat beside Willis Everett, the lawyer whose name became synonymous with an extraordinary performance of defending law. It took me long minutes to ease myself up along one side, to a point where I could look into the faces of the accused men—and, no surprise, I saw Peiper first.

When a uniformed court official called out the number forty-two, in English and German, Peiper stood up, respectful as a convent girl. Hands straight as knives by his sides, he nodded four times in response to four points being made from the bench to his interpreter. He said *"Danke"* each time. And then, to the bench directly, he said with impeccable pronunciation, "Thank you. I understand clearly."

In my peripheral vision, I saw through the window the rows and rows of neat roofs in the main camp, and beyond them the barbed-wire crowns of thorns that formed the fences.

I began to make notes—and I see now that I remarked at length upon "the force of the American defending counsel" and "the focus, the intentness of Joachim Jochen Peiper Number Forty-two," who, in a matter of shorthand minutes, became "JJPNFT" in my notebook.

After his courteous exchanges, JJPNFT was permitted to sit again. He crossed one leg over the other knee and looked around, as people do in court, searching for friends. He saw me—and after a tiny effort of recollection he recognized me, with a half-nod and a half-smile. Was there a hint of surprise too in his look? Perhaps. When he looked at me I couldn't hold his gaze.

Later I did; indeed I looked at him without a flinch, and he with his piercing eyes, he was the one who broke the link.

When the proceedings adjourned, I waited and approached the friendly officer whose mother came from Limerick. Willis Everett had begun a deep conversation with a member of the bench.

We strolled outside, to the camp gates, and I asked, "What are you here? Are you still a soldier or are you a lawyer again?"

He laughed. "Fair question. I'm both, I guess. But you know what they say: There's only three kinds of people in the world—good, bad, and lawyers."

"How did you get here?" I asked him, and he told me that he had been part of a detail researching German prisoners of war east of Berlin, finding out who "qualified" (his word) to be charged with war crimes, and escorting them down here to be tried.

"Think about it," he said. "If Hitler won, Ike and Patton and Bradley—they'd all be on trial here, or some other joint."

He asked me why I'd come to Dachau and I told him—the entire story, in detail.

I said, "Are you still in charge of the prisoners?"

He said, with a sigh, "I will be until they're hung."

"What?"

He said, "That's what the prosecution will say—that they're criminals, that they gave up soldiers' rights when they committed war crimes. They won't be shot like soldiers."

I remembered the impromptu firing squad on the streets of Saint-Omer—and didn't know what to think.

"Could I meet one of them?" I said.

He looked at me. "Can I guess?"

I said, "Peiper."

He smiled. "He's the prosecution's prize. I picked him up myself."

"There's a question I have to ask him."

He said, "Let me clear it with Everett."

I gave him some more information—Volunder and the bloodstained tunic; he told me about Peiper.

"His English is good, and he was actually one of their best commanders."

I said, "He seemed cold."

The officer laughed. "He's ice on legs, but he's smart. I got talking to him about what he did in Belgium, his campaign, the battle he fought, and he told me all about it. He damn near got through, and if he did, he'd have been on the coast of Holland before we could catch him."

"You sound as if you like him?"

"No," said the sergeant. "But he's a damn interesting guy."

"Do you think he'll answer my question?"

125

The next day, when the bench had adjourned for the night, the officer gave me a thumbs-up from the well of the court. He then directed me to a small room off the hallway, to which he brought Peiper—who smiled, inclined his head in a not unfriendly way, and sat down.

I began, "Colonel Peiper," but he cut in.

"Obersturmbannführer Peiper."

I replied, "I don't mean any offense, but I just can't pronounce your German title."

He began to teach me. "Ober."

And I repeated, "Ober."

"Shturmbann. Say 'shturm.' "

I said, "Shturm."

"Now say 'bann.' "

And I said, "Bann."

Peiper said, "Say 'Shturmbann.' "

I said, "Shturmbann."

The young officer stepped in. "Call him Colonel."

At the insult I saw the icicles flash in Peiper's eyes. He sat up, rigid and aloof. *A year younger than I,* I thought, *one year younger.*

"I can tell," I said, "that you remember me."

He inclined his head again.

"Did you personally kill Captain Charles Miller?"

Peiper shook his head.

"Did you give the order to have him killed?"

Peiper shook his head.

"But were your men responsible?"

Peiper spoke. "I was leading my men into battle. I could not see what went on behind me."

I began to say, "But Miller—"

Peiper butted in. "You're an intelligent man. You must know that a commander cannot see everything."

I said, "But you set the tone, you made the rules."

Peiper replied, "Not all soldiers obey all orders."

I said, "Do you know what happened to Captain Miller? His wife is my dearest friend. That's why I'm here."

Peiper said, "I can tell you this much. We did encounter him."

"Who's we? Do you mean Volunder?"

He smiled. "You do not need me. You know everything."

"Is Volunder alive? Can I reach him?"

Peiper spread his arms wide, to say, "I don't know. And that is truth."

I said, "That isn't good enough."

"Irishman," said Peiper. "I wasn't there. Your friend's husband—he wasn't tortured as I have been, he wasn't beaten as I have been. He was a well-trained intelligence operative. That is all I know."

I said, "Did you give orders to have him killed?"

Peiper said, "That was not my style. And he was the concern of others."

I said, "What became of him?"

Peiper looked puzzled. "I do not understand you."

"We're asking you what became of an American soldier," snapped the officer.

"We had his papers," said Peiper. "We needed them for our decoy operation. I think they must have been destroyed in battle. So if he is found—there was no way of identifying his body."

"Was that his tunic? With the blood?"

"Some people like taking souvenirs. But I already told you that."

I tried again. "Did Miller come after you and fail? And did Volunder then go after Miller and succeed?"

He showed no emotion. The war had aged him—he looked like a man in his late forties, not thirty-one years of age.

"You would have to ask Volunder that."

I realized that Peiper might have feared another war crime charge, so I changed tack.

"Please. His widow—his wife, my friend—she thinks Miller is still alive. Give me something to tell her. The war's over."

Peiper looked a little uncomfortable. He took his time about answering.

"He was a tough man," he said. "Very tough. If he'd been one of mine, I'd have given him great responsibility."

When I first met Sebastian Volunder, my skin had shrunk a little. With Peiper I felt none of that. I argued with myself as to why; *I've bathed and shaved,* I told myself. *I've even got new clothes. I'm human again, first time in almost two years. That's why.*

And whatever his coldness, and however dreadfully he'd infringed the rules of war, Peiper felt like a soldier, and I began to make excuses for him along those lines. And then I said to myself, *How tired I am from this swinging, this side-to-side movement of my allegiances; on this side for a time, then on that side; supporters of "our" armies for a time, then at least understanding "their" armies because I met "their" soldiers, and "their" ordinary, countryside people. Neutrality, or is it indecision, and worse, cowardice? I'm tired of it.*

Once in a while, though not very often, and never for long, I see myself clearly, and in that particular glimpse at Dachau, I had a flash of reason and objectivity. For a second or two, I knew where I stood on everything—the war, my own loss, the woman back in New York, and her dreadful pain.

126

Now I have to tell you a horrible fact about myself. I acknowledge it as such; I will accept any epithet you launch at me, even though I am your father. If I have a defense—and perhaps I shouldn't be allowed one— I will say that the war brutalized me.

Meeting Volunder, who was more thug than soldier, interviewing Peiper, who was more soldier than thug, associating with Killer Miller— all of that reduced my decent sensibilities, and I learned that, if given the opportunity, I could be as bad as they were. That's all I will say in my defense.

If you want to be kind to me, add in the years of stolen and lost youth, of tender love and innocence destroyed, the savage and cynical

plundering of two young people, and a vile and violent separation moti-
vated by greed and punishment.

All of these may provide understanding of what I did when I returned
from Dachau—but they do not excuse action. Yet, as I learned in war, action too often overstates motive. I know; I killed a man in the deep snow.
Yes, please allow me to defend myself by saying that I was morally reduced by the war. I knew that I could cross boundaries of an unspeakable
nature.

And so—have you guessed what I'm about to tell you? Have you
guessed that I went back to Templebeg, to find the house with the blue
door? And found Cody? Raymond Cody, the rat. The milk-faced,
snotty-nosed, hand-washing rat, the accountant planted on an unknow-
ing Venetia by her appalling grandfather, the rat who set up—or so I suspected—the plot that took Venetia away from me and, if she weren't still
alive, led to her death.

If ever you behave brutally—and I hope you never do—the emotional consequences will appall you. Observe how your ego will change
as you do so. You will believe that everything around you is conspiring
against you, and that therefore you have to act. In my case, I left Germany in a bate of rage—unsatisfied, unfulfilled, unsteady. Neither of the
two essential loose ends in my life had been tied, and I must have needed
to take it out on someone.

When I saw that Cody's brother had painted the blue door of his
house a dull white, I believed that he had done it to fool me, to make me
think that the house in Templebeg had never existed or that it now belonged to others.

It worked in part. I didn't go to the door, I didn't knock—I observed.
I watched to see whether the slobbering brother and his fool-faced wife
still lived there. Parking the car several hundred yards away, I went back
to my previous vantage point among the trees. I had to wait several
hours—and then I struck gold. Or lead. Or sewage. Or whatever I want
to call him.

You understand, don't you, that I had no evidence to implicate Cody
in Venetia's disappearance. I had nothing to go on beyond the fact that
he had disappeared at the same time and that he had been the one to tell
the members of Venetia Kelly's Traveling Show the troupe was dis-
banded. That's what they told me when I went to the trouble of finding

each and every one of them. As the years went by, I became persuaded and then convinced of Cody's guilt. Now at least one knot could be sealed.

Around eleven o'clock, with the sun choked by overcast, a light rain began to fall. The dull white door opened and somebody peered out. Not the brother, not the unmade bed of a wife—a different person. Moments later, clutching the collar of his raincoat to his chin, Raymond Cody emerged. Even at that distance I could tell the hooked nose, the pasty flour-and-water face. I watched—and judged that he intended to walk to the crossroads bus stop.

The rain thickened. I went to the car, turned around, drove in Cody's footsteps, caught up with him, halted, and opened the passenger door. Remember—I know every lane in the Irish countryside. I turned my face away from the passenger side and said, "Hop in."

"Oh thanks, thanks very much"—still the same nasal whine.

When he closed the door and again said, "Thanks very much," I accelerated and turned my face full on to him.

"Oh, Jesus," he said. "Let me out, I can walk."

I said, "You're walking nowhere."

127

Now and again on the road over the years, I've found myself far from a decent house at nightfall. It never felt ideal, and I knew that my own depression was causing me to damage myself in that way. It did, however, teach me where the old barns were all across the country, and ruined houses that still had portions of roof, or even old castles that could offer more than a smidgen of shelter.

In the wooded hills above Templebeg stood a derelict mansion that had once known delusions of grandeur. The roof had long fallen in, except on one tower, and I had found a way into that turret room by a staircase hidden in the ivy at the rear. Rain or no rain, I drove up the ruined old avenue, under low-hanging branches that swiped the windshield, and parked on the old terrace that had fronted the main door.

Twice en route, Cody had attempted to open the car door. The first time I reached across him and slammed it shut again. And the second time I did nothing, but said, "If you do attempt to get out, I will kill you. I will knock you unconscious and drive the car over your head multiple times."

I took my pens, and my toolbox, which had pliers, screwdrivers, wrenches, a ball of string, and a bradawl. I pushed him up the staircase ahead of me. Nobody would ever find him in this bleak place, not for months, maybe years. Forensic science hadn't yet advanced to a sophisticated level; even if they used dental records I'd have taken a bet that Cody had never seen a dentist in his life. He had teeth like a yellow rat, and even the front ones needed fillings.

This plan of mine had been laid over many years, and with the greatest possible care. And why not? He had conspired to destroy all that I held dear—he might even have been Venetia's killer.

We had almost no light in that damp, ruined room. Old furniture stood there—a broken armchair, a table propped against the wall because it lacked a leg. I twisted it around, so that it leaned against the wall propped on its two good legs.

Cody was small. With my big hands I was easily able to pinch his windpipe between finger and thumb, the means by which I pushed him back against the table. When I had him there, I held him by the throat as I tied him to the slanting wood and I didn't care if the cords cut him. He cared, though, squealing like a puppy.

"What are you doing?"

"You mean you don't know?" I asked. "Be patient, Ray, be patient."

Am I that cruel? I must be, mustn't I? Or was it simply that thirteen years of pain and loss and worry came flowing out of me like molten fire? Either way, I can't be proud of it—and I'm not. I hope you find some comfort in that.

When I had him tied, I ripped open his shirt. I'd allowed him to keep on his coat for no particular reason; I didn't care, provided I could get to some expanse of bare flesh, and now I had his chest exposed to me.

On the floor, I spread my tools—pliers, bradawl, wrench. He started to weep.

"Ben, don't. Ben, don't hurt me, Jesus' sake, Ben, don't. Ben, please."

Pliers in hand, I stood in front of him and inspected his chest—so scrawny that finding loose flesh might prove difficult. I found a patch, above his left nipple, took it between the jaws of the pliers, and twisted. He almost lifted the table off the ground, so hard did he squirm. And he almost blew my left eardrum, so loud did he shriek. I twisted the flesh above the right nipple much harder. Then I stopped and stood back.

"I will now do the same to every loose piece of flesh, tissue, or muscle in your body," I said.

"Why, why?" He could scarcely get the words out.

"If you ask me why again, I'll start on your eyes earlier than I intended."

"I didn't touch her, I didn't touch her."

"So you do know why you're here?"

"Two fellas came in a truck. We all had to hurry, people nearly saw us."

I said, "How did you do it?"

"They had a shotgun. Old Kelly's shotgun."

I said, "King Kelly's gun?"—meaning Venetia's grandfather.

"Yes, I had to take it back to him."

"Where did you bury her?"

"What? What d'you mean?"

This time I caught the flesh where it wrinkled next to his armpit and I twisted very hard and very fast.

"Don't ask stupid questions."

"She was never buried."

So I moved to the other armpit; he shrieked again. By now he was losing control of his body—and I had scarcely begun.

"She never died, Ben. We didn't harm her. We didn't, we didn't."

I stopped. It hit me like a blow. For all my hopes, I had believed her dead. In all the searching, and the digging in forests, and the endless questions, and the resisted mournings, and the volatile hopes—I had lived in the belief that they'd killed her, even though I fought it and fought it.

"What happened?"

"We took her to Galway. There was a ship."

When I heard this, why didn't my steady, controlled rage that I had been building so carefully to get me through this exercise, why didn't it begin to subside? I didn't feel it slipping one jot; I had no difficulty keeping it going. If anything, it mounted.

"A ship to where?" I reached for my bradawl and began to polish it on my sleeve.

"Ben. To America. She's in America, Ben."

"Where in America?"

"She's in Florida, Ben, Jesus, Ben, my skin, Ben, it's burning me."

"Big place, Florida. Where in Florida?" I could hear my own voice as though it came from a distant metallic source.

"A beach, Ben, an Atlantic beach."

"Florida is lined with Atlantic beaches."

He twisted and turned. I saw that his face was turning blue—with shock, I supposed, and a pool of urine had gathered at his feet.

"Tell me how to find her," I said.

So now you know. How many men of your acquaintance—indeed of your own blood—have killed and gone on to torture?

I made Cody write it down. Freeing him from the cords, I gave him a pen and made him write the name and the address in my notebook. He talked as he did so, and told me how, at the orders of King Kelly, Cody had paid certain people to tell me stories that would lead me to believe Venetia had died—or was still living. King Kelly knew that I was traveling the country, asking everywhere, and he chose a number of people who would plant false and conflicting information on me. When Cody told me, I saw the pattern, and recalled how many had done so—here, there, and everywhere.

My head began to hurt. I'd always been more right than wrong; I'd often had the suspicion that I was being manipulated. Now Cody was giving me the proof.

I asked him a series of questions: Venetia's health; her mother; how she lived. And I stopped, disgusted that I was receiving such intimate news from the man who had taken her away from me.

Suddenly the air in that old room smelled foul. I wrestled back the ancient shutters and let the breeze blow through the broken window-panes.

Fool! He was gone—gone like a bat out of hell. I hadn't finished with him, so I took off after him. He vanished. I heard him clatter down the old staircase and then silence, as though his feet had hit the long grasses outside.

Racing down the stairs, I tried to see a path in the grass, but found no trace. Had he turned and run into the old ruin itself? Where he could hide for years and nobody would find him?

I could sit him out—which would stop him getting away from me and going to the police. But if I sat him out, would I kill him? And then hide his body? Probably drop it into one of the deep ice-pits below the mansion kitchen floors? He might never be found—or be a skeleton if a rambler or a hunter or a nosy child eventually found him?

How fortunate that I'd had such experience of war, where decisions of massive emotional import were forced on me minute by minute. There I stood, wrestling with, on one hand, a decision whether to kill some-body—whom I'd just been torturing; and on the other hand to go and reclaim my lost and deeply beloved wife who was alive and well.

Note, by the way, that I didn't ask Cody how Venetia's pregnancy had borne fruit. Some things are just too much to bear.

At that moment, something good occurred—my inner voice began to return. It had been absent through most of Europe and the war. I'd scarcely heard it when we were shelled in France; hardly a cheep did it make in the forests of Belgium. Now it came back, in full voice and sharp as ever, my conscience, my sardonic adviser, my only means of control over myself. Its first words? *Well now, Venetia found, eh? Don't you know the old saying? Be careful what you wish for.*

128

June 1946

I admit to a poetic turn of mind. That explains the mode of travel I chose to cross the Atlantic—a freighter, a tramp steamer, and, I joked with my-self, I had such heavy freight, and I had picked it up in many a port—

Charleville, Saint-Omer, Germany, Belgium. She took fourteen days, had fifteen passengers, forty crew, and a captain so depressed that he had tears in his eyes every time I saw him. Perfect.

As was the main cargo—peat, from the bogs of Ireland, being taken to a manufacturer of grass and meadow fertilizer in the United States. See the connection? My country's memory lay in those bogs—villages, bodies, and even now and then somebody found a box of ancient butter, preserved by the bogs' natural chemicals. As I had preserved Venetia in the mire and mud of my own past ramblings and despairs.

And when I'd worked that set of ideas through, my inner voice said, *You're not exactly losing your taste for the ludicrous, are you?* The inner gentleman also preferred some of the other cargo—a dozen pianos, five thousand "foundation garments" going to a lingerie store in New York, and two thousand pairs of children's shoes. Six tractors pleased him too.

On the voyage, I spoke little, and to few. Instead I tried to pick my steps through the minefield of my own emotions. What would I feel when I saw Venetia? Did I have any idea what words might come out of my mouth? Was there a child?

Remember—I had spent every day of my life, and sometimes every minute of every hour of every day, thinking of little else but recovering the idyllic life that she and I once had. All the fears, all the anxieties, the pains, the sense of loss, the loneliness, the erotic remembrances, the sheer hurt—now what would become of them?

As I say, if I hadn't had the experiences of war so recently behind me, I might well have collapsed. Let me give you a measure of how absorbed I was on that ocean journey: Not for a moment did I have a flash of remorse over my appalling treatment of Cody. I've had many since, but none then.

Indeed, only one other issue found its way into my considerations—Kate Begley. How was she? Still in New York? Still waiting on the dockside every morning? Still arranging her working day so that she could be on hand whenever a likely ship came into port? And when would she give up? And what would she do then? Would I ever see her again?

After the huff between us, I'd stopped by our local bar and given the barman, Les Neenan, twenty dollars; he was to use it for a telegram to me if anything changed in Kate's life; it's what I'd have done back home.

No telegram had arrived. *She's fine,* said the inner gentleman, *and at the moment she isn't your business. Focus, Ben, focus on Venetia. Remember what James said about the circumstances you anticipate. Be alert, because this might not play out as you expect.*

129

Sometimes it may not have appeared so, but I am, at core, a careful man, especially when doing something of importance. In such circumstances, I prepare with diligence and caution. For instance, if I know that I'm about to visit a house that has a significant content of old stories, traditions, or music, I sit down the night before, prepare all my pens, notebooks, and questions, check the map to make sure I know where I'm going—sometimes I even find the house the day before I'm expected.

In Jacksonville I did likewise. There's more than one Jacksonville in Florida—or, more accurately, the place they call Jacksonville stretches for a long way down the coast. First of all I visited the town hall and began to search the electoral roll for the name "Kelly"; I found "Kelly, Sarah," and she had owned this property since 1933.

Easy enough to trace the development; Sarah and her long-term beau, Mr. Anderson, had been in the habit of wintering in Florida. When Venetia disappeared in 1932, they took her there to a rented property— this was my surmise and I later found it true—and then bought a house. To which Sarah eventually retired, and in which she would die.

Not trusting Cody, I reestablished the address—between Third Street South and Ocean Drive—not in Jacksonville, but Jacksonville Beach, a different place altogether, way south of the main conurbation (such as it was in those days), on a narrow, tree-lined street a few hundred yards from the longest beach I had ever seen.

Now what was I to do? Walk to the front door and ring the bell? *No,* said my inner voice. *Wait. Too much water has been flowing under all those bridges. Wait and watch.* So I waited and I watched. I had rented a convertible, and in glorious, unhumid weather, I parked down the street at ten o'clock in the morning.

At a quarter past the hour, a car drew up. The man who climbed out and went into the house using a front-door key stood about an inch taller than I, but thin as a rake—with a pencil line of jet-black mustache. He wore a white shirt and black pants, and he walked like a dancer. In none of my imaginings had I considered a man in Venetia's life; perhaps I'd come to the wrong address?

No. Minutes later, the door opened again and there Venetia stood, half-turned backward, speaking to somebody within—the mustache man, I presumed.

The choke of my breath, the sudden twist I made in the car seat— involuntary reaction, call it shock if you like, at this moment I'd so long and so desperately wanted. She hadn't changed at all—still the silver-blond hair, brighter if anything, still the long, loose walk that only angels have, still the serene air. All my systems, my metabolisms, physical, mental, spiritual—all seized. She turned left—not toward where I sat—and loped toward the Atlantic.

My mind began to compute the days we'd been apart. There was a time when I'd known the number of hours, but the war had shut down that daily calculation. And then I stopped, halted by my inner voice asking, *What are you going to do now? Dive into yet another pool of self-pity?*

I'd parked to keep the house between me and the beach, and therefore Venetia didn't walk past the car. My view of her remained clear, as I ran through my options: *Follow her. Or keep watching and ring the doorbell later if I've seen that Mr. Mustache has gone out? Or go away and never come back?*

I could still see her, though the distance between us had widened. Down the street, she turned right; she wore a light, airy shift and it wafted around her legs. She disappeared from view and then moments later, as I was about to start the engine, she reappeared, on a path that led to the beach.

I drove down, keeping her in my vision to my right. At the same moment as I parked, she emerged from the low dunes and began to walk across the wide, wide sands toward the ocean. You can't see where those beaches begin and end—they come from nothingness, and they drift on into nothingness, and that morning, nobody but Venetia walked there. Literally and metaphorically.

At the steady walking pace I knew so well, she reached the waves, and without a hesitation walked into the water. She was now perhaps a quarter of a mile away, and she kept walking until waist-high, and then began to swim, the shift flowing behind her like a shoal of colored fish; I guessed that she'd chosen it because the cloth was so light and dried so quickly.

I stood by the car and watched. A strong breeze whipped the waves; relentless small breakers trooped ashore and collapsed. She didn't look in my direction as she swam across and back, and across again, parallel to the shore, in waters of comfortable depth for such long legs. Venetia and I—I and she; an ocean, a sunny day of warm and strong-ish winds, and nobody else in the world.

And still I didn't know what to do. Soon, she rose from the waves and walked back in from the sea, as lovely a shape as the world has ever made. Holding the flimsy gown out from her, she headed south, in the opposite direction from me, showing no sign of returning to the lane by which she had reached this spot. I divined her purpose—she would walk until the sun and the wind had dried her, and then walk home: very Venetia, very like the woman I knew, practical but with style. By now, I dreaded seeing her face.

When she had walked so far that she seemed little more than a vertical dot, I drifted down toward the water. I peeled off shoes and socks and trod in the hissing shallows. At last, I too turned right and set off in the same direction. If I had a calculation in mind, it must have been that I imagined coming face-to-face with her when she came back. By then, her gown would have dried and become opaque again.

An hour she walked, before she turned. I recalled the sands at Le Crotoy, but this time no horse and rider came galloping by, no secret message fell at my feet—although, as I thought of it, I wondered whether kidnapping might arise. I could scarcely look out to sea in the strong glare; when I looked ahead, Venetia shimmered.

And my inner voice said, *Are you going to turn the whole bloody day into one long metaphor?*

She walked back; I walked on. Nobody I had ever known walked like Venetia did—that steady lope with her hands clasped behind her back, and her head sometimes down, gazing at the ground as if in thought, and that morning her face tilted up, looking for the sun.

When we were perhaps a hundred and fifty yards apart, she looked ahead, and she recognized me before I had prepared to greet her. Peering again, she slowed down, stopped, and brought her hands up to her mouth. She stayed like that until I got to within ten feet of her and halted.

"I knew," she said. "I knew I would see you today."

Here's the most bizarre thing: Neither of us moved to the other. We didn't rush into each other's arms. She didn't extend her two hands to me as she used to, and I didn't move to pick her up and swing her around as I used to do.

"How did you know?" I asked, because my inner voice was asking, *Did that bastard Cody tell somebody?*

She said. "There were other days when I hoped and prayed you were coming for me. But today—I just knew."

130

It's only fair that I report how she looked and how I felt. My first thought said, *The great actress in her is still alive. She holds herself the same way. Her eyes have much the same light.* My next thought said, *If you're to learn anything from this—learn the uselessness of self-pity.*

"I thought you were dead, Venetia."

"Oh, Ben, wasn't it awful what they did to us?"

Moving as one person, we squatted, hunkered down, looking at the ribbed sand beneath us and the white food-stains of the ocean's salt.

"How are you?" I said; that was about all I could manage.

She replied, "I—you—we—there were, are, twins."

"I think we joked about that possibility," I said.

"I think we did. Do you want to know their names?"

When I nodded, she said, "Louise and Ben."

Mother's name and mine. Oh, Jesus.

———

Only one question existed in the world at that moment. Despite my self-absorption, it wasn't, *How have you been?* Or, *Do you still love me?* Or, *Did you miss me?* Or, *Why didn't you come and look for me?* It was, *What do we do now?*

"They told me that if I ever tried to see you again, they'd kill you. That's what happened to me, Ben. They told me I had to stay here."

"Did you ever go back?"

"I want to live there, I want the children to have their own country."

"Can we go now?" I stood up and held out my arms; she stayed hunkered. And she began to cry.

"It's complicated."

I said, "We've had worse. And now I can fight them off. They can throw what they like at me. If they still want to."

"My grandfather's too feeble now. My mother won't care—she wants to retire and live here."

"Those aren't complications. Jesus, Venetia, I've just been in a war."

"Ben, I've remarried."

I stood up and walked away. And there, you see, is where the fault always lay. And there because of that fault, as I will now tell you, came my next great mistake. The fault lay in the fact that, all through those years, I could have found her—I know that. I could have found Cody, and I could have bribed or beaten the truth out of him.

But I preferred the martyrdom, the brooding self-pity, the wandering, lonely scribe. No wonder I had great violence in me—all sentimental people do. And it gets in our way, that sentimentality; on the Atlantic beaches of Florida that morning, I failed again to do the right thing—because I stood for a minute or two as she spoke to the back of my head, and I walked away from her without a word.

131

The words she spoke do matter—or, rather, it matters that you know them, now that I have "met" you, as it were. As I stood there, and before I took that dreadful, stupid decision, she explained.

"I met a man who wanted to look after me. He had a road show, we could work together. And sometimes we do. His name is Jack Stirling."

"Is it called Venetia Kelly's Traveling Show?" I didn't want the answer to be "yes."

She answered, "He calls it 'Gentleman Jack and His Friend.' He has a pickpocket act."

"How appropriate," I said, the words blurting out before I could stop them.

"He persuaded me to get a divorce in a city named Reno. Ben, I sent you a telegram. You didn't reply. I sent you five telegrams."

This was too much. My parents opened all my telegrams and letters—they had my permission, because Goldenfields was my only address. Either Venetia was lying or they had never told me. Too much. I walked away.

She called after me, "Do you want to meet the twins?"

And one last, fainter plea: "Ben, don't. Please. I always hoped—" and she didn't finish the sentence.

Could I have wanted anything more in life? Venetia and our children? And still I walked, my shoes and socks discarded behind me on the sand, ready to be sucked out to sea on the next tide.

132

July 1946

Kate Begley said to me once, "A Love Lost is an Angel hurt. Did you know that, Ben?"

By now, she must have had them weeping in buckets. And so did I, and that, I concluded, was what ultimately had kept Kate and me so friendly—in all the hearts and flowers and ribbons and bows, we had both lost the most important people in our lives. Such was my thought, as I drove from Jacksonville Beach to Jacksonville and took a train to New York. In short, cheap music had proved once again too potent for me—it was what I now wanted to hear. I waited for the devastation to sweep in, and hoped it never would; there must, I thought, be a way of keeping it at bay, or replacing it with something else.

She had stayed in the same apartment because, as she'd said, she could hear the ships coming in. New York hadn't changed her; in fact, she looked better than ever, and I thought I saw a certain calm in her, a new serenity. She still possessed the high energy, the bouncing around, the quick movements, the ready laugh.

On the last morning that I'd seen her, our brief acrimony had been severe.

"Go then."

"Kate, I've been through a lot with you."

"Have you?" She was as arch as a bridge.

"And I did it for you."

"But you don't believe in me, do you?"

To which I said, "What do you mean?"

"You don't believe what I believe?"

I knew that the appropriate phrase should be "That Charles is alive." After all—Venetia was. But I didn't say it. I couldn't say it. And I couldn't say it because I didn't believe it—simple as that. Which, I suppose, meant that I didn't believe in her. So, once again, I said nothing.

We'd had so many moments when I felt, *Now is right, tell her now. Look at all the evidence. Good God! Even his tunic was bloodstained.* But she had said to Peiper, my Number Forty-two from Dachau, "Will I tell you what that is? That's a bloodstained jacket, that's all it is. That doesn't prove anything."

Our parting had taken place as she prepared like a bride. But the waiting pen had long vanished because the need for it had long disappeared too. By several months, in fact.

"When you go down there this morning," I'd said, "look around you. There's nobody here." I should have said, "He's not coming back, he'd have been back by now." Instead, I made a sweeping gesture with my hand and asked, "Why do you think they've taken away all the barriers?"

She said, "There's still the wounded."

"Kate, they came back last year. The last of them. They told us."

"Go away," she said, "and leave me alone."

"Do you mean that?"

She didn't reply; she turned her face to the Hudson River and I walked out of her life.

Now, as I swept in from Florida, she said to me, "Ah, I knew you were coming." And since I'd so recently heard those words elsewhere, I almost turned my back and left. But I didn't, and I stayed—and went forward with her into her next and final act of faith.

Kate had this walk that I'd first noticed at Lamb's Head, a curious, unfeminine surging forward, planting each foot one step at a time, as though carrying a bucket of water in each hand; it entailed almost a personality change. I came to recognize that she walked like that when deeply focused on the task in hand.

Now, two days after my return to her, I saw the stride again on the sidewalks of New York, and it pleased and intrigued me.

"We're going to Brooklyn," she said.

"Why?"

"To meet a man."

"About a dog?"

She said, "No. Not a dog exactly, but you're fairly close."

I didn't count the hours, but this was no stroll. From time to time she pulled a piece of paper from her cuff, peered at it, put it back, and strode on. I had difficulty keeping up with her.

"Talk to me, Kate," I said.

She said, "No. I'm thinking."

"Well, tell me what you're thinking."

"I can't 'til I've thought it."

"Is there a scheme under way?" I asked.

She said, "What do you think?"

"That you have a plan."

"Yes, I have a plan."

"At least tell me the name of the man we're going to meet."

"His name is Bobby Bilbum."

I said, "There's nobody in the world named Bobby Bilbum."

She said, "You'll see."

Half an hour after crossing the greatest bridge I had ever seen, we stopped somewhere on a wide street, at a place that sold food.

"I have become devoted to the frankfurter," she said.

"Devoted?"

"I chose my word carefully."

I said, "Devoted suggests a spiritual dimension."

"So?" She looked up at me; on her lower lip hung a speck of golden mustard like the egg of a tiny, tiny, golden bird.

"People are devoted to God, or the Blessed Virgin Mary, or Saint Anthony of Padua—like your grandmother."

"Nana's only devoted to Saint Anthony because she's always losing things, and Saint Anthony always finds them for her."

"No, Kate. She finds them. He died six or seven hundred years ago."

"You're a heathen, Ben."

"Nevertheless, you can't apply the word *devoted* to a sausage."

"Why can't I?"

I said, "I like celery soup a lot, but did you ever hear me saying I'm devoted to celery soup?"

She laughed—and I had to look away, because when she laughed like that, and her eyes lost all their newfound age and caution, and the dimples in her cheeks sparkled, my heart turned over. A crumb from my own hot dog went astray, and I began to catch my breath.

"Cough it up, 'tis only a brick," she said.

What could I do? I couldn't tell her to stop being so appealing, so vulnerable, could I? *Charles Miller, you'd better be dead.*

We ordered coffee, to which, since Germany, I had taken a shine. The sun gleamed on distant tall buildings; not for the first time I thought of Hy-Brasil, the Irish legend of the man who saw golden towers out in the sea and set sail from the western shores of Ireland to find them—and never did. That day, and ever since, I have wondered if the golden towers he saw were the skyscrapers of Manhattan.

I knew that Kate was looking at me, and I knew that she had then followed my gaze.

She said, "Do you know about Hy-Brasil?"

I said, "You did it again."

"What?"

"You homed in on the thought in my head."

"Honed."

"Homed."

"No. It's honed."

"It isn't," I said. "Ignorant people say 'honed,' which means 'sharp-ened' or 'refined,' but what they mean is 'focused.' "

"Well—there's Hy-Brasil," she said. "You're looking at it."

"That's what I thought, too."

She said, "I've seen it so often from Lamb's Head."

"You've seen the island of Manhattan from the cliffs of County Kerry?" I didn't bother to keep the incredulous, even contemptuous tone out of my voice.

"So?" she said.

I replied, "But that's three thousand miles."

And Kate Begley said, "Only if you allow it to be."

To which I said, in a tone of resignation, "So there is a fellow called Bobby Bilbum?"

"There is," she said, "and he has a giraffe for me."

"A giraffe?"

"Name of Jerry," she said. "Young and not fully weaned. And a truck."

"To take Jerry the Giraffe?"

"Yes. Of course."

"Where?"

She took a breath and said, "Since you asked. Here's my scheme. Don't you remember? I told you already what Charles and I agreed. If the war parted us, and the absence became too much or too long, I'd go to the very center of the United States and wait there for him. And that's what I'm doing. We're going to Kansas."

"Kansas?"

"Lebanon, Kansas."

"Is that the very center of the United States?"

"To all intents and purposes, yes."

I said, "How do you know he's not there already?"

"He wasn't there two weeks ago."

"Did you go there?"

She said, "I've been there four times in the past year."

"Tell me that again," I said.

She looked at me with a frown like a cross little girl.

"Charles and I made a pact. We promised each other. If the war kept us apart we'd wait for each other in the most obvious place on earth—the center of the United States. I argued for Kenmare, we tossed a coin. He won and I'm keeping my promise."

"Did you also promise him a giraffe?"

"Ben, don't be stupid."

"But what do you want a giraffe for?"

She sighed, as though explaining something to a dimwit.

"I'm going to open a matchmaking business out there, and since they won't have seen many giraffes in Kansas, I figured a giraffe would draw crowds. It's called advertising, Ben."

I looked at her, amazed again.

"He'll certainly draw crowds," I said. And after a moment's thought I added, "Okay. Bobby Bilbum, here we come?"

She nodded.

I invite you for a moment to think of our age—how old we were. Young enough for all kinds of adventures, and old enough to be marrying, settling down, and having families. On the train from Jacksonville I looked at men my own age, and I looked at girls of Kate's age, and I knew that few of them had lived through anything like the experiences she and I had shared.

Those thoughts came back as we crossed the Brooklyn Bridge, and as we stood in the sun eating hot dogs. What I could not divine was the use to which I would put whatever I had learned, or what the war had done to me. To my bitter regret, I would soon find out.

133

I have never seen, nor expect to see, a fatter man than Bobby Bilbum. Nor a man who so enjoyed being fat. He wore dungarees big as a tarpaulin and a red check shirt. The brown dye from his extravagant pigtail ran down his neck because he sweated all the time, and he had perfect, perfect teeth. He showed them the moment we met him, as he slapped his stomach—the sides, not the front. Let me make it clear— he slapped the sides of his stomach like the man in the parade beats the big drum.

We'd reached his place by walking past the corner of Prospect Park, and, on the next long street, finding a deep lane somewhere off Montgomery Street. The long, narrow passageway opened out into a great yard full of dismantled trucks and vans all lying on their sides. Kate, once more sharp as a razor, picked up their significance.

"He wouldn't have been able to drive these down the lane—they're all too wide."

She pulled a bell rope outside a wide-open door, and cymbals clashed somewhere—so tuneful that she tugged again.

"Everybody does that," said Bobby Bilbum, whom we saw walking from the farthest point indoors, as light on his feet as a dancer.

They made their connection, he and Kate; and he went back and fetched her letter.

"I give a compliment to you," he announced. "Nobody writes proper English anymore."

I could determine no distinctive New York or American accent, and he later told us that he was half-Scottish, half-Polish.

"Do you sing?" he said to me.

"Should I?" I had picked up Kate's habit of answering one question with another.

"With that big chest," he said, "you should sing." He opened his mouth and warbled a scale as sweet as any blackbird. "I love to sing," he said, "and I do believe that I have in my repertoire a thousand songs and more. And essentially I call myself a crooner." Still addressing me, he said, "Have you acquainted yourself with the song, 'Beautiful Dreamer'?"

I said, "My father sings it."

With his hand on his chest and the other hand held out, fingers splayed, Bobby Bilbum launched into song like a nightclub singer.

"Beautiful dreamer, wake unto me, Starlight and dewdrops are waiting for thee; Sounds of the rude world, heard in the day, Lull'd by the

moonlight have all pass'd away! Beautiful dreamer, queen of my song—"
and then stopped. "Impressive, isn't it?" he said.

Kate applauded, and so did I.

"How many people answered your advertisement?" Kate asked.

"Alas, you and you alone."

"It said very little." She raised the famous eyebrow at him.

"The world is full of barbarians," he said. "Not everybody is suited to
this enterprise. And I suppose you require a viewing?"

"We walked from Tenth Avenue," she said.

"Oh, my goodness, oh, my goodness. How rude of me. Come in at
once, you need to come through the house anyway."

Bobby Bilbum had no furniture—of any kind. He lived in a completely bare house. The kitchen contained a refrigerator; cabinets lined
the walls; I could see coffeepots and utensils of all kinds on the long
counters—but no table, chairs, nowhere to sit.

He saw me looking around. "I sold everything," he said. "No chair
bears my weight anymore. I sleep in there. Or in the truck. With
THEM." He freighted the word so heavily that he might have been
speaking of mysterious beings—which, in a sense, he was. I looked into
the room that he'd indicated, and saw a mountain of rich and wild, red
and yellow bedding, a sultan's couch, taking up the entire floor of what
must once have been a dining or living room.

From the refrigerator he took a large stone jar and poured a drink that
I had never tasted—iced tea. He reached back in, took out a round box,
opened it, and began to cut slices of pie.

"Blueberry and apple," he said. "It sustains me. I have them made
specially for me by a woman from Vienna. She lives two blocks away and
delivers every day."

I ate my slice like a greedy pig—but I knew I wouldn't need to eat
again for many hours. Bobby Bilbum ate two slices.

"I get peckish," he said. "And now you have to tell me why you've
come to see me. I know you want to buy Jerry, but why?"

Miss Begley explained. Bobby listened, tears in his eyes.

She ended her tale by saying, "But how do I take care of a giraffe?"

"You are an inspired and inspiring woman," he said. "And your
dear husband has been helping to free my country from the depreda-

tions of the mighty Hun. I will do all I can for you, but it will be complicated."

My inner man went, *Uh-oh. Complicated. This will be interesting,* and sure enough, in Bobby Bilbum's application, the word *complicated* reached new heights.

"You've reached me through my backyard," he said. "The creatures live in the front."

We followed him, the floorboards shaking and bending under his feet, to a wide hallway, and a great front door with stained glass. He lived, I could see, in what had been a mansion, set well back from the street and shaded with abundant trees. From outside the large gate it would have been impossible to achieve a clear view of the house— or the building beside it, a tall, simple wooden shed, painted bright green. It looked like a loose box from an impossibly high stable yard. Beside it stood a truck, with a trailer and an equally tall structure made of canvas.

"Here we are," said Bobby Bilbum, "or should I say, here they are." And again he emphasized "they."

We crossed the gravel to the tall loose box.

"Good morning, children," Bobby called, and from inside I heard sounds of delight. He opened the middle section of the door—which, I saw, had been made in three ascending parts—and said to us, "Voilà! Meet the love of my life. Jerry," he called. "You've never met an Irish person before, my boy, have you. They're very civilized, you'll like them."

Four delighted creatures stood there, in that strange but somehow wonderful place that day—Bobby Bilbum, Kate Begley, Ben MacCarthy (even my inner voice said, *Aaaah!*), and Jerry the Giraffe. Within seconds a fifth called out for attention, squealing and scrabbling. Bobby opened the lowest door and out hurtled a small pink pig who began to paw Bobby's dungaree legs.

"This is Sydney," said Bobby. "Sydney is Jerry's constant companion— when I'm not. And sometimes we all sleep together, don't we, Sydney." He held the pig close to his face and Sydney began to kiss and lick Bobby—who then handed Sydney to me.

I knew pigs; Mother scrubbed hers every two days with a long-handled yard broom; and I knew how to calm them, because I had often helped her deliver litters of a dozen and more. Sydney relaxed in my arms at once and Bobby Bilbum squealed in delight.

"This augurs well. Sydney likes very few people, oh my dears! We shall have such fun."

Puzzlement began to cross Kate's face like a frowning cloud.

"How would all this work?" she began to ask, but didn't get far—because Jerry the Giraffe, who had eyelashes like back satin fringes, reached down and curled a long tongue across her right cheek. She stood; she all but froze. And then she began to blush.

"That," she declared, "is one of the nicest things that has ever happened to me."

I see now that I made a note on the margin of my private journal later that day—the single word *healing*. That remains my impression of that first encounter with Bobby Bilbum and "them"—it had a healing tone.

God knows I needed it. The train journey from Florida had been a slow, painful blur of loneliness, self-chastisement, and fighting off self-pity. So hurt did I feel at my own hands that I couldn't even begin to assess what had happened.

And yet—would I ever have a moment as huge again in my life? I had seen my wife, had caught my breath at her beauty—not undimmed but richer now, and I loved her, loved her, loved her. But I'd learned that another man had replaced me, and that perhaps my parents had conspired against me. How could I come to terms with all that?

No wonder I was looking for anything that would heal me, anything at all—and at least I fared better than Kate, because Venetia was still alive. Under the word *healing* I now find that I scribbled another note, one of Kate's sayings: "Where there's Life there's Hope."

134

I wish I could tell you more about Jerry the Giraffe. I wish I could tell you that he and I had long conversations—because I swear to God that he seemed fractions of time away from such a capability. And in those conversations, we'd have discussed his ancestry, in the wide-skied veldt of Africa, and he'd have told me how his grandparents would find the sweetest leaves on the tallest trees, and bend them down for him. I wish I could tell you that every now and then he'd turn to me and say, "D'you know what my biggest fear is, Ben? I dread getting a sore throat, and I'd love you to make some of that black currant jam gargle that your mother used to give you when you were a child."

You have no idea how close Jerry and I came to such chatting. You have no idea how often I felt that he was dying to talk to me, ready to say, "Ben, leave Venetia or Kate or any girl that you want, leave her to me. I'll flutter these eyelashes at her, and she'll be ours like a snap."

Yet, if I can't tell you about these chats that Jerry and I had, I can tell you other wonderful things about him—not to mention his relationship with Sydney, and Sydney's relationship with me.

Did you know, for example, that if you stroke a giraffe's coat, it will after a moment feel much silkier than you'd expect? At first, it felt not unlike hide to my hand—as, indeed, I hoped it would; and then, as Jerry and I became closer, he felt much silkier.

And how long was that tongue? I have no idea. My guess is, when Jerry became a full-grown adult (he was eight months old when I met him), it could reach to a foot. In Kansas, I often put a delicious ball of leaves on the porch table just to see Jerry stalk over and flick the tongue out to get it.

He was growing, Bobby said, at about an inch a day, and had only recently stopped weeping.

"You mean real tears?" said Kate.

"A thug in the audience shot a dart into his mother at the circus. She died of a heart attack. My brother owns the circus."

Bobby patted Jerry, and Jerry licked Bobby—and licked Kate, who was now smitten, and who reached up and put her arms around Jerry's neck. In my arms Sydney grunted and gave a little wriggle of pleasure.

I wandered off a little to look back and gain some objectivity on this unexpected scenario. Kate and Bobby entered a deep conversation; Sydney wanted a number of extra kisses; a sense of healing did indeed begin to flow over me.

As to how all this might yet work I couldn't begin to imagine—and had less of an idea when I strolled back and Kate told me, "If a giraffe hasn't been weaned right, you have to provide twenty gallons of fresh milk for it every day. Jerry was only four months old when his mother died. He should have been with her for two years. He's eight months now."

I asked, "How tall will he grow? How old will he get?"

"Bobby said he can go up to twenty feet, and if we look after him correctly we could get him to maybe twenty-five or thirty."

The use of "we" hadn't escaped me—I had experience of Kate's "negotiations" and I sensed that this "deal" had been done. How did I know? As you'll have gathered by now, when Kate truly wanted something she never consulted—she went after it with a purpose blind to all other considerations—such as how she'd get a giraffe halfway across the United States.

"What does Jerry eat?" I asked.

"Fruit," said Bobby. "And hay and grass and stuff like that."

Kate said, "Sixty pounds of food a day. I can tell you anything you want to know about giraffes. I've been reading about them all my life."

My inner voice had something to say to that: *So maybe you can tell us where you're going to get sixty pounds of grass and fruit and twenty gallons of milk a day as we drive a couple of thousand miles to Kansas—not to mention when we get there.*

135

Let me pause here for a moment and help you, Ben and Louise, to take stock. The year was 1946, and since I was born in 1914, I was, as I've said, thirty-two years old. By most standards of the time, I could consider myself too young for what I'd already been through, and most of it had been unexpected and impossible to predict. What had happened to me, and the things I'd done and the places I'd been had no precedent in the life from which I came. No ancestor had been recorded with such adventures; no emotional unhinging such as I'd known had ever been endured by somebody of my kin.

You have to look at that, said my inner voice to me one day around that time, as I mulled these thoughts. *You have to look at why such events occur in your life; why what happens to you happens to you, so to speak.*

My inner pest went on to say, *If you're to cope with the breathtaking error you've just made by turning your back on Venetia without exploring any possibility with her, you'd better grab any straw of help that comes your way.*

So—I took a measure of comfort from the unusualness of my life thus far. In my eighteenth year, that is, my final year at school, I had belonged to a class of twenty boys. Since we'd all left school, none of them, not one, had been living a life a tenth as exciting as mine. Now it seemed as though I might be about to travel across America with a darling giraffe, a charming little pink pig, a fat man with a pigtail and no other hair of any kind, and a war widow who could tell the future and find missing people using a needle, thread, and a map. In my tact and newfound kindness I didn't ask Kate whether she'd deployed her pendulum in recent times to search for Charles Miller.

136

August 1946

From inside Jerry's tall trailer, Bobby fetched three folding chairs and opened them in the sunshine. We sat with our backs to the trailer doors, and from time to time Jerry's warm tongue would curl down the back of my neck. Once or twice I had to hold up Sydney so that Jerry could lick her too—at which Sydney would shimmy a little and settle back into my arms with a tiny contented snort.

As in the past, Kate had shared none of her plans with me—the transport, the length of the journey, the feeding en route, what she intended to do when she got there. Now she seemed relieved at the prospect of Bobby traveling with us. It occurred to me that if she had him she didn't need me—but I needed her.

You're rudderless now, said my irritating voice. *You have no anchor either. This is the best you're going to get.*

Bobby, who looked fifty but might easily have been thirty, had the gift of assumption. It can be enviable, that confidence; useful too; it allows you to go through life more or less unchallenged. As he now did, and began to lay out the route.

Neither Kate nor I questioned him. We didn't ask him why he was traveling. We didn't ask him how he could afford to drop everything, close his house, and come to Kansas. We didn't ask him if he intended to stay out there.

It's not that we didn't want to—he never gave us the chance. As we sat there, he launched into the journey's details—Pennsylvania, Ohio, Indiana, Illinois, Missouri, Kansas; to Lebanon, Kansas, he believed it would take near to thirteen hundred miles and that would be about two weeks. He believed that we shouldn't rush, because Jerry and Sydney had delicate constitutions, and so had he.

"I'm a natural observer of life," Bobby Bilbum intoned, "and here we have an odyssey of natural observation taking us across this great land. I myself have often traveled such roads, and I have always found them rewarding."

Kate fidgeted, caught between looking back over her shoulder at her new love, Jerry, and trying to get a question asked of Bobby.

When he stopped for breath, she finally made it. "How will we arrange the food?" she said. "People won't be used to feeding giraffes out there in the countryside."

"Au contraire, my dear," said Bobby. "Every place in which we stop for the night will have had the habit of feeding all kinds of animals."

"Is there an American habit of keeping giraffes as pets?" I asked.

"Not at all, dear boy. But the route we shall follow is my brother's old circus route, and I have traveled it many times."

"Will we be meeting his circus?" Kate asked.

"I fear not," said Bobby, "I fear not," and I knew instinctively that we had encountered a mystery, which, large or small, might not be shared with us. Bobby felt like a man with many such mysteries.

He declared that it should take at least a week to prepare for this journey. In answer to our inquiries, he laid out a plan—of acquiring food and an additional trailer; of identifying the towns where we'd be stopping; of writing letters ahead, or, for the nearer states, sending telegrams, to secure accommodations with which he was familiar, and where the animals and ourselves could be assured of safe and good accommodation. And he had to close down this existence of his—"At least for some time," he added.

For a man who seemed chaotic in his living arrangements, Bobby proved a true surprise—he had the organizational gifts of a four-star general. I watched him closely, and became so intrigued by his gift of effectiveness that I found a tactful way of asking him.

"Bobby, you have a talent for this road organization, haven't you?"

I said this as I leaned against the wall in his stark kitchen, and I made sure that he saw me looking all around the disturbingly unconventional house.

"You're saying to yourself, Ben, how can it be that a man who has no furniture, who can't control his appetites, whose life is lived beyond the reach of his neighbors and their society—how can it be that such a man could be trusted to get a caravan of exotic animals and even more exotic people halfway across this great continent?"

I must have blenched or fidgeted or made some giveaway spontaneous movement.

"Don't worry, Ben, I shan't flinch with pain. In fact, you have liberated an answer in me that I have wanted to hear myself say aloud for some time."

Among his many pies, Bobby had a favorite—apple and strawberry, with some rhubarb to give it edge. He cut a wedge that would have chocked an aircraft's wheels and took his mouth to it, the cream whiskering his smooth cheeks. He chewed, his eyes aflame like a man who has love in his heart, and when he had motored through the pound and a half that the slice must have contained, he settled his ruby lips and delivered his explanation.

"Dear boy, when you travel with me to Kansas, you will see in me a creature without whom the world could not have happened, without whom the United States of America could never have been discovered or united. This creature stands as the criterion of Man's endeavor. Without such a being, and you may be one yourself, the cave would still be our home, the jawbone of a donkey still our plowshare."

He had become an orator, with an audience of one young Irishman and a small, wriggling pig.

"I refer to the figure of the traveler, the creature so restless that when he feels the world drawing in upon his shoulders, as though the walls of this room were to move inward to us right now—when he feels that vile constriction, he knows it is time to find the mountains. And the river-banks. And the quiet corners of the lakes. And the little dusty towns where even when it rains they have the siesta."

And now Bobby began to pace up and down.

"This figure, the traveler, he knows what power the road gives him—the power of never being owned, the power of discovery for himself. No matter that legions may have been there before him; it is the freshness of his eye that matters. To move, to travel, to find the point of the compass whence comes the freshest wind, and to turn one's face upward to that wind—that is the shape of my spirit."

Hand on heart, Bobby stood before me now, his other hand on my shoulder.

Sometimes—if not always—we have to depend on others to tell us the truth of ourselves. Bobby Bilbum, with his wobbling stomach and a jowl big as a briefcase, and his elegant, orotund speech, captured for me the essence of why I'd liked the road around Ireland. It had nothing to do with the outer world; it had to do with the landscapes within me, and my own mountains and rivers and lakes. No wonder I've so loved my Wandering Scholars. They understood the inner terrain that we all have—and the need to travel it.

I wrote down as much as I could remember of Bobby's speech (it was much longer than I have quoted), and I relayed it to Kate.

"The Safety of Princes comes from Kings, Ben," she said. And her reliance upon greeting-card sentiments told me how much pressure she felt at this brave new adventure. Nor did I understand at all what she meant.

I'd been watching her during that week of preparation, and I now didn't like too much how she seemed in her spirit. Her grooming, her care of her clothes and hair—nothing wrong with any of that, but she seemed to speak to herself much oftener, muttering, arguing.

Though we lived in the same building as I had shared with her during our days at the waiting pen, she had taken an extra room next door, and I slept in there, on a makeshift bed of two armchairs. Twice in the first week I woke to hear noises from that room. The first night I heard Kate pacing, walking, and talking; if I hadn't known better I'd have wondered if she had a visitor. On the second night the sounds had an upsetting familiarity—the same kind of sobbing that I'd heard for the first time one night at Lamb's Head.

137

Pennsylvania, Ohio, Indiana, Illinois, Missouri, Kansas—that was the way that we went, as the song says. We took two days to pack, including a crate with a hinged door for Sydney, to which she took as to a luxury suite.

In our last act, before Bobby closed the doors of his house and locked the gates of his "estate," as he called it, we walked Jerry into the wagon. He had plenty of room, and an ingenious structure of vertical curtain-rods enabled Bobby to make the roof of the cart a little higher every day as Jerry grew.

Bobby drove; Kate sat beside him; I beside Kate. The truck, though now painted a bright cherry, had done circus duty, and flakes of red and yellow road-show paint peeked through here and there. It had also been fitted for sleeping, and the bench seat on which we sat folded backward in sections. Once we had cleared New York, I took advantage of the comfort and slept.

That Bobby Bilbum had some kind of road plan in his head soon became apparent—even though he followed no map of any kind. When I later assembled the journey, I made the following list of major "destination points," to use Bobby's term, and they add up to as near a straight line westward as he could have followed; Newark, New Jersey; Harrisburg, Pennsylvania; Wheeling, Ohio; Richmond, Indiana; Hannibal, Missouri, and St. Joseph, Kansas. His driving system, if I may call it that, entailed getting the truck to a steady forty miles an hour and holding it there, no matter what happened all around him.

In New Jersey, he swung carefully off the road. He took the truck down a narrow road, which became a deserted lane by a lake, and in the lights I saw the flash of water.

"Here," Bobby said, "our caravan will rest. Please stay with dear Kate while I address the creatures."

Kate didn't wake, and I opened the satchel that Bobby had given us. It contained a bottle of milk and two sandwiches; we would eat and drink nothing else on the road except milk and sandwiches; we bought the milk in little country stores miles from anywhere, and the bread and the meat for the sandwiches.

When I'd finished eating, I eased from the truck and went to find Bobby. He and Jerry were standing side by side while Jerry, front legs splayed wide as a door, drank from a creamery urn that came up to my waist. From the crate, Sydney began to grunt, and I reached in, put on her collar and leash, and took her out.

Though with no moon to help us, we had light enough to see, and I could tell that Nowhere, New Jersey, had some natural beauty. Heavy rocks behind me, the quiet gleam of water before me, and wooded heights across the way—all spoke of peace and quiet.

Have you ever been on a long journey that became a slow and delicious blur? I had great anxiety underpinning our travels—What would Lebanon, Kansas, have to offer in the long term? Would Captain Charles Miller get there?—yet, I have glorious memories of that trip. In the blur of farms and farmers and their amazement at Jerry, and the delight of the wives and children as they stroked his neck and he licked their hands, it's the names that remain in my head.

They're the underlying music of America, they're the piano player's left hand, the marching band's big cymbals. Every day, the name of a town or a county would cause me to reach for my notebook, and I floated across the continent of North America on a cloud of word tunes.

They come back to my mind now, like the lines of some great, geo-graphical poem, and I almost recall them in the order in which I met them or saw their names. Birdsboro, Hopeland, Clay, and Brickerville; Highspire, Boiling Springs, Walnut Bottom, Pleasant Hall; Helixville, Husband, Seven Springs, Champion; Cadiz, Ohio, Deersville. Stillwater, Newcomerstown, a place named Warsaw, and another named Nellie.

Some towns offered to live up to their names. In Ragetown, Ohio, we had a moment of discomfort. We found a milk depot and refilled our creamery urn in the early morning. As the people, mostly farmers, gath-ered to admire Jerry (and ask if Sydney was to be our dinner), a reporter from the local newspaper came by on his bicycle. Bobby grew jumpy and annoyed, especially when the reporter hustled off to find his photographer. We left Ragetown, Ohio, faster than we'd arrived there.

"Maybe it was the name that provoked the mood," Kate whispered as we clambered back on the truck.

Here are some more names; Magnetic Springs, East Liberty, Zanesfield, and De Graff; Quincy, Sidney (which, we all agreed, had been named after the porker asleep in the back), Willowdell, and Fort Recovery.

Dublin, Indiana, sparked a debate about the naming of American towns—the unexpected number of Native American words in all melodies, the number of European suffixes -burg and -ville, the Irish and English and Scottish names, the names of people and families. And the names of girls; if there could be towns such as Nellie and Anna surely we might find a Kate—to which Bobby, by now more than half in love with Kate, said, "It will have to be a beautiful metropolis."

And so we traveled west, on a journey that soon became rhythmic, smooth, and grand. I, who lived on the road, found myself entering two new dimensions—altered space and altered time, the former causing the latter.

On foot in Ireland, as I'd spent so many years, thirty miles to the next town occasioned a day of walking at a stiff pace. Here, hundreds of miles opened up before us every morning. I amused myself by reckoning our averages; a speed of forty miles an hour gives a net thirty miles an hour; we drove twelve hours a day and that should have yielded three hundred and sixty miles, therefore a journey of four days.

Not at all. Bobby's route took us into highways and byways, and we averaged no more than a hundred miles in any given twenty-four hours. So much for the new dimension of time in my life.

The skies took hold of my imagination—and my heart. In Ireland, we're never too far from sea clouds. They seem high and they scud across the sky looking to join other cumuli. Out in the middle of America, those weren't skies that I saw—that was the edge of space, with sometimes no hint or trace that a cloud had ever been there. A sense of freedom that I had never known came down to visit me, and at one daytime break, Kate said, "I feel that a weight has been lifted from me out here."

I said, knowing what she meant, "It's because the sky is so high."

Bobby said, "And we're in Cloud County, Kansas."

The following day, raising dust on empty, long, unpaved roads, we reached Lebanon. Kate sat forward, completely focused.

"It's Sunday morning," she said. "Stop by the church with the tower."

Bobby turned left, pulled the truck in, and we sat there. Half an hour later, much of the population of Lebanon began to pour from the solid, red church. With no hurry on them, they stopped and began to chat to neighbors. I felt Kate start, as she did with a sudden thought.

"Quick. Get Jerry out."

Within minutes, the little town of Lebanon had something new and wonderful to talk about.

"I thought I was drunk," said one man.

"Does he have a name?" asked a lady.

The children said, "May we hug him?"

And when Jerry batted those eyelashes, and looped that tongue around the cherries in a lady's hat, I understood Kate Begley's shrewdness. Later, when the town came to know her story, and when she opened her matchmaking business, she became their beloved star.

I stayed for some weeks and helped; Bobby wondered if he might "linger forever and a day." We found a house for rent on the edge of town, just below the church, a farm where the husband had died; the lone son had been killed in the war and the wife had lost her spirit, as she put it. I take the credit for seeing it first—on account of the high barn at the rear, and when we knocked on the door, we found that the lady who answered had been the one who'd almost lost her hat to Jerry outside the church.

At the side, a separate building had once housed seasonal laborers, and on the wall of this bunkhouse Kate Begley put up a sign that said, MARRIAGES MADE HERE, and beside fashioned another sign—a large pink heart. Six months later, when the owner died, and her sister sold the place to Kate and allowed her to buy it by installment, Kate put out a board with a name: She called the house "Kenmare."

She still had that same blind faith.

138

I came back to Ireland and resumed my life as a collector of folklore, this time an easier career on account of the car. My journeys took less time, my stays could be longer, and I had no need of worry lest I didn't get in off the road before dark—because I could always sleep in the car even if I came to a town that had no room at the inn.

As I traveled, I mused so often on the life that I'd seen out on the plains of Kansas. Setting up the new Kenmare had been a delightful exercise, but where was I in all this? I had needed to come back home, and I felt, in doing so, that Kate now had a measure of safety and comfort—a new life and a resumed career.

In some ways, it mirrored what she'd had at Lamb's Head—becoming a matchmaker while waiting for her parents to return from the dead. This time, she had the additional reality of Bobby Bilbum living in the barn, with Jerry now close to fully grown, and the old grain barn being high enough for him; and Sydney having plenty of room to run around and get her little snout into squealing and happy things.

Kate wrote often to me—long letters in that careful, "best girl in the class" handwriting, and always with a little flourish of homily at the end, or a piece of advice, or—something on which she was very keen—a useful tip. Three examples:

"In Love, as in Life, Courage comes from the Heart, not the Head."

"Always polish your boots last thing at night, because their shine will brighten your Life next morning and make you feel prepared for the day."

"Now that you have a car, always carry a bottle of vinegar with you—it's useful for all kinds of cleaning and it gets rid of smells."

She often asked about my life and my work, but never about Venetia. In Kansas one night I'd told her what had happened on the beach that awful day. Kate looked shattered.

"Did I make a terrible mistake?" I asked.

She stood up and ruffled my hair, her way of showing maximum affection.

"There's no way of telling what will happen," she said, but she remained muted for a long time afterward and never mentioned Venetia again.

By then, no matter what we'd been through, my dominant feelings toward Kate could have been defined as "grateful"—not least because our exploits together had given me a new sense of proportion. I can't say that I didn't think of Venetia as often as I used to—but I moped less about her. In fact I moped not at all. I gnashed my teeth, yes, and I swore—but largely at my own stupidity.

And that awful, weakening pain of loss—that had gone; I assumed that it had been erased by the fact that she hadn't died.

As to my future, I put everything on hold until I could measure myself against what I knew, my own country, my own work, my own normal life. Soon, I told myself, I would know what I wanted.

Thus I went about Ireland in the year or so from September 1946, relatively calm, celibate, absorbed in my work, and able to pay increasing attention to my parents, to James and Miss Fay, and to my work. I finished the basic interviewing for my report on matchmaking in rural Ireland, and got on with writing it up—the little segment from our fraught and bombed German village piqued my interest all over again.

One day, I telephoned home. (By now Mother had trained Lily the housekeeper to understand that we didn't have to wait for the phone to ring before we could use it.) My father told me that a telegram had arrived for me.

I said, "Open it."

"I-I-I don't like doing that, Ben."

I said, "But it never stopped you before," and he dropped the phone. That was the only mention I ever made of the Venetia telegrams, and he proved the truth of it.

I never raised that fact with my parents, never discussed with them the notion that my father—and I suspect that my mother never knew—willfully and deliberately kept me from reuniting with Venetia. And he knew of my grief, I know he knew it.

Mother took over the conversation.

"What did you say to your father, Ben?" She sounded too agitated to open the wound.

"I believe there's a telegram for me, Mother." I'd already told her quietly one day that I'd "met Venetia and she's fine, there are twin grandchildren and she may be coming back to Ireland, but she's married again," and I hadn't allowed the conversation to develop beyond that. Nor had she.

"It's from your friend, Miss Begley."

"Read it, Mother." Why did my heart suddenly hammer?

"Nana getting married in Cork. Thursday, July 17. You're invited. See you there Imperial Hotel. Love, Kate."

139

A small wedding: The bridegroom looked like a retired general: Mrs. Holst bridal. Kate shining.

Those were my opening notes, written that night. No more than twenty people attended, fewer at the church ceremony—which was held in the sacristy, not in the main church, because the bride and groom had both been widowed. The wedding "breakfast," as we always called it, took place at two o'clock in the afternoon.

"Why gray? Why didn't she wear white?" I asked Kate.

"Ben, don't you know anything? Widows who marry again wear gray—out of respect to the dear departed. And white's for virgins, you know that."

"Then there's a lot of fibbing that goes on in wedding dresses," I said, and she punched me.

That was the old Kate, the Kate that I had first met. She radiated excitement and good humor, gave me a full briefing on Jerry and Sydney—and had found, or so she thought, a potential wife for Bobby Bilbum.

"Problem is—she's as fat as he is and I don't know what to do."

"Leave them alone," I said.

"But they want to have children—" and she began to laugh so much that we both ended up with streaming eyes.

Mrs. Holst bore down on us. Kate whispered, "And I have something marvelous happening which I'll tell you later—because Nana wants to talk to you, I can tell from the way she's walking toward us."

"Oh, God," I said. "Stay here."

But Kate said, "No, I want to talk to the bridegroom," and darted away.

Marvelous? I thought, *What can that mean? Marvelous? Miller? No. She'd have told me.*

Mrs. Holst (as she always was and would be to me) sat in Kate's chair.

"Now, young man." Her eyes gleamed.

She's had sherry and more, said my inner voice. *Watch out.* I hadn't seen or heard from her since that offensive letter she wrote after Belgium, more or less alleging that I had caused World War II in order to hurt Kate.

"Congratulations," I said, in a voice stronger than I felt.

"I want to talk to you," she said.

"Here I am."

"Why don't you go back to the States with Kate, marry her, make her sell that place, and come back here?"

I hadn't been drinking, yet I almost fell over.

"Kate has her own plans for her life."

Delia Holst grabbed my forearm. Jesus! *Was she once a wrestler?* asked my inner gent.

"Look. Mr. Miller hasn't come. And he won't."

"You sound glad about that," I said.

"That fellow worried me. There was danger in him."

I recollected that she had said something similar about me—Kate had written it in her ledger.

"Well, there may have been danger in him, but she married him. And she'll go on believing that one day he'll turn up."

Mrs. Holst grabbed my knee. "He won't. He's dead. I got the telegram. Missing in action. That means to all intents and purposes dead."

I gasped. "And you didn't tell her?"

"Why should I? Don't you know anything? What do you think has been keeping her together? Now do as I say. Marry her. She trusts you."

On several counts, including bewilderment, I shook my head—and came up with the right words. Or so I thought.

"But you don't even like me."

Mrs. Holst said, "What are you talking about?"

I said, "You've never shown me anything but a frown. Or a scowl."

"God in Heaven," she said. "You know nothing about women. If I were forty years younger I'd eat you. I've never been nice to men that I couldn't have."

She rose and walked away, saying over her shoulder, "Go on. Do what you're told."

I didn't tell Kate her grandmother's directive—not then, anyway. The encounter left me feeling shaken. What had all the hostility been about? And did she now want me to marry Kate to give everybody an easy mind? Where did I fit in?

As I tried to sleep, I began to calculate the possibility. I can't say that the idea had never crossed my mind, and now the circumstances had offered level ground, so to speak—no Charles, no Venetia. Kate took another step in the direction her grandmother had suggested—by inviting me to come to Lebanon, Kansas, and observe the "something marvelous happening" that she had mentioned.

140

October 1947

Two weeks later, I traveled with Kate Begley for the last time. Our final journey together. We, who had been such intrepid traveling companions, would never do it again. This time, we did it with greater flair—on the SS *Ansonia,* as exquisite a liner as ever sailed the sea. We took a suite, all velvet and leather; Kate paid, because her grandmother had given her a gift of cash, she didn't say how much. In New York, we stayed one night, then I rented a convertible car, and with the roof down we drove to Lebanon, Kansas. Wide skies. Open roads. Wonderful.

The bunkhouse had expanded into a much stronger building with a porch and two waiting rooms, one for the men and one for the women. Somebody, perhaps Bobby, had improved upon the great pink heart—it seemed less vulgar, more alluring. The crude KENMARE sign had been replaced with a swinging board and delicate sign-writing. MARRIAGES MADE was new too, with delicate scrolling and ladylike borders. If Kate had done all of this in little more than a year, business must have been fine.

Which of them gave me the warmest reception—Bobby, Jerry, or Sydney? It has to be Sydney, who refused to leave my arms all evening. Jerry was cooler about these things, and by now had become a giant; yet, how he fluttered those eyelashes when he saw me. Bobby wept, and produced a hug close to suffocation; it felt like having a tent fall on me.

"Have you told him our marvelous news?" he asked Kate.

"Yes," she said.

"Wait until you meet her, dear boy, you will be so jealous. Ethel—isn't that a glorious name?"

"And," said Kate, recovering fast, "he also knows about the ball."

She hadn't told me until aboard ship—"to keep up the suspense," she said.

Her "customers," as she called them, knew her story—of her "waiting for Captain Miller." Many of them, from all over that part of the state, had formed a little committee, and they'd begun a search. Kate understood the kindness of their motives, and no matter how it hurt her soul, she humored them by going along with it.

Now they had raised funds to bring every Charles Miller they could find to empty, lonely, little Lebanon, Kansas, in the wild but kind and deep hope that somehow the gods who manage these things would find her Charles Miller and bring him along too.

She saw it for what it was—a cockeyed idea, with its roots in great kindness. I wondered whether they had another motive—that in their searching they had established the truth from the U.S. military and were in fact saying to Kate, "Give up—there are other fish in the sea."

I'd asked her on board ship whether she'd ever heard from the embassy in Dublin.

"No. Which supports me, Ben, doesn't it?"

I said, "I see your point," and didn't say a word about her grandmother.

"How actively have you been searching?" I asked her.

"I've left it to Destiny now," she said. "I've done all I can," and she closed down the conversation in her usual style. "Fate is kind, Ben, as often as it's cruel."

And we sailed on—two people who, as she might have put it, had bobbed about like corks on the Sea of Fate. Or, as I preferred, had been subject to the same vagaries of life as one of my beloved scholars; *Carminis hic fienem lacrimis faciemus*—"Let us now put an end to songs of grief, but not an end to love."

To say it another way, her grandmother's exhortation to me had begun to make a lot of sense. Kate might well have been thinking so too, and given our open affection toward each other, anybody who had seen us as we'd traveled to and through America, and now in Lebanon, Kansas, would have assumed married love.

With new power in my heart, and a feeling that many things of the worst kind in my life had come to an end, I set myself to observe Kate. I wanted to see how she had taken to life on the prairie. If the matchmaking business had become a success—and signs of prosperity abounded—how was she doing it? Was her approach here any different from how she operated in Ireland? Whence came her customers?

From what I could see, Lebanon sat in the heart of farming country, and the little interaction I'd had with local people when we first came here suggested decent, straightforward folk who worked hard. I didn't yet know, though, some of the relevant social factors, such as the general level of financial comfort, the ratio of single women to single men, the popularity of marriage.

Perhaps the most likely noticeable difference would be in the practice of religion—or so I thought. In the Ireland that Kate had known, close to 100 percent of the rural population attended Mass on a Sunday; here I didn't know how many denominations existed or the depth and zeal of observance. The plains hold many worshippers.

All things considered, I could scarcely have been more interested in anything in the world when, on that first morning, I sat in the back room of her "office," as she liked to call it, and listened through the open door to the first marriage candidate of the day.

Nothing in Kate's practice of matchmaking had changed. Had we been in Borneo, she would have said the same things—or so I felt. Here, though, in Kansas, something unusual did happen—the first man to arrive brought his mother.

He had the same shyness, the same awkwardness as Neddy the Drover. His name was Jubal Johnson—had Kate not asked him to spell it I should never have known how, and however deeply American his accent, he spoke so slowly that I had no difficulty in understanding every word.

Not that he said much at all; his mother did most of the talking. Jubal sat there as if he were mute; his ears, thinned by the weather, looked like wide, semi-transparent leaves. Mrs. Johnson said that she wanted him to find a wife; she was getting old; the farm was now too big; he needed help; and he needed to have children, and stop being a child himself. Those were his mother's words.

Kate said, "Let me talk to your son alone, right, Mrs. Johnson?"

She had to ask twice. First, the mother said, "He don't talk for himself." And then she said, "No secret questions, now."

Kate said, "I'm sure you have no secrets, Mrs. Johnson."

Jubal relaxed—that was Kate's gift. He'd have told her anything, and he did say that the reason he hadn't married was because he wouldn't put any woman he liked under the same roof as his mother. Kate told me afterward that she had difficulty in not laughing out loud.

"How do you handle something like that?" I asked her.

Kate said, "A girl came to see me a few weeks ago looking for a husband. She said that most men are frightened of her. She's six feet tall, built like a small castle, and although she has a kind heart it's well hidden and she shows to the world an eye so cold I needed a fur coat. That's the girl for Jubal Johnson."

Next came the weekend, busy beyond endurance. They came from all over the state to see her, and from northern Missouri, and from southern Nebraska, and from northwestern Colorado—and one youngish woman had come all the way up from the north of Arkansas. On Sunday afternoon, Bobby Bilbum sold hot dogs and ice cream, and encouraged people to hand fistfuls of grass and pieces of fruit to Jerry, who batted his eyelids at them all.

They came from farms and feed stores and grain mills and grocery stores, from church congregations and sporting clubs, from the plains and the prairies; she brought Catholics and Protestants and Shakers and Quakers and Lutherans and Baptists and Buddhists.

"Where are the Jews?" I asked.

"They have their own matchmakers," said Kate, "and they came here to meet me. I learned so much from them."

"How did you get so busy, so fast?"

She laughed. "Ben, d'you remember the look on your face when I first told you I was buying a giraffe?"

"I can never see the look on my own face, Kate."

"Jerry packs them in," she said. "About three weekends after you went back, people started arriving here at six o'clock on Sunday morning. The state police had to come and regulate the traffic, there must have been five hundred cars and trucks and tractors. In this dusty little place! Bobby thought that he'd died and gone to Heaven."

Let me describe her to you, as she sat there that twilit evening, the last marriage seeker gone. The sun of the plains had ended her pallor and yet had given her white lines around her eyes from squinting against the glare. She still cared for her hands, which didn't look like they belonged on the land. We sat on the porch, maybe two hundred yards from the nearest house in that small town, and yet she looked as though she'd come from a salon in New York. Her long skirt of charcoal gray barathea rustled every time she moved; and I tried not to look at the bosom beneath the embroidered cream blouse.

Her command impressed me more than anything—that calm, level air, changed only by a sudden thought, question, or laugh. Call me fickle, call me disloyal to my past life, but my heart turned over that evening. I could understand, and longed to replicate for her, every caring act my father had ever done for my mother. Even now, such a long time afterward, I wish I hadn't.

141

I'd planned to stay two weeks—until the day after the ball. It would mark the end of the search—or so I learned, because as Kate and I stood on the porch of the house, and watched a group of happy men string a banner that shouted THE CHUCK MILLER BALL, she said to me, "If this doesn't do it—nothing will."

"Meaning you've stopped searching?" I asked, as my mind said, *At long, bloody last.*

"Ben, you've been such a patient man."

"The things that happened to us, Kate. The things that we did, Miss Begley."

I spoke as though we'd been married, and settled down out here, and were looking back over our past. Although we were about to have a ball that might bring the right Charles Miller to Kansas, I felt it wouldn't. With Kate, however, who could tell anything? Nevertheless, I asked the question that had been rolling around in my mind.

"What do you think will happen at the ball?"

She smiled. "Aren't these the nicest people out here?" Lowering her voice, she said, "The Charles I knew would make his own way here. If that was what he wanted to do."

I reached a hand out and rested it on her shoulder.

"What was it you said to me once? There's one thing we can't stop, you said."

"You mean the world from turning?" She laughed. "I'm pleased you remember it."

I wanted to say, *Kate, I recall every word you ever spoke to me*—but it would have come out sardonically, and that would have broken the mood.

"Of course I remember it. Miss Begley. I make you sound like a teacher, don't I?"

"I wasn't, Ben. That's what you made me. I always felt, from that first day, that I was sent into your life to teach you."

Clearly, there is no God. For if there were, He would have taught me how to challenge that. I let it go. We watched the men drag the banner across to the other tree, trying to keep it up from the dust of the street. She had one more question.

"Do you remember when we told the Canadian soldiers that we were neutral?" No laugh accompanied the question, and that told me she had something else in mind.

"That whole neutral business," I said. "It probably saved our lives but I don't know how to judge it."

"Do you mean it's wrong not to take sides?"

"Probably. Given all we know now."

She didn't look at me—never did when she wanted to achieve something large with me.

"I often thought that you were 'neutral' with me." She stressed the word.

"But you wouldn't have wanted anything else," I said.

"No," she replied, dragging out the word. "No, not then." She quit the porch and went indoors.

To my own credit, I knew that I was being manipulated. First the grandmother had mended her fences with me, and had then proceeded to do what she knew best—get two people on the road to marriage. Then Kate's behavior and attitude on board ship—coy and affectionate but keeping a flirty distance—bore no resemblance to her past ways with me.

She also referred to our past deeds together—France, Mr. Seefeld, the snow in Belgium, the night in the cellar of the hut. My inner man said to me, *Tell her that you see what's going on.* In short, I knew that I was being set up—and I went along with it because that was what she wanted.

She danced her legs off that night. From the first bars of the fiddle she took to the floor and danced. Her hair, now longer than I'd ever seen it, flew out like a banner and caught the light, and her eyes reflected back that gleam to every man, woman, and child in the room.

Only about 50 percent of the people who came could fit into the barn at any one time—and that barn was fifty feet long and forty feet wide. Bobby Bilbum had spent weeks building a separate loose box for Jerry at the southern end, and from there he looked out in his lovely benign way at the band on the northern end. We put out a tub of apples and pears and oranges, and everything we could lay hands on outside the door of his box, and all night long, supervised by Bobby, people fed Jerry.

Sydney fared less well. She didn't like the crowds or the noise, and spent much of the early evening shivering in my arms. It occurred to me that perhaps some race instinct (perhaps I should call that "breed instinct") told her that most of the people there would have been only too pleased to take her home and serve her for Sunday lunch. At about nine o'clock, I took her back to the house, set out a massive dish of food for her, hauled her bed down the floor, and left her to it, knowing that she'd eat and then fall asleep.

It ranks as one of the most bizarre evenings of my life. For the first hour, Kate danced with all the neighbors, all the men who had proved so kind to her when she arrived (though when they came to offer help, she told me, they were usually accompanied by their wives).

Next, she danced with the men who had come to look for help in finding wives. Some of her successful couples showed up—"Still happily married," as she said later—and she danced with the wives as well as the husbands.

She danced with Bobby Bilbum; he surprised them all with his fluid, light-footed steps—but not me; I had seen how Bobby moved from the day I first met him, and I've frequently observed how delicate on their feet big men can be.

Kate danced with me too. You're familiar, I expect, with the traditional image of a society girl who likes to dance. Venetia and I—we'd never danced; the opportunity had never arisen. I bet that she was a wonderful dancer, though, those legs, that easy carriage with that long neck, and the head raised like a swan. Well, that image, of the girl dancing, her head thrown back laughing as she twirls and swirls across the floor, delighting everybody with her gaiety—that's how Kate looked that night.

"Did you ever have such a good time?" She laughed up at me. And we both said together, "Better than Killarney."

"I'm watching you," she said.

"I'm throwing no punches tonight."

"Or ever again," she said, mock-scolding.

"Except to protect you," I said.

We whirled some more.

"Are you all right?" I asked. She greeted every person past whom we waltzed, and they smiled, laughed, applauded, waved to her.

"You're worried for me, aren't you?"

"In case you're disappointed," I said.

"That would only happen if I had an expectation," she said.

In fact, I was the apprehensive one, and I should have listened to that feeling and its implications, and I didn't.

———

The band played something as close to a fanfare as they could get. Bobby Bilbum, by now the master of ceremonies, took the stage, and with him a lady of his own height and girth.

"Ladies and gentlemen, I pray your attention." Applause spattered and somebody whistled on fingers. "I wish to make two announcements. The first will be an invitation to share my joy—because this magnificent creature, Ethel Pampling, has agreed to become my wife."

Wild cheering broke out, and Kate ran up to the stage and tried to kiss both of them—they had to make considerable accommodations of height and girth for her to get to their cheeks. At the urgings of the audience, the happy couple then kissed, and a man behind me remarked, "It's like two ships meeting at sea."

When this delight had settled, Bobby proceeded to the next announcement.

"Now you all know why we're here. A long time ago, our dear Kate here made a vow. She said to her new husband, an American officer, that if the war separated them, she would come here and wait for him in the heart of his own country, the very center of the United States."

The women made oohing and aahing sounds and much applause rose again.

"Kate got here first," declared Bobby, "and what an adornment she has been, and what a service to society—bringing people together to love each other. Tonight, we want to see whether, by any chance, we have found for her the man she's been seeking—Captain Miller. We formed a committee—we only told Kate this quite recently—and with letters in all directions, to all kinds of people, we sent for every Chuck or Charles Miller we could find. Out of the goodness of their hearts, seventy of them turned up—and they've been fed and watered in the church hall for the last two hours."

142

Perhaps they expected gaiety to attach to this notion—but it didn't happen. In fact, the guardian of that barn's mood would turn out to be Kate, because, of a sudden, people became tense.

The remarking man behind me said, "Whose dang fool idea was this?"

A woman answered, "This is just gonna hurt."

Bobby, usually sensitive, picked up the change of atmosphere, but too late to affect the proceedings. As he watched, the big doors opened and, directed by somebody outside, a line of men began to file in, one at a time.

Bobby called, "Kate!"

She answered his beckoning finger and went back onto the little stage, where she stood between Bobby and Ethel like a shrub between two oaks. I, and I alone, could see the anguish on her face; once again, she hadn't thought it through.

The men, who must have been briefed, headed for the little bandstand, walking as confidently as they could muster. For a moment, each one stopped in front of Kate.

"I'm Chuck Miller—from Smith County, Kansas; my hometown is Jacksonburg, just up the road a ways."

"I'm Chuck Miller—from Wallace County, Kansas."

"I'm Chuck Miller—from Ness County, Kansas; my hometown is Wellmanville."

"I'm Chuck Miller—from the town of Coldwater in Comanche County, Kansas."

"I'm Chuck Miller—from Sedgwick County, Kansas. I have a farm near the town of Ruby."

There had been times in my life when I'd almost wished to die; I don't need to go into such moments again, but the embarrassment I felt in that barn might well be included among them. Not a man among the early arrivals looked remotely like the Charles Miller whom Kate had married;

one was at least seventy years old, another stood no more than five feet two inches tall—and on it went.

Men in suits, men in cowboy clothes, men in bib-dungarees, men in uniform—I began to wonder what they thought they were doing there, what they had been told.

When two or three more from the counties of Kansas had declared themselves, the extent of the trawl began to show. A man strode to the bandstand and announced, "I'm Chuck Miller from the great state of Arkansas." Two more Arkansans followed, and now the parade was up and running. Chuck Miller, Charles Miller, Charlie Miller, Chuck Miller—they marched in through the great main door of the barn at ten-second intervals, walked to the bandstand, and declared themselves.

Just as I was beginning to think that these men aspired to Kate's hand in marriage, a couple came along.

"I'm Chuck Miller from the great state of Illinois and this is my wife, Marge—and ma'am, I know I'm not the Chuck Miller you wanted to see, but all of us have come here to tell you that if he's not here tonight, Marge and I'll do everything we can to find your own Chuck Miller for you. That's why we came—and I know that's why a lot of the other Chuck Millers came. To tell you that."

Two more couples arrived on their heels, and then two more, and soon I counted at least fifteen Chuck Millers who had brought along their wives. Now the true purpose had begun to surface. They might not have known it when they first began the enterprise, but the committee members thought that if they didn't find the real Chuck Miller, at least they'd bring Kate the comfort, as they saw it, of surrounding her with men who bore her beloved husband's name.

But it wasn't over yet. One of the organizers at the barn door responded to a signal from Bobby Bilbum and held up nine fingers. Now the incoming men slowed down, and the first of this last nine to walk in at least belonged in the same age bracket as the Charles Miller I knew—and he too wore a uniform, even if it was U.S. Air Force and not army.

I shivered a little, not so much at the uniform, but at the possibility that they had in fact found the real Charles Miller. Given the way they'd structured it so far, were they keeping him until last?

Bobby compounded this anxiety in me by sidling over and whispering, "They're very excited out there."

And what of Kate in all of this? She had never impressed me more. With all the rights in the world to fall apart, she stood there as composed as a queen, smiling, shaking hands, sharing a brief joke with each Chuck Miller who came along. Every man among them responded to her. Many said, "I wish it had been me. He's a lucky guy, the real Chuck."

And if the men showed their appreciation in smiles, laughs, and little smatterings of solitary applause, the women loved her even more. Each wife stepped up on the bandstand and hugged her and wished her luck.

After the wives, all of the men who now came in wore uniforms—army, navy, air force. The intervals between their appearances grew longer and longer—and the men began to look more and more likely. I moved forward a little, to stand right behind Kate in case Charles appeared—or didn't.

From the pace and tension of the parade, it was clear that the organizers thought they had found at least a replacement—and in fact the last man through the door looked, in the distance and at first glance, not unlike "the real Chuck," as Bobby had begun to say.

Big, fair-haired, and in an impeccable army uniform festooned with decorations, he stood for a half-second framed in the doorway and there was a flash, a lightning flare in that half-second when I said to myself, "Jesus God!" I know that Kate had the same thought because her body leaned forward in that direction and her hands flew to her mouth. She sagged when she saw him clearer.

He halted before her, saluted, and said, "Ma'am, I'm Lieutenant Chuck Miller, from the town of Fontana, in the County of San Bernardino, in the great state of California."

She said, "And you've come all this way?"

He said, "Ma'am, in a cause such as this, in the name of a fellow officer, it was a short journey."

He snapped off another salute, turned with robot steps, and marched the few feet to join the others.

I whispered, "Are you all right?" and she reached a hand back for me to take, and she held on and held on.

———

They all stood there in a group and applauded her—it seemed they might never stop. When, eventually, they responded to her gestures, Kate took a deep breath and spoke.

"Thank you—thank you all for coming here. And thank you too, the organizers who dreamed up this lovely plan. I've never known such kindness, and even though you must have all known that none of you was ever married to me—at least I hope you'd have remembered if you had been—it was kind beyond measure of you to come here, and many of you from so far away. If my Chuck Miller were here, he'd be in tears, I know it. For all his bravery as a soldier, he was a very tender man. And he'd now tell me something—he'd give me an order. Well, he was an officer, wasn't he? He'd order me to dance with every Chuck Miller here tonight."

And she did. She stepped from the little makeshift stage—hand-hewn by Bobby Bilbum—and, with the grace of Heaven itself, approached sixty-year-old Chuck Miller from Jacksonburg, "just up the road a ways," and spun him through the barn.

I'm guessing that Lebanon's population in the late 1940s came to about two hundred voters and their children. They ate dinner early out there; they lived their lives in an admirably calm way, regulated, undramatic people, good neighbors, and better friends, who all went to bed early, rose at the same time, and worked hard.

The Chuck Miller Party dented all that for a night—the last person left the barn around half past two in the morning, and even then the fiddler, a man named Rufus Quisenberry, whose fingers I could scarcely see on the neck of the fiddle so fast did he play, didn't want to stop. And was it my imagination, or did Jerry the Giraffe actually sway in time to Rufus's fiddle?

Kate stood at the door and said good night to every person.

"Good night, Margie, you should always wear your hair up like that—now we can see your lovely neck."

"Eddie, nobody told me you were such a good dancer."

"Girls, I know why you're giggling, I saw you with the boys."

Her warmth, her laughing good humor, her compliments to men, women, and children—no wonder the little town of Lebanon loved her. She kissed every Chuck Miller on the cheek, and she teased their wives about the trials of being married to a man of that name, and when it was all over she stood in the barn doorway and whispered, "Ben, I need you, I need you, I need you."

Some men are good at being needed, some not—I didn't know either way until that night. Or perhaps it's more accurate to say that I'd never stopped to think about it. When my father left home, Mother said to me, "I need you to go after him and bring him back. For me." That had been my only encounter with the word *need*. Venetia had never used it— and Venetia certainly didn't need me now. I shied away from that bitter arena as from a cloud of poison gas.

We went into the house, leaving Bobby and Ethel to tend Jerry, who was wide awake, as he was most of the time.

"He needs one hour of sleep in twenty-four," Kate told me, and I never saw Jerry sleeping—which he did, they told me, by sitting down and resting his head on his haunches for a few minutes at a time.

Sydney was sprawled flat out; she had licked the bowl clean and looked as pink, fat, and debauched as Nero. A little whistling snore came from her as we stepped over on our way to the staircase.

I had been sleeping in a small room with a deep mansard; it looked out onto the wide, wide fields of Kansas with not an object in sight, not even a tree; Kate's room, in front, overlooked the street. Moonlight gave me all the light I needed and, too hot to wear anything, I stripped and climbed into bed.

A moment later, I heard a knock on my open door, and Kate said, "It's your turn tonight. Last time I went to your room."

"Kate, I'm wearing nothing."

"Do you want to borrow a nightdress?" And she laughed. "Come on, Ben, you can't be shy of me, can you?"

I took no care to hide myself or be modest, nor did she react in anything but an ordinary way. We didn't sleep until dawn. For hours we talked, revisiting every phase of our lives in each other's company.

After a period of prolonged kissing, I said, "You chided me once for not being bolder with you."

Kate raised herself on an elbow. "I wouldn't chide you now. But I want to wait."

I said nothing, merely waited.

"Aren't you going to ask me, 'Wait for what'?"

I said, "Wait for what?"

"Guess."

"Guess what?"

"Ben, what is it women want to wait for?"

What could I reply, other than, "So we're to be married, is that it?"

She said not another word, but rolled closer to me and soon fell asleep on my chest.

And I? I judge my mood by the words that cross the screen of my mind, and now I saw *rhapsody,* and *companionship,* and *natural,* and, yes, *love.* In truth, the word *matchmaking* crossed my mind too. I had joined the ranks of Neddy the Drover and Miss Mangan from the bakery, and the men who came up from the sea.

143

December 1947

We had arrangements to make, and we made them with quiet and firm pleasure. Our first agreement came mutually—to tell nobody until we had married, which would happen quietly in a few months, once all the paperwork had been arranged. As she was now resident in the United States, she could acquire, in my name, the Venetia divorce papers from Reno, Nevada. I said not a word about the documentation that she would need—too painful for her. I was to go back to Ireland for a month or so, to close Lamb's Head and make it weatherproof. Her grandmother had gone to live in Cork and Kate now owned the cottage; we agreed that we would always keep it as a home in Ireland should we ever wish to return.

I had many questions that I wanted to ask. Had she been officially informed of Charles's death? His family—had she been in touch with them? And—of great personal interest to me—did we know how he had died? I should very much have liked to establish that Volunder had killed him; and Peiper's case still dragged on as Willis Everett fought and fought— such an unpopular cause—to get the death sentence commuted.

My questions remained in my locker, so to speak; I never asked them, because, as ever, Kate set the ground rules.

"I sense," she said, "that the Venetia business has left you in pain. So why don't I promise that I'll never talk about her, and you'll never ask about Charles?"

Even if I hadn't consented—and I didn't entirely wish to—I knew that nothing would be gained by disagreeing. Kate had decided on her method of dealing with the past; on a topic so delicate and fraught, I could never change her mind—nor could anyone else.

A week later, I kissed Sydney good-bye, and kissed Jerry good-bye, and kissed Kate good-bye, and took the train to Chicago, another to New York, and the steamer home to Cork.

Let me reflect for a moment on what I recall of those months. Last week I had the fiftieth anniversary of meeting Kate, and I know that I've done the right thing by recording her life as I knew it—or at least that period of her life that I've shown you. I also believe that by leaving behind for you these memoirs, reminiscences, chronicles—call them what you wish—you'll come to understand your father better, but by the unortho-dox route he has chosen.

After all, I haven't hidden any of my emotions in anything I've writ-ten, and by now I've made it clear, even in my digressions, how I con-ducted my life—and my heart. It's possible that at this moment you may feel some pain on behalf of your mother, and the way things were as we left them on that beach, and I would certainly understand that. And it's possible too that you'll feel critical of me, find me at least care-less, at most reprehensible. But I hope you'll believe that I tried to act in a responsible way—most of the time.

144

January 1948

You'll recall, I'm sure, my obsession with wolves. Therefore you'll know that I had unfinished business, in which James Clare expected to play a part—namely, the collection of a famous but as yet untold story in

County Donegal. As I crossed the Atlantic once more, I made another good decision; not only would I accompany James to the storyteller's house, I would ask him to help me wrap this past segment of my life, Venetia included, into a package I could carry without pain.

I sent him a cable from New York, told him that I'd be at my parents' house, and gave the dates. If he would let me know when to meet him in Donegal, we could try to collect the wolf story. As ever, the arrangements with James worked smooth as butter, and I met him in the town of Glenties in the middle of August.

He looked as healthy as a dog, though still with the long black coat that he wore winter and summer. The story, he said, existed in a place out on the shoreline; a man by name of Peter Magee had it, who, according to James, "definitely wanted money."

I asked, "How will you handle that?" We operated under strict "never pay" directives.

"He'll tell us the story, we won't note it down, but if it's good enough I'll find a way of compensating him."

"Will he trust us not to go away and write it?"

James said, "He has to. Otherwise how can we trust him that the story is genuinely old?"

The storyteller lived alone. He described himself as "a retired jobbing fisherman"—that is, he used to work on trawlers for anyone who would give him a day's work. He also said that he was "a quiet man" and "a listener, not a talker." Never married, he lived in a new house provided by the Donegal County Council, because his old house had begun to fall down around his ears.

At James's prompting, he said that he had many stories, but he never told them.

"Who'd want to listen to me?" he said over and over.

"I've met few men whom I'd rather listen to," said James, who had brought him gifts of food.

How this man had ever worked a trawler I shall never know. He had a girl's hands, and a dainty way about him in general. Apologetic for himself and his house, he had a hesitant air.

"Now, Peter," said James. "Do you mind if Ben here takes notes as you speak?"

"I don't mind at all," said Peter Magee.

"And do you mind if we publish what you say in our annual journal?"

"Not a bother on me," said Peter Magee.

"So," said James. "Off you go, then, we'll be listening like children."

"And what'll you be listening to?" said Peter Magee.

"To your famous story about the wolf," said James.

"Well," said Peter Magee, "you can listen from now 'til the middle of next week, but you'll not hear that story."

James said, "But I thought, Peter, that's why we're here."

"I know you thought that," said Peter Magee. "But a man may think what he likes."

James and I looked at each other and all we could do was smile. He offered to put the storyteller's name in the folklore archives, but Peter Magee, a gentle man, and so timid, refused, saying that he had no liking for being named in public.

"Besides which," he said, "I had a gentleman come here from Los Angeles, and he's paying me good money for my stories. And I have a lot of them."

"Where and how did you hear them?" we asked.

"Nobody had any interest in anything I ever had to say," he said. "So I listened. And I was always with old people. My great-grandfather lived to be a hundred and two, and I remember him saying that he got that wolf tale from his grandfather."

As we said good-bye, promising to come back, he asked, "Now the two of you—are you father and son?"

James laughed and replied, "I'd like to think so."

By now I had a roof rack on the car—one of the first in the country. With James's bicycle still on top of it, we drove back into Glenties and found a place to eat and a place to stay the night. James drank whiskey and I lemonade, and we laughed many times over Peter Magee and his Hollywood friend, and how we'd been taken for a ride.

When the laughing was done, James asked the usual question: "Now, tell me about your own self."

I had so much to tell him, and he sensed it.

Together we began to rehash all that had happened to me in my life. And yet, having described the Venetia meeting—and parting—and having told him how ship after ship after ship had arrived to the docks in

New York with Kate looking so hopeful and then so forlorn, and having described what it was like to drive halfway across America with a pig and a giraffe, I chose not to tell him about my American plans and my forthcoming marriage. However shoddy and disloyal I felt about that, something held me back.

Knowledge of him had told me that James was about to make one of his epic comments—so I waited. "Did you do what I taught you?" James asked.

"Did I keep a record? As much as I could. It's fragmentary. I salvaged her notes and mine such as they were."

"How did you do that?"

I laughed. "In the lining of my coat."

"That's appropriate," said James. "That's how Marco Polo brought jewels back from the East." He paused. "But I was asking you something else."

I waited. He said nothing. I knew this game.

"Go on," I said.

"Did you measure what's happened to you on a legendary scale?" he asked.

I said, "I haven't tried yet."

James said, "Well, it's all there waiting for you."

Again I said, "Go on," knowing that he needed only the prompting.

He sat back, a sense of relish about him. "You're the scribe, aren't you? You're the Homer watching all this and reporting it."

"Not Homer, James. Not at all."

"Yes. And not only the scribe but the warrior, too. You know what I mean. First of all, you go out of your way to observe an age-old tradition—matchmaking. One of the most ancient customs in the world, a true life force. Then the warrior arrives from over the sea. Paris seeking his Helen of Troy. He asks her to undertake a task to prove her worth. You go along—scribe, but also faithful companion. And by now you've surely crossed seven seas, haven't you?"

"That's certainly true."

"And you've been a warrior in the forest, haven't you? And the leader who led the princess to safety."

I hadn't told James that I'd killed a man, and I never told him.

He continued, "And by fair means or foul you discovered where your own heart's desire was, and you went to see her."

"Hold on," I said. "Fair means or foul?"

He patted my arm. "People talk, Ben. Ireland's a village. But 'tis all right. Ray Cody's a dirty little scut, and everybody knows it."

I must have looked stricken—I certainly felt that—because James piled on the reassurance.

"He won't open his mouth again. Does he want to be charged with kidnapping?"

I shook my head. "Probably not."

James said, "Now comes your only mistake. And it's a big one. If you see your life as a legend, you have to listen to the words of the principal characters."

"What do you mean?"

"If you can bear to," he said, "listen again carefully to the words Venetia spoke. I don't think you have."

"James, you're right in this respect—I can't bear to. And that's over. She married another. Is that legendary too?"

"Oh, Ben, you sound bitter," said James.

"Maybe I am."

Next morning, as I unloaded his bicycle from my roof rack, James told me that he was taking a year's sabbatical; it would begin in two months, and he asked me to take over his duties. That was the moment to tell him—that I wouldn't even be in the country, that I would have joined the ranks of exile and gone abroad to seek my fortune. But I didn't—too cowardly. Instead, I thanked him for the compliment, and he thanked me for having always been so trustworthy.

145

The symbolism that James had aired stayed in my mind as I drove away. I began to see myself as Odysseus, Ulysses, Homer's wanderer, at last on his way to his Ithaca and his Penelope, except that it was Lebanon, Kansas, and she was Kate.

And I had even had some tasks to complete before my odyssey ended.

In fact, that day could be counted as part of it, because from Donegal to the west of Kerry is almost the longest journey one can take in Ireland. I stayed in Killarney; Mrs. Cooper still had the suitcase we'd packed before leaving for Germany and Belgium—I'd completely forgotten it. I assumed, as I opened it, that the new and savage beating of my heart came from the memories stirred by the suitcase.

Next morning, with the sun high in the sky, I set out for Lamb's Head. By now, the long, low house had been vacant for almost a year—perhaps more, because I didn't know the precise date that Mrs. Holst had ceased to live there.

A squall hung on the sea out beyond Caherdaniel. The lane had weeds growing in it. A seagull perched on the chimney, something that could never previously have happened because the fire burned all the time. A tiny corner of the thatch had grass peeping through; if that weren't soon corrected it would overgrow the roof. The red paint of the door had peeled away in part, possibly from salt pitched up here during a storm in the winter.

On a windowsill at the back of the house, beneath a geranium pot now grown wild, I found the key where Kate had told me. She was needed again, with her stick of chalk—the ants had invaded the kitchen, and a line of them walked across the floor looking like a thin, flowing trail of gunpowder.

I propped the door wide open, flung up all the windows, and opened the other doors to get as much air through the house as possible. I caught the faint odor of a fire long gone out. I went from room to room, checking for ceiling damage; everything seemed very sound. I felt no alarm. Not yet. The furniture hadn't been covered with dust sheets, therefore no ghosts.

Mrs. Holst must have visited somewhat recently, and she'd left a single cigarette in a packet on the table, together with a box of matches. She hadn't left any food, however, and I sat in the open air, grateful that I'd had the foresight to have Mrs. Cooper make me a sandwich. How that outdoor nook got its shelter I never could tell, but from the first moment I sat there, the day when Kate touched my arm and asked me to tell her my troubles, it had had a sense of calm. I didn't feel it now.

Before I locked up the house again, I decided to do one last tour of inspection. Something was getting at me. I picked up the cigarette packet. *Mrs. Holst doesn't smoke. So whose cigarette packet is that?* I dismissed it. *Perhaps her new husband smokes.* It didn't quite go away.

Under an old pile of newspapers in Kate's room, and the magazine clippings we'd used for our researches before Belgium, I saw her red book. Here is the last entry she'd made.

I will not give up, and I know from the ancient power of matchmakers that Charles is alive. He lives in me, that's how I know. That belief comes from the same faith I have when I introduce people to each other, and have faith in them to conduct ordinary decent lives for each other. None of them has ever let me down. I was given this power of understanding from a greater force than the world can translate, it is a power as old as the oldest gods, and Charles and I were born with those silver cords around our ankles, and the gods haven't finished wrapping those cords around us together yet. Those were the cords that drew us toward each other. Charles admitted to me that when he first met me he was as drawn to me as I to him. No death can end that power. So I will go on looking for him, and waiting for him, and I will do both in equal measure. Even if I marry Ben—which is Nana's suggestion—he, though as kind a man as has ever lived, will never have the power over me that Charles has. Ben will be practical and affectionate and he will look after me. But he will never make me catch my breath.

My father had an old saying, "Listeners never hear good of themselves." Meaning that eavesdroppers may hear people speak of them in unpleasant terms. My children, dear Ben, dear Louise—never read somebody's intimate journal, especially if you know and love them. You won't be portrayed as you'd wish to be.

I closed the book, shut all reaction from my mind, refastened all the doors and windows, locked the house, and drove down to Kenmare. On the edge of the town, I found my way ahead blocked—in every possible sense.

146

His face had a few moments earlier loomed into my mind, his kind, decent face with its smile backed by rented teeth. Neddy the Drover was taking twenty head of cattle to a yard on the other side of Kenmare, and for the next few minutes they blocked the entire sloping street.

I bipped the horn at him, he waved a casual hand back without looking, as much as to say, "This will only take a few minutes," so I bipped again. Harder. Louder. He looked back—puzzled, because Neddy could never reach annoyance. When he saw me, he didn't wave, he ran back.

"Mr. Ben. It is, isn't it?"

"Neddy, how are you?"

"Sir, you're the man I want to see, the very man."

"You look good, Neddy."

"Sir, these'll take me about ten minutes. Ten minutes and no more. Can you meet me at MacCarthy's?"

"The name is good anyway," I said, but Neddy didn't catch—or, more accurate, didn't want—the joke. He looked agitated.

When he trotted into the pub and found me, before I could offer him a drink, he grabbed my wrist.

"Sir, were you up at the house at all?"

"That's where I was coming from."

"Was it all right?"

"There's grass in the thatch," I said.

"Jesus, sir, don't go up there again. Not on your own anyway."

I laughed. "Is there a ghost there?"

He looked at me wide-eyed and nodded.

"Kind of," he said.

How did I know? Nobody rational can answer that question. I knew with that part of me that I can't define or locate, the part of me that tortured and killed, the part of me that knows about remorse, the part of me that had those brain-spattering fantasies of violence, the part of me that's ashamed of all that.

It is my fervent hope that you never feel shame—by which I mean shame that you've deserved. It covers the soul like slime. You can't shake it off. It lasts for a long, long time. Try the detergent of justification if you like, but it doesn't work. I'm ashamed of what I did to Cody— ashamed of the actual violence, ashamed of the greater and terrifying threat. I'm ashamed of killing that soldier in the snows, even if it were Sebastian Volunder. Shame's time lies deep in the night, at four o'clock in the morning, the time that the Norse legends call "the hour of the wolf"—that's when most people die. It's when I'll die. And from the place I keep such knowledge—that's how I knew.

All of those thoughts came rushing in that afternoon—as much to remind me of my capacities as of my shame.

147

Neddy the Drover had extensive detail. When he and his bakery love had wed, they'd gone to live in a house between Lamb's Head and Kenmare. With the house came a small boat, and Neddy delighted to row out and fish. One morning early, edging around the point at Lamb's Head, he saw a figure standing down by the water.

"Not doing anything, Mr. Ben, just standing and looking at the stones. On the little dock, like."

Neddy assumed that it was some fisherman—but he saw no boat. He then assumed that it was some tourist, some camper. But when, a week later, and then two weeks later, and then three weeks later, the man could still be seen there, standing, smoking a cigarette, and staring at the rocks on the jetty, the little dock to which fishermen came seeking a wife, Neddy assumed a ghost. He hadn't gone near the place, too frightened.

"Didn't Miss Begley's father die at sea, and wasn't he a big, blondy man too, by all accounts?"

But I knew what the "ghost" was looking at: a little plaque with a tender message from a bereft child.

"And then, Mr. Ben, didn't I hear tell, like everyone else along here, that Miss Begley's new husband, wasn't he killed in the war, like? And was it his ghost?"

"When did you see him last, Neddy?"

"Mr. Ben, wasn't he there every day, like? It's a shock that he hasn't fallen into the ocean by now."

"Is he there all day?"

"I can't say, Mr. Ben. I'm not all that inclined to go there that much at the minute."

What choice did I have? Decency had nothing to do with it. Powerful self-interest, self-protection—even curiosity—all kicked in. My life had suddenly become unsafe, as it always had been, I realized, when I'd been in Captain Miller's company. Remember those fantasies of violence that I'd had when he and Kate married in London? I'm certain they came from not feeling safe. And back then, I hadn't even known that they called him "Killer."

Halfway up the lane, I stopped the car and switched off—even though the wind off the sea was blowing the engine sound away behind me. I walked the rest of the journey, I tiptoed. This time—no key; the pot had been moved and the key taken. When I went around to the front, the door stood wide open.

Do officers carry guns? was my first thought.

In the gloom of the kitchen, he sat by the cold and empty fireplace— in Kate's chair. He looked up—a shattered man; January outside, January in his eyes. When he stood, he still had the same height, but he looked like an effigy from which the straw had been taken—hollow-chested, and his shoulders hunched, like a man expecting a blow. The straw-colored hair, the color of Kansas, was ragged with gray. If I hadn't known better I'd have said that somebody had drawn black shadow lines down his cheeks.

"Where's Kate?" he said, in a voice that sounded ready to cough.

And I thought, *Did ever a man so dwindle?*

———

I didn't know what to do. Was he dangerous? He didn't look it. Did he know me? I didn't think so at first. Was he sane? If he was, it was a reduced sanity, a lurching from one handhold to the next, barely hanging on. This was a man who needed to die; nobody could go on through life in that shape, a member of the Silent Ones. This was also a man whom I'd so admired and now he had come down so far; where once there had been gold, I now saw only lead. The loss seared me—the loss of a man whom, whatever my doubts about his role in war, I had so admired. My mind raced faster than it had in the forest snows. Who knows he's here? Neddy the Drover. And Neddy believes that this ghost will fall into the sea. I sat.

"Do you know who I am?"

He sat too; it is a characteristic of shell shock that the victim frequently mimics the actions of a person nearby.

"Do you know who I am?" he repeated, but he said it in an ambiguous way—he could have been parroting me, or he could have been asking me the same question. With his next words, he saved me from answering. "When will Kate be here?"

Let me try to count the currents flowing in torrents through my brain as I sat there.

Why should Kate be lumbered with this husk? How weak is his mind? Who would miss him? The scar on his throat has turned blue. Does he have any menace left in him? Is he to be pitied? Could he fight me off? Those are the sorts of clothes I saw the men wearing in the German villages. This would hurt her, to see him like this. This would ruin her life. Can he ever recover? I doubt it. Who knows that he's here? Only Neddy and me. Who knows who he is? Apart from me, probably nobody. Not even himself. And I was unreliable—I, after all, had become a brutalized man.

148

While I sat looking at him and thinking, he lapsed into gloom, staring at the sullen hearth.

I stood again. "Come with me."

He followed me from the cottage and I walked across the little plateau, and down a few steps to the part where the path grew steepest. Nothing on the sea, not even a gull, just the waves still trying to come ashore and subdue the land and retreating in failure.

I looked back. He stumbled a little, and now he stood where I had first seen him entreating Kate, persuading her into the adventures that had ultimately scarred us all. She had lost a husband, he had lost his wits, and I had lost my soul—or part of it. The gods of war had had a field day with us. And now they would close the book with a flourish.

Charles Miller held out his hands to me, a child afraid of falling. He stood exactly where Kate Begley had stood on the day she'd held out her hands to me in forgiveness for my drunken brawl. I went back up the dangerous slope and took his hands.

149

Good and bad, we all do things without thinking. I can't and I won't claim deliberate action that day; I can't and won't say that I took such actions as I did for the greater good or ill of anybody. All I will do is report. And I report that I took Charles Miller's hands, and I pulled him a little toward me and got him into my arms. Then I turned him around and walked him back up the slope.

I led him into the house, I sat him down in Kate's chair, I opened the neck of his filthy, army-issue shirt, and I left him sitting there for a moment. From a corner of the kitchen, I took the blue pitcher that they used for milk, and I went out to the butt of rainwater that stood at the corner of the house, filled the pitcher, came back in, found a towel in Kate's room, and began to bathe Charles Miller's face and neck.

He sat like a child. He sat still as a dog. As softly as my large hands would allow, I cleaned his face and his neck and his head, and his caked-with-dirt hands and wrists, and he sat there, tears in his eyes, not quite comprehending—and yet knowing something, because he said, "Thank you."

I left him for a moment, saying, "Charles, sit here. I'll be right back." He nodded, like one of those missionary collection boxes where the saint's head bobs when you drop in a coin.

Down the lane, I retrieved the car, backed it up to the front door, and installed him in the passenger's seat. I locked the cottage and put the key under the geranium pot and we drove away from Lamb's Head. The danger—my danger to him, my greater danger to myself—had passed. Did he ever return to Lamb's Head? I do not know.

What to do now? Like hay on a pitchfork, my mind kept tossing up the word *understanding*. I stayed with it—and its different interpretations opened out until one dominated.

In Kenmare, I drove to the house of Hans-Dieter Seefeld and parked in his driveway, careful as a clerk in case I mowed down one of the many cats.

He came to the door, blinking like an owl.

"Ben!" He hugged me. "Come in, come in."

"No. I can't. But I need you."

"For why?" It remains the only linguistic error that I ever heard Hans-Dieter Seefeld make in English.

"There is somebody in the car with me who needs help. You may not like this."

He looked at me in the same slow way as one of his cats.

"I heard he was in the vicinity."

"The war is over," I said, registering too that Neddy's hadn't been the only sighting.

Here's a fact: Some people make the effort, some don't. Some can and will. Some can and won't. Mr. Seefeld couldn't—but did.

"He frightens me."

"Not now he can't."

"I heard he's like a ghost. But I'm still frightened."

I said, "He probably saved your life."

Slow as contemplation itself, Mr. Seefeld nodded his big head with its big brain. "How can I help?"

"That German doctor," I said. "His English skills are as poor as my German."

Charles Miller didn't—or didn't want to—recognize Mr. Seefeld, who tried to hide his distaste and huddled in the back, trying to shrink his large bulk into a corner. We drove to Castlemaine in silence. Charles— Chuck, as I now supposed he'd forever be—fell asleep, and I, who'd always set such store by the weather, looked out at the rain and felt the length and depth of my own gloom.

Dr. Kortig and his wife had aged more than I'd have expected. And they seemed to have withdrawn somewhat into themselves. They remembered me, and of course saw Mr. Seefeld often—with whom they now held a deep and whispered conversation on their own doorstep.

Mr. Seefeld walked back to where I stood by the open door of the car, with my passenger still inside, and said, "Yes, you guessed right. He was a doctor in the first war. And he has seen this condition."

"What am I to do?"

"He doesn't want you to think that he's unwilling to help, but there is little he can do. He can observe, he says, and make recommendations. But if you will bring the American into the house, and agree to stay here with him for a few days, he will make every effort to find the right treatment."

It rained for those four days. I never left the house. Mrs. Kortig and I played endless card games and board games with Charles Miller, and when he left off, or failed to start, or fell asleep, we accepted the doctor's admonishments to "keep him in the game, keep his mind working." Mr. Seefeld arranged to go back to Kenmare, and I thanked him, and agreed with him that the world was a very strange place.

150

March 1948

And so it began, the rest of my life. Again, I will report, I will not interpret. Having accepted Dr. Kortig's recommendations, and his letter of introduction, I drove Charles Miller to a nursing home in Killarney. The home was run by Mrs. Cooper's cousin, and I got the best of attention— and took a bed there myself for a few days, though only as a next-of-kin resident.

The doctors who came reported that as far as they could tell, Captain Miller had survived many infections, and though poorly in terms of immediate vitality, showed no signs of anything but dementia and mental fatigue.

To pursue Dr. Kortig's next recommendations, I went to the bank and found that I had just about enough money left to get us to the States in some comfort—and get me home again, if that's what was needed.

I hadn't dared to address the thought, but I was by no means certain how Kate would react when she saw that her man was not the man she'd married—or when she viewed him in comparison to me, in all my big, rude health and vigor.

We sailed from Cork, on a little tender out to the liner. I liked the irony that the SS *America* had just come from Bremerhaven. The suite that I'd booked had two bedrooms, and I'd paid for a nurse from the shipping line to give Charles extra attention. Buying clothes for and with him in Cork had been trying, but he looked better, to say the least. I kept aside the best outfit for his arrival in Lebanon.

During the voyage, I walked him up and down on deck at night. The word got around that an "unwell American war hero was traveling," and people stopped us to pat him on the arm and shake his hand. And I fought off fantasies of having him fall overboard.

He began to eat well—"a good sign," Dr. Kortig would have said. No wider or deeper lucidity did I see, until we sailed up the Hudson and he applauded for a second or two, no more. By the time we caught a train to Chicago next day, he was again sleeping heavily.

From Chicago, I sent a telegram: BOBBY: MEET THE TRAIN IN LEBANON, 10:30 TUESDAY. DON'T TELL KATE. Bobby loved romantic conspiracies and I knew he'd agree.

On the train, Charles asked, "Are we going to Kenmare?"

I said, and it was true, "We are, Charles."

He managed the sleeper bunk on the train better than I'd thought he might; he managed the bathroom too, for almost the first time. Progress, Dr. Kortig, progress.

Bobby brought Sydney on her leash. Bobby sat down on a bench with a dangerous *plop!* Bobby wiped his brow when he saw Charles.

"Oh, Jesus and Christ, dear boy. This is him, isn't it, this is him. And I was just building a special bed," and he dropped to a whisper, "for you and Kate, oh, Jesus and Christ."

I picked up Sydney, and she kissed me. Many times. Charles put out his hand, and she kissed him, and then struggled from my arms toward him.

"Off with the old love, on with the new," said Bobby Bilbum. "I dread to think what Jerry will do."

We drove to the house. I reached back, tapped Charles's knee, and pointed to the sign, KENMARE. My inner gentleman swore like a seafaring drunk. *The hearts and flowers won,* he said. *Cheap music is dangerous indeed. I told you but you wouldn't listen.*

Had I anticipated the moment? Of course I had. But my mind always turned from it—in dread, in bitterness, and, it has to be said, in some pleasure for my dear friend, Kate.

Did it happen like Hollywood? No, children, that never happens, not in my experience, anyway. I've seen partings, I've seen reunions, I've even had them myself, and they're never like the movies.

Bobby Bilbum, though, wanted a part in it. He leapt ahead of me and opened the back door into the kitchen.

"Dear Kate," he called. "Look who's here."

She turned from her work—baking, I think. And then she turned back again, shaking her head. I walked around Bobby and Charles and crossed the floor to her.

"It's all right," I said. "But he's not well, he needs looking after."

She couldn't move. Her arms didn't work, her legs didn't work. She did that hand-washing thing again, up and down her arms. She began to mutter.

"What?" I said.

She said it louder. "One must Drink as one Brews."

"Come and sit down," I said, and I led her to the table.

To you, my children, I repeat: I'm merely reporting.

Kate looked nowhere. I gestured to Bobby, who pulled out a chair for Charles and sat him down, and when he had done so, I led Bobby from the kitchen, in part because I could hear Sydney squealing where we'd left her in the truck. But I'm only human, and when I walked past the kitchen door on my way to see Jerry, I looked in, and Kate was standing with her arms around Charles's head, and her cheek in his hair.

For the next half hour or so, I chatted to Jerry, received multiple and very wet kisses from Sydney, and then I said good-bye to them all, and Bobby took me to the train station, where I handed him Dr. Kortig's letter to me, summarizing Charles's condition and his recommendations that military doctors be consulted. I slept all the way to Chicago, and all the way to New York.

Postscript

My house on this hillside gets two-thirds of the sun's daily circuit. I had it built this way, and on the terrace just outside my door I grow geraniums in clay pots that I used to make; my hands aren't up to throwing pots anymore. When I think back on what happened to me in my twenties and thirties, I appreciate all the more this place and its peace, and my long life. Others of my age didn't fare as well.

Joachim or Jochen Peiper, Prisoner Forty-two, spent many years in jail, under sentence of death. His military defender, that ascetic-faced man I saw at Dachau, Willis Everett, fought and fought—not out of compassion for Peiper, but out of a belief that Peiper's legal rights had been breached by the way he and the other captured German officers had been abused in custody.

Everett kept this case between his teeth for a decade. He risked everything, he forced a U.S. congressional hearing, and he got the death sentence commuted.

Peiper became an executive with a major European sports car manufacturer, but those who pursued war criminals soon uncovered him, and he was forced out of that job. He went to live in a small French town not far from the German border, where he was known only to a few of his former comrades, who also lived nearby. Just before 14 July 1976, he sent his wife back to Germany in a packed car, and on Bastille Day itself, the attack that he had long expected came.

From inside the house, lying on the floor, with his weapons beside him, he defended himself against the wild gunfire—but the fireball they launched got him. Had the French Communists, who had just recently "outed" him—had they known that he was nicknamed "Blowtorch"? The flames shrank his body to a third of its natural size—the firemen thought that a child had died.

Charles Miller was close to me in age too—and for years my greatest act of willpower lay in not inquiring what became of him.

Kate wrote many letters to me at my parents' house, and Delia Holst wrote too. I never read them. In time, they stopped writing, and my interest in what became of them faded to an occasional idle: "I wonder . . ." What would my life have been like had I married Kate? Excellent, I think. We understood each other so well. Or, if I'm as truthful as ice, I understood her, and she liked me. I knew that I didn't ignite her. The barb still lay embedded in me, though, as I drove around Ireland. But that wound healed too, and I can tell you now that it's only the self-inflicted injuries that are unlikely to mend.

Which, of course, as I hear you thinking, brings me to Venetia.

My willingness to be advised by James Clare was always both a strength and a weakness. I believed so much in what he said that I tended to follow it blindly. Miss Fay even pointed that out to me once.

"My lovely James is not infallible," she said. And then she wrecked her own argument by saying, "But he's always right."

James had said to me, remember, that I should have listened to Venetia's words. In time, I summoned up the courage to play them back—and then I put them on a loop of tape in my head. Her words tormented me. Do you recall them? I'll play the "tape" for you—after all, you are her children. Ours.

There were other days when I hoped you were coming for me. But today—I just knew . . . Ben, I sent you a telegram . . . I sent you five telegrams . . . Ben . . . I always hoped . . .

The road can be the best life—and sometimes the worst, especially if you have an inner voice as scalding as mine can be. My inner adviser made me play those words over and over—he gave me no quarter, no letup. In some ways he proved fiercer on me with those words than with "torturer" or "killer": *Ben, I sent you a telegram . . . I sent you five telegrams . . . Ben . . . I always hoped . . .*

You see, he truly loved Venetia, that inner man of mine. How do I know? I'll tell you how I know—because one day, in the early 1950s, long after all these events, as I was driving through the city of Wexford, my inner voice began to laugh, and when you hear your inner voice laughing like a maniac, be sure, my children, that mischief lies ahead.

Sure enough, I saw the cause—a sign that said, COMING SOON: DRAMA! EXCITEMENT! YOU WON'T BELIEVE YOUR EYES! BOOK NOW FOR THE SENSATIONAL GENTLEMAN JACK AND HIS FRIEND.

ABOUT THE AUTHOR

FRANK DELANEY is the *New York Times* bestselling author of the novels *Venetia Kelly's Traveling Show, Shannon, Ireland,* and *Tipperary,* and his nonfiction work, *Simple Courage: A True Story of Peril on the Sea,* was selected as one of the American Library Association Books of the Year. Formerly a judge for the Booker Fiction Prize, he worked for many years as a broadcaster with the BBC in England, where he also wrote many fiction and nonfiction bestsellers. Born in Ireland, he now lives in the United States.

ABOUT THE TYPE

This book was set in Garamond, a typeface originally designed by the Parisian typecutter Claude Garamond (1480–1561). This version of Garamond was modeled on a 1592 specimen sheet from the Egenolff-Berner foundry, which was produced from types assumed to have been brought to Frankfurt by the punchcutter Jacques Sabon.

Claude Garamond's distinguished romans and italics first appeared in *Opera Ciceronis* in 1543–44. The Garamond types are clear, open, and elegant.